Buffalo
Gordon

Buffalo Gordon

*The Extraordinary Life and Times of
Nate Gordon from Louisiana Slave
to Buffalo Soldier*

J. P. SINCLAIR LEWIS

A Tom Doherty Associates Book / *New York*

BUFFALO GORDON

Copyright © 2001 by John-Paul Sinclair Lewis

This book is printed on acid-free paper.

Design by Heidi Eriksen

A Forge Book
Published by Tom Doherty Associates, LLC
175 Fifth Avenue
New York, NY 10010

www.tor.com

Forge® is a registered trademark of Tom Doherty Associates, LLC.

Library of Congress Cataloging-in-Publication Data

Lewis, John-Paul.
    Buffalo Gordon /John-Paul Lewis.—1st. ed.
        p. cm.
    "A Tom Doherty Associates book."
    ISBN 0-312-87376-X (acid-free paper)
    1. United States. Army. Cavalry—Afro-American troops—Fiction.
2. United States. Army. Cavalry, 9th—Fiction.   3. Afro-American
soldiers—Fiction.   4. Fugitive slaves—Fiction.   5. Reconstruction—
Fiction.   6. West (U.S.)—Fiction.   7. Louisiana—Fiction.   I. Title.

PS3562.E9478 B8 2001
813'.6—dc21   00-048458

First Edition: February 2001

Printed in the United States of America

0 9 8 7 6 5 4 3 2 1

To my deceased father, Michael, who taught me to seek historical grit.
To my wife, Sue Ellen, and my mother, Bernadette, who sustained me.
To my friend Peter Cooper, who showed me the way.
To Dr. Jon Sumida, who gave me the confidence to start this project.

Buffalo Gordon

Part One

THE
RECRUITMENT

NEW ORLEANS, SEPTEMBER 1866

Nate Gordon felt anxious as he stepped off the gangplank from the Federal side-wheel gunboat U.S.S. *Mohawk*, and paused as a putrid wave of humidity and stagnant air engulfed him. He quickly removed his kepi and pulled frantically at the red bandanna lodged in between the two shiny central brass buttons of his cavalry shell jacket.

"Gawd almighty," he muttered, wiping the perspiration from his face. He then shook his head in disgust and whispered to himself, "*Damn this air and humidity*."

"A Southern black boy likes you should love the heat," jibed a barefooted sailor moving past Nate as he pulled on a thick rope and tied it around a piling.

"*Yeah*. Guess I forgot," responded Nate, shading his eyes with his hand as he gazed at the sky. "Haze and heat. Nothing . . . but haze and heat."

As Nate glanced back at the U.S.S. *Mohawk*, he already missed the gentle river breeze that made the voyage from St. Louis pleasurable. The bobbing gunboat, still covered with tin planking from its service in the war, resembled a beetle struggling in a murky pond. Sweat continued to pour down Nate's neck and chest, soaking his undergarments and blue wool cavalry shell jacket.

Three long years had passed since Nate left Louisiana to join the Union army. He was born a slave not far from the Crescent City, on a plantation in St. Charles Parish. He had escaped, fought in the war, and was now returning as a sergeant major in the Tenth United States Negro Cavalry. When he was ordered by the regimental commanding officer, Gen. Benjamin Grierson, to go to New Orleans and assist in the recruitment of able-bodied men of color to form the Ninth Negro Cavalry, he looked forward to the task but loathed the prospect of going back to the Deep South.

The wharves of the Crescent City, recovering slowly from the devastating effects of the war, once again teemed with activity, and the chanting of barefooted cotton rollers rose above the din. Nate forced his way into the flow and wound his way through the maze of cotton bales, barrels of rum, sacks of rice and grain, and hardwood timber, all being hauled by hundreds of blacks dressed in rags or stripped to the waist. The riverfront was choked with all manner of steam vessels, moored together, single file, forming a long line of paddle wheels bellowing black smoke into the hazy sky, their piercing whistles resonating a deafening sound throughout Jackson Square and the French Quarter.

His forgotten New Orleans now came back to him through his nostrils. When he was a slave, Mas'a Hammond often brought him to the slave markets and to purchase items that were only available at the French Market. Now, and as was the case when he was in bondage, the Crescent City stank to high heaven. He covered his nose with his moist bandanna against the stench of rotting food and human waste as hundreds of screeching seagulls hovered and swooped down to investigate cargo and feed on trash. Nate walked slowly and remained alert. He always walked as if he had eyes in the back of his neck, a practice developed when he was a slave and sharpened during the war. Nate began to notice that the eyes of his black brethren were upon him, stopping their work to simply stare in amazement as if a gaudy whore dressed in red had just meandered by, leaving cheap perfume in her wake.

"Nev' see a black man with high boots and carryin' a big pistol," cried one tall and very muscular, coal-black dock worker.

"Where you from boy?" asked another, older man with enormous arms and a barrel chest, wearing a large weather-beaten straw hat. Several hundred-pound bags of rice rested on his left shoulder as if they were pillows.

"I'm jest like you." Nate stopped and smiled. "Come from these parts, sorta."

"You ain't like me," retorted the big man, laughing. "Shit, I lived here all my life and I sure 'nough don't talk like no white man."

The response caught the attention of several workers, and a small crowd of gawking laborers had begun to gather around Nate when a white pier supervisor with rotting teeth and wearing a filthy beige frock coat appeared.

"What in Sam Hill is goin' on here?" His eyes widened, then narrowed, when he spied Nate. The supervisor spit out the big wad of spent chewing tobacco and blurted to his workers, "You boys arn't paid wages to mill 'round an' stare at blue-belly niggers all day long. Now git to work, or ah'll fire de bunch ya."

The crowd slowly dissipated and fumed silently. Nate continued through the commercial district toward Union Headquarters on Canal Street. He missed the protection of the tin-clad gunboat, felt exposed and mildly endangered by the hostile stares of white Southerners.

He patted his Walker-Colt revolver several times, a practical talisman, and kept his eyes peeled for trouble. Although the presence of federal troops on the streets would surely deter any rascality on the part of the local populace, Nate nevertheless felt a sense of foreboding. He cursed his commanding officer. Why had old man Grierson sent him back to Louisiana? When he escaped from that miserable plantation in St. Charles Parish he swore he would never return to the land where he and his ancestors were kept as slaves. All he wanted now was to complete his mission in Louisiana and return to the openness of the frontier.

Across the street, he heard a rattling screech. A haggard, middle-aged woman, was ranting and raving as she paced up and down Canal Street. Her frail body listed forward as if she were a hunchback, and her long tangled gray hair came all the way down to her waist, covering the back of her tattered clothes. The old woman's appearance made her look like a medieval sorceress, and her once delicate hands were gnarled with arthritis and fingernails crusted with dirt. As she dragged her feet along the brick pavement she would point her long and bony index finger and shout accusingly at passersby.

"What would you do if your family was murdered by the government?"

Onlookers shook their heads and avoided her. Unable to find a listener, the hag cast about until her wild eyes locked on to Nate. She screamed again, jabbing her finger in Nate's direction.

"You nigger blue bellies murdered my son and husband at Milliken's Bend." Nate froze as the women covered the distance between them without seeming to touch the ground. Before he could cover his face, the hag spat at him, then raised her hand and cracked him on the side of the head, knocking his kepi into a watery gutter.

"Stop!" he ordered, wiping his face with the bandanna and fixing her with a malevolent stare. "You crazy hoodoo white woman!"

Although insane, the hag appeared startled that a black man had not bowed his head in submission and actually dared to look her in the eyes. She staggered backward, shaking her head and muttering an unintelligible mixture of curses and complaints.

A second crowd gathered around Nate and the crazy woman. Nate glanced around slowly, taking in the odd vestiges of Confederate uniforms—shredded evidence of both the losing side's poverty and remaining pride.

"The nigger *insulted* the lady," came a voice that seemed to rise up from the ground behind him.

Nate turned and glanced down to see a man who'd lost both his legs at the hip. His pathetic torso was supported by a hand-hewn cart with tiny primitive wheels, propelled by concave blocks with leather straps. The man's severed body wore a soiled Confederate cavalry shell jacket with yellow corporal stripes, and his head was wrapped in bandages. He had a rough face that had not been shaven for days, and his right eye had a patch over it. He began hollering to the crowd while pointing his finger from his dwarfed position at Nate.

"Ain't you boys goin' do something about dis nigger insultin' a white woman?" he bellowed defiantly as he moved the little cart in tiny circles around Nate with his concave blocks.

The remark sparked the crowd and the mood grew increasingly hostile, with many of the citizens jeering and waving clenched fists.

"*Tue le noir!*" shouted a man in thick Cajun French, who was holding a stiletto and whose face was hideously disfigured by burns.

"This nigger Yankee come down here an' tell us what to do an' abuse our kinfolk," yelled the cripple in the cart.

"I done no such thing," retorted Nate. Stunned by his baritone voice, the crowd became temporarily silent. "You all can see dat's she touched in the head," he pleaded.

"That gives you no right to abuse a white woman, nigger! I say we string dis black blue belly in Jackson Square as an example," commanded the amputee, still rolling around in his cart as if he was in a circus. The crowd roared in agreement and tightened the circle around their prey.

Nate was coming perilously close to disaster, and although holding his ground, the crowd was becoming larger and more aggressive. Several men sporting dirty red fez hats, once part of the uniform of the Louisiana Tiger Zouaves, pulled out concealed weapons. One very fat former Zouave drew a pair of brass knuckles from the inside of his sash, while another man with a fez hat and a long mean scar on his right cheek was stepping closer to Nate as he drew a well-worn black-jack from the inside of his frock coat.

"*Tue le noir!*" yelled the Cajun again, egging on the mob. He had removed a small derringer from a concealed pocket that was stitched to the inside lining of his right boot, and was trying to get close to Nate.

Lt. Zachary Hennessy was on the opposite side of Canal Street, about a block south of where all the commotion was occurring, when his attention was diverted by the noise up the street. He proceeded up Canal to investigate. As he came closer, he noticed a large black man in the middle of the crowd, wearing a sergeant major's cavalry uniform. The soldier was obviously in trouble. Hatless, and moving his huge frame in a small circle as if he was a cornered bear trapped by vicious hounds, Lieutenant Hennessy realized that this was a lynch mob about to string up a federal noncommissioned officer.

The sight of a Union colored soldier being bullied by the former enemy made Hennessy's blood boil. His lips tightened and his eyes became intense. These immoral Southerners will never let the black man be, he thought to himself. They went to war to keep them as their personal chattel, and now that they had lost the greatest challenge that the history of the republic ever faced, were still trying to reconstruct the past.

He decided that the best course of action was to locate a Union patrol or some of the off-duty soldiers who were milling around drinking establishments and whorehouses in the Quarter. He spotted a corporal with two other men talking price with a harlot on St. Louis Street. The prostitute was dolled and painted up to look like a little girl. She had pigtails that were tied at the ends with lavender bows, and was giggling as the corporal whispered in her left ear.

"You there—Corporal! I want you and the other two men to follow me and break up that mob up the street."

The corporal and his comrades looked stunned; they had been drinking all afternoon in the French Quarter, and all they wanted now was to have a woman and pass out before it got too hot. The last thing they had in mind was some popinjay officer ordering them around on their leave.

"We-wer-werrre offf d-duty, suhhh," said the inebriated corporal pathetically, as he struggled to sound sober.

"I do not care, mister. You will obey orders and proceed with me to disperse that mob."

"Wwhaa-what crowd, Lootenat?" said the corporal as he tripped over his left foot.

"That crowd over there," replied Hennessy sharply, pointing up Canal Street. "You men fall in and report now, or I'll have your stripes and you'll be up on charges for public drunkenness."

That got the corporal's attention. He had lost his stripes twice before during the war, and was not prepared to lose them again. He realized that he had better detoxify himself quickly and obey orders. While contemplating his predicament, the corporal noticed that his right hand was leaning on an overflowing rain barrel underneath a gutter. He decided to soak his entire head in the barrel, and hoped this would chase away the effects of the spirits. He gave the barrel a long look, stepped back, and removed his forage cap. He then plunged his head into the water, and after what seemed to be minutes to an anxious Hennessy, raised his head from the container, opened his mouth, and uttered a crude groan of relief as if he was discharging urine after a long wait.

"What are we goin' use as weapons, suh?" said the corporal as he pulled back his wet hair with the palm of his left hand and placed the forage cap back on his head.

"You fools are not fit to carry arms in your debauched condition," scolded Hennessy as he shook his head. Realizing however, that these men would have to do, he commanded them, "Follow me into the fray." With his hasty, reluctant, tiny detachment, Hennessy lead the way up Canal Street toward the commotion.

Nate realized that he had to do something to free himself from the mob. With his right hand, he slowly reached for the pommel of his Walker-Colt revolver and gently unsnapped the holster flap. Then with his large thumb he cocked the hammer back into the safety position and rapidly pulled the weapon from its holster. When the tip of the barrel was free, he quickly raised the gun in the air and placed his right elbow on his hip. The sight of the huge Walker-Colt once again silenced the crowd.

The former Tiger Zouave who was carrying the blackjack managed to weave his way through the mob and got within striking distance of Nate. He had the weapon fully raised and was about to crack it on the back of Nate's head when Hennessy grabbed the blackjack and brought the man's arm down on his knee. This forced the weapon from the attacker's hand. Hennessy then pulled his Navy Colt .44 with his right hand and pistol-whipped the brute on the back of the neck, sending him facedown, rolling into the gutter. Lieutenant Hennessy then said in a loud and forceful voice to the rest of the crowd, "*Enough.*"

Nate turned around and faced Hennessy, who was looking straight at him. "Thought you needed some assistance, Sergeant."

"Yes sir, I was in a real fix. I was 'bout to use this horse pistol. . . ."

"There will be none of that, Sergeant. The corporal and his men will disperse the crowd."

Hennessy then turned and faced the now largely silent mob and bellowed, "This is an unlawful assembly. You must clear the street now, or I will start arresting people and you will be taken to the provost marshal."

The mob, now cheated out of their amusement, grumbled and slowly scattered back into the French Quarter. The amputee was still circling around Nate, however, using his concave blocks to propel his pitiable cart. Although the little ex-Confederate bastard almost had him lynched, Nate felt sorry for the maimed soldier, who surely must have suffered greatly when he lost his legs. The war had devastated his way of life and condemned him to a miserable existence as a bitter, crippled beggar.

"Where did you lose your legs, Corporal?" asked Nate.

"Pittsburg Landing," retorted the amputee defiantly, then as an afterthought added with pride, "I was with Gen'ral Albert Sidney Johnston."

"I h'ard he was one hell of a gen'ral," commented Nate as he slightly lowered his head in respect.

"Hell of a general," bellowed the cripple. "Difference is, dough, I'm still alive an' livin' in dis hare cart, but old Gen'ral Sidney got kilt, dyin' fer what was right."

"Sure, Corporal, sure," acknowledged Nate, feeling sorry for the ex-Confederate who had sacrificed everything for a cause that was venal at best.

Lieutenant Hennessy was astonished that this colored man, who was nearly murdered by a crowd of rabble rowers led by an ex-Confederate, would take the time to even speak to the man, let alone feel sympathy. "What is your name, Sergeant?" demanded the lieutenant as he holstered his service revolver. "And who is your commanding officer?"

Nate quickly retrieved his kepi, which was lying on its side near where his attacker was lying in the gutter, and slapped the hat against the side of his sky-blue trousers to wipe off the water. When he placed it back on his head, Hennessy noticed the brass insignias on the flat top of the kepi. Above the brass crossed swords, the number ten stood out.

"I see that you are part of the Tenth Colored Cavalry. I have heard of your regiment," remarked Hennessy.

Nate snapped to attention and saluted.

"Sergeant Major Nate Gordon, Tenth Cavalry. My commanding

officer is Colonel Grierson. We're currently stationed at Fort Leavenworth, sir."

"I presume that is one of the newly formed black cavalry regiments for service in the west?" Hennessy was intrigued, almost envious.

Nate was pleased that the word had gotten out that Congress had approved the formation of two colored cavalry regiments, the Ninth and Tenth, for service on the frontier.

"Sergeant, did you say that Colonel Grierson is your commanding officer? Is that old Ben Grierson, of Grierson's raid into Mississippi?" inquired Hennessy enthusiastically.

"One 'n' de same, sir." Nate smiled.

Lieutenant Hennessy was impressed. Benjamin Grierson was a real war hero. His daring cavalry raid, with seventeen hundred troopers, penetrated deep into the heart of Dixie. His command destroyed over six hundred miles of railroad track and supply depots, and diverted Confederate troops away from Grant, enabling him to take Vicksburg.

"What are your orders, Sergeant?"

Still at attention, Nate replied, "I'm carrying dispatches for Lootenant Colonel Wesley Merritt, sir. Beggin' de Lootenant's pardon, can you tell me where I might locate him?"

Hennessy was interested in this black noncommissioned officer. He was articulate, and his accent was southern but did not have the long drawl that was so characteristic of southern speech. He was also handsome and extremely muscular, but most curiously, what was he doing in New Orleans, and how was he connected to such high officers? "Lieutenant Colonel Merritt is at Union HQ on St. Charles Street," replied Hennessy finally. "I am on my way there now; you may accompany me, Sergeant."

"Much obliged, sir," acknowledged Nate as he saluted. He was relieved that this officer had helped him escape the madness of the mob and reassured that he had an escort through the streets of a hostile city that only weeks earlier had rioted against his brethren and hung dozens of newly freed innocent colored.

Two

Army headquarters was only a few blocks away. The structure was an imposing but gaudy Victorian mansion that General Butler had confiscated when he was military governor of New Orleans during the early part of federal occupation. He had lived like a European baron, and the mansion reflected his tawdry tastes. During the war, Nate had heard that the general made an infamous reputation for himself among the citizens of the Crescent City, resulting in much hatred toward the Yankee occupiers. He remembered reading in the newspapers how the local population bestowed upon him the name "Beast Butler" for his issuance of General Order No. 28, which declared that all women of the city of New Orleans be treated by his soldiers as prostitutes if they demonstrated any sign of disrespect to federal authorities. At the time, Nate had considered this order rather harsh, but after his own unpleasant altercation with some of the "good" citizens of New Orleans, he heartily agreed with "Spoons" Butler, as his own men called him after he was accused of stealing silver bullion from some of the city's most prominent citizens.

With Lieutenant Hennessy leading the way, and Nate following closely behind, they passed some warehouses guarded by federal troops. As they approached army headquarters, military activity increased. Infantry and cavalry troopers were camped on both flanks of the mansion, and their white Sibley tents were pitched in neat long rows in front of stacked Springfields. Young, barefoot black orderlies were lazily brushing and grooming sleek cavalry chargers, oiling tack, and polishing brass bits, stirrups, and spurs. Cook fires were burning and Nate could

21

smell roasting pork and chicken, which sadly reminded him that he had not eaten anything since the night before, and if he did not get some grub soon, the familiar hunger pain in his stomach would begin to bother him.

Nate noticed that cavalry and infantry officers of all ranks were milling around the great exterior stairway of the mansion and leaning on the wrought-iron fence that surrounded the property. Young lieutenants and captains were laughing, joking, and generally radiating the sense of great confidence typical of an occupying army.

A tall and muscular black man dressed in clean work clothes and well-oiled boots had been following Nate and Hennessy along the sidewalk at a close distance. Sensing that the two men were about to turn and enter the grounds of Union headquarters, he called out to them.

"Pardon me! Ah . . . Lootinent . . . Sergeant Major."

Both Nate and Hennessy halted and turned around.

"Sorry to disturb, but I was wondering, where can I enlist?"

"Why do you want to sign up?" replied Nate as his eyes examined the man.

"I was in de army once," answered the stranger confidently.

"What's your name, mister?" interrupted Hennessy as he pulled on the wide cuffs of his gauntlets.

"My name is Jesse," responded the stranger, coming to attention as if he was still in the army. "Jesse Randolph, sir." His voice then became hesitant. "I saw all the com'otion back dare on the street, with all dem angry white folk getting ready to lynch ya. I wanted to help . . . but felt powerless, Sergeant Major." Jesse Randolph bowed his head as if he was feeling a sense of shame. "I'm sorry 'bout dat." He then lifted his head and his eyes became wide with admiration. "But the way you . . . all handled yo'selfs back there on the street with the mob an' all . . . made me recall the days when I was in de army. Dat sense of strong confidence reminded me when I was in the war. Soz I want to sign up with that new cavalry outfit that I heard 'bout."

"This is your lucky day then, 'cause if you are referrin' to the Ninth, they are recruiting in Greenville and I'm going to be in charge," stated Nate with authority.

"Well then, I best be makin' my way there then," replied Jesse with a smile. He saluted, which bemused Nate considering that the man was not in uniform, and turned around and proceeded to walk back toward the river on St. Charles Street.

"Do you think he will really enlist?" asked Hennessy, still tugging on the cuffs of his gauntlets.

"Maybe, maybe not. Lots of men claim they goin' do something but then do nothing."

Nate followed Hennessy up the stairs toward the portico and double doors of the mansion. He noticed that there was a long line of pushy civilians waiting to go inside. Most of them were dressed in what seemed to Nate their Sunday best, and some of them were carrying little suitcases, made out of carpet fabric, while others clutched folded documents and maps. They were waving them as if they were passes to some great event or spectacle.

"Beggin' de Lootenant's permission, sir, who are these civilians waitin' in line?" inquired Nate, puzzled.

"They are Northerners who are here to assist us in the reconstruction of the South," replied Hennessy.

"They don't look like gov'ment officials to me sir."

"They are not," said Hennessy curtly. "These gentlemen seek commercial opportunity here, and they need our permission to conduct some of their affairs."

A young ordinance noncommissioned officer was standing by the door admiring his new boots. He spotted Hennessy and snapped to attention while Nate and Hennessy entered the mansion. Immediately the light and temperature changed. The interior was dark, and smoke filled the air with cigar and pipe aroma. The great entry hall's ceilings were extremely high and the ornate wainscoting, huge plaster medallions, impressive brass fixtures, and fine furnishings reminded Nate of the days when he was a slave on the plantation. Many, many times he had to go to the Big House to see Mas'a Hammond to receive his work orders or be chastised for some infraction, real or imagined. Now he felt the same sense of uneasiness. He sighed while whispering to himself, "It seems so long ago."

The great entry hall was choked with military personnel moving up and down the wide and winding stairway, and coming in and out from the side parlor rooms that had been converted into makeshift offices. A bespectacled corporal was sitting behind a huge, ornate desk a few feet from the front entry. The piece of furniture was obviously borrowed from the library, since even its large size was too small for the area where it was currently located. The corporal, engaged in clerical duties, was scribbling madly away. He kept dipping his plume into the inkwell and leaving a trail of ink all over the blotter pad and various documents. Not a very neat worker, Nate thought. Lieutenant Hennessy and Nate approached the desk.

"Corporal, the Sergeant Major here has dispatches for Lieutenant Colonel Merritt."

Without moving his little head from its bowed position, the clerk responded in a lame manner. "Hold your horses, mister. I got to finish this report before my commanding officer has my ass. Besides, I thought all you carpetbaggers are supposed to remain outside until you are called upon."

Hennessy's face suddenly turned red. Before he could respond however, Nate jumped into the conversation.

"Stan' at attention, damn you, 'fore I make you clean up horse manure." This startled the clerk, and he raised his head only to find Nate's big black face a few inches away from his spectacles.

"I'm Sergeant Major Gordon and this here is Lieutenant Hennessy. Yo'll render him every consideration, and respect these stripes. Is that clear, Corporal?!"

The clerk bolted from his comfortable velvet chair and stood erect and saluted. "Yes, Sergeant Major!" He then turned toward Hennessy, his frame ramrod straight. "I am sorry, sir, I did not realize you were army, sir. It's just that these . . . damn carpetbaggers keep pestering me all day with requests, and . . ."

"That will be enough, Corporal, an' button your collar," interrupted Nate.

Nate was enjoying this little dressing down. The surly clerk deserved it. Besides, he wanted to show the lieutenant that he was in control of the situation. "Now then, where kin I fin' Lieutenant Colonel Merritt?"

"Up the stairs, second floor, third door to your left." The corporal was still at attention and in the salute position.

Nate returned the salute and then turned to Hennessy. "Thank you for your assistance earlier, sir. I'll be on my way now."

The lieutenant held out his hand toward Nate. "Good luck, Sergeant Major."

Nate was astonished that an officer wanted to shake his hand. This had never happened to him before. It was considered quite unmilitary for officers and NCOs to show any sign of personal warmth while communicating. Nevertheless, Nate reached for Hennessy's stretched-out arm and warmly clasped the officer's hand. Both men squeezed hard and gazed in each other's eyes. Hennessy nodded and Nate replied, "Thank you, sir."

Nate made his way up the long, ornate stairway. He thought to himself how strange it was that Hennessy wanted to shake his hand. He wondered for a moment to ponder if this had ever happened to him before and decided that it had not. During the war, he had become fairly close to some white officers, but any overt expressions of friendship between the officers and himself never occurred. He pulled out his pocket watch that his mother had given him and pondered what she had told him when he was a boy. Her distant, soft voice echoed in the back of his head. "Always expect the unexpected."

Three

Lt. Col. Wesley Merritt was staring out of the window in his cramped office and feeling melancholy. He had arrived in New Orleans only a month before Nate, and his assignment was to assist Colonel Hatch in forming the newly created Ninth Negro Cavalry and get them ready for duty on the frontier. He was daydreaming again about the war, and especially about his former commanding officer, friend, and mentor, General John Buford. Merritt pondered on Buford's courage on that first day at Gettysburg. He admired the decision that Buford made in taking a stand against the rebel invaders and fighting the arrogant Confederates to a standstill. This action prevented Bobby Lee's advance forces from taking the high ground and gained time for reinforcements to come up. Merritt sighed as he thought about the men and officers who paid the supreme sacrifice during that battle, and how sad it was that General Buford died a few months after Gettysburg. Merritt still felt his mentor's loss.

Outside in the hallway next to Merritt's door there was a clerk seated on a chair that was too large for his frame. His body was pulled up tightly against the rim of a very large mahogany desk, and he was preoccupied with stacking and organizing files and communiqués. Nate walked up to the little table and large chair.

"Sergeant Major Nate Gordon with dispatches for Lieutenant Colonel Merritt."

"One moment, Sergeant Major, I will see if General Merritt will see you," commanded the clerk, addressing his commanding officer by his wartime rank of major general.

A moment later the clerk emerged from the office and signaled Nate to go in. Wesley Merritt was still staring out of the window daydreaming about Gettysburg when he heard Nate's crisp voice.

"Sergeant Major Nate Gordon reportin' for duty, sir."

Nate had heard about the exploits of Wesley Merritt in the newspapers, and had picked up information about this famous cavalryman when he would listen to officers talk about him. He knew that he was a graduate of West Point, went on to receive seven brevets, and finished the war as a major general of volunteers. He had been told by Colonel Grierson that Merritt had been recently attached to General Sheridan's staff until he accepted a new commission as a lieutenant colonel in the Ninth Cavalry. Nate had also learned through rumors that the same commission was offered to Gen. George Custer, but the boy general had scornfully refused, stating that he did not "want to lead no brunettes."

The moment Nate walked in he was impressed by Wesley Merritt's military dress and demeanor. The lieutenant colonel wore an immaculate, dark blue, double-breasted military frock coat with black velvet cuffs and collar. His general staff eagle brass buttons were polished to a high gloss and reflected the dim light of the room. With his strong facial features, high cheekbones and forehead, pale blue eyes, and delicate fingers, Nate liked the way this white man looked. Merritt possessed an aura of quiet confidence and Nate sensed that in a hot fight, this officer would be as cool as spring water on a hot July day. Nate also noticed that unlike most other white cavalry officers, who preferred to have their mustaches wavy and waxed, Merritt's light brown mustache was clipped very short, so short that it was hardly visible in the ill-lit room.

The door and single, window in Merritt's office were kept wide open due to the stifling heat and humidity. He had hoped to create a slight draft but this proved to be totally in vain. Although the air was hot and stagnant, Nate noticed that Merritt kept his crisp white shirt collar, which protruded from his dark blue frock coat, buttoned. When Nate entered the room Merritt immediately rotated on the heels of his boots and faced the sergeant major. They exchanged salutes, and Nate removed his kepi. Nate did not mind that the lieutenant colonel did not ask him to sit down in the chair facing his bureau, but he did expect to be ordered to be at ease. "Sergeant Major, you have dispatches for me?"

The lieutenant colonel sat back down in his chair at his bureau and folded his arms. He rested his elbows on the table and folded his left hand over his right, as if he was waiting for a student to respond to an oral examination question.

"Yes sir," replied Nate. "From Colonel Grierson, sir."

"Ah, Ben Grierson." Merritt repeated the name with an air of great reverence. "He wrote me about your arrival, Sergeant Major. I have been expecting you." Merritt paused and then continued. "Are you not two days late?"

"The ship's main boiler broke down at Caro, sir."

"I see. Well, that seems to be a consistent problem with our beloved navy's river gunboats, huh, Sergeant Major?"

"Yes sir, if you say so, sir."

Nate felt Merritt's pale blue eyes scrutinizing his size and physique. He chuckled to himself as he thought, Surely this white man must be thinking that I'm the biggest black man he had ever seen. He also knew that Merritt was examining the state of his uniform and his high flap cavalry boots that were polished to a gloss, as were the brass loops and buckle on his well-oiled 1851 dragoon saber belt. Nate however, remained confident that his custom-fitted dark blue shell jacket with high collar and yellow braid, sky-blue wool trousers with thin yellow piping along the seams and reinforced calf-skin seat, made him "perfectly regulation."

"I see that you have modified your dragoon belt to accommodate a Spencer carbine cartridge box," observed Merritt, as Nate handed the dispatches to him. "I was not made aware that the Tenth Cavalry have been issued Spencer carbines," Merritt added with astonishment as he opened the sealed envelope.

Nate was not surprised that Merritt had noticed the Spencer cartridge box hooked to his dragoon belt. The seven-shot, fifty-two-caliber rim-fire Spencer repeating carbine was a prized possession for those regiments who were fortunate enough to obtain them, and Nate thought it was quite normal that Merritt would be amazed that a black regiment would have them.

"No, sir. We've not been issued any Spencers. Fact is Colonel Grierson's requisition requests have been repeatedly ignored."

"Then how did you obtain yours, Sergeant Major?" Merritt inquired curiously.

"My reg'ment, the fo'mer Fifth Negro Cav'lry, was issued Spencers in late 'sixty-four. I kept my carbine after the reg'ment disbanded, sir."

"Then where is your Spencer, Sergeant Major?"

"I took m'ah carbine and broke down the weapon and wrapped the barrel and stock with an oil cloth so it would fit snugly in my haversack, sir," responded Nate proudly as he remained at attention in the stifling room while flies buzzed around his head. "I thought it be best dat de weapon remain outta sight while I'm in New O'leans."

"I see." Merritt nodded in approval as he glanced at the bulging haversack. There was a tightly wrapped object protruding from the corner of the haversack, and Merritt assumed that it was the barrel. "That was probably wise. This city is full of thieves and lowlives who would think nothing of cutting your throat for such a weapon."

"Yes sir," acknowledged Nate.

"Colonel Grierson speaks very highly of you, Sergeant Major. And if you are as resourceful as he says you are, and you are able to disassemble a complicated weapon such as a Spencer carbine to fit in your haversack, I think you will not disappointment me in my efforts to recruit good men and build a regiment."

Nate was still standing at attention in the suffocating room and longed to pull out his bandanna to wipe his face, but as he was not ordered to be "at ease," he had to tolerate the beads of perspiration that soaked his face and the irritating flies that kept swarming around the crown of his head.

"Did Colonel Grierson explain to you the difficulties we are experiencing in recruiting men of quality?"

"Yes sir, the Colonel explained that you were experiencin' difficulties in recruitin' reliable men."

"That is only partly correct, Sergeant Major. The Ninth Cavalry is a shell of a regiment and I am plagued by unenthusiastic officers who are on temporary assignment until the regiment finds permanent ones. Among the recruits themselves, I have cutthroats, thieves, drunkards, gamblers, and men with very weak constitutions who are often physically violent. I fear, Sergeant Major, that these men are not fit for military discipline or the ardors of frontier life."

"Yes sir, I understand sir," nodded Nate trying to be accommodating to Merritt's line of thought.

"In short, I need some one of your experience to weed out the troublemakers and attract quality recruits to fill the regiment. Colonel Grierson mentions that you can read and write. I will expect a written report every week on the progress of the regiment's readiness. You are to depart for Greenville, assess the situation, and assist Captain Frederick Graham, who is in charge of the recruitment center."

Nate remained stone-faced, still at attention. By now the air had become so stagnant and humid in the small room that his clean-shaven face glistened with perspiration that started to drip on his high collar. He still longed to take out his bandanna and wipe his face dry, but resisted asking permission.

"Beggin' de general's pardon, sir, I'm to act as liaison 'tween de command at de recruitment center and yourself, sir, and do I have de authority to recruit men of my own choosin'?"

Merritt sat back in his chair again. "Yes, Sergeant Major, you will serve as my eyes and ears and have full authority to aggressively pursue what you deem necessary to improve the quality of the regiment.

"Sergeant Major." Merritt's face manifested signs of strain and became melancholy. "The eyes of the nation are upon our regiment. There are many elements in the military establishment and in the press who are waiting to pounce on us if we fail in our duty. The slightest mistake that the regiment might make in terms of conduct or field performance will be picked up by the press and bull-horned to the public. They will attack us like venom, claiming that black soldiers are useless and unworthy to wear the uniform." Merritt removed a white handkerchief from the inside of his frock coat and wiped the streams of perspiration that crowned his forehead. Nate wanted to do the same but decided that he would continue to resist asking permission, even though some of the beads of sweat were now dripping down the point of his nose. "I am not insensitive to your position, Sergeant Major," continued Merritt. "I realize the difficulties you will encounter. I am not indifferent to your position as a black man in the South wearing a Union uniform. However, in view of your distinguished war record, and your commanding officer's positive report on your courage and resourcefulness, I have reasoned that you will be of great service to me personally and to the formation of the Ninth Cavalry."

"Yes sir," replied Nate.

Merritt handed him his orders. "I have included orders for the quartermaster sergeant so you can secure a mount and all necessary supplies and equipment. And if there are no further questions, you are dismissed, Sergeant Major."

"Yes, sir. Thank you, sir."

Nate saluted, placed his kepi back on his now-soaked head, and marched toward the door. Merritt then bowed his head and resumed reading his dispatches as if Nate never appeared.

Four

As soon as Nate started on the road to Greenville, he saw the recent signs of war and the effects of three years of Union occupation. He knew that since last year, a formal policy of reconstruction had dug deep into Louisiana's traditional plantation society. He was saddened, however, to see so many plantations in ruin. One Creole plantation that looked particularly pillaged and decrepit caught Nate's eye. Although lush with greenery and plant life, the once-manicured grounds were now overgrown with weeds, vines, and grass grown wild, giving the place a melancholy appearance. Many of the old estates that once graced the roadway, such as this Creole plantation, now lay abandoned with their doors missing as rotting shutters dangled precariously from broken hinges that banged against the exterior walls. Windowpanes were cracked or missing, and scavengers had stripped the interiors of these once-magnificent estates of most furnishings, brass-and wrought-iron fixtures, glass panes, and building materials such as windows and planking. As Nate gazed at the abandoned fields and store houses he whispered to himself, "Yeah . . . King Cotton is sure gone."

He was further downhearted by the condition of the once-serene landscape that had also borne the scars of war and neglect. Most of the cypress rail fencing had been either stripped or left rotting on the soft ground, and thousands of acres of fertile land remained unattended. Nate was glad he was not traveling by night, for the shoulders of the roads were littered with human waste, and makeshift campsites occupied by refugees and homeless people were everywhere. He had been told that the area was filled with local cutthroats who would kill someone for their shoelaces, and all local authority was more-or-less powerless to contain the growing banditry, murder, and vigilantism that plagued southern Louisiana ever since the Yankees invaded the state.

Although Nate managed to procure all the necessary supplies he thought he might require on the journey, and certain creature comforts he decided that he must have such as a folding camp chair and bureau, he had to deal with a very disagreeable and boorish quartermaster sergeant at the New Orleans horse depot. He was an Irishman from New York City who was not only insolent and uncooperative but attempted to cheat Nate on stolen camp furniture that he had taken from a widow of a dead Confederate general's house on Napoleon Street.

"I'll sell ya the table, chair, and chest for twenty-five dollars," was his reply when Nate asked how much he wanted for the items.

"Twenty-five dollars?" replied Nate, outraged. "Ain't that a *thief's price?*" Nate towered over the gruff quartermaster sergeant, who had a yellow beard that Nate thought needed trimming.

"You *black* bastard! Don't you be calling me a thief. This is *war booty,* and I's the one who is in possession of these goods. Now, if you want them, you'll just have to pay my price."

Nate smiled, but his eyes remained intense as they stared down at the Irishman's green eyes. "I'll tell *you* what, *Sergeant.* I'll give you ten dollars for de camp chair, foldin' desk, and de chest, and I promise not to report you for underfeedin' the horses."

The Irishman's ears began to turn red with embarrassment and rage as Nate continued to grin while his eyes remained transfixed on the quartermaster's face.

"Why you . . ."

"Why what?" interrupted Nate, the smile vanishing from his face. He placed his right hand near the pommel of his Walker-Colt while pointing his left index finger at the quartermaster sergeant's face. "I knows full well that you been stealin' army forage and sellin' it to the planters and takin' advantage of old women and widows . . . trading oats fo' furniture and gold. Now, considerin' that I hate thieves but I *really* hate men who mistreat horses and dogs even more, I want you to throw in a good horse, mule, and a decent McClellan with a seat dat ain't worn out, and *I won't report your sorry ass* to General Merritt."

Stunned, the quartermaster's jaw dropped open. "General *Wesley* Merritt?"

"The same," replied Nate with satisfaction. "An' he happens to be mah immediate superior. Now, do we have an arrangement, Sergeant, or . . ."

"Goddamn my fuckin' luck for dealin' with a *smart nigger,*" whined the quartermaster as he removed his forage cap with his right hand and pulled on his yellow beard with his left, bowing his head in thought. "All right, all right. Damn it! Pick your horse and mule and I'll sell you the stuff for the lousy ten dollars," sneered the Irishman as he put back his forage cap and held out his hand for the money.

Nate slapped the greenbacks into his hand with such force that the quartermaster dropped the bills onto a fresh pile of horse dung.

"Thank you, Sergeant, for your cooperation," said Nate sarcastically, as he made his way toward one of the corrals to select a horse, leaving the Irishman from New York swearing racial profanities as he picked up the greenbacks that were stuck to the steaming green pile of horse manure.

Most of the mounts were windblown relics of the war, and Nate finally had to settle on an old gray gelding that had been wounded in the hip joint during the last months of the conflict. Although fully recovered, the animal had a slight limp in his gait when he walked, but seemed to be all right when he trotted or cantered. Nate thought about the boorish Irishman from New York who had just tried to cheat him by overcharging for stolen war booty and stealing government property. Not that he was taken by surprise by the quartermaster sergeant's criminal actions. During the war, he had witnessed and, on occasion, had dealings with greedy black marketers and thieving sutlers who preyed on enlisted men's camps as if they were buzzards perched on a tree limb awaiting the afterbirths of newborn livestock.

He was eager to get on the road to Greenville, a little faubourg a few miles west of New Orleans. The way to Greenville was a narrow, single-lane dirt road that frequently flooded during heavy rains. Nate noticed that on the south side of the road as far as the eye could see, miles of endless and expanding bayou flora and waterways typified the landscape. He could smell the stagnant water and the aroma of rotting wood coming from the hundreds of lagoons and miles of marshland. Wide cypress trees, tilting precariously away from the road and leaning over the water, had long and thick branches draped in Spanish moss. A slight wind coming from the west picked up, and the Spanish moss moved gently in the direction of the breeze. Nate smiled at the blowing moss, which reminded him of a picture he saw in *Harper's Weekly* of a distressed clipper ship with torn sails.

Nate had to constantly maneuver his horse through the human traffic throng and take care not to let his horse step into any of the large pools of water left from daily torrential downpours. Dozens of black families were on the move, and their wagons, pulled by over-burdened oxen, strained to haul primitive furnishings, blankets, farm implements, cooking utensils, and other worldly belongings.

Most of the traffic, however, moved on foot, and represented a tapestry of human activity and misery. People of all descriptions, ages, and color, walked along the shoulders of the road at a slow pace, usually with bowed heads. Their tattered hats were the only shield against the hot sun. Colored women were carrying tremendous bundles of clothes wrapped in patchwork quilts on top of their heads, and many of them, especially the younger ones, held the hands of their barefoot toddlers.

There were also poor white farmers on their way to market in New Orleans, and Yankee officers in requisitioned buggies, seen frequently with overdressed and overly made-up women. Competing for space were also Union cavalry patrols and fast-moving military couriers mounted on thoroughbreds, galloping up and down the roadway delivering dispatches.

A few miles out of the city's limit the traffic began to die down, and Nate started to daydream about the past as he gazed at the surrounding scenery. Although it was only seven-thirty in the morning, the humidity, which formed a layer of haze, could be seen rising from the ground like a fog moving in from the sea. In a few hours, the hot sun and the moisture would mix together and form an oppressive heat. Nate's attention was suddenly drawn by a sound that originated from a dense clump of large banana trees dead ahead of him on the lefthand side of the road. The noise sounded as if someone was shaking the leaves of the banana trees in order to draw his attention. Nate commanded his gray gelding to a slow walk and maneuvered the animal toward the sounds. As he approached the banana trees he noticed what appeared to be a slender brown log until it moved slightly, as if attempting to conceal itself.

"All right, child . . . come outta there now, 'fore I come in and gets ya!" shouted Nate playfully. The moment he saw the brown log move, he knew it was the limb of a black child. He waited for a few seconds but nothing emerged from the clump of banana trees, so he hollered again, "Chil', I ain't foolin'! Come outta dare, now!"

The face of a little brown boy appeared from behind one of the lower leaves of a banana tree and smiled at Nate.

"What you doin' dare, *boy?* What yo' hidin' from?"

The boy emerged from the clump of trees and stared at Nate as he sucked on his thumb. He was barefoot and his shirt and trousers were patched with many different kinds of fabrics.

"Come here, son," beckoned Nate softly.

The boy remained motionless, still sucking on his thumb.

"Don't be 'fraid. I ain't goin' harm you."

"You a Yankee sold'er?" queried the boy, finally taking his thumb out of his mouth.

"I'm a soldier, but no Yankee man." Nate smiled. "What you doin out here?" inquired Nate, concerned that the boy might be lost.

"Playin' hide-an'-seek wid my broders," responded the lad.

"*Hide-an'-seek?*" responded Nate, reassured that the boy was not lost. "Where are your parents, son?"

"Down yonda by de creek," he replied, pointing his little right index finger in the designated direction. "Did yo' eva play hide-an'-seek?"

Nate thought for a moment. "Oh, yeah. I played hide-an'-seek, but it was no game."

"What yo' mean?" The boy was puzzled and kept staring at Nate's wide sergeant major's chevrons and high-top boots.

"Never you mind, boy, yo' get back to yo'r folks now, yo' hear? These roads ain't safe, an' besides, never leave your mother alone. Now go on . . . get," commanded Nate as he threw out his right hand in the direction of where the lad had indicated his relatives were camped. The boy hesitated at first but Nate kept staring at him, so he grudgingly obeyed.

Nate watched the boy walk away while his horse snorted violently several times from the pollen. "Hide-an'-seek. Hide-an'-seek. Yes, sir. It was a mawnin' like this one that I ran 'way and I was hidin' aw'right . . . from de goddamn patrollers!" The lad's innocent little game had forced Nate to ponder the circumstances of the day he escaped from Mas'a Hammond's plantation in St. Charles Parish. He turned up the sleeve of his shell jacket and gently ran his fingers along a deep and long scar that marked the under side of his left arm. A wide groove started from his palm and ran up to his elbow. The groove resembled a ravine, indicating a loss of flesh and muscle in that area.

"Well, could have been a hell of a lot worse," he thought to himself as he lifted and turned his head in the direction of the sun. He pulled out his bandanna and removed his kepi to wipe his head. His thoughts turned to that predawn day when he fled Mas'a Hammond's plantation and made his way toward the swamps. He shivered briefly when he pondered how he was pursued by the horrifying and incessant barking of the bloodhounds, the yelling of the patrollers, and gunshot sounds and bullets whizzing by his head. Nate sighed as he contemplated how his flight to freedom all seemed like yesterday.

Nate's predawn escape from the plantation did not go as he had planned. He had only traveled a few miles when the alarm was sounded; one of the drivers couldn't sleep because he had consumed too much stolen white lightning with some of his friends. As a consequence, he had to get up earlier than usual to urinate. Since the driver was also dehydrated, he made his way to the well to quench his burning thirst. As he passed Nate's shack, he noticed that the door was not completely shut, and found this strange since it was a damp and cold night. He decided to peek into the window and see if Nate was there. The driver approached the window and lifted the burlap cover; to his horror, the bed was empty. His eyes frantically searched the room but saw no signs of Nate. He began to shout out Nate's name in the quarter as he made his way toward Nate's mother's cabin, where he knew they would clandestinely meet to read books. Nate's mother, a tall and frail woman whose once-nimble hands were now knotted with arthritis, pleaded total ignorance on the whereabouts of her only son. After a quick inspection of her cabin the driver ran to the overseer's house, who in turn informed Mas'a Hammond of Nate's absence. When told that Nate had run, the supreme being of the plantation was outraged and ordered the overseer to ride like hell and engage the slave catcher, Bloodhound Jack, and alert the patrollers.

As Nate leisurely rode his gray gelding along the road toward Greenville, different thoughts wandered about in his mind. He thought about how carefully he had planned his escape, and with the help of his mother, they had packed a tight bag that Nate could tie around his waist so could run faster with his arms and hands free. The wraparound bag was made from heavy quilt cloth and sturdy burlap, and contained all they thought would be required for Nate to make his way north and avoid capture by the patrollers. Nate thought how instrumental his mother was in scrounging up about a pound of corn, stealing several small hambones from the smokehouse, and raiding Mas'a's garden to collect yams, onions, turnips, and sugar beets. Other items that his mother had insisted on packing were a needle, thread, and a clean blouse. Nate felt a little melancholy as he remembered saying good-bye to his mother. He could still feel her strong arms around him as she embraced him and commanded, "Go, boy . . . you run an' not stop till you get to Kansas an' fight to *free* de rest of us!" Nate bit his lip, located the north star, and started to run.

Nate vividly recalled the conversation that he had had with a traveling free black preacher, who informed him about how he had heard that the Yankees were recruiting escaped slaves and freemen in Kansas into military units for service against the Secesh. Nate had wanted to run since the war had broken out but when he privately conversed with the preacher after a Sunday service in the quarter, his motivation to flee peaked.

The most harrowing point on his long journey came on that first day of his flight. Nate only had an hour headstart on his pursuers. The bloodhounds had picked up his scent immediately from one of his old shirts, and the chase was on. The slave catchers were on horseback and were gaining on him fast. Although Nate moved quickly through the thick saw grasses of the marshes, his level of fear and desperation increased as the sounds from the dog's barking and howling, grew louder and closer. The canines, led by Bloodhound Jack's lead dog, Socomo, sensed that they were closing in on their prey. Desperate to gain distance on the dogs or loose their scent, Nate decided to take his chances of getting lost in the bayous. He plunged into the lagoons and waded knee-deep into the brackish water.

The moment Nate splashed into the water, the alligators, who were quietly sunning themselves along the banks of the bayou, were aroused by his movements. Sensing breakfast, the reptiles quickly slipped into the swamp from their high ground positions. Nate was about a hundred yards away from the other side of the lagoon when he noticed that a half a dozen gators were swimming rapidly toward him. Their scaled bodies partially submerged, the gators were swinging their tails back and forth to gain speed as they sensed that a meal was on hand. Nate saw their deep red eyes fixed on his person, and realized that he was going to be torn to pieces if he did not reach higher ground on the other side of the lagoon.

He decided that he was not going to outswim the gators. Chest heaving and adrenaline flowing, he could hear the bloodhounds approaching and the sounds of moving brush as the slave catchers' horses plowed through the vegetation and water pools of the bayou.

"Tell them bitches of yours to move faster, Bloodhound!" ordered the head slave catcher.

Nate heard him and knew his prospects looked grim as his mind raced with apprehension. Either he would be torn to pieces by the gators or shortly captured by the patrollers. Exhausted and resigned to make a final stand, he halted next to a big cypress tree surrounded by cattails and giant water hibiscus. He persuaded himself that he would rather die fighting gators then be forced to return to the plantation in chains and face a whipping by the sadistic overseer. He believed that if he could kill the lead gator, a ten-foot bull the others would be diverted by the smell of his blood, and give Nate enough time to escape.

The howling and yelping bloodhounds were very near now, and the slave catchers not far behind. Nate pulled out his homemade bowie knife and prepared to meet his reptilian attackers. He grabbed the pommel of his knife in his right hand, and rather than wait for the lead gator to make the first move, decided to lunge at him with his knife and plunge the blade into the back of his neck. He screamed at the top of his lungs and lunged at the gator, "You *bastard!*"

He moved his right arm and body forward as if he was a grizzly, ready to pounce on a snake. He aimed for the neck of the reptile and bellowed, "You're not goin' to git me!"

Nate yelled and grunted as he repeatedly plunged the huge bowie again and again into the tough hide of the gator until the water around them was red with blood. Because the gator moved so quickly and his scaled skin was slippery from the murky water of the swamp, Nate failed to mortally wound the reptile in the neck because the blade kept slipping against the hide. He was plunging the big knife all the way up to the pommel when, on his fourth thrust, his hand slipped past the grip and he seriously gashed three of his fingers on the razor-sharp edge of the knife.

The bull gator, although seriously wounded, was not dead. The reptile quickly slipped under the water line and circled around Nate. His giant mouth was wide open when he leaped from the water, seized Nate's left arm, and held on, wiggling his body in an attempt to tear off a piece of meat. As Nate desperately tried to pull his left arm out of the gator's mouth and avoid being dragged into the water, he plunged his Bowie with his right hand into the gator's soft underbelly, ripping the beast's stomach as if he was butchering a hog. This finished the reptile.

By now the dogs were approaching the banks of the bayou, and Bloodhound Jack's favorite bloodhound, Socomo, dived into the lagoon. The remaining members of the pack followed him into the water, oblivious that the swamp was infested with alligators. Although Nate's arm was seriously ripped open and bleeding profusely, his adrenaline flowed as his instinct for survival remained paramount. He climbed out of the lagoon and started to run as fast as he could without looking back. The other gators' attention now turned to the movement in the water and noise made by the dogs.

By the time the bloodhounds were in the middle of the lagoon, the gators were upon them as if they were flies lured by a rotting carcass. Slow to maneuver in water, the hounds were defenseless against these reptiles. A dog paddle was no match for fast, slippery tails, and the hapless animals became easy prey. The reptiles surrounded the pack, and when they came within striking distance, they dived and pulled the hounds down beneath the water line, where one by one they ripped and disemboweled them in an orgiastic feeding frenzy. The usual tranquil insect and bird sounds of the bayou were interrupted now by horrific howls and yelps of dogs being disemboweled. Although Nate moved quickly and deeper into the swamp, he could hear the sounds of the dogs being butchered and devoured. He did not want to look back, so he just pushed on as fast as he could, pressing his left arm against his chest in an attempt to minimize the bleeding.

In the brackish water of the lagoon, oozing pools of blood appeared mixed with dog parts. Paws, legs, and tails were floating on the surface, and some limbs became wedged in the saw grass and the exposed roots of cypress trees.

As the slave catchers approached the lagoon, Bloodhound Jack was perplexed that he could not hear any of the yelps, barking, or howling that were characteristic of his dogs when they were close to their quarry, but as soon as he arrived at the lagoon's edge he noticed the red water and the entrails and pieces of meat floating around. Already the birds and other scavengers that inhabit the bayou were picking and clawing at the meager remains.

As the posse stared in total disbelief at the carnage, Bloodhound Jack started to cry and repeat over and over again, "My dawgs, my poor, poor, hounds. They all gone. *Butchered!*"

The leader of the posse, a tall, clean-shaven man wearing a planter's hat and a heavily soiled white duster, noticed an oval object wedged among some exposed roots of a cypress in the middle of the lagoon. The murky water was lapping around the object. In his haste to start after Nate, he had forgotten his spectacles, so he had to squint his eyes in order to focus. His eyes were suddenly wide open and he nearly swallowed his wad of tobacco when he identified the mysterious object. "Holy Mother of God," he exclaimed. He rubbed his face and covered his eyes with his right hand, as if he could not bear to look at the object, for the sight might upset his stomach. "Jack. Look ov'r there yonder, among the roots of that big cypress." The leader meekly pointed to where the object lay lodged. "I think, I think, it's . . . Oh *lawd,* it's ol' Socomo's head!"

Bloodhound Jack stared toward the spot where his prize dog's head rested among the exposed roots of the tree, and started to weep and sob as if he were a child. Tears running down his scraggly beard, mouth quivering, he began to chant as if he was participating in some solemn religious ritual.

"Gawd have mercy. Gawd have mercy. Oh Lawd! Please Lawd. That can't be my Socomo's head!"

Bloodhound Jack's eyes were aflame with anger and his face soaked with tears as his eyes oozed water down his cheeks. He walked up to the edge of the lagoon and opened up his mouth wide, exposing his heavily tobacco-stained yellow teeth. He started to yell at the top of his lungs in the direction where Nate had disappeared into the bayou.

"I'll kill you, *nigger!* I'll make you pay for killin' my dawgs! I swear to Jehovah, I'll hunt you down if it takes till the second coming."

Bloodhound Jack was shaking his fist in the air as if he were swearing an oath. Frustrated and furious, he grabbed a shotgun from the rifle pouch of a nearby horse. He cocked both hammers all the way back and fired each barrel into the swamp, frightening hundreds of birds that fled the tall branches and tops of nearby trees. He then demanding more shells and kept loading and reloading the shotgun and firing blindly into the bayou, knowing full well that Nate was out of range. Finally a companion, embarrassed that one of their own was losing his senses, forcefully led Bloodhound Jack to the rear of the group as he continued to sob and demand more shotgun shells.

"Well, boys, that's the end of this chase," said the leader of the slave catchers as he hurled a big wad of spent tobacco into the lagoon. He had been chewing the wad throughout the chase and now was glad to be rid of it. Then as an afterthought, in order to calm Bloodhound

Jack, he tried to be reassuring. "Least for now, Bloodhound."

"The hell it is," retorted Bloodhound Jack as he sniffled and wiped the tears from his face with his sleeve, leaving brown streaks on his cheeks. "I'll come back wid mo' dawgs and run the darkie bastard straight to hell."

"You'll do it on your own time, Bloodhound. The country is full of runaways and we don't have time to try and catch this one buck."

Five

As Nate approached Greenville, which was not a town but an undeveloped faubourg that was part of Orleans Parish, his eyes focused on a building that appeared melancholy. The brick building stood detached near the edge of the dirt road surrounded by dozens of hitching posts for horses and buggies. Tall clusters of banana trees that were no older than a few years sprouted near and around the structure, giving the place an aura of neglect.

As his gelding walked toward the building, he noticed Old Glory flapping in the slight breeze from the second-story window, and an overhead faded sign with capital letters painted above the main entrance, which he could not make out.

"That would be the recruitment office," he said to himself softly as he patted his mount's neck. Nate always felt better expressing his joy and sorrows with horses rather than with people. During the war, he had ridden many different horses. It saddened him to think about the number of noble animals that had been shot from under him while engaging the enemy.

Nate decided to dismount from his horse and walk the remaining hundred or so yards in order to cool off the animal. The lettering on top of the main doorway still remained indecipherable so he squinted his eyes to try and make out what the old lettering spelled. As he led his tired gray gelding by the reins, he saw three pickets clustered together, laughing, a testimony to the structure's once central importance in the Parish's economic and cultural life.

As his gray gelding approached the building that flew the stars and stripes from the central second-story window, Nate felt his heart sink. He was close enough to read the faded painted lettering above the main entrance: LAPORTE & SONS, DEALERS IN SLAVES.

Nate's face tightened and his body stiffened in anger. He halted, loosened his hold on the reins, pushed back on the rim of his kepi, and shook his head in irate disbelief. "Gawdforsaken place. Can't believe af'er every thing we been through, that they converted a slave pen and auction house into a recruitment office to *enlist black men!*"

Nevertheless, he was determined not to pay any attention to the fact that this structure represented wickedness and a place of earthly hell for many of his black brothers. He proceeded to the entrance, where he dismounted and signaled to an orderly to take care of his horse and pack mule.

The three sentries were leaning against the wall near the middle doorway, their arms resting on the curvature part of the socket bayonets that were fixed to their Springfield muskets. The corporal of the guard, who was wearing white gloves, was in the process of telling his comrades a joke.

"Dare was dis mas'a who axed his driver how he kin keep firm for a *long time* when he does it with de missus. The driver said, 'Mas'a . . . youz *gots to take your time*. Youz gots to git up from time to time an' have smoke, an' get back into it. An' when de missus is all hot an' beggin' you for moe, you get up *again* an' look at de moon or have a shot of brandy.' So de mas'a goes back to de big house an' starts a doin it wid de missus an' she gets all hot an' begs likes she's a cat in heat, an' de mas'a gets up an' lights up a seegar an' stares out de window lookin' at de moon. He takes a puff or two an' puts out de seegar an' starts doin' it *again* wid de missus. Well . . . de missus is now *real* excited an' begs him not to stop. But mas'a get up one moe time! An' dis time he drinks a little brandy, leavin' his wife on de bed a-turnin' an' a-rollin' around in de sheets all *excited*. At last, de missus can't take no moe an' she cries out to de mas'a . . . Gawddamn you, you fuckin' me like a nigger!" The sentries erupted in laughter, back-slapped each other, and one of them had to hold his gut as he howled uncontrollably.

When the corporal of the guard noticed Nate, however, he abruptly halted his laughter and came to attention.

"I hope you boys had a *good* laugh, cause it's de *last* one you all will tell while on duty," said Nate sternly.

"Yes suh, Sergeant Major," said the corporal, smiling while the others were still snickering.

"Never call me sir, boy! That's reserved for off'cers, not for non-commissioned men. *And take dat grin off yo face*," barked Nate, looking into the corporal's eyes as if he was about to devour him. Chastised and fearing for his two stripes, the corporal immediately puckered his lips to be rid of the grin. "That's it, boy. Good. Now, is de commanding officer inside?"

"No, Sergeant Major. Wez 'spect him soon, though. He comes 'bout nine o'cock."

Nate's eyes wandered all over the building. He could not help but take note of the wrought-iron bars on the windows of the adjoining slave pen, and the elevated brick platform, now covered with tropical vegetation, that was once used for auctioning humans into bondage. Although he did not feel as if he was entering a military establishment, Nate stepped inside the recruitment center.

The interior paint of the main building was peeling and the walls and ceilings had wide cracks in the plaster. The air smelled of musk mixed with the reeking aroma of old urine. It was dark, and hundreds of flies were crawling on the walls and buzzing loudly. The wide central hallway had two large rooms on either side, and Nate peered into each one. The rooms were scantily furnished. Some camp desks, requisitioned chairs, and a few beat-up file cabinets made up the offices.

In one of the rooms, several old and faded recruitment circulars left over from the war were displayed. One poster, which Nate recognized immediately, was the "Come and join us, brothers" recruitment announcement. The painting showed a company of black infantry soldiers standing at attention with a white officer and Old Glory in the center. Nate chuckled. He found it amusing that in every military enlistment circular he had ever seen designed to encourage colored men to swell the ranks of the Union army, white officers were always taller than the black troops he commanded, while in reality, Negro troops were often much taller than the white officers.

Nate slowly walked to the center of the building where the

entrance of the slave-pen annex was located. The pen, as it was called by locals, was where they once kept the slaves before they were placed on the auction block. He opened the huge door that led to the annex and entered hesitantly. The place looked as it did before the war. The room was extremely dark and was divided into several large pens that resembled animal stalls. They were sealed by thick oak doors with little sliding cast-iron viewing windows. The slots served as peepholes.

At the very end of the annex was the punishment cell. This was where they kept the "difficult" slaves in cast-iron shackles fastened to the walls with large rings. The chains were encrusted in rust and shrouded in cobwebs now, and as Nate stared at the corroded manacles and watched the spiders crawl about on the dusty oak floor, he thought about how many times he had seen his brethren chained by their necks, ankles, and wrists, to hitching posts as if they were cattle, or to the rear of wagons and forced to run in order to keep from falling down and being dragged.

"Damn place should be burned to de ground," Nate whispered to himself. Then in a brief fit of rage bellowed, "*Hell.* All you need are some whips, thumbscrews, handcuffs, iron yokes, and some stocks and this place be jest like de ol' days."

The condition of the building forced Nate to recall the occasions that he had to go into New Orleans with Mas'a Hammond and pick up supplies and, of course, new slaves that were purchased at the auction house for the running of the plantation. On one particular occasion, Mas'a Hammond, after a lengthy and heated bidding war with a rival planter, lost the possibility of buying a Mandingo. The slave was smuggled to the continent via Cuba by a rogue Dutch slave-ship captain who could not resist the lucrative pay off of selling prime captive black men. Ignoring the international ban on slavery, the Dutch man persisted in engaging in the illegal commerce of human flesh, and specialized in high-priced captives such as Mandingos, who were particularly tall and muscular and were in high demand for field work. Nate, being the biggest slave on the plantation, was called on by Mas'a Hammond to accompany him to the slave auction, and be available in case one of his new chattel's became unruly on the way home.

Nate remembered how the auctioneer, a man with a ghoulish face, hawk nose, and bad skin, dressed completely in black with a stove-top hat, introduced the Mandingo to the buyers. "Gentlemen! I have here today," announced the auctioneer, grinning. "A *surprise*. A genuine Mandingo . . . fresh from the Niger river valley of West Africa." Some of the planters' wives expressed delight, exclaiming *ooh* and *ahh,* while many of the men remained skeptical. The auctioneer continued, "Now, I know that you gentlemen *know* that the Mandingos are *superior* to all other blacks. And they are *prized* for their great *strength, stamina*, and *longevity*." Several planters nodded their heads in approval. The auctioneer saved his best line for last, as a means to drum up a buying spirit among the bidders. Nate watched with great curiosity as the auctioneer raised his long arms above his head as if he was a preacher beseeching the all mighty and yell, "*Hell!* They can do the work of ten fieldhands!"

The auctioneer's salesmanship talent paid off. The first planter, a gray bearded man with a beige frock coat, shouted, "I'll bid five hundred for that buck." "One thousand," responded another bidder coolly, as he smoked on a cigar and slowly blew smoke into the air. "Twelve hundred dollars!" proclaimed one well-dressed slave buyer confidently, as his heavily painted lady friend fanned her face with a huge Spanish fan. Mas'a Hammond's top bid was two thousand dollars, but he lost to another planter, a man from Natchez, who offered two thousand five hundred, which settled the matter.

During the bidding, the Mandingo stood in the middle of the auction block virtually naked except for a tattered, filthy loin cloth. His body, black as coal, was wet with perspiration and gleaned in the midday sunlight. Standing erect, he towered over the auctioneer. Chest heaved forward, his face and eyes were filled with pride, and the Mandingo's muscular formation made Nate feel weak and small. He was well over six feet, and Nate recalled how his packed arms, legs, and neck resembled the branches of an oak tree.

When the auctioneer's thin, freckled hands tried to open the Mandingo's mouth to show off his teeth to the gaping crowd, he defiantly bolted and threw up his shackled arms into the air. He brazenly yelled at the spectators and bidders in a language that Nate had never heard before. The crowd was startled and drew back, while some of the women led their gaping, open-mouthed children to the rear. The auctioneer became alarmed and decided to postpone the bidding. He ordered the slave handlers to whip the Mandingo into submission and drag the man to the punishment cell in the pen, where he would be restrained by wall chains and choke collar until he had what the auctioneer called "a change of attitude."

Nate sighed as he thought about the Mandingo. If there was one person in the world besides his mother and the cowardly death of his father that influenced him more than anyone else, it was the figure of that unknown, big black man in chains. Nate remembered how he felt humiliated at the sight of the stripped man standing perfectly erect on the auction block. At the time, the poignancy of what he had witnessed so deeply affected him that he feared for years that this might happen to him or to his mother. The Mandingo taught him, however, that although his feet and hands were in irons, and he was completely naked except for a rag that served as a modest loincloth, his spirit remained free because he still possessed pride and defied his tormentors. The episode was traumatic to be sure, and placed fear into his heart, but it also instilled new resolve within Nate. If there was one moment when he made up his mind to run and gain his freedom, it was when he saw how the shackled Mandingo comported himself against the hostile crowd, the whip, and brutal treatment.

Mas'a Hammond was impressed with the Mandingo in the same way a horse owner would be with a prized stallion, workhorse, or bull. His eyes glowing, he commented to Nate enthusiastically, "That giant darkie sure would have been my most *prize* possession, come cotton-picking time." His mood suddenly turned solemn. "Damn that fellow from Natchez. How *dare* he come down here and buy up our precious stock!"

Nate was astonished that Mas'a Hammond should show any signs of respect toward the Mandingo. Granted, it was a perverse form of esteem, but Nate never forgot that episode and the lesson he learned that afternoon. For a slave to keep his self-respect, the colored must not only endure daily injustice, frequent physical brutality, and spiritual degradation, but also denial of his or her worth as a human being. It was then that Nate made up his mind that when the opportunity presented itself, he would run, and take his chances in either being free or dead. He wanted to be like the Mandingo who had refused to submit to bondage even though he probably knew it was futile.

Six

Capt. Frederick Graham was late this morning arriving at the recruitment center. He was hungover and felt physically ill. All he really wanted to do was stay in bed and to hell with responsibilities. He had lost his left hand during the Battle of the Wilderness and was bitter that he had to wear a wooden substitute that neither functioned nor fit properly. As a consequence, it always took him a long time to dress. The scion of a once-prominent Baltimore family, Captain Graham had grown old and tired in the army. His red hair was thinning, and there were deep circles around his eyes.

This morning, Captain Graham's black orderly had not appeared, so he had to struggle to put on his new boots with his only good hand. The task was made even more difficult by virtue of the fact that he was addicted to a liquid narcotic called wine mariani. A drink derived from the coca leaf, wine mariani, if consumed in small dosages, was said to lift the spirit of the weary, and provide greater physical energy for those who felt tired or weak. When consumed to excess, however, as was the practice with Captain Graham, the abuser would experience severe withdrawal if the craving was not satiated on a regular basis. The addict would then have to resort to strong spirits in order to induce sleep. It was Captain Graham's pathetic habit to consume too much of the narcotic when he started to think about the companions he had lost during the war, and wallow in self-pity that he was an amputee. Alone, at night, in his humid, insect-infested room, he would brood in silence and consume wine mariani until he slowly became intoxicated and passed out.

When his left hand was amputated in a Washington hospital by an Italian immigrant doctor, the well-meaning physician felt compassion for Graham's constant suffering and depressed mood caused by his wounds. The doctor started to administer small dosages of wine mariani to him, which he took from his private stock that he had brought with him from Italy. The narcotic greatly improved the patient's mental disposition, but Graham discovered that he simply could not go through the day without it. He became a drug addict, and hated himself for it.

He also despised his post as the officer responsible for the recruitment center. Graham would lie on his bed alone in his wretched room at night, usually intoxicated, and bitterly reflect on his circumstances. How could the military do this to him? he would ask himself over and over again. He had become obsessed with what he considered a great injustice, and as time passed, he grew increasingly embittered about how the military was treating him, especially when he had sacrificed his right hand for the preservation of the Union. He felt he could be no more isolated than if he were exiled to the other side of the moon.

He resented the task he had been ordered to do. He cursed the politicians in Washington and the fools at the war department for forming two new "nigger" cavalry regiments. Drunk on wine mariani, he would cry out loud in his room at night as a means to vent his deep anger and frustration. "Recruit darkies for duty on the frontier? Absurd! What next? Black officers?" Graham also felt vexed that all the brevet ranks earned through merit during the war were being reduced in rank and pay. He had been a lieutenant colonel during the last year of the conflict but was now reduced to the level of captain, and consequently detested the diminishment of his privileges.

Partly out of revenge and spite against the army, and partly out of the need to compensate for his monetary losses as a result of being demoted to an inferior rank, Captain Graham became part of a ring of black marketeers. Several months prior he had been approached by the quartermaster sergeant of the New Orleans horse depot, who boasted that he had contacts all over the Crescent City engaging in siphoning off army property and selling the goods to merchants in all of the major cities in Louisiana. Military equipment such as McClellan saddles, bridles, army great coats, blouses, boots, cookware, and food were being diverted from the troops and sold to dealers who had eager customers. Business was good for the quartermaster sergeant and his business cronies, but they harbored larger ambitions. They wanted to sell horses and mules from the main depot, which fetched a premium among desperate planters who needed draft animals to plant and harvest crops. The planters were so frantic to get their farms in working order after four years of war that they were willing to lien their properties to the black marketeers if they could obtain draft animals. In order to fulfill their long-term ambitions however, the black marketeers needed a senior officer in a colored regiment to order horses and mules on paper—to protect themselves in case they were ever audited. They decided that no one would notice or care if they diverted horses and mules from a negro regiment and sold the animals on the market for their own personal gain. Considering that Graham felt cheated and resentful of the army for what it had done to him, it did not take him very long to decide to cast his lot with the black marketeers for a share in the lucrative profits. The arrangement was that he would draw up orders once a week, requesting horses and mules for the regiment, and made sure to mention that previous mounts that had been delivered had died of diseases. That way, if there was an investigation, there would be a proper paper trail, and if the auditors would inquire why there were so few horses or mules for the regiment, Graham would simply state that they had perished and that he had burned the carcasses.

Captain Graham finally arrived at the recruitment center with his adjutant in tow. He was dressed as if he was on parade. He wore a black felt hat with three ostrich feathers on the left side, and his double-breasted frock coat was buttoned all the way up to the collar. As usual, he had his wooden left hand wedged in between the two middle brass buttons of his coat. He discovered Nate inside the main office going through dossiers of recent recruits with the corporal of the guard.

"Who in the hell are you, Sergeant?"

Nate could see that Graham was furious. He knew that this officer was probably thinking, Who is this darkie noncom upstart rifling through my files? Graham removed his felt hat and placed it on the edge of the bureau.

"Sergeant Major Nate Gordon, on special assignment from the Tenth Cavalry, reporting for duty, *sir*."

Nate stood at attention but felt a little awkward getting caught perusing recruitment dossiers by the commanding officer. He reached within his leather haversack, pulled out Lieutenant Colonel Merritt's orders, and handed the envelope to Captain Graham.

Graham took the yellow envelope and handed it to his adjutant, who broke the wax seal and began reading the orders. While the adjutant was reading the orders, Graham was scrutinizing Nate. He circled him as if he was some raw recruit about to be chastised for some infraction.

"The Tenth Cavalry, eh?" Graham was in his usual cynical mood, and he felt particularly abrasive this morning. "Who gave you permission to rifle through my files, Sergeant?"

"Beggin' the Captain's pardon, sir, my orders come from Lieutenant Colonel Merritt, and I believe that when you examine de dispatches, it will be clear, sir, that I'm here to assist you in your efforts to recruit able-bodied black men for service in de United States Cavalry, sir."

Nate was very composed. He knew he had Merritt's support in assessing what needed to be done here, and implement changes he considered necessary to raise the Ninth Cavalry to full strength.

The adjutant finished reading the orders, and raised his head to interject, "It's true, sir, Headquarters has assigned Sergeant Major Gordon to be of service to us in making improvements at the recruitment center."

The adjutant handed the documents to Graham, but the captain waved them away with his wooden hand. He wanted to make sure that Nate saw that he had paid a price in the war for *his freedom!* "Make *improvements,* eh?" Graham was outraged that his powers might be usurped by a black noncommissioned officer. "And . . . what improvements would you make, Sergeant?" said Graham sarcastically.

Nate was aware that Graham wanted to provoke Nate into a response that would expose him for a dressing down. Nate, however, remained at attention, and his voice stayed composed.

"The sign, sir. The outside sign should be painted over, and the chains removed from the walls, and the bars should come down . . ."

"That's enough, Sergeant Major!" Graham was becoming as red as a beet. Nate however, was insistent.

"With respect, sir, my people will never come here and enlist, considering that this place is a former *slave pen* and auction house."

By the expression on Graham's face, Nate saw that he was unmoved by the argument that the sign was offensive and scared blacks from enlisting.

"Well, Sergeant, then how do you explain the fact that Negroes have been signing up in droves?" demanded Graham as he sneered at Nate.

"Again, beggin' the Captain's pardon, sir, according to Lieutenant Colonel Merritt, de qualities of mos' of the men are questionable, sir."

"*Questionable*? Well, Sergeant Major Gordon." Graham started to circle Nate again. "We will see if you can make a difference under the adverse circumstances we have had to endure here. . . . Now get out of my office, I have work to do."

Nate gave Graham a crisp salute, turned on his heels, and exited the room, followed by the corporal of the guard.

Seven

The verbal confrontation with Captain Graham left Nate unsettled, but after viewing the recruitment encampment, he realized that his task, converting the flea bitten camp into something resembling a proper military post, would be difficult. The encampment was located a short distance from the center of Greenville and situated on an abandoned cotton plantation in sight of the Mississippi River. Captain Graham and his staff occupied the Big House, while the recruits and most of the noncoms were bivouacked in old cotton compresses and dilapidated farm buildings that leaked like giant strainers when the rain poured, which was almost daily in Louisiana. Nate could not help but be reminded that this situation was comparable with his former state of slavery. The white officers, like the master's family and his toadying house niggers, were in the Big House calling the shots, while the recruits, like the fieldhands, were in the quarter, lodged in miserable shelters. Nate was appalled when he saw some of the recruits using badly rotted Sibley tents left over from the war.

What really outraged Nate were the dozens of wandering farm animals that were at liberty to roam the camp and defecate where they pleased. Chickens scratched around in the dirt and perched where the men slept and had their meals. Goats spent their days and nights nibbling at tents, uniforms, and leather. Most of the physical damage and general health threat to the men in the camp however, were the dozen or so pigs that routinely escaped their poke and rooted all around the camp. As a result, small pools of standing water filled with mosquitoes dotted the camp. The swine especially enjoyed wallowing in the shallow lagoon that also served as the camp's main water supply. They devoured all vegetation in sight, turned over camp equipment, and occasionally invaded the barracks to bite a trooper's leg or arm during the night.

After Nate had settled in at the noncommissioned officer's cabin, he was led on a tour by 1st Sgt. William "Willie" McKlintock. The first sergeant pointed out other signs of disorder and unhealthy conditions, such as laundry lines that crisscrossed the camp, festooned with all sorts of different articles of clothing and rags. Piles of rubbish, infested with maggots and millions of flies, were too close to the camp's only source of water, the nearby lagoon that emptied into the bayou. Most of the laundry, bathing, and drinking water came from that source, and a hastily dug latrine ditch that was swarming with insects and parasites was only a few yards away from the lagoon.

"*Gawd almighty*. This place is ripe fo' chol'ra!" Nate remarked to Willie, incensed.

"If you tink the campsite's bad, wait till you meet some of the men. We've a real problem here. Mos' of de recruits will nev' make good soldiers. They here fo' the thirteen dollar a month and the *blue suit*. They got no sense of whut kind of commitment it takes to be a United States soldier. *Ev'ry day* I gots to break up knife an' bottle fights 'tween them. I spend mo' time jest tryin' to keep de peace then drilling the men."

"What 'bout Captain Graham? Don't he know 'bout this?" queried Nate in disbelief.

Nate already knew the answer but he wanted to hear what Willie had to say. After all, he seemed to be the only man here who knew what was really going on.

"The captain?!" Sergeant McKlintock bowed his head, removed his kepi, and wiped his head with a bandanna. He then sighed and bowed his head in disgust. "He nev' comes here. He thinks we all a bunch of no-good niggers and should be back in the fields. All he wants is be transferred to Wash'ton, and wear a pretty uniform." Willie paused, then added, "He don't give a coon's terd fo' us. We can all rot here 'fore he gives a damn."

"I don't know why I'm not surprised," said Nate cynically.

Sergeant McKlintock nodded his head in agreement.

"Well, I've a few surprises fo' him." Nate's eyes wandered around the camp. He was determining how he could do some immediate improvements.

Willie however, started to laugh. Nate just smiled, nodding his head back and forth, and waited until Sergeant McKlintock finished his foolish laughter. Willie could not help himself. He thought he knew better than Nate that it was virtually hopeless to make changes if white officers wanted to keep you down. He had seen many injustices during the war. The Negroes were more often used as cannon fodder and for digging ditches. How could this single noncom make any changes?

"I can make a difference." With cold seriousness, Nate calmly told Willie some facts. "I'm goin' to be de eyes and ears of General Wesley Merritt." Nate paused and then looked Willie squarely in the eyes. "And I've got the authority."

"Authority to do what?" exclaimed Willie skeptically.

"We need to keep what I'm goin' to say to ourselfs. You can help me make it better here, so we can git on with de business of fightin' Indians on the frontier." Nate paused, then with a heavy voice said, "Durin' the war, we were of'en given the worst duties. Manual labor was the only t'ing they thought we could do, till we prov' to them over and over again that we could not only stop a bullet like a white man, but fight just as well, maybe even better than them. I'm determined, with the help of some good and important officers, not to repeat that pattern and git this regiment out of this filthy camp." Nate grinned again. His smile was the most attractive feature of his face. "I've Merritt's full confidence to make de necessary changes we need to complete our training and git the Ninth movin'." Then, as an afterthought, Nate added, "And the first ting I'm goin' to do is paint over that damn sign that reads LAPORTE & SONS, DEALERS IN SLAVES."

After the bugler sounded taps that first night at camp, Nate was busy writing Lieutenant Colonel Merritt a long letter describing the conditions of the camp and his initial impressions of the general poor quality of most of the recruits. Nate was a slow but careful writer. During the war, he used to write most of the reports concerning the condition of his men, as well as writing letters informing widows and relatives of the death of their men. Most of the letters never reached their destinations, however; many families were displaced from their place of origin and lingered in freedmens camps throughout the occupied South. Even if some of the letters did get through, the only people who could read them would be preachers, and they were often hard to find.

Each time Nate would put pen to paper, he thought of his mother. During the war, every time he would help his brethren by either reading to them or writing letters to their loved ones, Nate considered this as a way to pay back his mother and the risks she took to teach her son how to seek knowledge, because she knew that there was nothing more powerful in the white man's world than the printed word. Like his grandmother, Nate's mother passed on and practiced one of the main cardinal sins that was prohibited in the plantation system; the ability to read and write. Nate's mother taught him the basics of reading, writing, and all the arithmetic she knew, which was not much. Nate's mother, Mary Reynolds, was a house servant and Mas'a Hammond's wife's "favorite darkie." As was the case with her mother, Mary Reynolds was responsible for the dusting, polishing, and mopping of Mas'a Hammond's sizable library. Once or twice a week she would "borrow" a book from the library when she cleaned the room. As she carefully dusted each volume she would open the work and read a few sentences to determine whether the book would benefit her son's education. As she softly sang songs to herself she would gently place the leather-bound editions in her washbasket and smuggle them from the Big House.

Nate's mother would then go home and dust and broom-sweep the dirt-floor shack and make supper from the leftovers that Mas'a Hammond's wife would insist she take home with her because she liked her "big, strong son Nate," and thought that he was not getting enough to eat.

After all the lights of the slave quarter were extinguished, Nate and his mother would sit in a corner of their rude little shack and cover themselves with a patchwork blanket that Mary Reynolds had lovingly sewed together. They would prop up the quilt with the broom stick to create a tent and light a candle stub on the floor so they could read.

They would have to stop reading, however, when the searing vertical heat from the candle threatened to ignite the quilt and start a fire. Nate's mother always feared that a fire would start and the shack would burn down. All reading and talking were conducted in low voices and whispers. To be discovered would mean severe punishment, the worst being forced separation from Nate. Mary Reynold's fear of a possible fire and punishment for being discovered, however, did not curtail her determination that her son should read and write. They would read for about five to eight minutes and then blow out the candle and remain still in total darkness. Rather than remain quiet, though, Nate's mother would use the time to talk about what they just had read as they waited for the quilt to cool down so they could resume their reading. As the years passed by, they had read many books, and Nate's favorites were Washington Irving, Nathaniel Hawthorne, Henry David Thoreau, and other "Yankee" writers, as Mas'a Hammond often referred to his wife's preferred literary tastes for northern authors. Nate most particularly liked Herman Melville's *Moby Dick*. His favorite character was the occasional cannibal and tattooed "savage" harpooner, Queequeg, who came from the mythical island of Kokovoko. Nate identified with Queequeg because he was unpredictable, independent, and different from the white or black man. He was also a traveler, and Nate had a burning curiosity to travel and see what was beyond the nearby plantations.

Nate and 1st Sgt. Willie McKlintock had arrived at the recruitment building well before reveille. Nate had ordered the premises to be entirely broom-swept and dusted, and had personally removed the wall chains in the old punishment cell and buried the items deep in the ground. Nate wanted the place to have some appearance of decency and create a more militarylike environment. He inspected the guards and weapons and had to reprimand one of them for not properly cleaning his Springfield.

"*Boy* . . . The nipple is *choked* with *dirt*. The weapon will *misfire* and prob'ly blow your face off," he yelled, standing inches away from the guard's face.

"Yes, Sergeant Major," replied the guard, fully chastised.

Since First Sergeant McKlintock could not read or write, Nate sat behind the table with a huge ledger notebook that was used to inscribe the names and details of the recruits.

By late morning several men had arrived at the recruitment center and stood in line outside of the office.

"All right. Bring the first man in," ordered Nate as he waved his hand at the corporal of the guard.

The first man who entered the room was drunk, and stank from stale beer and vomit. He scratched his crotch with such frequency that Nate knew that the man must have a bad case of scabies. "Ah, ah, ah . . . wants to join up, ah . . ."

"*Corporal*. Escort this drunkard out the back door, and if he should resist, use your bayonet," barked Nate. The drunkard's facial expression became perplexed and confused as he was escorted from the room by the corporal of the guard.

"Next man," ordered Nate.

A tall man dressed in city clothes with a gold watch chain protruding from his vest pockets entered the room. As Nate watched the man walk toward him, he thought that his gait possessed a rhythm of arrogance and slyness. Nate also noticed that the man's boots were of good-quality leather and were polished to a high gloss. He halted at the very edge of the table and smiled. Nate knew that his smile was a ruse to hide something, and he became irked when the man halted so close to the edge of his table.

"You want to enlist in de United States Army?" asked Willie as he folded his arms across his chest.

"I want to join de cavalry, and gets the thirteen dollars a month. I figure dats good pay fo' ridin' a horse and chasin' Injuns."

"If we decide to ac'ept you, you'll earn ev'ry cent of that money," retorted Willie.

"What's your name, boy?" asked Nate as he stared into the man's eyes.

"Percy-Ray Pridgeon," he replied, his mouth twitching slightly to the left.

"You running 'way from de law?" Nate's instincts told him that this man might be a no-good drifter, a thief on the run, or simply an opportunist.

"I ain't runnin' from de law, lest not de white man's law," he replied defensively.

"You seem fit 'nough, though somtin' tells me that you are a liar an' been up to *no good*." Nate hesitated to enroll him, but he needed strong men, and this Percy-Ray Pridgeon appeared to be solid enough for soldiering. As for his questionable character, Nate decided that he just had to take a chance and try and mold him into a disciplined cavalryman. "All right Sergeant McKlintock will explain the conditions of your service in the United States Army, and if you agrees to the terms, make your mark in this book. Have all ready wrote in your name, but I need your age and occupation, 'fore I let you make your mark."

"I's born twenty year ago. And my occupation?" Percy-Ray thought for a moment and replied, "I's a boatman."

"A boat man?" echoed Willie. "Youz a rivaboat man?"

"*Yeah*, that be right!" insisted Percy-Ray, lifting his head proudly.

"And where's you from, riverboat man?" asked Nate skeptically.

"I's from Mis'sip'i."

"Make your mark, then," ordered Nate as he turned the ledger book and pointed to where Percy-Ray Pridgeon had to write in an X. "Now, you go with de sergeant here, and he'll explain de rules and send you to de quartermaster for your uniform."

"What 'bout a rifle? Don't I gets to carry a rifle?" demanded Percy-Ray.

"You'll be shootin' soon 'nough, Private," retorted Nate. He then smiled and stared into Percy-Ray's eyes. "When I say so."

"Next man."

A little man with spectacles carefully entered the room and removed his felt hat. Nate was disappointed that he was not very tall, maybe five foot seven inches at the most, but appeared to have an amiable quality about him, and even though the man was wearing spectacles, Nate noticed that his eyes showed great intelligence.

"You want to join de cavalry, son?" asked Nate softly.

"Yes sir, I wants to be a soldier," replied the little man.

"Never call me sir, son. My rank is sergeant major, and I expect to be ad'ressed accordingly. Do I make myself clear?"

"Yes, Sergeant Major," replied the little man.

"What's your name?"

"Mathias Pryor."

"Well, Mathias Pryor, where do you come from?"

"Charleston, South Carolina," responded Mathias Pryor smartly.

"Age and occupation?"

"Twenty-two years old."

"Occupation?"

"House servant, Sergeant Major."

"*Hey boys*! We gots a house nigga who wants to join up," yelled one man who was waiting in the line and overheard Mathias's response. Most of the prospective recruits started to snicker and catcall insulting comments to Mathias.

"Whats you gonna do boy? Clean assholes all day long?" added another man who hollered uncontrollably with laughter.

"Silence, out there!" bellowed Nate as he partially lifted his body from its sitting position behind the table. The laughter died down after a few moments and Nate resumed his questioning.

"Can you read and write?"

Mathias bowed his head slightly, his eyes shifting toward the line where the other prospective recruits were standing. He mumbled softly, somewhat embarrassed, "Yes, Sergeant Major, I can read and write." He did not want the other men to know about his literary qualities, because many of his brethren were denied the opportunity to acquire the forbidden fruit of learning, and consequently he felt that his relatively privileged position produced resentment and envy.

"*Speak up, boy*. Can't hear you," ordered Nate, slightly irritated.

"*Yes*. I can read and write," he repeated with confidence.

"*Good*. Good," acknowledged Nate. "The regiment needs men who can read and write. Sign here." Nate turned the ledger book around and handed Mathias the quill pen. Mathias adjusted his spectacles and took the quill pen from Nate's giant hand. He signed his name with great care and placed the pen on the table. Nate smiled and leaned back into his chair.

"Welcome to de Ninth Cavalry, Private Mathias Pryor."

Although Nate avoided any open criticism of Captain Graham in his dispatches to Merritt, he felt compelled to mention that the officer appeared to be indifferent to the task of training colored men into becoming soldiers. Nate was not completely surprised by Graham's comportment. During the war, he frequently witnessed officers who had nothing but contempt for colored soldiers, and frequently abused their power in defrauding them by cheating the men in their pay and stealing their equipment to sell on the black market. Nate's instinct led him to believe that Captain Graham was one of those officers. The man did not even appear once during the day to witness the progress of the recruitment, and his peacocklike appearance contrasted sharply with the overall condition of the regiment. Nate went on to explain to Merritt that he agreed that the recruits needed additional officers to instill discipline and authority, and that many of the men were indeed, cutthroats and rabble-rousers. He emphasized, however, that he would maximize his efforts, along with the other noncoms, to weed out those recruits who were physically weak, and those who "lacked character," from the ranks.

Nate also requested uniforms, boots, and military equipment that still had not arrived yet in sufficient quantity to supply the Ninth. None of the officers seemed to know when, or if, the needed equipment and uniforms would arrive. He wanted to request Spencer carbines but thought this might be premature in view of the unreadiness of the recruits. He felt that if he could just obtain basic cavalry accoutrements, and essentials such as mess equipment, uniforms, and boots, it would go a long way in establishing regimental cohesion and boosting morale. In conclusion, Nate suggested that Merritt make a surprise inspection at his earliest convenience so he could properly ascertain the situation for himself. He believed that he would have to fight Captain Graham for every improvement request he would make. It was his hope that if Merritt would directly intercede, Captain Graham would either be replaced with another officer better suited to the task, or ordered to perform the duty that he was assigned to.

A courier would ride to Union headquarters in New Orleans at first light and deliver the dispatches to Merritt's sleeping quarters by the time the lieutenant colonel heard reveille. Nate sealed the envelope, pulled off his boots, and collapsed backward on his cot. He eagerly looked forward to the little project he had in mind for some of the recruits before reveille was sounded.

Eight

As Nate pulled back the canvas entrance flap on one of the Sibley tents, and shined the bright folding lantern in the faces of Pvts. Percy-Ray Pridgeon and Mathias Pryor.

"Rise and shine, boys, fatigue duty in five . . . *five minutes.*"

It was five o'clock in the morning, a half hour before reveille. Dawn was just breaking. The white light filtered through the big cypresses in the bayou and the thick ground fog became visible.

Nate had told Sergeant McKlintock about his plan to wake up a few of the recruits and detail them to paint over the offensive sign on the recruitment center. Nate decided that it would be best to wake accomplish the task before any of the white officers were awake. He did not want any interference from them, or orders for him to abort his mission. After all, what could they do once the deed was done?

Back at the Sibley tent, the two recruits that Nate and Sergeant McKlintock had rudely woken up rubbed the sleep from their eyes in disbelief.

"I no hear no fife an' drum," said Pvt. Percy-Ray Pridgeon as he scratched his ass and played with his enormous erect penis.

"That's because there was none," responded Pvt. Mathias Pryor smugly as he placed his spectacles on his face. He had a little grin on his face that Percy-Ray found obnoxious.

Percy-Ray resented the way Mathias talked. He would whisper to himself over and over again: "Toadying, educated house nigger . . . so proper and *white!*" Percy-Ray told Mathias a little about where he came from and what he did before and during the war. The night before, after the men were ordered to their quarters for the night, Percy-Ray told Mathias that he had spent most of his adult life as a slave for a boatman on the Yazoo River. As he lay awake in the flea-bitten bedroll staring at the ceiling, Percy-Ray started to talk about his past.

"I was a slave fo' a red-hair Scotsman. He move goods on de Yazoo 'tween Greenwood an' Vicksburg. Dat white man would whup me *good* with a *long* bull whip ev'ry time he'd overload the boat. He'd holler at me to . . . *purrt yourr back into the pole . . . ya different colored bastard!* I ken still hear his *gawddamn* voice to this *day*." There was a moment of silence in the tent as Percy-Ray smiled to himself. "Well, during the war . . . I made sur' that he gots his for whut he done to me."

"What happened?" asked Mathias, intrigued by his tentmate's tale.

"The Scotsman, he be transportin' food fo' de Secesh at Vicksburg at night an' selling the food at high prices fo' *gold*. But durin' the day, he'd sell food to the Yankees, an' make believe that he was on their side. One night, I was able to leave the boat when he fell 'sleep after he drunk too much whiskey. I found some Yankee of'icers an' told them that my Mas'a was secretly sellin' food to de Rebs at Vicksburg." Percy-Ray started to chuckle with ghoulish satisfaction. "The blue bellies com' an' ar'ested him in de mawnin' an' took the boat. The blue bellies then put his ass on trial an' shot de bastard full of holes fo' de sun gone down. After that, I lived in freeman's camps, tryin' to survive by sellin' what folks needed in the camps."

"You mean you were selling food at high prices and made a lot of money," quipped Mathias, knowing full well that Percy-Ray was the kind of man who only thought of himself. During the war, when Charleston was under siege, Mathias had often seen men cheat helpless people who were in dire need.

"*What you mean?* You sayin' that I cheats my own kind?" protested Percy-Ray, his torso abruptly rising from the bedroll, his head turning toward his accuser. Mathias could see the whites of Percy-Ray's wild eyes, and became a little frightened.

"I mean . . . you made a profit for yourself," replied Mathias, trying to diffuse Percy-Ray's anger.

"*Yeah. That's right.* I made money to *survive like I's had to,*" responded Percy-Ray as he lay back down on the bedroll.

70

Nate was making an entry in his journal. He was sitting at his camp desk, writing away, when his train of thought was momentarily interrupted by the hooting sounds made by an owl somewhere in the nearby bayou. He had started keeping a journal during the war because he wanted to keep a record of his thoughts, events, and the people he encountered as a means of pretending he was talking to his deceased mother. Nate felt that the only real form of relaxation from the stress of being a leader and teacher was to write to vent his anxieties. Tonight he was writing about the new recruit, Mathias Pryor, whom he had spoken to a few hours after he had enlisted.

> *Pvt. Mathias Pryor is a relatively slender lad with delicate hands. He wears spectacles, and I have noticed that the boy frequently removes them from his nose to clean the lenses with a white handkerchief. He told me that he was born and raised in Charleston, South Carolina, in one of those great big houses. He told me that his parents were third-generation house servants, and lived in the back of the house. Unlike my mother, his family was well treated, well fed, and allowed to read! His father was responsible for all the duties regarding the running of the big house. His mother was the personal maid to the missus of the house, and confident.*
>
> *The mas'a of the great house was a former high-ranking diplomat who served in Paris and London under President Buchanan, while the missus spent her days in social activities.*
>
> *What really interested me, though, was the way Mathias was abused by his mas'a and missus. They would dress him up in silk knee socks and velvet britches with a little vest and peacock feather stuck into a big wavy hat to amuse visitors. Old Mas'a Hammond would never waste time on such foolishness.*
>
> *Mathias started to get real sad when he spoke of the federal bombardment and siege of Charleston. For almost six hundred days, the city was shelled by union gunboats, and by the end*

of the war, much of the city lay in ruins. Mathias started to cry when he told me how his family suffered and starved, and how the big house took several direct hits from Yankee naval gunfire.

After the war, Mathias's family took to the road, but both parents were too old and frail. His father longed for the days when life was simple, when they were well provided for by their generous masters. Weakened by the poor diet due to the siege, he died from a broken heart shortly after the war ended in one of those wretched freedman camps. Three days later, Mathias's mother followed her husband to the grave.

I believe that the hardships produced by the war and the sudden loss of his parents matured the boy quickly. By '65, he was 21 years old, and gone thru the terrible siege of Charleston. I asked him how he heard about the Ninth Cav., and he told me that when he was passing through Wilmington, North Carolina, he read a newspaper announcing the formation of new colored regiments. That caught his attention because he told me that the day when the Federals finally entered Charleston, the first troops he saw were black! He told me how proud he became when he saw black men marching down the street, banners and flags flowing, fife and drums playing. The boy made up his mind to go to New Orleans and enlist in the Ninth. I guess he decided he wanted to be like those black soldiers.

Nine

Lt. Donald Smith was having his coffee poured by Julius, an elderly black servant whose hair was so white it matched his white cotton uniform and white gloves. Lieutenant Smith was about to order breakfast when Captain Graham walked into the officer's mess. As usual, his wooden right hand was buried in between the two unbuttoned central brass buttons of his frock coat. Lieutenant Smith noticed that the captain looked very pale this morning. He was about to rise from his chair when Graham waved his hand in a horizontal motion, instructing him to remain seated. Julius helped him pull up his chair to the table, which was lavishly set with confiscated china and English silver.

"Good morning, sir," Smith loudly proclaimed, trying to show the commanding officer that he was fit and in control. He also wanted to irritate him by taking advantage of his obvious hangover by speaking in a boisterous manner. Graham winced a little but decided to ignore Smith. He turned his head and whispered to Julius, who was still standing by, "I'll have the usual, Julius."

As Julius started to pour the coffee, Graham turned and asked Smith, "Have you met the new sergeant major yet?"

"No sir, not formally. Although I heard him wake up some of the recruits this morning before reveille. I thought he showed initiative on his part. I believe that he formed a detail and proceeded to the recruitment center."

"He's a real Jim Dandy, ain't he? Real bright-eyed and bushy-tailed," Graham responded sarcastically as he stirred his coffee cup.

"Any word yet from Headquarters regarding my requests for uniforms and other military equipment, sir?"

"*Julius!*" Graham called out for the servant as if he were some wounded soldier begging for water on a battlefield. As he rubbed his face with his good hand, he responded, "*Nooo*, I have not received any word on the matter, Lieutenant."

"Sir, I don't know how much longer I can maintain the situation without additional officers," said Smith firmly.

"Well, you have that new sergeant, don't you? You think very highly of him, don't you—mister? As for additional officers, one is due in a few days. A certain Lieutenant Hennessy has applied for this regiment." Graham then lifted his head and raised his arms toward the ceiling in an air of wonderment. "God knows why any officer would want to be part of this regiment."

"I suppose that is good news, sir, but I still think we have an explosive situation here. The conditions that exist at camp are ripe for a cholera outbreak. I have seen it before; during the siege of Petersburg . . ."

"I am very well aware of what happened at the siege of Petersburg, *Lieutenant*," interrupted Graham. "Besides, it is beyond my control." Lieutenant Smith noticed that Graham's left hand shook as he struggled to bring the cup of coffee to his lips. "I have told you time after time that Headquarters will not move us from this swamp-infested area. They want us out of public view so we will not upset the local population. As for the farm animals and harlots that infest the camp, I believe that if we take any disciplinary action, we might provoke a riot, and I will not have that on my record."

"It is our duty to see that these men are fit for duty on the frontier as soon as possible . . ."

"*Lieutenant*, these men will never serve on the frontier in the capacity as cavalry troops. They will be relegated to digging drainage ditches, cutting wood, and hauling freight. And as far as I am concerned . . . that is where they belong."

Smith's face winced with that last remark, and it disgusted him that Graham was now spreading a pile of butter on his biscuit.

"They will certainly not fight Indians," Graham further added, taking a bite from a big piece of ham that Julius had cut for him. As he was chewing with his mouth half open, Smith began to feel like striking this man for his ignorance but decided that it was best to continue to listen to his patronizing lecture.

"I know; I have read up on the matter, Lieutenant," Graham continued. "And believe me, the Negroes just do not have the backbone and moral fiber required to fight Indians."

Smith finally snapped. "Oh yes suh, oh yes suh . . . Mas'a be right . . . an' us niggers mighty happy to lie down by the corn! Is that what you really think, sir? Is it?" Smith rose from his chair and slapped his linen napkin on the table. He stood erect and stood over his commanding officer. "Because if so, sir, I warn you that I will be making my own report to General Merritt."

"Threats, Lieutenant?"

Lt. Donald Smith did not respond. He had heard enough and decided to quietly walk out the room.

"*Lieutenant. I have not given you permission to leave.*" Smith did not stop. What little respect for Graham he had had evaporated like the water from the bayou in the hot Louisiana sun.

Ten

Jesse Randolph was carrying a pole over his right shoulder. Dangling at the opposite end of the rod was a large cloth bundle filled with clothes and personal effects. A giant knot kept the packet tightly bound, and although dusty from his long walk on the road, his clothes were not tattered, as was the case with most of the people who walked the withered and hot road. He was wearing a new beige linen vest, and his wool trousers were light blue with dark blue piping down the seams.

Jesse was on his way to Greenville to enlist. He had heard about the formation of the regiment in a circular and decided that he would return to military service. As his feet kicked up dust from the road, he thought about the war. He missed being in the army because he wanted to be a leader of men. Jesse cherished the memories associated with being a first lieutenant in the Ninth Louisiana Native Guards, a regiment that he was very fond of because it was composed of free African slaves and was the only black regiment to have its own colored officers.

Jesse reminisced about joining the Ninth Louisiana Native Guards when Louisiana seceded from the Union, and how he and several companies of militia made up of freemen were organized and desired to serve under the Confederacy. He smiled to himself as he recalled how proud he was when the Yankee army occupied New Orleans, the colored militias voted to switch their allegiance from the Confederacy to the Union.

Jesse became sad however, when he started to think about how the Yankees forced all the officers to resign their commissions because they considered black men unfit to command their own men in battle. As

77

his eyes wandered down the road that led to Greenville, Jesse became more melancholy when he thought about how he had written a petition to Gen. Nathaniel P. Banks, the military governor of Louisiana, pleading with him to reinstate his rank and those other officers who organized the regiment, and how it was all in vain.

Jesse was becoming hungry and decided to have some lunch. He got off the road and made for a tall cypress tree that looked inviting; its branches were low and offered shade from the searing sun. He placed his back against the trunk of the cypress and carefully untied the knot that held his bundle of worldly goods and reached inside. His hands wandered a bit, and he became a little frustrated that he was unable to locate what he was looking for. His anxiety ended when his hand finally touched the item he was looking for, a can of peaches that he had purchased in New Orleans. He removed his pocket knife and quickly hacked at the inside rim of the can to open it. He then found his spoon and started to devour the contents with great contentment. Jesse savored each peach as if it was his last. When the can became empty, he drank the juice and became disappointed that there was no more. He placed the can on the ground and unbuttoned the two top buttons of his blouse, because he was really feeling warm now even though he was in the shade. Jesse started to doze off, and within a few moments he was dreaming about the battle of Milliken's Bend.

Jesse saw himself standing on top of the breastwork, jabbing and thrusting the long bayonet that was fixed on his Springfield at a Reb officer, when he caught a minie ball in his left shoulderblade. When the Confederates breached the Union works, the Ninth Native Louisiana Guard, equipped with deficient muskets that would not fire, were forced to defend their position at the old levee with bayonets and knives against superior numbers. Lying there wounded, Jesse felt paralyzed and helpless in his misty dream as he watched many of his comrades converting their useless rifles into clubs as they were being shot where they stood. Jesse started to moan lightly in his sleep but the groaning became louder and louder as he saw his comrades swinging their rifles, yelling and cursing at the enemy. Jesse now started to cry out in frustration because he was too badly wounded to render assistance to his doomed comrades. Through the haze of sulfur, smoke, and shot, he saw his beloved Native Guards regiment, armed only with bayonets, fall back to the river and undergo a red sheet of infilading fire on their flanks, decimating the regiment.

Jesse woke up violently. As his eyes popped wide open he bellowed, "*Jeez Crist* . . . those *poor men*." His head, which was resting on his chest as he dreamed, abruptly snapped back, hitting the trunk of the cypress. The howling of wounded and dying comrades around him had become too much for his mind to remain asleep. The scene of thrusting bayonets, close-range gunshot, knives ripping flesh, and rifle butts cracking skulls had tormented Jesse ever since the battle. With only slight variations, the nightmares of the fighting at Milliken's Bend were unceasingly the same, and Jesse always felt guilty that he had survived while his comrades chose slaughter over surrender. He stared at one of the big branches of the cypress and noticed that his blouse was sodden with perspiration. He removed his slouch hat and pulled out his blue bandanna to wipe his face and neck. He then got up, tiredly tied his bundle together again, lifted his long pole, placed the rod on his left shoulder, and headed down the road toward Greenville.

After a few more miles of walking in the dust and heat, Jesse approached the recruitment center, where he noticed that there were two soldiers dressed for fatigue duty whitewashing the facade of the building while a big sergeant major supervised the work detail.

"Well, well, well," Jesse said, smiling as he gently lowered his pole and bundle to the ground. He gave Nate a big grin and then looked up at where once there had been a sign advertising the selling of slaves.

"What you got there, gold!?" retorted Nate as he took a quick glance at Jesse's bundle. He was a little bemused by this fellow, and wanted to know more about him.

"Nope, jest my worldly goods," replied Jesse, responding with a big grin.

"Don't look too worldly to me," mocked Nate.

"I edmit, it might be small now, but I hope 't'll grow soon." Both Jesse and Nate started to laugh.

Eleven

Nate and Willie were drilling C and K companies when Lt. Zachary Hennessy appeared on the parade ground riding a fine gray mare. It was late afternoon and the sun's last rays of the day were shining through the cypress's thick branches.

As Hennessy approached, the lieutenant noticed that the men were drilling not with rifles, but with long withered sticks and old spent brooms. He also remarked that the men were dressed in ill-fitting surplus Union infantry uniforms. What troubled him most, however, was that he hardly saw any signs of horses, riding paddocks, stables, feed, horse equipment, etc. He thought this very strange, considering that this was to supposed to be a cavalry regiment. Although there were many big men in the ranks, Hennessy was troubled that many of them looked frail, unfit for the rigors of cavalry life.

Percy-Ray was standing in the middle of the front-row rank. He was whispering to another enlisted man when Nate caught him.

He bellowed, "Hold your tongue, Private! No talking in de ranks!"

Percy-Ray ceased his low-voice chatter, but as soon as Nate had turned his back, he puckered up his lips as if he was preparing to kiss someone and made a noise that sounded as if he was calling an animal. One man laughed, and a few others smiled and giggled.

"Quiet in the ranks," said Hennessy sternly as he dismounted from his horse and adjusted his saber.

Nate had his back turned, and was about twenty feet away when he heard the lieutenant's voice. He knew in an instant who it was. He turned around and saw the face of Lieutenant Hennessy.

As Nate approached the lieutenant, he cried out, "*Private Archie Vaughn.*"

"Yes, Sergeant Major?" Private Vaughn replied rather meekly. He was a little fellow who barely made the physical height requirement when he enlisted, and had mischievous eyes that tended to wonder about aimlessly. He was standing next to Mathias in K company.

"You will take de lieutenant's horse and rub the animal down and corral him with de other officers' mounts," ordered Nate.

"I, I don't no how to rub down no hoss, Sergeant."

Several of the men started to laugh and Percy-Ray offered advice. "Just like a woman, but seein' that you nev' ben with one, I ain't surprised."

The statement created even more laughter and commotion as some of the men started gesticulating and adding their own observations and comments.

"I haven't ben wid a woman fo' a couple o' weeks, Lootenant— ah rub yo hoss," said one private, laughing.

"*Silence in de ranks or you all will be doin' extra fatigue duty till de rooster crows.*" Nate was irate and picked out Percy-Ray to vent his wrath. He approached him, placing his face just inches away from Percy-Ray's nose, and started to yell loud enough for all the men to hear. "*You African baboon!* If I ketch your black mouth worken without my permission again, I'll take a needle and sew it up."

"An' I'll give him my sewin' needle," added Sgt. Willie McKlintock, marching up to where Percy-Ray and Nate were standing.

This silenced the men, and Percy-Ray's obnoxious smile disappeared.

After Nate supervised Pvt. Archie Vaughn's removal of Hennessy's horse, he walked up to him and saluted.

"It's a pleasure to see you again, Lieutenant."

"Thank you, Sergeant Major." Hennessy returned the salute and started to look around the camp.

"Lieutenant Colonel Merritt spoke to me about the problems here at camp, but I had no idea that things were as bad as you stated in your dispatches to him."

"We doing improvements, but we need better food, clothin', and enough horses for the men," said Willie anxiously.

"Supplies will be coming shortly, Sergeant," responded Hennessy.

"It's the truth, sir," intervened Nate, trying to calm things down a little between Sergeant McKlintock and Lieutenant Hennessy. "My immediate problem is the lack of support in gettin' rid of the harlots and miscreants that infest the camp, sir."

Nate was firm in his explanation of the wretched conditions that plagued the military compound. What he really wanted above all, however, was to move the encampment away from the mosquito-bitten site, and discharge half of the men.

To Hennessy, this sounded all too familiar. His brief experience with black regiments taught him a valuable lesson: The army and the war department always gave black regiments the lowest of priorities regarding essential supplies, equipment, and horses.

"We will speak of this matter later on, Sergeant Major. Right now I need to report and find accommodations," responded Hennessy somewhat anxiously as he pulled off his gauntlets. The lieutenant felt a little overwhelmed by Nate's complaints and the obstacles that had to be crossed. He welcomed the challenge, but dreaded the task of fighting the military bureaucracy.

"Yes, sir. I be happy to escort you to Captain Graham, sir," replied Nate, who was put off that Hennessy was not really in the mood to hear what had to be done to improve conditions at the camp.

Twelve

It was just past eleven o'clock at night and Private Percy-Ray lay wide awake in his Sibley tent, wondering how he could sneak out and find that quadroon woman he saw while on fatigue duty at the recruitment center. As he played with himself, he became obsessed with various erotic fantasies that turned in his head. He eagerly pondered how many ways he could abuse her if given the opportunity. The very thought of having his way with the quadroon made his organ huge and firm, and Percy-Ray became hot with lust. All day long he thought about the high-yellow girl, who was petite and very shapely. He liked the way her hair was cropped short and the manner in which she swayed her tight fanny. Percy-Ray had never been with a quadroon woman before, so he was very eager to taste and devour this elusive fruit. A few hours before, he had gone to see Pvt. Isaac Moore, a recruit who had been one of the first to enlist into the regiment and was known by some of the men as the Voodoo Man. Percy-Ray purchased a potion Isaac Moore had concocted that promised to make his balls firm and resistant to premature ejaculation, while his penis would remain as hard as a freshly picked cucumber.

Percy-Ray was contemplating the morning events as he masturbated. The vision of him whitewashing the recruitment center as the quadroon girl drifted past, carrying a tall ceramic water jug on top of her head, preoccupied him. She was barefoot and moved very slowly as she passed the building. Her firm, round buttocks swayed with grace in her tight burlap dress, which hung very low on the shoulders, exposing her deep cleavage.

"You gotta man?" Percy-Ray recalled inquiring. He was standing on the ladder, his brush dripping whitewash all over the ground beneath him.

The quadroon halted and raised her arms to stabilize the jug on top of her head. "My man, he ran off," she responded in a tone of voice that delighted Percy Ray. "He won't be back," she further advised. The quadroon then turned her delicate head as if indicating a direction. "My man . . . he gon' north."

"Where you live?" Percy-Ray sensed that she was making herself available for him.

"I live down the road, over by the church with m'ah pappy." She paused for a moment, then added with pride, "My pappy is a preacher." By now she had lowered her big jug down from her head and placed the container on the ground.

"My name's Lizzie, but my friends call me Izzie." She was moving her big toe on her right foot and drawing a circle in the dust of the road. That was as far as the conversation went. When Nate emerged from the interior of the building and saw what was going on, he exploded.

"What do you tink this is? Church social?" Nate paused, then turned to Percy-Ray.

"*Private*. You're going do extra guard duty till you drop."

After he had browbeaten Percy-Ray, he turned his attention to Lizzie and said in a more conciliatory tone, "And you, ma'am, please, no frat'nization with my men while they are on duty."

Lizzie became a little flustered, but she understood. As she picked up her big jug and placed it delicately back on top of her head, she gave Percy-Ray a big smile. She slowly walked off down the road. Her firm buttocks swung back and forth in perfect rhythm to the tune she was humming to herself.

Nate's interference in his flirting, and subsequent extra guard duty, fueled Percy-Ray's growing resentment toward the sergeant major and the army. Unable to fall asleep, due to his overwhelming sexual impulses and fantasies, Percy-Ray made up his mind to sneak out of camp and find Izzie's father's shack. As for the possibility of running into the preacher; well, he decided that he would confront the situation, if and when it occurred. All he wanted now was to physically possess the quadroon girl with the shapely buttocks.

Sneaking out of camp was not difficult. He moved swiftly among the cypresses and banana trees, and in no time he was on the road toward Greenville. It was a moonless night and the clouds were hanging low. The air was thick with humidity and the sounds of millions of insects coming from the bayous filled the darkness with their repetitive racket. As he weaseled down the edge of the road, he noticed an old cemetery. Percy-Ray's heart jumped at first, but then he thought about how this would be an excellent place to conduct what he had in mind. As he pondered how quiet and private the cemetery was, he reached for his pocket knife that was lodged in a sheath stitched to the inside of his right boot. He removed the item and flicked the blade free from its casing. He stared at the sharp, slightly curved blade and spoke to it. "You and I goin' have some fun tonight."

It took Percy-Ray about twenty-five minutes to locate the Black Methodist Church where Izzie indicated her father's cabin was located. Behind the church was a cemetery where freed Negroes were interred. Her father's home was on the west side of the church. A lantern placed in front of the cabin's only window, which was missing a pane, was turned down low.

Percy-Ray crept up to the window on his hands and knees. As he crawled toward the window he heard faint mumbling coming from inside the cabin. When he reached the south side of the wall where the window was located, he slowly raised his head until his eyes became level with the windowsill and was able to identify the silhouette of a man sitting at a crude table. When Percy-Ray's eyes finally adjusted to the lighting in the cabin, he noticed that the man was old and bald. He was sitting at the table reading passages from the Bible to Izzie.

Percy-Ray quickly lowered his head from the window and sat on the grass to think. He could take a chance and signal Izzie that he was outside waiting for her, or he could simply wait until the old man went to sleep, enter the cabin, and fetch Izzie.

He decided to wait for a while and see if the old man might nod off or retire to his room. As the minutes passed by, he could hear the old man recite the ten commandments from the Bible.

"Gawd almighty! When's the bastard goin' to bed?" he whispered to himself, frustrated.

Fortunately for Percy-Ray, Izzie's father was only citing the commandments, as he always did before retiring. When he had finished the recitation, he kissed his daughter on the cheek, bidding her good night, and then closed the door to his room. Izzie was alone in the kitchen.

When Percy-Ray heard the door close, he raised his head to the window and began tapping on one of the glass panes. Izzie was at the opposite end of the cabin, spreading ashes on the dying embers in the fireplace to preserve the heat of the coals. When she heard the tapping, Percy-Ray noticed that she thought it was the wind blowing against the cabin, so he placed his face tightly against the glass panes and glared into the interior. He smiled when Izzie turned and saw him because he knew that he had startled her. Percy-Ray was concerned that she might cry out, so he placed a finger against his lips, signaling her to remain silent. Izzie's eyes squinted toward the window for a moment and when she recognized Percy-Ray, grinned with delight. She quickly ran over to the window and opened it.

She lifted the hem of her burlap skirt and placed her left leg on the windowsill. Percy-Ray then lifted her tight and slender body from the casing and placed her on the ground. Izzie closed the window behind her, giggling softly, and Percy-Ray felt like Lucifer anticipating the abduction of some innocent soul as he seized her hand and led her to the cemetery that he had seen earlier.

They cautiously entered the old cemetery and Percy-Ray noticed that most of the headstones were either seriously eroded or crumbling, and although much of the ground was overwhelmed by high weeds and grass grown wild, the place smelled sweet with the aroma of blooming oleander.

They walked among the graves, giggling and whispering to each other. They finally stopped by a headstone that was split in half. One part of the ancient stone lay on the grass, leaving the other part buried in the soft ground, tilting slightly forward. Percy-Ray's hands reached for Izzie's breasts as he felt his penis grow long and firm. He was looking forward to putting into practice the benefits of the voodoo potion that he had taken earlier, so Percy-Ray moved his right hand and lifted Izzie's burlap dress over her waist.

Meanwhile, Izzie became intensely preoccupied with undoing Percy-Ray's buttons on his blue wool trousers, squeezing his long and thick organ, which was bulging against the front of his breeches. She quickly, almost frantically unfastened one button at a time, and when she finally succeeded in lowering his pants and drawers, Percy-Ray's long, curved black penis emerged as if it were a large eel looming from its place of seclusion. Izzie's eyes bulged with excitement and anticipation.

"Turn aroun' an' bend ov'a," Percy-Ray instructed as if he was maneuvering a hog's rear end into a stall.

Izzie obeyed immediately. She turned around and placed her arms firmly around the partially eroded headstone. She wanted to brace herself from the anticipated thrusts of his pelvis. The outline of Izzie's light-skinned buttocks in the dim moonlight drove Percy-Ray wild with lust, filling him with adrenaline and making his cock feel as if it were on fire. He placed his big hands on her buttocks, one on each cheek, and mounted her. He drove his huge penis into her and started to pump his lower body as his kneecaps dug into the soft ground. Izzie gave out a loud cry, signaling Percy-Ray's initial penetration. She then started to moan and her grin turned into a crooked expression, converting her face into an almost animal-like appearance. There was no breeze, and the air was heavy with humidity; their perspiration and sexual juices produced a strong aroma and the odor of their bodies wafted, hovering above the two. As Percy-Ray thrusted his penis in and out, first slowly, then quickening the pace more vigorously, his sexual appetite increased. He felt the skin of his scrotum slap against her buttocks as Izzie began to moan.

His face aflame with ecstasy, he suddenly craved more intense pleasure. Instinctively, Percy-Ray pulled out his small pocket knife from its canvas pocket from inside of his boot. He flicked the blade open and smiled at the knife. He raised his arm and started swinging back and forth as the blade slashed at the yellow flesh of Izzie's buttocks. At first, she felt a slight burning sensation; then, as Percy-Ray inflicted longer and deeper cuts, the pain became more acute. When she finally realized, that he was cutting her flesh with a razor-sharp blade, she stared to scream and pleaded with Percy-Ray to stop.

"Stop your screamin' you light-skinned bitch, or I'll use this knife on your throat and cut ya like a pig."

Izzie became afraid. She wanted him to stop slicing her. She began to feel the blood run down the inside of her thighs as he held his left hand on her neck and used his right arm to slash the knife as if it were a pendulum. As he carried on his grisly task, Izzie managed to stop her screaming but started to whimper like a child. Her face, soaked with tears, which only a few moments ago possessed an expression of intense pleasure, was now grimacing with pain.

Percy-Ray's slashing came to an abrupt end when he felt his hot cream shoot through his organ. He let out a giant moan and his muscles became rigid and bulged. He remained in that position for a few seconds, then quickly pushed Izzie away as if she were some disgusting creature he had mistakenly found. He rose to his feet, pulled up his trousers, and buttoned his fly. He looked at Izzie, who was quietly whimpering by the headstone, and as he whipped the sweat off his face with his sleeve he commented casually, "C'mon now, baby, that was not too bad, stop your whinnin', ye 'ear! Why, you was screamin' like a cat in heat earlier. I thought you liked it."

Thirteen

Lt. Donald Smith was at breakfast, having his coffee poured from a silver decanter by Julius' steady hand.

"This morning, Julius, I would like the boiled ham, and that bizarre mashlike food I tried the other day; what was it called again?"

"Grits, sir," responded Julius with his usual good-natured smile.

"*Yes, grits,*" pondered Lieutenant Smith happily.

Julius was about to leave the dining room when he noticed Lt. Zachary Hennessy enter the door.

"He's going to want his breakfast right away," Julius thought to himself.

Hennessy was dressed in his campaign uniform which was ill-suited for duty in the tropics. He wore a tight, single-breasted dark blue jacket with gold braid adorning the sleeves. His trousers, bright red and pleated at the waist, were modeled after the French Chasseur uniform. He wore high-top cavalry boots made from heavy bridle leather, and had them custom made while he was on leave. As he placed his kepi on the hat rack, Julius inquired if he wished him to pour his coffee.

"Yes, that would be fine, thank you." Hennessy pulled up a dinning room chair across from where Smith was spreading butter on a warm biscuit.

"Those boots will make your feet swell in this climate," scoffed Smith as he took a bite out of his biscuit. Although he did not look as military as Hennessy, he was dressed in a more appropriate attire for the climate: a loose-fitting white flannel shirt under a light sack coat, with no military insignia except for his first lieutenant's shoulder boards.

"We have not met. I'm Lieutenant Hennessy, newly assigned to the regiment."

"We have been expecting you. I'm Lieutenant Donald Chancellor Smith."

He rose from his chair and stretched his right hand and arm across the table, holding his napkin with his left. Hennessy also rose and clasped Smith's hand.

"Welcome to the Ninth, Hennessy, or may I call you Zachary?"

"Zach will be fine." Hennessy paused, then asked, "May I call you Donny?"

"Ah, absolutely not! Too many bad memories of being teased when I was a schoolboy. I would appreciate it if you would just call me Don."

Hennessy wanted to keep the conversation going; he wanted to make friends fast. In fact, if the man possessed one weakness, it was his overeagerness to befriend his peers and gain their approval. "I see— were you the victim of the town tough?"

"No, just the major source of amusement in the school yard," replied Lieutenant Smith, becoming impatient for Julius to bring him his breakfast.

Julius came back with Lieutenant Smith's breakfast. As he served, Hennessy could smell the ham and fried potatoes. He noticed that there was a strange white substance next to the ham.

"It's called grits, Zach. Julius here," Smith pointed in the direction of the old black servant, "who by the way, is the only good thing about this place, made me try it. I found it quite good, especially with butter or some red-eye gravy."

Julius was way ahead of Hennessy.

"Would the Lootenant desire the same order?"

Hennessy hesitated, then quickly replied, "Yes, yes, that will be fine, thank you."

"Have you inspected the camp yet?" Smith inquired. He wanted Hennessy's support against Captain Graham's intransigence.

"Yes, I have," Hennessy replied. He clasped his hands and placed his elbows on the white tablecloth. A slight breeze came through the open double louvered doors, allowing for the air to move around the room a little more than usual. Hennessy now wished that he had not worn his tight-fitting shell jacket, red Chasseur pants, and high boots. After a few seconds of reflective silence, Hennessy lowered his arms onto the table.

"I have never seen so much filth in a military encampment. Even during the war, officers would not allow their men to live under these conditions. What is going on here?" Hennessy paused, then continued, "This morning, I was not awakened by the bugler, but by a chicken scratching at my window ledge! Why is the camp in such shape?"

"*Ah*," said Smith sarcastically, waving his hand in the air as if hailing someone from a distance. "Our beloved leader is washing his hands of the whole affair, like Pontius Pilate at the trial of Christ."

"Surely we can at least start by confiscating the loose livestock, removing the worst apples in the barrel, and putting some discipline into these boys. I know that some of the noncommissioned officers such as Sergeant Major Gordon and First Sergeant McKlintock are slowly making a difference in that regard. I think that—" but before Hennessy could finish, Lieutenant Smith interrupted him.

"Zach, you are new here. I appreciate your eagerness and I am in complete agreement. But the reality is that we are talking about nearly two hundred very green recruits, and most of them are not worthy to wear the uniform." Smith raised his fork and pointed it at Hennessy, using the utensil as a prop. "If we had twenty noncoms such as Sergeant Gordon, we would still face a situation of acute danger. As it is, the regiment has only two noncoms, and we lack sufficient officers and proper equipment. For God's sake, man! We don't even have enough horses to start training the men to be cavalry troops!" Smith returned the fork to the edge of his porcelain plate and lifted his delicate coffee cup to his lips. The brew was steamy hot, and Smith was afraid that he might burn his lips or tongue. He slurped the coffee and placed the cup back in the saucer. "What is really lacking in the regiment, Zach, is esprit de corps." Lieutenant Smith started to calm down now and commenced cutting into his big piece of ham, which was staring back at him on his plate. "The only hope that this regiment might have— and as you know, our military careers are also on the line—is to leave Louisiana in some military condition as soon as possible."

"And what would that solve? We would be transporting rabble to the frontier, not soldiers," retorted Hennessy aggressively.

"Well, first of all, we would be rid of our beloved commander," replied Smith with a smirk on his face.

Hennessy was a little uncomfortable when Smith showed outward signs of disrespect toward a superior officer, especially when the man was not even present to defend himself.

"Second of all, we would leave this wretched place and hopefully be stationed somewhere with a drier climate. And third of all, the next part of the regiment's training will be to teach these men to be cavalrymen. Right now they are being treated as if they were going to be infantry, or used as manual labor to dig ditches."

"Yes, I noticed that there were only about fifty horses in the coral." Hennessy then added, "Why are the horses in such poor condition?"

Smith put down his fork and knife and bellowed. "Why? Because we live in this glorious climate of perpetual humidity, rain, humidity, and more rain. Most of the horses have thrush and rain rot on their coats, stripping them of their fur and exposing the raw skin."

Before Smith could finish his tirade, Captain Graham strolled in, looking pale as usual. His stumped left arm crossed the middle of his waist. Both Hennessy and Smith started to get up from their chairs but Graham waved his wooden hand. "At ease gentlemen, at ease." The captain took his place at the head of the table. He then cried out, as he usually did every morning, "*Julius.*"

Julius was right behind Graham with his coffee.

"Yes sir, Captain, ah have your chicory."

Captain Graham was startled by Julius' close presence.

"*Goddamn it, man.* Don't ever creep up behind my back like that." Graham was easily irritated by the slightest noise, and loathed being surprised when he was hungover.

Julius responded in his typical polite and accommodating demeanor.

"Yes sir, so sorry, sir. Shall I git your breakfast?"

Graham nodded in approval, and Julius disappeared back into the kitchen.

"I trust you gentlemen have become acquainted and are making plans for the regiment?" Graham was always cynical when referring to the Ninth. He really did not want to be part of this so-called military experiment of using black troops for frontier service. His only concern was that expected staff position in Washington that his uncle, the congressman, promised him. Lieutenant Smith took the opportunity to badger Graham regarding the regiment's shortages in basic kitchen utensils, bedrolls, cavalry uniforms, shoes, and weapons.

"Sir, it has been over a week since I inquired about the supplies I requested to properly equip the Ninth. Has there been any word yet, sir?"

All of a sudden Graham cracked a grin, the expression of a child with mischief on his mind.

"As a matter of fact, Lieutenant, you will be pleased to know that I have heard from Lieutenant Colonel Merritt. He has informed me that our commanding officer, Colonel Hatch, has been informed by General Sheridan that all twelve companies will be leaving for Texas sometime by the end of February, early March at the latest."

"*Texas?*" Lieutenants Smith and Hennessy said the word as if it meant some kind deliverance from desolation.

Julius reappeared with Graham and Hennessy's breakfast. Captain Graham was clearly enjoying keeping the two junior officers on edge, watching their eyes, which were full of anticipation. As Julius carefully served them their breakfast and refilled empty coffee cups, Captain Graham halted his briefing. He did not want Julius to overhear the conversation. He suspected him of spreading rumors among the men, and the last thing that Graham wanted was more rumors. Finally, when Julius completed serving the officers and had left the dinning room, Graham resumed his briefing.

"The details have not been completely worked out yet. As the situation now stands, some companies will be stationed at Brownsville on the Rio Grande, and some companies will depart for San Antonio for further training."

Lieutenant Smith was quick to voice his usual concerns. "What about the supplies and additional officers, sir? As the situation presents itself, we only have six officers for eight companies, and when the regiments reaches full strength at twelve companies, we will not have a regiment, sir, but an undisciplined rabble of over two hundred men."

Graham stuffed his face with the smoked ham as he listened to Lieutenant Smith's concerns. He hurriedly finished chewing the piece that was in his mouth and blurted, "If you have any complaints regarding the situation here, mister, I suggest you put them in writing and go through proper military channels; in other words, follow the command structure, Lieutenant, and let me have my breakfast in peace!"

Fourteen

Izzie's father was in a state of shock and rage. The preacher had discovered his daughter weeping on her bed when he had risen and noticed that there was no fire in the hearth. He went to her room and
found his beloved child crying on her back. When he approached the
bed he noticed that the sheet that covered the goosefeather mattress
had large red stains. He took his index finger, touched the stain, brought
the finger to his nose, and smelled the substance. "*My God, girl*. Where
did this come from?" The preacher's eyes grew wild with bewilderment
as Izzie sobbed. He asked the question again, but Izzie refused to answer and continued to whimper. Losing patience, the father turned his
daughter's body over and lifted her burlap dress, revealing her buttocks.
Dozens of tiny crimson cuts crisscrossed his daughter's behind. The
fresh wounds reminded him of the days of slavery when he had to help
and console slaves that had been whipped. "*God have mercy. Who done
this to you, child?*" he demanded.

Izzie wailed in shame. "One, one . . . of the soldiers cut me."

"Who? What is his name?"

"He, he calls himself Percy-Ray," she replied, trying to control her
sobbing.

"The Lord will punish the wicked and the lustful," he vowed,
raising his hands in the air and lifting his head toward the ceiling. He
then seized Izzie's right arm and forced her to her feet. "We are going
to *get down on our knees and pray*," pledged the preacher as he coerced
his daughter to the floor of the cabin. "Then . . . we will *seek out* the
sinner and punish him."

Percy-Ray Pridgeon, his new sidekick, Archie Vaughn, and Isaac Moore, the Voodoo Man, were sitting around a fire devouring some leftover chicken meat when the preacher and Izzie stormed into camp. Dragging his whimpering daughter by the hand, the preacher had frantically searched the encampment for Percy-Ray when they stumbled upon the three enlistees eating their breakfast.

Percy-Ray knew he was in trouble when he spotted the tall, thin black man marching toward him, leading Izzie by the hand. "Jesus Christ," he exclaimed, arousing Archie Vaughn and Isaac Moore's attention. The preacher was dressed in a well-worn black frock coat and vest, black trousers, and heavy boots.

"*Oooweee*. The man sur' looks like a big ol' mean crow," commented Archie Vaughn as he licked his fingers clean from leftover bird residue.

"*Yeah*. And he come to pick my innards," replied Percy-Ray as he wiped his mouth with the sleeve of his undershirt and tossed a chicken-leg bone into the fire.

"I will take care of dis, my broder," offered Isaac Moore reassuringly. He then pulled out a little neck charm and rubbed the charm and muttered, "*Donne moi la pussiance . . . Oh MAKANDAL.*" Percy-Ray was stunned by the change in Isaac Moore's eyes. He turned to Archie Vaughn and noticed that he was also transfixed by the mesmerizing metamorphosis. The Voodoo Man's eyes had changed from a dull brown to a vibrant green, and the pupils exploded to twice their normal size.

"Which one of you miscreants calls himself Percy-Ray?" demanded the preacher, outraged. His weather-beaten skin tightened and his jaw tensed as he stared at the group. Izzie had ceased to whimper but her face was marked with dirt and dried up tears, and her head remained bowed. She refused to identify Percy-Ray.

"*Speak up. Who is responsible for abusing my child?*"

"What abuse?" scoffed Percy-Ray as he touched his boot at the spot where he concealed the knife. He wanted to make sure that his precious instrument of abuse was snugly lodged in its hidden pouch.

"*So it is you. You!*" exclaimed the preacher as if he had found the devil in his house. He seized his daughter's hand, turned her backside around so that her cheeks faced the men, and raised her burlap dress, revealing dozens of fresh crimson-red cuts that crisscrossed her buttocks. "*Do you deny this outrage?*"

"*Wait,*" interrupted Isaac Moore as he suddenly stretched out his right arm and placed the palm of his hand in the preacher's face. The Voodoo Man's eyes were now focusing on the preacher, and Percy-Ray was pleased that Isaac Moore was intervening on his behalf by distracting Izzie's father. As the Voodoo Man stroked his neck fetish with his left hand, he started to chant a curse:

> "Eh! Eh! Bomba hen! hen!
> Canga bafio, te
> Mal a toi chretien, mal a toi chretien
> Toi, va mourir bientot!"

The preacher was not impressed with Isaac Moore's curse or with his wild looking eyes. "*Stand aside, you servant of Lucifer!*"

Percy-Ray decided to run and lose the preacher while Isaac Moore beguiled him. He slowly turned around, watching Isaac Moore and Izzie's father confront each other from the corner of his eye. He started to stride away when the preacher clamored, "*Stop sinner, you will atone for your transgressions against my flesh and blood.*" He took a step toward Percy-Ray but Isaac Moore slapped the preacher across the face with the palm of his hand, knocking him down as Percy-Ray disappeared within the confusion of the camp. Mortified on seeing her father collapse to the ground, Izzie commenced to wail in horror. She placed her hands on her tear-streaked face and kept lamenting over and over again, "Oh lawd, Oh lawd, this all my fault." She kneeled down and attempted to revive her father by shaking him and trying to lift his tall frame up from the dirt.

"Go now," commanded Isaac Moore to Izzie as he pointed his bony finger at the preacher's body. He then motioned to Archie Vaughn, who was sitting on a stump and had watched the whole scene in a state of dumfoundedness. "Dis man will help you bring dis ol' man home." The Voodoo Man's ferocious eyes then stared into Izzie's face. "You will neva return here. If you do, I'll hex your father to the grave."

Fifteen

Jesse Randolph was plucking the feathers off an old hen for breakfast. As the food in camp was generally deplorable—cooked in open fires and poorly stored, leaving the flour, meat, and produce to deteriorate— the old hen was the only source of decent nourishment he could find. One of the enlisted men in K company, Pvt. Isaac Moore, was raising chickens near his tent. He was selling the scrawny birds at high prices to enlisted men and noncoms alike.

Jesse met Isaac Moore the night before at his tent with two other enlisted men. They spent the night gambling and passing around a bottle of tafia, strong, raw alcoholic beverage favored by the devotees of voodooism. They also shared two sluts that Isaac Moore brought in from New Orleans. The sluts, as well as the dozens of others that infested the camp, came from New Orleans to prey on the thirteen dollars a month pay that many of the men freely spent on women, rot-gut alcohol, and gambling. As Jesse methodically plucked away at the chicken carcass, he thought about the previous evening. He regretted sharing the slut with the others and felt disgusted that he was so hung-over. Jesse was not in the habit of drinking to excess and wenching, and after last night's experience, swore he would never repeat that mistake again.

"*Damn* that Isaac Moore. He's one *bad* nigger," said Jesse softly to himself. Jesse was also upset that he was lured by Isaac Moore to gamble, something he loved to do but had promised himself that he would refrain from.

"Bastard got most of my money."

Isaac Moore had told Jesse that he enjoyed influencing and be-guiling men and women, and that he came from New Orleans and lived near Congo Square, where he practiced voodoo openly. He claimed that his father was the legendary Dr. John who originally came from Senegal, and that his mother was white. Isaac Moore also claimed that Dr. John had taught him how to place and lift curses and how to make *gris-gris* in order to attain the power of the Zombi. What in-trigued Jesse the most about Isaac Moore, however, was his boasting that he was engaged in the black market and that he sold wine mariani on a regular basis to one of the officers in the regiment, whose name he teasingly refused to divulge. The only clue he would give regarding the identity of the officer in question was his swaggering remark, "I gots de man in m'ah pocket where I wants him! And whut's more, my broder, I knows dat dis officer is in *le marche noir,* like myself."

As Jesse was stripping the bird, Nate and Sergeant McKlintock appeared dressed for fatigue duty. Although it was Sunday morning, they had decided to implement a sneak inspection on companies A, E, and K. Captain Graham had forbidden roll call on the Sabbath, but Nate took the order because he wanted to determine who was present and who had deserted the night before.

"Damn deserters. Leavin' ev'ry nite night in droves . . . and Gra-ham not giving a shit," lamented Willie.

"Hell, McKlintock. Let de bad apples go. Most of de deserters are foolish men, an' de regiment don't need 'em," scorned Nate as the two noncoms approached Jesse.

"What's the matter? Still hungry after that big breakfast?" Willie was trying to make a joke, but Jesse was not amused.

"You call that gruel breakfast?" Jesse started to pluck the feathers with violent pulls, using his entire hand rather than his thumb and index finger. "Mean no dispect, Sergeant Major." Jesse stopped plucking the hen with his fist and looked up at Nate and Willie. "No wonder the men are desertin' ev'ry night. Like Moses and de Jews of ol', fleein' de Egyptians, these men are leavin'! De food's poison. Harlot's coming into camp ev'ry nite, stealin' money, and no-good swamp niggers sellin' rot-gut alcohol. It's got the men down. I suspect 'fore long the reg'ment will wither 'way like a severed vine. What's more! Is dat I *know* that an of'cer is at the mercy of one of the enlisted men!"

"What you mean, mercy?" demanded Nate, stunned by Jesse Randolph's accusation.

"I mean that I knows that an officer in the regiment is involved in purchasin' an' maybe sellin' stolen goods! Hell, if the of'cers are bad, what's de use? What's de use?"

The corner of Nate's mouth twitched in anger on hearing this information. He did not need to know the name of the particular officer who was in the take. "Graham!" he muttered to himself in a tone that confirmed all of his suspicions.

Nate approached a little closer to Jesse, careful not to step in the pile of chicken feathers.

"Your responsibility is to me and de reg'ment. You ought to know that." Nate paused, and then in a reconciliatory tone, hoping to woo Jesse, "You told me that you were once an officer in de Ninth Louisiana Native Guard."

By now Jesse had stripped the old hen of all the feathers and was getting ready to butcher the bird with his knife.

"That was a long time ago." Jesse cut open the hen's belly and started to clean the bird and dress it for the spit, so he could roast it over the small fire he had prepared.

"Well, yo have de opportunity to be someone again, if you want to."

Sixteen

Nate decided that it was time to break Pvt. Isaac Moore's voodoo practices. He was determined to put an end to his nightly rituals of witchcraft and the use of fetishes to hex certain individuals of the regiment who would not follow his spiritual leadership. What also infuriated Nate was Isaac Moore's business practice of placing and lifting curses for a fee, not only for enlisted men but for civilians who would come to camp and engage his powers.

For several weeks Nate had concentrated on catching Isaac Moore in the act of practicing voodooism. One night, he overheard Pvt. Archie Vaughn talking with another enlisted man about a hidden altar, a kind of shrine dedicated to the power of Pedro, the militant vodun spirit, that Moore kept hidden deep in the swamp. Nate became obsessed with finding the shrine and destroying it, before Moore's spiritual grip on many of the younger recruits grew stronger and, consequently, further eroded discipline.

The opportunity came one night when Nate and Willie decided to follow Pvt. Archie Vaughn into the swamp. They knew he was going to the location where Moore conducted his voodoo ceremonies. They cautiously followed him in the moonlight at a safe distance through the bayou.

The night was humid and mosquitoes and other unpleasant insects swarmed about Nate and Willie as they moved through the vegetation and shallow pools of water, shadowing Archie Vaughn. After they had traveled for about twenty minutes, they began to hear the faint, erratic, but rhythmic sounds of drum beating and waves of chanting. As they continued to advance through the tall grasses and thick water plants, Nate noticed a slight, multicolored glow of light filtering through the vegetation and cypress trees. They made their way through the marsh until a small clearing became visible to them. About a dozen men, all of them out of uniform, naked except for loincloths, and several octoroon and quadroon women, who were virtually stripped bare of clothing, were dancing furiously around a large, burning cauldron, located near the makeshift altar. Nate and Willie decided to crouch behind some willow trees and observe the affair.

Through the trees and undergrowth, they noticed an illustrated altar constructed in a series of tiers between two oak trees. Although it was dark and the noncoms were several dozen yards away from the altar, the multitude of flickering candles that had been deliberately, spatially arranged enabled Nate to see quite clearly the contents that decorated the shrine. On each tier, an array of items such as old jugs and jars were displayed, as well as many gnarled and twisted roots. On the top tier of the altar, the surface was covered with liquor bottles and empty glass bottles with tiny crucifixes within each one. What really disturbed Nate, however, was the decrepit skull of a human and the head of a eel freshly killed cat suspended on a string. Its glossy eyes stared right at him.

Nate and Willie arrived right in the middle of the ceremony. The men and women were dancing as if they were in a trance. Some of the devotees' faces were covered by crude masks that invoked fear and death. Near the shrine, Nate spotted Privates Percy-Ray and Archie Vaughn. They were squatting and staring intensely at Isaac Moore, who was holding and caressing several serpents of different sizes. He was wearing a crimson hat and a red loincloth as he chanted and encouraged the men and women to participate in the dancing and drinking of tafia. He was speaking in a language that Willie could not make out. Straining to hear, he finally whispered to Nate,

"What's he sayin'?"

Nate could not make out what Isaac Moore was saying initially either, but after listening intensely for a few seconds, he recognized some words.

"Seem to be part Creole French and part African," whispered Nate to Willie, "and he's prayin' to his god, Makandal, to destroy all whites."

"I've seen enough," said Willie. "Let's go in dere an' break this ting up."

As Willie started to rise from his place of seclusion, Nate grabbed his shoulder and held him back.

"No, not yet. This is not the way to stop this."

Suddenly a large bang exploded, resulting in a cloud of smoke. The air smelled of sulfur.

"*Gunpowder,*" exclaimed Nate.

It was the signal for the participants to commence more chanting.

> Eh! Eh Bomba hen hen!
> Canga bafio te
> Danga moune de te
> Canga do ki li!
> Canga li!

Isaac Moore emerged from the shadows and placed himself in front of the altar. He was scattering gunpowder with his right hand, followed by a servitor who ignited the powder. In his left hand, Moore was shaking a ritual rattle and shouting in Creole French.

> L'Appe vini, le Grand Zombi,
> L'Appe vine, pou fe gris-gris!

Isaac Moore was appealing to his god, Zombi, to grant him the power to defeat his enemies and to welcome new converts.

"*Vie la puissance de Tousissant L'Overture. Mort aux blancs!*"

Nate and Willie had seen enough. While Willie was visibly disturbed by the strange rituals that he had just observed, Nate was irate. They decided to leave and return to camp. Nate would deal with Pvt. Isaac Moore in his own way.

Nate had trouble falling asleep that night. His mind kept wandering, engrossed in thought about his assignment and its importance. He kept contemplating how he could break Isaac Moore's influence on the men and expose Graham's corruption. The last words that Colonel Grierson said to him before he left Fort Leavenworth for New Orleans haunted him, made him restless as he shifted his weight from side to side in his bunk.

"I am depending on you to make a difference, Sergeant Major!" Grierson kept repeating over and over again. "The successful formation of the Ninth Cavalry is instrumental in the overall achievement of bringing the members of your race within the rank and file of the army on an equal basis with whites. When you have finished your task with the Ninth Cavalry, you will return to Fort Leavenworth and continue to assist me in training the Tenth."

Returning to Fort Leavenworth and the open spaces of the West is what kept Nate going, and the likes of Isaac Moore and Captain Graham were not going to delay that prospect. As he tossed and turned in his bunk thinking how he could get rid of Graham, an idea came to Nate as he was staring at the ceiling. "Hennessy! I can trust him, and *together*, we can expose him."

After the officer of the day had dismissed the companies of the regiment from morning inspection, Nate accosted Hennessy and asked permission to speak. "Sir! Beggin' the lieutenant's indulgence, sir. I have something to report. May we walk a spell?"

"Certainly, Sergeant Major. Lead on, please," replied Hennessy waving his right hand forward.

The two men walked slowly toward a grove of oak trees that offered shade from the brutal sun and humidity.

"Sir, I think I knows why de regiment don't have no equipment an' horses," explained Nate.

Hennessy looked perplexed, and for a moment was at a loss for words. "Make yourself clear, Sergeant Major."

"Well, sir, you know how durin' the war there was a lot of black marketin' and thievry by civilians and officers at the expense of the rank and file."

"Yes, Sergeant Major, I am aware that such malfeasance took

place," replied Hennessy, annoyed that Nate was not getting immediately to the point.

"Well, lieutenant, its happening right here, and that's why we got no horses, saddles, cookin' utensils . . ."

"*Proof*, Sergeant Major, *proof!* Do you have evidence to base your findings?" interrupted Hennessy skeptically.

"I only have half of the beast, sir. I knows the tail end but I'm not sur' who's at the head."

The lieutenant's curiosity was aroused by Nate's information. "Continue, Sergeant Major," commanded Hennessy as he folded his arms against his chest.

"One of the enlisted men tol' me that Private Isaac Moore is sellin' wine mariani to one of the officers, and that this same officer is in the black market."

"Sellin' wine mariani is not a crime as far as I know, Sergeant Major.

"Beggin' de lieutenant's pardon, sir! It is against military regulations for an enlisted man to sell *anything* to *anyone* as long as they are in uniform, *sir*."

Hennessy was taken aback by Nate's assertiveness and realized that he might be on to something very serious. "Do you know the name of this officer?"

"Sir, I believe that it's Captain Graham, though I don't have any proof that it's him."

Hennessy was not entirely taken by surprise by this intelligence. He had seen the captain painfully hungover almost daily, and had suspected since day one that there were other reasons why horses and equipment were not being delivered to the regiment other than the war department's ineptitude and the regiment's low priority. Nevertheless, Hennessy did not want to jump the gun, so he remained hesitatingly dubious. "Sounds like rumors to me, Sergeant Major. How certain are you of your source?"

"Beggin' de lieutenant's patience, sir, but my source is reliable, and I *know* that Private Isaac Moore is a no-good huckster and hoodoo peddler. The problem is sir, I need your help in exposin' Graham for what he really is."

Hennessy unfolded his arms and rubbed the sweat away from his face with his right hand in pensive thought. "Yes, I see. You need an officer to report his conduct to his superiors. But Sergeant Major, without proof, my hands are tied. We need evidence that he is engaged in black marketeering."

"Lieutenant! I can only get evidence if you help me. Sir, I have a plan, and I know how to get the information."

Hoping to surprise Private Moore in his sleep, Nate decided to wake him an hour before reveille. "Nothin' like su'prise!" he said to himself with a little chuckle as he put on his boots. He sipped down some coffee that Julius had prepared for him and marched toward Private Moore's tent. Nate's plan was simple. He convinced Hennessy that the best and most direct way to obtain the necessary evidence to connect Graham with the black market ring was to shake the tree. If he was successful in bullying Pvt. Isaac Moore into revealing some evidence of Graham's complicity, Hennessy promised he would back him when he went to Gen. Wesley Merritt with the evidence.

"I knew that you was comin' to see me this mawnin'," said Private Moore as he fed his scrawny chickens with stolen horse feed. It was an hour after the bugler had sounded reveille, and Moore was still not in uniform. Nate noticed that he was not only out of uniform but barefooted, and that the stupid chickens were pecking around his feet, scrounging for the oats. He was disgusted by the unmilitary nature of the place. "I've been hopin' that you would see the light, and join us, my broder," said Moore in a patronizing manner.

"I'm not your broder, and when you address me, you call me Sergeant Major!" Nate was cold as ice, and almost as an afterthought, abruptly seized the feed bag from Moore's hands. "This is stolen federal property, *Private*, and you're not in uniform!" Nate slightly lifted the visor of his kept and placed his face next to Moore's. "I can chuck your ass in de stockade. Did yo' know dat?"

Issac Moore's attitude was smug. "Oh yes, Sergeant; you could do that, but I knows you won't!"

"Oh, you think I'm foolin'?" Nate slowly circled around Private

Moore as if he was a cat stalking prey, and in a low and menacing tone said, "I'm goin' put a placard 'round your neck dat says *thief!*"

Stunned and outraged, Isaac Moore's eyes widened; he then blurted, "*Thief!* You can't do that, I knows my rights—I'm free man!"

"Oh?" responded Nate contemptuously. "You think that the Yankees and the sacrifice of thirty thousand dead black men that fought the Secesh bought your ass freedom?"

Isaac Moore was about to blurt out something, but Nate was quick to cut him off. In his usual dressing-down manner, Nate placed his face within a few inches from Private Moore's face. His eyes became wide and intense. Even though his adrenaline was flowing, he spoke slowly and deliberately. He knew that raising his voice would only work in Private Moore's favor.

"I'm sick and tired of your foolishness! You been spookin' de men with your witchery and hoodoism. I want that altar of yours in de swamp destroyed, now! And if I ketch your ass involved in any mo' mischief, like incitin' rebellion and pushin' de men to kill whites, I'll put your ass in de stockade—eatin' rotten bread and drinkin' putrid water."

Private Moore did not move a muscle. He was not intimidated by this Uncle Tom nigger who coveted the white man's respect. He became defiant and stood in front of Nate. The two men were now facing each other as if they were roosters in a cockfight pit.

"You can't harm me. Vodun and the spirit of Dompedre, who speaks through me, will protect me from my en'mies! We'll triumph over your kind, and take what has been denied us fo' hun'reds of years . . ." But before Private Moore could finish his rhetoric and threats, Nate quickly stomped his right boot on Private Moore's naked left foot. Moore yelled in pain and instinctively cocked back his leg. Nate then reached for Private Moore's right leg and yanked the limb violently forward, causing him to fall backward. Nate then placed his boot on Moore's throat and pressed down, choking him to the point where he started to gag for air.

Nate stared contemptuously into Isaac Moore's bulging eyes. "Feels good, don't it boy? I outta know, cause my ol' overseer used to do de same thing to me, when I was a youngin. *Hell*, the stupid bastard would make my face look like a *blue* catfish and I thought that he was goin' to *kill* me!" Isaac Moore tried to dislodge the boot from his throat but Nate held it tight as he watched his victim gag and gasp for air. "Now listen up! I'll release my boot from your scrawny little neck if you answer my questions." Isaac Moore nodded his head vigorously and Nate removed his boot. "I wants some information from you no-good black ass, and if you're lyin' to me, I'll make sure that you're gator food."

It took several moments for Isaac Moore to get his breath back as he stood on his hands and knees, breathing heavily. He felt dizzy and disoriented and lacked the strength to get to his feet. Nate thought he looked pathetic on all fours and decided to grab him by the scruff of the neck and prop him up against a large banana tree.

"Which officer you been sellin' wine mariani to?"

"What officer?! I, I don't know nuttin' 'bout no officer."

Nate slammed his boot again on Isaac Moore's bare feet, causing him to cry out in pain. "That will teach you to walk around without shoes, you hoodoo huckster. Now, don't bullshit me! Who's the officer in this regiment that's in the black market?"

"*Graham,*" replied Isaac Moore desperately as he continued to struggle with getting enough air into his lungs, rubbing his foot against his leg to soothe the pain.

"That's good, boy, real good. Least you're not lyin' to me on that score. And how you know it's Graham?"

" 'Cause of, of, the horses."

"What 'bout de horses?"

"Graham gave me orders to take the best horses and hide them in the swamp."

"The swamp?!" Nate became very still for a moment while his eyes wandered in thought. "The swamp? What de hell fo'?"

"A quartermaster sergeant," responded Isaac Moore meekly as he held his sore leg. "He, he, brings them dare at night, and I reports back to Graham that the delivery was made."

"Then what?"

"Then they sell them to civilians."

Nate nodded to himself as an expression of confirmation on what he had wanted to find out from Isaac Moore. Satisfied that he had a solid lead, he leered at him while pressing his index finger in Moore's chest. "This will do fo' now, *Private*, but if I catch your mutinous tongue a-waggin' one mo' time, I'll cut it out and put the damn thing on that altar of yor's—candles aflame and all!"

It did not take long for Nate to find the hidden corral in the bayou. He located the site near where Isaac Moore held his voodoo ceremonies. The corral was nestled among some large oak trees, and the crude fencing was hidden behind short tupelo trees. Nate noticed other signs of horse activity, such as old and recent piles of dung, some hay, and cribbing on the cypress fencing.

He immediately reported his findings to Lieutenant Hennessy, and together they decided to ambush the quartermaster sergeant when he collected or delivered the next string of horses. The only problem with this plan, Nate pointed out to the lieutenant, was that they were ignorant of when a delivery or pickup would be made. They needed reliable information to act on, so Hennessy told Nate that he had a plan of his own.

Lieutenant Hennessy decided to sneak into Captain's Graham's bedroom while the commanding officer lay fast asleep. It was during the middle of the night, and Hennessy found the man lying on top of his bed still in uniform, clutching a half-bottle of rum against his chest as he snored loudly, his mouth making unbearable noises. Hennessy gently rifled through Graham's desk and fingered through his files. He was fortunate that there was a bright moon in the sky, so the bedroom was flooded with white light. Finding nothing out of the ordinary, he quietly started to search the pigeonholes of his desk for paperwork that might be incriminating. "Nothing! Absolutely nothing here," he whispered to himself. He looked at Graham, who was still snoring and clutching the bottle of rum as if it were a helpless baby. His tunic and trousers were unbuttoned, and the room reeked of the smell of cheese—which came from his stinking feet. "Disgusting disgrace to the uniform!" Hennessy scoffed in a low voice as his mouth twitched in disgust. He started to leave the room but his boot tripped over a brass tureen at the foot of the desk, causing the lid to come off and roll around the room in small circles. "*Damn* it!" Hennessy exclaimed. Graham, however, remained undisturbed. He shifted his body and head to the left and stopped snoring for a moment while Hennessy stared at the lid that had come to a halt in the middle of the room. He delicately stooped down, picked it up, and was about to place the lid back on the tureen when he noticed some folded papers with heavy black ink script protruding from the opening. "Hello?" Hennessy removed one of them and unfolded it. He moved to the window where the glow of the moon was greatest and held the papers close to his face. It was a copy of a regular requisition form, signed and dated by Graham, requesting six horses for the Ninth Cavalry from the New Orleans horse depot. He unfolded the other papers, and all of the copies were almost identical except for the dates, all of them requesting a half dozen horses to be delivered immediately to the regiment. The latest order was dated yesterday, so Hennessy surmised that the horses would be delivered tomorrow. "Got you!" Hennessy smiled to himself and returned the forms back into the brass tureen. He then tiptoed out of the room, gently opened Graham's rickety door, and stepped into the hallway, leaving his commanding officer in the same drink-induced sleep that he had found him in.

Nate, Lieutenant Hennessy, and two troopers were armed and waiting near the clandestine corral in the bayou. They had been hiding behind several large magnolia trees since dark, and Nate thought that the mosquitoes seemed more avaricious than usual because they had to remain motionless and secluded in the brush in order to catch their prey by surprise. Hours passed and the two troopers started to fidget with impatience.

"Stop that!" whispered Nate to one of them, who was scratching a fresh mosquito bite on his face.

It was past midnight and Lieutenant Hennessy was about to give the order to retire when the faint sounds of shod horses could be heard approaching.

"Here they come, Lieutenant. Sure as rain, Lieutenant." Nate tapped the black leather of his holster flap, reassuring himself that his Walker-Colt was ready in case there was trouble.

"We will wait until the horses are in the corral before we arrest them, Sergeant Major. Tell the troopers to be ready with their carbines," ordered Hennessy as he pulled down on the brim of his kepi so the hat would be secured properly on his head when he was ready to move.

"Sir!" reaffirmed Nate.

Nate could see a rider at the head of the string of horses through the vegetation of the bayou, and as the man came riding closer he recognized him as the quartermaster sergeant from the New Orleans horse depot, who had tried to cheat him. "Well, he's goin' get his now," he thought to himself.

The quartermaster sergeant was whistling the tune "Molly Malone" as he sat heavily in the saddle, his gut so enormous that he had to stretch his arms to hold the reins. "The fat thief needs a gawddamn wagon to carry him, not a hoss!" Nate whispered to himself and one of the troopers started to giggle. "Shut up, boy, and pay attention," admonished Nate.

The fat quartermaster sergeant dismounted when he reached the gate and opened it to let the horses in. "Get ready, men, keep a sharp eye," instructed Hennessy as he pulled his army Colt from the holster. "Let's go!"

Hennessy charged ahead and the four men emerged from behind the large magnolia trees at a run, making for the corral. "*Hold it right there, Sergeant!* You are under arrest for stealing and selling government property."

"*Holy shit,*" cried the quartermaster sergeant, who was stunned by the surprise. He raced toward his horse and attempted to mount the animal to escape, but was too slow and fat to get his boot in the stirrup. Panic stricken, he decided to let the animal go and started to run in flight into the bayou. Nate pursued him and quickly caught up. He seized the quartermaster sergeant by the back of his neck and pulled him back with such force that he fell backward on his ass.

Nate kicked the fat man as he sat on his backside. "*Get up.* De lieutenant wants to meet you." As he grudgingly got up to his feet,

Hennessy walked up to them and ordered Nate to remove the quartermaster's side arm. "Search him, Sergeant Major!"

"No nigger is goin' to put his filthy black paws on me, Goddamn it!" he protested loudly.

"*Shut up man*, or I will have you bucked and tied," replied Hennessy. "Search him!" he repeated.

Nate went through the pockets but found nothing except some coins, a pocket watch, a tobacco pouch and a ceramic pipe. He then ripped open the quartermaster sergeant's shell jacket, forcing several of the brass buttons to pop off, and a folded piece of paper that had been wedged in between the jacket and undergarment fell to the ground. Nate slowly picked up the piece of paper, opened it, and handed it over to Lieutenant Hennessy.

Hennessy's anxious eyes examined the piece of paper. "Excellent!" he proclaimed. "This has been signed by Graham, ordering these horses. Sergeant Major, we have our proof."

Seventeen

Nate was sitting at his camp desk in his quarters, writing a lengthy entry into his journal. The lamp oil was running low, and he raced to complete his entry before the wick died.

The rainy season has come early this year. The weather is still humid, the marshes and bayous have overflowed their banks, and much of the countryside is experiencing flooding. For most of the recruits, poor bastards, quartered in those cramped cotton compresses and old tents, and getting their water supply from the polluted swamp, this has produced deadly consequences. Cholera! The camp's water supply is known by all that it was declared unsafe, but some of the men have continued to drink without boiling. In addition, the practice of cooking in open fires and not properly washing utensils only furthers the advance of this deadly sickness.

I noticed that this epidemic was going to break out during drill period last week. I was with Lieutenant Hennessy, conducting target practice with companies A and B. They were shooting infantry Springfields, the only firearms that the lieutenant managed to procure.

While we were firing the Springfields, Corp. William Walker suddenly collapsed, holding his gut in pain. The poor wretch fell to his knees and his torso buckled so far forward that his mouth was almost in the dirt. He started to gag and make hideous discharge sounds. For several days he had com-

plained about painful watery diarrhea and cramps. Last eve-
ning, he told me that he was experiencing vomiting. I ordered
him to the dispensary, but Corporal Walker refused, claiming
that he actually felt better and fit for duty. He died last night,
and I found his body at his post.

For most of October and all of November, the men have
been dying at a rate of one every third day. As these weeks pass
by, the dreaded disease, which first strikes its victims with ag-
onizing diarrhea, is then followed by vomiting and cramps. The
stricken experience acute dehydration and the body becomes
pale and emaciated. If bodily fluids are not replaced, the victim
finally dies a slow and agonizing death. God? How many more
times am I going see this? Lord knows I saw enough of it
during the war.

Nate paused for a moment and thought about his mother. He
pondered what she would have said if she were still alive and was able
to witness the effects that cholera had on people. Whenever Nate entered his thoughts and feelings in his journal, he tried to be as deep-
thinking as possible, because his mother told him over and over again
that "if you can't write 'bout som'ting smart, don't bother to write at
all." Thus Nate would spend long moments staring at his journal, contemplating how he should express himself correctly in the written word.
He tried to be a different person when alone with his journal. He knew
that at times his speech was crude and limited, but felt confident and
prided himself in his ability to write clearly and perhaps express a touch
of primitive philosophical thought and observation.

When human misery and suffering prevail in its ugliest form,
such as a deadly infectious disease, the manner in which indi-
viduals react to a crisis situation either brings out the worst or
the best in them. This cholera epidemic in Greenville is no
different from any other collective human drama—certainly no
different than the choleras that I saw during the war. While
some of the officers shrugged their duty in caring for their men,

others, such as Lieutenants Hennessy and Smith, worked diligently to halt the spread of the pestilence, and worked hard to keep the regiment from falling apart. Captain Graham, our soon-to-become former commanding officer, on the other hand, approached this crisis in his traditional style. He chose to hide in his room, soaking his brain with wine marinari and cheap rum. He knew of the arrest of the quartermaster sergeant, so he knows that the game of stealing government horses and writing false requisition forms for a cut in the profits is over. Lieutenant Hennessy and I have written General Merritt about Captain Graham's conduct and involvement in the black market. We expect his arrest very soon. Graham is truly tormented. I overheard, as did the servant Julius, his pathetic crying out during the night:

"Not my fault. I . . . didn't want this."

Pvt. Percy-Ray Pridgeon, never one to pass up an opportunity for material gain, took advantage of the misery of others by robbing those men who had cholera. Although he possessed no firm evidence, Nate had observed Percy-Ray's behavior over a period of several days and believed that he was plying his natural skills as a rogue. Nate had overheard some of the recruits talking about Percy-Ray and how, while posing as a concerned comrade, he would promise to send what few valuables the dying men possessed to their families. Then, at night, he would sneak into the dispensary and lurk in the shadows near the severely stricken. After the dying had finally expired, Percy-Ray would quickly proceed, rodentlike, and steal what he thought was valuable—usually homemade primitive jewelry, small sums of money, and modest personal effects. Nate was frustrated that none of the recruits came forward with any testimony, and he believed the reason was because they feared the close association and symbiotic relationship that existed between Percy-Ray and Isaac Moore—the Voodoo Man. He knew that the recruits feared being hexed by Moore, and many told him that they thought the Voodoo Man was responsible for the cholera outbreak. Nate was also told by some of the members of the burial detail, which burned the corpses, that some of the bodies had ghastly mouth wounds, indicating that someone had hacked away at the gums and bone to remove gold fillings.

While Pvt. Percy-Ray Pridgeon was robbing the dead, and Isaac Moore was busy with his voodoo shenanigans, Pvts. Mathias Pryor and Jesse Randolph were models of diligence, assisting Nate and Lieutenants Hennessy and Smith in attempting to halt the spread of the disease. Although exhausted from the dual tasks of training raw recruits and containing the ravages of the cholera, Nate always found time to make an evening entry into his journal.

> *We've isolated the sick and made sure that all the water in camp was boiled before drinking and cooking.*
>
> *Good news! Captain Graham has been arrested on orders from General Merritt. He was taken under guard to Regimental Headquarters in New Orleans. Based on Hennessy's and my report, along with the copies of the fake requisition doers, Merritt has convened an immediate court martial and investigation into the black-market ring.*
>
> *Merritt also used his influence to contact General Phil Sheridan, commander of the department of the Gulf, and release the back pay that was due to the regiment as well as accelerate equipment and weapons procurement. Thank you, Lord! Merritt also ordered that a surgeon leave at once from New Orleans and come to Greenville.*
>
> *Today, Hennessy gave me some of his own money to purchase fresh meat and vegetables from local farmers. And unlike the other white officers, he has spent hours and hours overseeing cleaning details to scrub all the buildings with soap and water.*
>
> *This evening we had a big pile of bodies. The biggest ever! I hope it is the last, because I am getting tired of watching the men pour kerosene on the bodies and lighting the torch to burn those dead men who should not have died.*

Pvts. Jesse Randolph and Mathias Pryor took it upon themselves to catch Percy-Ray in the act of stealing from the dead. Jesse and Mathias had agreed to hide outside the dispensary and watch to see if Percy-Ray made his nightly appearance. They waited until almost dawn and were about to give up when, sure enough, the rogue private made his appearance and crept into the building through an open window.

"There he goes—jes' lake clockwork. That sun-o'-bitch sure is predictable," said Jesse cynically.

"I can't wait to catch that bastard and hand him over to Sergeant Major Gordon," responded Mathias.

"No use disturbin' the sergeant major. We can teach this boy want he needs to know!" advised Jesse.

They waited a few minutes and then quietly slipped through the back door. They caught Percy-Ray pilfering through a haversack that belonged to a private, who just had died a few minutes before his arrival.

"Fixin's to rob anoder dead man, Percy-Ray?" said Jesse matter-of-factly. He felt cocky and a little triumphant that he had finally caught this macabre thief with his hand in the cookie jar. He quickly struck a match and touched the wick of a nearby oil lamp, partially illuminating the room. Percy-Ray was on his knees near the cot where the dead man lay. His hands were holding the haversack.

He was startled and his face suddenly flushed with embarrassment. He had to clear his throat before he finally blurted out, "I, I, was jest goin' to pack the man's belongin's-up and . . ."

"And send them to his family?" interrupted Mathias. The light from the oil lamp flickered on his spectacles, making him look like a youngster rather than an outraged adult.

Jesse and Mathias did not wait to hear Percy-Ray's lengthy, bogus explanation of how he was only fulfilling the promise that he made to the fatally ill. Without any hesitation, Pvt. Jesse Randolph, being much larger than Percy-Ray, threw his right arm around his adversary's torso and used his left hand to cover Percy-Ray's mouth. Mathias instinctively grabbed his feet and legs, and they carried him out of the building. Percy-Ray was wiggling like a panicked hog, but Privates Pryor and Randolph had rehearsed their little plot thoroughly, and Percy-Ray

Pridgeon, although strong, was not going to break free.

They carried him a good distance from the dispensary to a place where there was no human activity. When they arrived at an old, dilapidated carriage house, they released Percy-Ray and threw him on the ground.

"Well, now. You ready fo' your beatin', boy?" inquired Jesse, his face tight with rage.

Percy-Ray went for his concealed boot knife, but Jesse anticipated that. He knew that Percy-Ray carried a homemade knife in the lining of his right boot. He overheard him boasting to Archie Vaughn how he used it to amuse himself on Izzie's buttocks that night in the graveyard.

Jesse seized his wrist and quickly twisted the limb as if it were a piece of leather. Percy-Ray yelped like a dog and released the knife; the blade dropped to the ground. Mathias picked it up and pointed it at Percy-Ray. Mathias felt better now that he possessed Percy-Ray's weapon. Percy-Ray's anger finally surfaced.

"I'm not some helpless woman, you-son-of-a-bitch! Come and try and cut me!"

"That's not the way to pull a knife," said Jesse slowly. His face cracked a big, sly smile. Percy-Ray however, remained defiant.

"You big baboon. I'm goin' to kill you."

He started to rise, but like a bolt of lightning, Pvt. Jesse Randolph opened up his huge right hand and smacked the side of Percy-Ray's head with such force that he was thrown back to the ground. His body remained motionless for a few seconds, and then he started to moan.

"If you get up, I'll knock you down again," growled Jesse.

Meanwhile, about twenty yards away, Nate was observing this little event with great interest. He was hiding behind a cluster of banana trees, smoking his briarwood pipe, slowly blowing the blue smoke in the air as if he was contemplating some great concept. Taking his nightly constitutional, he just happened to stumble upon this scene. He was delighted to watch Percy-Ray finally get his, and best of all, the punishment was inflicted by his peers. He momentarily toyed with the idea of intervening, but decided that it was much more enjoyable watching Percy-Ray get a beating than throwing all three men in the guard house, which would have been the proper procedure. So Nate reasoned that in this particular case, this form of "natural" justice was much more effective in imposing punishment on the guilty than measures used by a military court.

Jesse was still towering over Percy-Ray, who remained lying on the ground, his head slightly tilted upward. Jesse adjusted his forage cap so that it was slightly cocked to the right side. He was preparing to whack him again, when Percy-Ray pleaded, "Don't hit me no mo'." He put his hands up so that his face was protected from any blows that Jesse might inflict.

"You're a coward and thief," interjected Mathias in his usual urbane, patronizing manner. "How can you graveyard-steal from these unfortunate men?" Jesse began to lose patience with Mathias's school-like lecture. He suddenly grabbed Percy-Ray's collar with both hands and pulled his body from the ground. He slapped his face again as if he were disciplining a dog.

"If I ketch you robbin' the dead one more time, you'll have to answer to me." Jesse paused, pointed his index finger down at Percy-Ray, and said, "And next time it won't be a few slaps 'round your little head."

FEBRUARY 1867

Lts. Zachary Hennessy and Donald Smith had retired after dinner to the parlor of the Big House. They were in full dress uniforms, smoking cigars and sipping port. They hovered over a small fire burning in the grate in the fireplace to fight off the dampness of the air and the perpetual and annoying drafts that permeated the house. The other officers in the room were either playing cards or reading newspapers. Some of the officers were gossiping about the recent dismissal of Captain Graham from his position as chief recruiting officer and commander of the military encampment in Greenville. Lt. Col. Wesley Merritt had decided to implement court-martial proceedings against him for dereliction of duty and for conduct unbecoming an officer.

Hennessy and Smith were conversing in low voices so that the other officers would not be able to hear. It was always a problem in keeping gossip down to a minimum among soldiers. Rumor and innuendo had a tendency to fester like a bad stomachache among troops closely quartered, and at Greenville, where the enlisted men were still unruly, surly and highly volatile, this proved to be a special problem.

"Well, Zach, in a couple of weeks from now we will be in San Antonio with ten companies," said Lieutenant Smith, flicking the long ash of his cigar into the fire grate.

"Yes, but we still do not have enough line officers or noncoms who can read, and the men are still undisciplined." Lieutenant Hennessy paused; then, when he finished pulling on his glass of port, remarked with an air of concern, "If it was not for Sergeant Major Nate Gordon, I believe the regiment would have completely collapsed weeks ago."

Hennessy took another sip from his glass and added. "His efforts have been splendid."

"Yes, I agree," interrupted Lieutenant Smith. "He really took the initiative in stopping the spread of the epidemic." He paused, then in a rather melancholy tone added, "Too bad that he will never be an officer."

"Oh, you don't think that will last long, do you? I mean there are blacks being elected to the House of Representatives, occupying judgeships . . . they're becoming landowners and farmers . . ."

"That's just on the surface," retorted Lieutenant Smith, dismissing his companion's argument with contempt. "Don't be so naive, Zach. Abolition was one matter; full rights as American citizens is another." Lieutenant Smith was beginning feel the effect of the port. He was on his third glass and was feeling much warmer now—so warm he even toyed with opening a window. His voice started to rise. "Real change for the African will come in decades, maybe centuries. Do you really think the country—north or south, for that matter—is ready to be really led by blacks in the officer corps and in high places of government? Mark my words, Zach, as soon as federal troops leave the South, our former enemies will be up to their old tricks again."

"What do you mean?" Lieutenant Hennessy was a little amazed at Lt. Donald Smith's sharp sarcasm.

"Look, Zach, it's really very simple. Most white people believe, and will continue to believe, that the black man has only come down from the trees twenty years ago. They do not believe, and will probably never believe, that they can be our equals." He was really feeling the port now, and loved to pontificate when his mind was turned loose from the alcohol.

"Well, I really think you're mistaken on this account, old man. I mean, the country just fought a war to free the black man, and . . ."

"Freedom don't mean equality!" Lieutenant Smith shouted. That caught the attention of the other officers. They interrupted their reading and card games and looked up at Smith.

"What's the matter, Smith? Darkies gotten under your skin?" derided one of the new officers who had only arrived two weeks earlier. Several of the other officers started to laugh and chuckle.

"What the hell do you know, mister? You only came to the Ninth because of its promise of faster promotion."

"Didn't every one us?" replied the new officer. The room fell awkwardly silent.

Nineteen

Nate was in New Orleans for the day. He was instructed to meet with the Ninth Cavalry's commander, Col. Edward Hatch, and Lt. Col. Wesley Merritt for a final review of details before the regiment was to be shipped off for San Antonio for further training. He planned to use the extra time in the city to purchase a few items he thought he would need before leaving for Texas.

He arrived at Union headquarters on time and was ushered immediately into Colonel Hatch's office. The commander of the Ninth Cavalry was sitting behind a heavy oak table, signing papers. His adjutant was standing to his left, feeding the forms to him one by one. Lt. Col. Wesley Merrit was also present, sitting cross-legged on a horsehair chair at the left end of the table, holding a large white handkerchief in his right hand. Although Nate had been with the Ninth for about five months, he had never met the legendary Colonel Hatch. He knew that he was a close friend of Nate's commanding officer, Col. Benjamin Grierson, back at Fort Leavenworth, and that Hatch had ridden with Grierson through Georgia on that six-hundred-mile raid back in 1863. Nate remembered reading in the newspapers how Hatch, like Benjamin Grierson, enlisted to fight for the Union and rose through the ranks to become a major general of volunteers. Nate was pleased that this capable abolitionist had sought to become the commander of the Ninth Negro Cavalry.

When Colonel Hatch put down his pen and raised his head to look up at the sergeant major's towering physique, Nate noticed that the commander's face was square in shape with a strong jaw. His hair was

129

cropped very short; the top of his skull resembled a gentleman's fine hair brush. Nate came to an extra-crisp attention and saluted. Hatch returned the salute as his pale blue eyes gazed into Nate's. The commander of the Ninth came immediately to business.

"I have heard much about you, Sergeant Major Nate Gordon. Lieutenant Colonel Merritt has forwarded all of your correspondence, and he has a high opinion of your capabilities. I thought your observations and recommendations were timely indeed."

"Yes sir, thank you, sir," responded Nate. Then, without asking permission, he interjected, making sure that he used Hatch's war-time rank, "Beggin' de general's pardon, sir, I have serious concerns regarding the overall discipline of the men. I—" Before Nate could finish however, Hatch interrupted him, and in his slight, drawn-out Maine accent, tried to be reassuring.

"That is one of the reasons why the Ninth is going to Texas, sergeant major." Hatch paused and stroked his bushy mustache with his right index finger. "We must leave Louisiana and leave the past behind. We must restore hope and morale among the men."

"Yes, sir. Hope is what de men need most, sir." Nate was immediately impressed with this man. It was not often that he felt this way upon meeting an individual. There was good reason. Colonel Hatch was a physically imposing man, and when he spoke his voice resonated with decisiveness. He had the appearance and essence of a Prussian officer. Although Nate knew he was not a West Pointer, Hatch looked every inch the soldier, and Nate thought that his face was handsome. Certain facial traits were very distinctive such as his large nose, cleft chin, and very thick but groomed mustache and eyebrows. Nate felt his eyes focusing on Hatch's chest, on the several medals that he had earned during at the battles of Franklin and Nashville.

"At the suggestion of Lieutenant Colonel Merrit, I have approved most of your suggestions and all the promotions you recommended," declared the commander of the Ninth as he leafed through his papers. "I believe . . . yes, here it is . . . Private Jesse Randolph to be promoted to first sergeant . . . and Private Mathias Pryor to be promoted to Corporal." Hatch looked up at Nate with his peering blue eyes and inquired, "Are you certain that the promotion of Private Jesse Randolph to first sergeant is not soon?"

"Sir, he has demonstrated leadership abilities, and durin' the recent sickness among the troops he further demonstrated his abilities for carin' fo' the men, and . . ." Nate suddenly paused in midsentence. He was unsure whether he should mention that Jesse Randolph had been a lieutenant in the Louisiana Native Guards. Hatch realized that Nate wanted to say something, encouraged him to speak up.

"Yes, sergeant major? Is there something else you care to add?"

"Yes, sir. Private Randolph was an officer in the Ninth Louisiana Native Guard."

"Yes, I read that in his dossier. His regiment performed well at Milliken's Bend. It is my hope that he will fulfill his potential." Hatch looked up at Nate but before he could say anything more, Lieutenant Colonel Merritt intervened. He noticed that Nate looked a little anxious.

"Is there anything else?"

"Yes, sir. What 'bout those companies that still don't have officers?" Nate paused and then his voice suddenly became grave. "Beggin' de colonel's pardon, but I'm still very concerned 'bout the mutinous nature of some of the men. I've been watchin' some of the mo' troublesome suspects, but I can't help but feel that trouble is on its way."

Part Two

MUTINY!

One

ON THE TRAIL TO SAN ANTONIO, MARCH 1867

On the day of departure from the Texas port of Indianola for San Antonio, the regiment was not ready for the one-hundred-and-fifty-mile march. The ship-transport trip from New Orleans to Indianola on Lavaca Bay, although short, proved to be a miserable experience for men and horses. Most of the green troopers became seasick and spent their time leaning over the railing, throwing up and complaining.

Upon arrival at Indianola, Texas, a wretched port located in the west side of Matagorda Bay close to the mouth of the San Antonio and Guadalupe Rivers, the soldiers were allocated horses from the military horse depot. The first night on the soggy west Texas plain, Nate made an entry into his journal.

> *The troopers are still green and poorly equipped, and the men are mostly mounted on windblown horses leftover from the war! Colonel Hatch and Lieutenant Colonel Merritt decided that the men could learn how to ride en route. I believe that this is a good but also hazardous proposition that entails all sorts of risks for both man and beast. The biggest problem is going to be keeping the column together. The senior officers, however, considered that this was still better than letting the regiment slowly disintegrate in morale and discipline in Louisiana. True enough! When the orders finally arrived for the Ninth to move out and proceed to San Antonio for further training and eventual deployment on the Texas frontier, the*

news was received by the officers with jubilation as if they were freed slaves. I swear, though, my sixth sense is telling me, and I know that my mother would agree, that the journey will be marked with all kinds of perils. Many of the troopers in company K, such as Privates Percy-Ray Pridgeon, Archie Vaughn, and Isaac Moore, are still up to the same foolishness and having a bad influence on the men. I asked Lieutenant Hennessy to be assigned to company K 'cause I know that those men need the most work in discipline and drill. I want to keep a sharp eye on those troublemakers, and be present to intercept them like a dog surprising a fox in the coop, if they cause any problems on the trail to San Antonio.

When the Ninth moved out from Indianola, the regiment consisted of about eight hundred men organized into ten companies. Company strength is about average, each squadron consisting of seventy men. But the shortage of line officers is bad. Instead of one captain, one lieutenant, and one second lieutenant for each company, we had to depart with almost no line officers and several of the companies only had one lieutenant. The burdens for overseeing discipline and drill, while instructing the men in horsemanship, has fallen on us noncoms. This situation is much worse than during the war.

Good news! Several weeks ago I taught First Sergeant Jesse Randolph and Corporal Mathias Pryor the basics of rudimentary cavalry horsemanship. Both men learn quickly, and their manner of sitting in the saddle tells me that they will be fine horsemen. In fact, those recruits who managed to get some horse training at Greenville have learned quickly. I believe this is a good omen and one of the few positive developments since I have been assignment to the Ninth. It gives me hope to see that the men are quickly learning to ride and master the tactics and practices of cavalry horsemanship. I am concerned, though, that most of the troopers tend to be a little rough with their horses. I know that the recruits had not yet learned that the horse is a trooper's best friend, and that they must be dependent on the animal's well-being. To ignore a sick or lame horse is the car-

dinal sin in the cavalry. Army regulations are clear in this matter. Any soldier or officer that permits a horse to be badly ridden or ill treated is to be severely punished.

Nate put away his quill and closed his journal. "That's enough for tonight," he whispered to himself, satisfied that he had completed his duty to make at least one entry a week in his journal. The air in his Sibley tent felt damp and the aroma of mildewed canvas permeated the space. He decided to step outside and get a breath of fresh air before retiring. It was several hours after the bugler had sounded taps and he felt tired. He pulled back the tent flap, stepped outside, and marveled at the millions of stars that filled the southern Texas sky. His mind began to wander again and he recalled how, during the war, he often saw men mistreat their horses. Even officers were not immune from abusing their mounts, and Nate held particular contempt for them since he thought that they should know better. He had witnessed on many occasions how brash young lieutenants and arrogant senior officers, dressed in their custom-made, perfectly fitting blue uniforms, dug their shiny eagle brass spurs into their horses' ribs to the point where their mounts' flank hides became soaked from the bleeding while leaving a thin coating of red on the spurs of the riders.

He then pondered how Mas'a Hammond had recognized Nate's particular quality that enabled him to communicate with animals. The one true gift that God gave him was his ability to speak to horses. He relished talking to them and gaining their trust as if they were real people, and even when he was a child—much to his mother's horror— he would play underneath the hooves of the plow and draft horses at the plantation. Nate recalled how as he grew older, Mas'a Hammond began to notice his extraordinary horsemanship qualities, and would watch him mount and trot his big bays in the fields without a bridle or saddle and lead them out of fields and paddocks without the assistance of a lead rope or halter. Most of the time, though, the horses would just naturally follow him when he called out to them. Nate recalled how one of the few joys that he ever experienced when he was a slave was when he was thirteen years old. Mas'a Hammond, recognizing his strength as a horseman, made him responsible for overseeing the overall care of all the horses and mules on the plantation.

Nate stepped back into the Sibley but left the door flap tied open, hoping that a breeze might blow into the stuffy tent, chasing away the stagnant air. First Sergeant Jesse Randolph was already asleep and snoring heavily. Nate sat down on his cot and removed his high-top boots before resting his huge frame on a cot that was too small for him. As he lay awake staring at the canvas wall, he thought about his old nemesis, the overseer, John Leach.

John Leach was envious of Nate's ability to ride any horse on the plantation, and of the trust that his boss had placed in the boy. As Nate tried to sleep he could not help but think about how mean and sadistic Leach became when intoxicated. Every day at around noon, he would start hitting his flask, which was filled with moonshine, and become increasingly abusive to the fieldhands and stock. Nate recalled how Leach loved to sneak up behind him when he was riding a horse, remove the cigar from his mouth, and flick off the ash. He would then blow on the tip until it got red hot, and then hold the stogie in between his thumb and index finger and ram the red-hot tip into the hindquarter of Nate's mount, watching the animal bolt. The roaring, boorish laughter that always accompanied this act, and the way Leach would slap his knee and exclaim, "*Jesus Crist.* Love to see that nigger hol' on or dear life!" still made Nate's blood boil. "But then again," he thought to himself, "the bastard did teach me how to stay on a horse." He reminisced on the first time Leach did that, and how surprised he was and how it resulted in being thrown from his mount. The big bay reared up and Nate rolled off the animal's rump, landing on his backside in the mud. The horse then charged off half crazed, bucking his hind legs as if he was being attacked by a swarm of bees. Humiliated, Nate vowed never again to be surprised on horseback. Every time he mounted a horse he rode as if he was expecting Leach to sneak up and burn his animal. This habit saved him quite a few times during the war.

It was not long before Nate was in a state of deep sleep. He was dreaming that he was once again on the outskirts of Prestonburg, Kentucky, when he was with the Fifth Negro Cavalry in 1864, only this time he was a spectator at the scene and not a participant. He witnessed his patrol ambushed by a squad of Confederate pickets, and saw the horse that the green lieutenant, who was leading the reconnaissance patrol, spook and bolt at the first sounds of gunfire. The other horses followed by panicking, and with the exception of Nate, all the troopers were thrown from their mounts. Nate watched himself hold on to his horse's mane and ride out of the ambush through a hail of gunfire, frightened horses, and yelling men as he witnessed all the other troopers get shot or captured by the Confederate pickets.

Nate suddenly woke up. His eyes popped open and he found himself staring at the stained canvas ceiling of the Sibley to the sounds of Jesse's loud snoring. The back of his neck was soaked, and the pores in his chest were staring to ooze perspiration. Nate seized his bandanna and wiped his face. "Goin' be one of them nights?" he whispered to himself contemptuously, dreading the prospect of spending another night accompanied by multiple nightmares about the war. He decided to get up from his cot and go outside and take a few puffs of tobacco from his pipe. He located the pipe and tobacco pouch from his haversack, cautiously walked outside, and proceeded to load a pinch of tobacco into the bowl. He fired it up and inhaled vigorously. The hit of tobacco made him feel more relaxed and he stopped perspiring. Nate took a second deep hit from the pipe and exhaled the smoke into the air, watching it dissipate among the stars. "That was a Gawdawful battle," he whispered to himself as he loaded another pinch of tobacco into the bowl. *"Prestonburg,"* he said to himself softly but firmly. He started to think back about the battle.

He remembered how the Rebs were dug in behind stone and wood breastworks and awaiting the anticipated charge. One hundred and fourteen men and officers died taking the rebel position, while his regiment, the Fifth Cavalry, was mounted, as all black cavalry regiments were during the war, on poor-quality horses. He bitterly recalled how the troopers were also low on ammunition because colored units were given the lowest of priorities in equipment allotment.

He thought about how as the regiment was preparing for a mass attack, the senior federal officer had his head blown off by a cannon ball. A second lieutenant from New Hampshire, fresh from West Point and dressed in gleaming high-top boots and spotless gloves, took command and the regiment formed two columns. Nate smiled as he pondered how the green lieutenant positioned, himself front and center of the front line and pulled his saber from its scabbard. Nate remembered how impressed he was when he saw the young officer rise from the saddle by standing in his stirrups and wave the blade in a wide circular motion in the air. The lad then turned to the command and bellowed in his native New Hampshire accent, *"Draaw sabers."*

At the time, Nate was stunned that this order was given. With the exception of some rudimentary saber exercises such as cuts in the air and so forth, none of the men had any real experience in using sabers, let alone any battle experience wielding the big, heavy 1840 dragoon sabers that were called "old wristbreakers." Nevertheless, the men drew their weapons smartly, and the loud crisp sound of steel being removed from their metal scabbards gave the troopers supreme confidence. The light reflected off the cold steel as they rested the back of their blades on their right shoulders. The second lieutenant wielded his horse to face the rebel entrenchments and roared, *"Charge."*

The men roared in unison, then spurred their mounts forward, racing across the open field, waving and pointing their sabers. As they closed in, Nate remembered as if it was yesterday that the Confederates changed from canister ordinance to grape shot, and the hot fire poured through the attacking horse columns. The regiment, many of the troopers yelling like wild Indians, galloped nevertheless toward the enemy's entrenchments. When the black cavalrymen approached the breastworks, small-arms fire decimated the first wave. When the second and third wave finally breached the enemy's position, bloody hand-to-hand combat ensued that pitted mounted men with long sharp blades and Colt revolvers against heavy-caliber-rifle Minie balls fired within inches of their targets.

The wounds inflicted to man and horse were horrific. It still made Nate nauseous when he reflected on that bloody and chaotic engagement. He shuddered every time his mind turned to those memories of men screaming in terror and pain when a limb was blown off or a chest opened up as if it was a can of tomatoes. With the exception of artillery fire, wounds inflicted on faces and chests by close range shot from .44 and .54-caliber Colt revolvers and cavalry carbines created the most ghastly wounds. Pieces of flesh, blood, tissue, and bone from both man and horse were thrown into the air like wedding confetti and landed on the combatants' clothes and faces.

Nate formed part of the first wave, which suffered the heaviest casualties from grape shot as they charged across the field. When surviving members of his squad breached the enemy's breastworks, they had to fight off dozens of Confederates who were sent in to repel the attackers. The black cavalrymen quickly emptied their Colts into the swarming mass of Confederates, and had to resort to using their sabers to defend themselves against thrashing bayonets.

Nate was holding his wristbreaker dragoon saber while remaining in control of his horse when a big Reb corporal, with a huge, braided gray beard that seemed to touch the ground, lunged at him with his long quadrangular bayonet. Nate was successful in paring the pointed blade from his body while maneuvering his big bay, but the Reb got tired of trying to stick him with the bayonet and decided, instead, to stab the horse in the chest. The poor beast whined in terror and pain and stumbled forward, throwing Nate, saber in hand, onto the ground. He rolled for a short distance, then quickly jumped to his feet like a cat escaping from a dog. The big Reb with the long beard came running toward him, wide-eyed, yelling as if he was in a state of mental derangement. His long, quadrangular bayonet was coming right for Nate's face. He drove the blade at him but only managed to scrape Nate's right cheek and severely cut his ear. As the Confederate corporal surged past him, Nate ran his saber with all his strength right through the Reb's lower back, and the curved tip of the blade emerged from the middle of his stomach. The Reb screamed in horror and clutched his gut where the tip of the sword protruded. He stumbled for a few paces, then dropped to his knees, moaning hideously as blood pumped out of his stomach, staining his butternut blouse. Nate sighed and whispered to himself as if he was confessing to a priest. "First time I ever kilt a man with a saber . . . an' what a bloody mess it was."

His mind turned to that horrifying moment when he could not dislodge his wristbreaker from the back of the Reb's torso. The saber simply failed to budge, and he grew alarmed as he frantically jerked at the pommel of the blade. Each time Nate attempted to wrench the saber from the Reb's torso, the hapless man would cry out in pain, convulse, and wiggle. After several unsuccessful attempts at dislodging the weapon, Nate decided to use his right boot to push on the dying Confederate's buttocks. He placed his right foot below the entry point of the saber, squeezed hard on the grip, and heaved on the wristbreaker, but the weapon remained too tightly wedged in the Reb's back. Hand-to-hand combat was occurring all around him and men were yelling, shooting, stabbing, choking, and clubbing one another. Eager to get back into the fight and kill Rebs, and realizing that any further effort was useless in retrieving his weapon, Nate decided to leave the saber in the Reb's torso and rejoin the affray. He unholstered his revolver and began shooting at any Confederate that came within sight.

Nate's mind focused on the green second lieutenant who initially led the charge. The picture of the man, who was shot through both hips by buckshot at close range by a Confederate artillery cannoneer, emerged clearly in his mind. As Nate puffed on his pipe he could see in his mind the Reb cannoneer blasting away with the lower barrel of his LeMat's .63-caliber smoothbore as the second lieutenant was about to spur his horse and jump over the Confederate breastworks. The impact of the buckshot threw the officer off his horse, and the new gleaming high-top boots were now filling up with his blood. Since his hips were shattered, the hapless man could only painfully drag his body very slowly across the ground.

As the officer was pulling himself with his arms and hands in the dirt, Nate saw much to his horror, a runaway quartermaster wagon pulled by panic-stricken mules heading in the second lieutenant's direction. The wagon's canvas cover flapped wildly and there were no drivers to control the vehicle. The officer frantically tried to remove himself from the path of the runaway wagon but could not pull his crippled body fast enough. When the mules were almost on top of him, they made an abrupt turn to avoid trampling the man, but the rear wheel slid sideways in the dry dust and the spinning iron rim struck him in the head, causing it to crack as if it were a walnut.

The only good thing that emerged from that battle, Nate decided, which gave him some solace, was that the white troops that participated in the engagement had stopped their jokes and jeering. The Fifth Negro Cavalry had earned their respect. They had paid a heavy price in blood, and those critics that said black cavalry was not worth the poor horseflesh they were mounted on were silenced.

Two

Lt. Col. Wesley Merritt had told Nate that the Ninth Cavalry Regiment's marching route from Indianola to San Antonio followed the old San Antonio–San Diego mail line route. Merritt had explained that this entailed crossing the Guadalupe River, then marching the column in a north west direction by following the San Antonio River. If the regiment proceeded at a leisurely pace, Merritt had emphasized several times to Nate, of fifteen miles per day, they would arrive in San Antonio within ten days.

They had discussed that although the regiment was issued new cavalry uniforms and boots, many standard accoutrements, such as cooking utensils, mess equipment, and camping necessities were insufficient to fully supply the regiment. Nate expressed deep concern that there were not enough tents and bedrolls, and what blankets had been issued were filthy and carried lice. "Bad for morale" he had told Merritt, who agreed but felt helpless to immediately remedy the situation. Nate knew that the lieutenant colonel was preoccupied with other matters, such as the lack of rifle slings, saber belts, percussion cap boxes for .44-caliber Colt revolvers, canteens, gauntlets, ponchos, and saddlebags. Consequently, many of the men were not fully equipped to military specifications and were unable to transport sufficient horse feed to supplement their mount's diet. This caused much ill will and resentment among the troopers. There were other problems as well. The military wagons provided to carry supplies were in very poor condition. Many of the wooden wheels' spokes were dry-rotted, and as a result the iron rims would simply fall off when a wagon rolled over a big stone or bump in the road.

Most of the supplies, however, were transported by green mules that kicked, bucked, and brayed incessantly when the mule skinners attempted to load equipment on their backs. The worst problem, though, was the quality of the horses. Although Lt. Col. Wesley Merritt managed to procure enough horses and mules to supply the regiment, many of the beasts were suffering from thrush, a nasty form of hoof rot. In addition, most of the mounts were poorly shod; their shoes would become loose on the trail and fall off. This slowed the progress of the column and produced stragglers.

Privates Percy-Ray Pridgeon and Archie Vaughn were on guard duty near the horse picket line. It was a cool night, and the sky dominated the horizon. Although there was no moon, the sky was filled with thousands of stars. The regiment was a day's march from the Sabine River and both men were teeming with resentment. Although Nate was successful in splitting up the troublemakers in the regiment by placing the men in different companies rather than bunching them in just two or three units, they still remained a problem.

Lt. Donald Smith's company K was worse in terms of discipline and low morale among the raw recruits. They were the worst equipped, and Private Percy-Ray, with his sidekick and flunky, Pvt. Archie Vaughn, were the most vocal in expressing their bitterness and discontentment among the men. Percy-Ray was still looking for a way to seek revenge on Sgt. Jesse Randolph and that weakling Cpl. Mathias Pryor for what they did to him that night outside of the dispensary. "I show them they can't kick me 'round like some mangy dawg," he often said to himself. He would bad-mouth the officers and all of the noncoms and complain to anyone who would listen about the poor quality of the food and how the "white man never want to see a nigger 'mount to anything, 'cept his servant." He would spread rumors about how the men were going to be used as "ditch diggers in the blazing sun." Although most of the men would say nothing when Percy-Ray ranted on about how bad the army was, a few of the troopers did grow more restless, and resentment festered.

Tattoo was sounded two hours earlier, and most of the troopers were sound asleep near dying camp fires. Percy-Ray and Archie Vaughn were standing in the middle of the horse picket line. Percy-Ray was vigorously scratching his head with a horse curry comb. He called out to Archie Vaughn who standing about twenty feet away, in a low but desperate voice, "*Pissst. Archie. Pissst.* Archie! Come over here."

Like a servant responding to his master's call, Archie Vaughn walked over to where Percy-Ray was standing. "What's the matter, P. R.?" inquired Archie Vaughn in a obsequious manner.

Scratching madly, Percy-Ray responded with an air of desperation. He sounded as if he was going to lose his mind. His head bowed, he scratched his scalp with great intensity. "Damn lice are eatin' my scalp as if I was a corpse!"

"I'll pluck 'em out," responded Private Vaughn eagerly. He placed his carbine on the ground and hurriedly walked over to Percy-Ray with his arms extended as if he was sleep walking. Private Percy-Ray was agitated and impatient.

"You can't do a thing without any light, *fool*."

"Yes, I can. I'll fetch a lantern. J'st you wait," said Private Vaughn devoutly, although he spoke those words with some reservation. Earlier he had noticed a lantern that was turned down low at the entrance flap of Lieutenant Smith's Sibley tent. With wild and bulging eyes, he anxiously tiptoed over to the spot where the lantern was located, turning his head spasmodically from left to right looking for any signs that might stop him from "borrowing" the lantern from any officer's tent. He snatched the lantern and ran back to Percy-Ray.

"W're in the hell have you been?

"I gots the lantern; lower your head," retorted Archie Vaughn with surprising authority.

Percy-Ray obeyed. He bowed his head and Archie Vaughn started to pick at his scalp with his index fingers. He pinched at Percy-Ray's curly hair and removed several of the flat-bodied, wingless, sucking insects from his head. He would then drop them into the lantern and watch the parasites burn up in a flash. Both men would then laugh like two mischievous brats torturing spiders in a schoolyard.

Nate's pipe was lodged in between his teeth in the right side of his mouth. He was making his nightly rounds when he came upon Archie Vaughn and Percy-Ray. Private Vaughn was still picking away at Percy-Ray's scalp. Nate was furious when he saw that the men were not at their posts and were burning an oil lamp for their personal use. The oil was in short supply, and they still had several more days of travel before they reached San Antonio.

Just as Private Vaughn picked out an unusually large louse from Percy-Ray's head and was to drop the parasitic insect into the flames of the lantern, Percy-Ray was sent flying across the ground as if kicked by a mule.

"I told you I'd kick your black ass if I caught you messin' 'round while on duty," said Nate sternly. He calmly struck a match with his fingernail and lit up the bowl of his briar-wood pipe. He drew on the stem until the flames from the tobacco protruded from the rim of the bowl. A light blue smoke cloud engulfed Nate's head, making him appear surreal in the low light provided by the lantern.

"I see that you boys stole Lieutenant Smith's lantern," said Nate rather matter-of-factly as he gazed at the lantern.

Pvt. Archie Vaughn started to stutter and stammer. "Wez, Wez, were j, je, jest bor, bor, borrowin' the lantern for little while . . ."

"Shut up you idiot, 'fore you end up like him," said Nate, pointing to Percy-Ray with his pipe. "Next time I finds your no-good black asses not at your posts, I'll have you both bucked and gagged. You know what that means?"

Percy-Ray got up from the ground, brushing off the dust and grass that covered the front of his uniform. Archie Vaughn stared at Nate wide-eyed, his mouth open.

Nate was calmly puffing on his pipe. "When a man is bucked and gagged he's fo'ced to squat on his ass in de dirt. His feet are flat on the ground and his knees are pushed up tight 'gainst the chest. His wrists are then bound in front, real tight like, so it cuts off de blood in de hands. A large log is then shoved across the bend of his arms and beneath his knees." Nate removed the pipe from his mouth and used it as a prop to illustrate the action of stuffing a log in between the back of a man's knees and the bend of the elbows. He paused for a moment. He wanted to make sure Percy-Ray and Archie Vaughn visualized this humiliating and painful punishment. His face then cracked a wide, malicious grin. As was his habit when he was ready to verbally abuse surly or complacent recruits, he circled the two hapless men twice, then turned abruptly to face them. His nose was just inches apart from the two troopers' faces.

"Then de man would be gagged with a soap or a piece of scrap wood and left for six hours in de sun with no hat."

Both enlisted men were standing at attention now, and while Private Percy-Ray's face still revealed a contemptuous smirk, Private Archie Vaughn's eyes clearly manifested fear of the thought of being bucked and gagged.

"You boys think I'm always on your ass 'cause I'm jest some kind of Tom with authority." Nate paused for a moment, then took out his pipe again from his teeth. He waved it at Percy-Ray and Archie Vaughn as if he was threatening a mule that was about to buck.

"What you fools don't understand is that I'm tryin' to pass on my experience's soz you can survive on the frontier. Supposin' I would have been some Commanche buck, out with the mind to stealin' horses. *You'd be dead by now. That's what!* De Comanche buck would have slit your throats." Nate pointed the stem of his pipe at his neck and jerked it across his Adam's apple. "And lifted your hair 'fore a hungry man finishes a meal. And then he would piss on your sorry asses and brag fo' years to his friends how he kilt and peed on two stupid niggers who were fucking 'round 'stead of mindin' de horses." Nate felt like using his boot to kick Percy-Ray and Archie Vaughn, but decided against it. "Get back to your posts. Now." Both Percy-Ray and Archie Vaughn picked up their rifles and obeyed Nate like whipped dogs. They had had enough for one night.

Nate's eyes were aflame with anger. During the war, he often had to scream at green recruits and belittle them for their own good. There were countless times when he had to confront an arrogant enlisted man who thought that he was better than anybody else and "cou'd lick da whole Secesh army" just because he wore a new blue suit and shoes and carried a gleaming Springfield rifle. Nate knew that this was dangerous thinking that resulted in quick death on the battlefield.

Lieutenants Smith and Hennessy were preparing to go to bed. They shared a Sibley tent, and had become close friends through their mutual respect and their shared desire to make a difference in building the Ninth Cavalry into a reliable, disciplined fighting force. Lieutenant Smith was cleaning the cylinder of his Starr army revolver. The tent smelled of cleaning oil and there was a collection of small dirty rags at the foot of his bed. Lieutenant Hennessy was reading a well-worn copy of *Ivanhoe*. It was past midnight and Hennessy wanted to blow out the lantern and sleep.

"Are you almost finished cleaning your side arm, Donald?"

"Almost. I just have to wipe the barrel with oil," responded Lieutenant Smith.

"If I had known that this was going to be a nightly ritual I would have never agreed to share this tent with you. Every night the tent reeks," stated Hennessy as he turned over toward the tent wall and pulled his blanket over his neck.

Smith could not have cared less what Zach Hennessy thought about his fetish with cleaning weapons every night before he retired. It was a practice he had developed during the war. Experience taught him that any soldier who neglected his weapon was a dead man.

"Well, Zach, at least I know that my weapon will not misfire due to jamming or wetness in the firing mechanisms. If I were you, I would be a little better prepared than you have been. I have not seen you once take the time to clean your revolver since leaving Greenville."

"I gave my Colt a good cleaning when we left. I see no reason to stink up the tent with sperm-whale oil when there is no immediate danger."

"No immediate danger?" Smith was perplexed at how Hennessy could be sometimes so naive. He quickly loaded his Starr revolver and turned the cylinder to make sure that it revolved smoothly. He then placed the Starr into its flap holster and hung the saber belt on a nail protruding from the tent pole. "You can never be too confident, old boy. There's always danger lurking. I am not going to be caught unprepared."

"Prepared for what? There are no Indians in these parts."

"I'm not talking about Indians, Zach," interrupted Smith. "It's the two-legged rats that are in this regiment that worry me." Smith blew out the flame in the oil lamp and lay down in his camp bed. Hennessy did not want to respond to that last comment. Was Smith right? His eyes were wide open, staring at the soiled tent wall, wondering.

Three

The regiment was five days on the trail following the banks of the San Antonio River, and although the horses were in poor condition at first, they seemed to improve during the march. Many of the troopers concocted old-time recipes that improved their mounts' health and gave them greater energy. These former slaves brought their knowledge of the care of horseflesh to the cavalry and devised remedies for cuts, sore hooves, and gastronomic problems such as worms and poor digestion. For cuts, some of the men would apply pine tar or soft mud mixed with garlic; for battered hooves some of the troopers would mix rich grasses and ironwood in their mount's feed; turpentine was widely used for deworming. In addition, much to Nate and the white officers' delight, most of the troopers genuinely became very fond and protective of their horses, which made the animals happier, thus improving performance.

The countryside, flat and very watery, was also lush, and water fowl and game abounded. For the first time in months, the regiment had fresh meat and fish, and Colonel Hatch gave permission that certain "trustworthy" men should go on short hunting expeditions and supply the troops with fresh food. Hatch, on the advice of Merritt, thought it would be good for morale, and Nate was ordered to lead one of the hunting excursions. The regiment had not been issued any carbines because they were not available, so the troopers carried only army Colts and sabers. Only officers and noncoms carried a hodgepodge of carbines ranging from .50-caliber Sharps to .54-caliber Burnsides and Nate's .52-caliber Spencer repeater.

153

Nate shot a deer, a lean, two-year-old buck, with his Spencer. He hit the animal in the head with one shot, and the beast collapsed immediately. It was the first time he used his carbine since target practice at Fort Leavenworth. He had kept the repeater disassembled in his haversack while he was in Greenville and on the boat crossing. Once in Texas, however, he reassembled the barrel and stock, and to the delight of the troopers, fired off a whole Blakeslee tube magazine in rapid succession at a makeshift target. While Nate worked the lever and hammer at lightning speed, firing all seven rounds in less than twenty seconds, some of the men exclaimed; *"Ooh-wi! Jesus Christ. And man!"* Nate would simply smile at the raw recruits and say, *"Now*, if *you boys* are *real* good, an' *prove* yourselves *worthy* of bein' *real* soldiers in dis army, maybe, just maybe, you'll gits de chance de use one of dese."

Nate had shot the buck about two hundred yards into the marsh. He then tied the animal's hindquarters together, attached the carcass to a rope, swung the rope over his right shoulder, and proceeded to walk out of the marsh with a stick in his right hand, poking and feeling his way through the tall grasses and murky water. As he was thrusting his pole into the mud of the marsh to avoid the deep parts, he thought how he once before had to do the exact same thing not too long ago. Nate sighed, shook his head, and spoke to himself, "Only back then . . . I was a *runaway* and no-account nigger and fleein' from Bloodhound Jack and the patrollers. Now . . . I'm carryin' a Spencer and I got chevrons on my sleeves that one can see for *miles*." Nevertheless, memories of the past started to come into focus whenever he was reminded of an action or scene that had occurred once before. He bowed his head and struggled through the mud as he dragged the deer carcass through the marsh, his thoughts returning to his memories of escape from Bloodhound Jack.

Nate had known Bloodhound Jack all of his life. He was the local slave catcher, and his dogs were renowned as "the best nigga-catchin' hounds in de parish." Mas'a Hammond had frequently used his services to track runaways and bring them back. It was known among the slave community that every time Bloodhound Jack caught a runaway, part of his price was cutting off the left ear of the captured fugitive and nailing it to the side of his privy. Nate hated Bloodhound Jack more than any man he had ever met. When he was very young, his father had run off. He wanted to escape his state of servitude, make a new life for himself up north, and gain enough resources and means to eventually help his wife and son gain their freedom and join him. Without telling his spouse because he wanted to protect her by keeping her ignorant of his plans, he bolted in the middle of the night, making for a safe house he heard existed. An older fellow slave had told him that a family of Quakers lived on a farm on the main road that ran through St. James' Parish. The old man explained that he would recognize the place because the Quaker family had hung a large quilt on the front of the house depicting the leaf patterns of Jacob's ladder. He was told that this was the sign that the Quakers used to indicate that this was a "safe house" and part of the underground railroad.

Nate's father never even made it to the St. James–St. Charles parish line. The alarm was immediately sounded when one of the house servants saw him running north clutching a bundled blanket filled with a few of his personal effects and some meager supplies. Mas'a Hammond immediately summoned Bloodhound Jack, and the slave catcher appeared at the big house with a one-year-old hound called, Socomo. Slapping the horsewhip against his tall boots, Bloodhound Jack explained to Mas'a Hammond that he had been training a new hound, Socomo, for slave catching, and told the planter that he was eager to put his new prize to use.

Bloodhound Jack departed immediately on horseback with his pack of hounds and quickly caught up with Nate's father. The young hound was proving himself worthy of his master's expectations by quickly picking up the scent and taking the lead in the chase. The pack ran down the fugitive slave and had him cornered against a thick grove of canebreaks, where he could not advance any farther. Nate's father held off Socomo and the crazed, barking hounds by wielding a long stick until Bloodhound Jack arrived.

The slave catcher's habit was to dismount and point his revolver at his prey's face while he pulled his skinning knife from its sheath.

Grinning hideously, he then approached the hapless fugitive, placed the end of the barrel in between the eyes, and slowly cocked back the hammer as if he was going to shoot. Usually the runaway would begin to beg or close his eyes, fearing imminent death, and Bloodhound Jack would then raise his skinning knife and swiftly slice off the left ear of his victim.

Nate's father had seen other runaway slaves return to the plantation by Bloodhound Jack without their left ears. The slave catcher would bind the fugitive's hands together with a rope, wrap the other end on the pommel of his saddle, and trot his mount back to the plantation, forcing the runaway to keep up in his exhausted state. If he fell, or was too injured to keep pace, Bloodhound Jack would simply drag him—with Mas'a Hammond's approval, because the planter wanted to set an example. Nate's father, however, had made up his mind even before he escaped that he would not let this humiliation happen to him. He had made up his mind that if he should be caught by Bloodhound Jack, he would either resist and fight him off, or be killed in the attempt. Either way, he was determined that he would not be returned to the plantation with only one ear, tied like an animal, and face disgrace and shame in front of his wife and son.

Bloodhound Jack dismounted and walked up to his victim, pointing the revolver at Nate's father's face while he pulled out his skinning knife.

"You know what I'm goin' do with that left ear?" Bloodhound Jack grinned as he slowly walked toward his quarry while the hounds barked and growled. "I'm goin' give it to my *new* hound as a *reward* on his first chase!"

"*The hell you will,*" yelled back Nate's father defiantly as he swung his stick at the slave catcher. Bloodhound Jack fired his revolver into Nate's father's face, and when the smoke had dissipated, Nate's father's body lay on the ground with the top of his head blown off. The slave catcher then calmly bent over the body, sliced off his dead prey's left ear, and proudly gave the organ to Socomo, stroking and speaking to the young dog softly as if he was a newborn baby. "Dat's a *good* boy, dat's a *good* boy."

After Nate fled the lagoon, losing the patrollers and hearing the cries of Bloodhound Jack's dogs being devoured by the gators, he ran in the marshes, keeping a northwest pace guided by the sun and stars. He had hurriedly packed his gaping gator wound with soothing swamp mud on his deeply lacerated arm, and waded through waist-deep marshland. The bayou was covered with miles of water hyacinth, lilies, and duck weed. In the evenings, when torrential rains would raise the water level and drench him, he sought shelter in the coulees among the big cypress and tupelo trees that grew on higher ground. At night, his only company were usually curious minks and raccoons, while more nocturnal animals such as owls and armadillos hooted and scurried about. In the mornings for breakfast, if he was unsuccessful in hooking a catfish for his breakfast, he would forage for swamp root and eat palmetto and hyacinth blooms so he would at least have enough nourishment to travel and not feel the gnawing hunger pains in his gut. He had traveled for five days living like a hunted animal, and although the risk of infection to his arm was much reduced, the limb remained very sore. In addition, he had started to become concerned that he might not find sanctuary and perish in the bayou wilderness.

What kept Nate moving and his determination strong was his will to succeed where his father had failed. His hatred for Bloodhound Jack and for what he did to his father equaled his desire to be free from bondage. While he slept at night hiding in the damp and cold bayou, hungry and miserable, his mind would always turn to that horrifying moment when he saw his father's lifeless body being dragged behind Bloodhound Jack's horse.

He shook his head sadly as he recalled the moment he and his mother were in their cabin, finishing their breakfast of cornmeal and bread, when they abruptly heard some of the slave women wail and cry out in grief. Nate's mother knew what the hysteria was about. She bolted from the table and tripped over one of its legs, jerking the table and causing her bowl to tumble onto the dirt floor. At first Nate was puzzled by the growing verbal pandemonium in the middle of the slave quarter. Then it came to him, and his soul filled up with dread. He slowly raised himself from the table with great foreboding, listening to his heart beat rapidly against his chest. He walked toward the bright light pouring through the entranceway where his mother had left the crude door open and stopped at the threshold. He shielded his eyes from the strong light as he watched the women weep in hysteria while Bloodhound Jack trotted his horse down the main lane of the slave quarters, dragging his father's broken body. His mother was standing immediately outside, and when she saw her dead spouse, she sobbed loudly and frantically ran toward him. Bloodhound Jack halted his horse, pulled out his skinning knife, and neatly sliced the rope, leaving Nate's father's carcass in the dust. Bloodhound Jack's pack of hounds trotted up from the rear and stopped to mill around their master's horse as Nate's mother cried and held her husband's battered head, which was crusted with dried blood, dirt, and straw.

Nate did not move a muscle but stared hatefully at his father's killer, who in turn was watching Nate's mother. Nate's fists were clenched in rage, and although he wanted to drag Bloodhound Jack from his horse and beat him to death, his body felt paralyzed as he stared at the murderer. He watched the slave catcher dismount and go up to his new young hound, Socomo, who was joyfully wagging his tail. In between the front part of his snout, the dog was holding what appeared to Nate as a dark piece of meat. Bloodhound Jack patted Socomo on the head and rear and loudly proclaimed to Nate as he pointed to the item, "See this, tar baby?! This here is your dead daddy's ear!" He then squatted next to Nate and added, "That's what you git, if you run!"

Jean le Fou was skinning some muskrats and preparing them to hang on his stretch lines so the skins could dry out. It was about six o'clock in the evening, and there was a beautiful red and orange sunset toward the east. He was smoking a pipe and humming a Cajun bastard version of a mid-eighteenth-century song that was once a popular among Napoleon's troops in Russia.

Plaisir d'amour, ne dure qu'un moment,
Chagrin d'amour, dure toute de la vie.

Outside, directly in back of the cabin, an iron tripod was support-
ing a medium-sized cauldron. A small open fire was burning in the
middle of the support structure, while red hot embers and tiny blue
flames slowly cooked Jean le Fou's favorite dish, gumbo. His old aunt
Elsie taught him the way the Indians used to prepare this traditional
feast of the bayous. The tropical stew was prepared with okra, onions,
garlic, tomatoes, black pepper, salt, bay leaves, thyme, crab claw meat,
and shrimp. After frying the okra in oil until there was a brown crust
in the cast-iron skillet, onions would be added. The crust would then
be glazed and transferred to a pot. Crabs, tomatoes, and seasonings
would be added with water, and the pot was allowed to simmer for
two hours. Peeled shrimp was then added and cooked slowly for an
additional hour. This dish of herbs, vegetables, and shellfish, diluted in
water while stewing over a slow, open fire, created a rich aroma that
could be smelled for miles.

Nate thought that he had put enough distance between himself
and Bloodhound Jack and the slave catchers. He was preparing to bed
down for the night, too tired to even try and catch some catfish for his
dinner. He found some high ground along the banks of one of the
many tributaries that flowed into Bayou Teche, and decided it was a
good spot to sleep. He was about to pass out next to some oak stumps
when he smelled the tomato-and-shrimp bouquet of Jean le Fou's
gumbo. Nate immediately ceased to feel tired and began to sniff the
air as if he had become a dog. His longing for food overwhelmed all
of his other physical pains, and he dragged his body from its sitting
position and looked over the horizon. He noticed a sliver of white
smoke climbing toward the sky in the northwest. He sighed and whispered to himself hopefully, "That's not far from here. Lawd, I hope
they can help me."

Nate stumbled in the marsh in the direction of the smoke. With
every step he took, the thick mud of the swamp became heavier and
heavier, making it more difficult to press on. As he neared Jean le Fou's

cabin, the aroma of the gumbo became stronger, and he could hear a man humming a tune. He decided to hide behind some tall saw grass, which was about twenty feet from the south side of the cabin, and reconnoiter. He wanted to determine if the occupants would be possibly proslavers or folks who might be sympathetic to a runaway.

Jean le Fou was still skinning muskrats and puffing on his pipe. A gentle breeze from where Nate was hiding blew by, and the Cajun stopped skinning. He took out the pipe from in between his teeth and turned his nose in the direction of the wind. He sniffed the breeze like a well-trained beagle seeking to pick up a scent, and after a few moments he whispered to himself, "*Hhmm, Noir, la bas!*"

Jean le Fou was famous for smelling odors of all kinds: animals, alligators, birds, and humans. He knew that a black man was hiding among the tall saw grass. Without flinching, he put back his pipe in between his teeth and gently turned around to resume his skinning. He would wait for a few minutes and see if the individual made a move.

Nate, squatting as low as he could, was growing increasingly weak and, above all, hungry. He was at the point in which he really didn't care if the man was a slave catcher or not. If he was a slave catcher, so be it, just as long as he could have a bowl of that food that was simmering in the cauldron.

When it became clear that the individual who was hiding behind the grasses was not going to make any movement, Jean le Fou decided that he would take the initiative. He turned toward Nate's hiding place and shouted in a heavy patois, "I know you dare. Come out, now."

Nate was stunned. He whispered to himself, "How in de hell di' he fine me?" Although he was sweating profusely, his body remained frozen in a squatting position.

"*Allez! Sort de la,*" said the Cajun, growing more irritated. He was puffy more vigorously now and held his skinning knife firmly. He waited for about fifteen seconds and then decided to throw his knife in the direction of Nate's hiding spot. The long, sharp blade landed tip first in the soft dirt in front of the saw grass where Nate was hiding. He heard the knife make a thumplike sound directly in front of him, just a foot away.

"*Merde*. Come out now or I'll come after you!" said the Cajun with intensifying vexation.

Nate decided to come forward. There was nothing else he could do. He took a deep breath, held his head high, and stepped into the clearing. He was sorry sight to behold. His clothes were in rags and splattered with mud. His feet were bleeding, and Jean le Fou noticed that his arm was caked with dried blood and mud.

"You had some trouble, *mon ami noir?*" The Cajun took out his pipe and pointed to Nate's arm.

Nate cracked a smile. "I had a run-in with a big ol' gator."

Jean le Fou returned the smile and teasingly remarked, "And de gator? Did you bite him back?"

Nate could not help but chuckle. He began to feel more at ease. He sensed that he was out of any immediate danger. If this man were a slaver he would have already used a gun.

"I half starved, sir. Please, if I could have a bowl of that there whats you have in de pot . . . I be on my ways," beseeched Nate humbly.

"My *gumbo?*" teased the Cajun as he emptied the ashes from the bowl of his pipe by tapping on the heel of his left boot. "You can have some of my gumbo, my black *ami*, but your arm, *c'est infecter*, if you not clean. *Viens avec moi*," instructed Jean le Fou as he pointed his pipe at Nate, beckoning the tired, wretched-looking runaway to follow him inside the cabin. Nate was all too happy to oblige. He felt safe now.

Bloodhound Jack was devouring the last few remaining beans on his plate with his spoon. Earlier, he had fed his three dogs and given his horse some feed mixed with molasses. He licked the spoon, wiped his plate and tin cup with an oily rag, and stuffed the remaining cooking utensils in one of his saddlebags. He checked his horses' tether and threw some dried oak logs into the fire so he would have some large, hot embers to heat the water for his morning coffee.

The loss of his oldest and favorite hound, Socomo, plagued Bloodhound Jack intensely. The vision that kept appearing in his mind of his old four-legged companion's head wedged in between some exposed roots of a cypress tree stump still brought tears into his eyes and made him sob like a child. As he lay awake on his back in the bedroll, staring at the Spanish moss that drooped down from the thick and gnarled branches of giant oaks trees, he cursed Nate and started to rave.

"*Goddamn nigger*. Killin' my dawgs. I'll fix you. I'm goin' hunt you down no matter how long it takes. And when I finds your black ass, what I did to your father will be nothin'!" Bloodhound Jack paused in pensive thought for a moment, breathing heavily. "I'm goin' cut out your privates and feed your balls to my pups."

After Bloodhound Jack lost his dogs in the bayou, he had returned home and resupplied himself with a fresh horse, provisions for a month, and his twelve-gauge shotgun. He took three remaining hounds that he had left behind and started out to track Nate. As he rode toward the direction where he hoped to pick up his prey's scent, he kept whispering to himself over and over again, "Vengeance is mine, said the Lord. Vengeance is mine, said the Lord. But today, I am the Lord."

Nate's wound was on the verge of becoming infected. The mud had stopped the bleeding, but the bacteria was starting to do its work. Jean le Fou scrubbed Nate's lacerations with soap and water, then soaked the whole arm in white-lightning alcohol. He used a fishing-net needle to stitch the wound closed and wrapped the arm in shreds of clean linen. The Cajun was impressed that Nate didn't flinch an eye or a muscle when he inserted the long needle into his patient's arm and ran the thread through his skin. As he sewed the wound, Nate stared at him with great intensity. It was his way of dissipating the pain.

By concentrating on not recoiling while the Cajun sewed him up, Nate could not help notice that this was a different type of white man. As best he could remember, he had never seen a white person do any hard physical labor or anything that required finger work. He also had never seen a white man who was so tall and muscular. Most of the white people he ever had any contact with, Mas'a Hammond's family, overseers, some townsfolk and hardscrabble farmers, were either fat, gaunt, or shorter than he was. This man, however, was different. Not only did he speak a language Nate had never heard before, but he was taller and bulkier than himself. His arms, torso, and neck filled out his shirt tightly. Unlike most of the white men Nate had seen, this man's face was clean-shaven, and the color of his skin resembled a well-used saddle seat. His forehead had long deep vertical lines and numerous tiny ones surrounding his eyes. Although his hands were huge, his nimble fingers worked the needle as if he was a seamstress.

Nate's eyes wandered around his host's primitive cabin. Except for a bent-up brass bed lodged in the corner and a cast-iron cooking stove in the middle of the cabin, the man had no luxuries. The walls were covered with fishing nets and all sorts of animal traps. A few shelves hung around the interior of the cabin and were stocked haphazardly with large preserving jars, strings of onions, garlic and peppers, oil lamps, fishing hooks, and skinning knives.

After Jean le Fou stitched up Nate's arm, he applied a dressing of two layers of lint, saturated with the tincture of opium. This soothed Nate's pain.

"*Maintenant toi,* no more pain. *Plus mal au bras.*"

Jean le Fou departed from the cabin and went to the back of the building to get his unexpected guest a bowl of gumbo. He stirred the pot slowly for a moment with a huge wooden spoon and tasted the stew with a cast-iron ladle. After pausing for a brief moment in deep reflection, he exclaimed, "*C'est bon.*" He then picked up a deep, hand-made oak bowl and filled it with a large helping of gumbo. He returned to the cabin's interior, gently transporting the bowl with both hands as if it were some religious relic. Exhausted, Nate was about to pass out at the table where he sat, but was awoken by Jean le Fou's footsteps on the creaky wooden floor.

"*Allez,* my black friend, *mangez.*" Jean le Fou put the steaming hot bowl in front of Nate and gave him a spoon.

Nate hesitated for a moment before he took the spoon and looked at the Cajun right in his eyes.

"Thank you!"

Jean le Fou and Nate were slowly paddling the Cajun's *perogue* through the bayou. It was early dawn, and a thick fog hovered over the water like a cloud. Three days had passed since Nate stumbled onto Jean le Fou's cabin, half dead. Thanks to his host's cooking, Nate managed to gain back most of the weight he had lost since he fled the plantation. Although he was still not up to full strength, he felt his arm slowly healing. The tincture of opium bandage that Jean le Fou placed on his arm made it stiff, and he experienced a sharp pain every time he attempted to turn his forearm from left to right or vice versa.

Jean le Fou wanted to show his guest how to hunt gator. They paddled the narrow wooden boat to where the Cajun knew there would be an alligator hole, and instructed Nate to hold the boat steady as he stepped into the bayou. Although the water line came up to his chest, he waded toward the alligator hole holding a hatchet in his right hand. He started to call out to the reptiles like a farmer talking to his pigs, only instead of calling out *soueee, soueee,* he would open his mouth in a contorted manner and call out like a crow, *"Kaaa, kaaa, kaaaa!"*

Jean le Fou knew that alligators had special eyelids that closed when they were underwater, making the reptiles virtually blind. As they swam from their tunnels they would bump into his legs. They would then slowly emerge to investigate, and the Cajun would be waiting for them. At a precise moment, in a flash, his left hand would pin the alligator's mouth closed while the other would end his life with a hatchet right between the eyes. Nate was amazed. He was fascinated at how the Cajun went about his business as easily as if he was picking berries. After he had dispatched one gator by splitting his head with the hatchet, he would throw the reptile over his shoulder and wade toward the *perogue*. He would throw the body in the boat, go back to the alligator tunnel, and repeat the process all over again until he had accumulated six of them, filling the middle of the perogue.

"Now you know why dey call me *le Fou!* Crazy!" he said as he twirled his index finger near his temple and threw the last gator in the boat.

"I've never seen anything like that before," Nate responded enthusiastically.

"Je le connais, donc je peut l'attraper. I know him . . . so I can ketch him," smiled the big Cajun. "Before you leave, you will know him, too."

Jean le Fou and Nate spent the remaining part of the day skinning and stretching the gator hides. That night for dinner, the two men had alligator stew. Never at a loss for whipping up concoctions, the Cajun had prepared the stew with onions, potatoes, peppers, and hot spices. Nate thought that the meat was the best food he had ever tasted. Better even than gumbo. It was tender and tasty and he had several bowls, gulping the juices dry from each serving. After dinner, the two men lit up pipes. Jean le Fou loaned Nate one of his hand-carved briarwood pipes and fired the bowl for his guest and newfound friend.

"I've nev' met a white man like you," remarked Nate as he pulled on his pipe while the big Cajun fired up his own bowl.

"Why? Because I treat you *comme un homme*, a man!? Let me tell you som-ting, *mon ami*, I don't give a swamp rat's asshole damn if a man is black or white. Back here, in de bay-you, a man must prove he can survive. There is no place for bullshit slavery. In de bay-you, all de animals are free, so man must be free also. I have only treated you as any man should treat an-other when he needs help."

The Cajun suddenly got up from his place at the table and walked over to the shelf where a bottle of rye rested between a can of spices and a sack of flour. He seized the whiskey and two shot glasses and returned to the table. He filled both glasses to the brim and proposed a toast. "*Toi*, always *bienvenue chez moi.*"

After spending ten days with Jean le Fou, Nate had slowly managed to somewhat understand his Cajun host's French patois and even picked up a few words. He especially liked the phrase, "*toi*, always *mon ami,*" and repeated it frequently.

Both men spontaneously smiled at each other and raised their shot glasses in a toast. They then pulled back their heads with their glasses to their mouths and emptied them with one gulp.

Bloodhound Jack's remaining three hounds had no trouble picking up Nate's scent. The dog slave catcher returned to the spot where his pack was massacred by the gators and located a small, bloody piece of his prey's shirt in the saw grass. Although Jack's remaining hounds were young and inexperienced in tracking, they had no problem locating their quarry's scent. They lost some time, however, when the hounds became distracted by the appearance of small mammals or by some of the more curious sounds that came from the swamp. The dogs would wander off for hours and he lost time getting his young hounds to concentrate on the scent. Nevertheless, he made relatively fast progress by using maximum daylight, and was finally closing in on Nate.

At sunset on the tenth day of his pursuit, his dogs located the place where Nate had rested, smelled the aroma of Jean le Fou's simmering pot of gumbo, and spotted the line of smoke that came out of the Cajun's chimney.

"So that's where that bastard been hidden all this time. Problay some Goddamn coon ass is hiding that nigger murderin' son-a-bitch," he said to himself as if he was really saying, "I got you now!"

Bloodhound Jack decided to probe the area surrounding the cabin. He placed muzzles on the dogs' snouts to keep them quiet and tethered them with his horse to a tupelo tree. He then unfurled his shotgun from an oil-soaked cloth and checked the percussion caps. Before he started, though, he removed his bowie knife from its sheath and ran his forefinger along its bottom edge to verify the blade's sharpness. His crowlike eyes brightened, and Jack's mouth cracked a malicious grin on his repulsive face as his forefinger drew blood.

"That will do," he said as he wiped the edge of the bowie on his trousers and placed the weapon back in its sheath, which was strapped to his belt on his left side. He then pulled down on the ripped flap of his weather-beaten hat and continued toward the Cajun's home in a crouchlike position. Using the dimming light of sunset, he moved like a snake in the tall saw grass and made his way toward the cabin.

Nate and Jean le Fou were drinking. The Cajun was recounting one of his alligator stories and how he had miraculously, yet again, escaped from being torn apart by a gator's razor-sharp teeth. He was feeling his liquor now, and started to act out the scene where he had to wrestle the reptile to the death in order to save himself. Nate was laughing, and for the first time in months, he felt relaxed. Although he felt his body temperature rise, he did not feel the whiskey as strongly as his host, who was now very boisterous and gesticulating wildly with his hands and arms.

Bloodhound Jack was moving slowly toward the cabin. Crouched forward, stepping carefully among the saw grass, he followed the light in the cabin's window. As he approached, he began to overhear laughter and voices from within, but couldn't distinguish what was being said. He moved yet closer. He wanted to peek in the window and see if that "Goddamn nigger" was hiding there. The clatter of millions of insects and bird calls from the marshes drowned out the sound of his movements, so Jack was able to move without being detected.

Jean le Fou's cabin was built on stilts. Seven wooden steps led from the front porch to the small dock where the *perogue* was tied to a post. Jean le Fou and Nat decided to go and pee from the edge of the front porch into the bayou. As they were urinating into the water, Nate had a thought. "I can shoot longer than you," he bragged teasingly.

"*Merde a toi, mon petit ami noir,*" responded the Cajun, accepting the challenge.

Both men lifted their penises for maximum elevation and tried to arch the path of their urine as if their organs were cannon barrels preparing for long-distance bombardment.

Bloodhound Jack was observing the two men from his concealed position behind the tall, thick saw grass. He was amused by what he saw, and even cracked a smile, as if he was a child getting ready to pull off the wings of a butterfly or some other hapless winged insect.

"Pee well, nigger, pee real well, 'cause it'll be your last time. Come mawnin', I'm goin' to cut it off likes I did to your dead daddy's ear."

Dawn is the most beautiful time of the day in the bayou. The bright early morning sunlight flickers on the trunks and vines of huge moss-laden oak and cypress trees; graceful water fowl glide through the murky waters of the swamp, searching for food. Bloodhound Jack was rubbing the sleep from his eyes when a thick mist meandered through the watery landscape and the drooping Spanish moss that dangled over the calm water moved as if they were veils blowing in a slight breeze. As he stared at the water, he noticed that the rays of the sun served as a signal for the lilies and water hyacinth flowers to surrender their blooms to the light as hungry, red-eyed alligators lurked in the bayou, remaining vigilant. Bloodhound Jack immediately noticed that his young hounds had escaped during the night by wiggling out of their collars. "Probably out chasin' swamp coons, *Gawddamn it*." Nevertheless, he was so looking forward to the task ahead that he decided to skip breakfast and immediately saddled his horse.

As dawn was breaking over the marches, Nate could hear the sounds of dozens of mallards congregating all around the Cajun's home. The wild ducks were floating in the water and walking about at the edge of the bayou near the cabin. Nate was wide awake thinking about Bloodhound Jack. As he gazed at his host's cabin's ceiling, examining the oak beams and cypress planks, listening to the mallards outside squawking among themselves, he fretted in his quilt about how the murderer of his father was also his mother's rapist and the father of his half-sister.

A week after Bloodhound Jack brought in Nate's father's body, the slave catcher had caught Nate's mother alone, at night, in the cold meat storage house stealing a small ham. Mas'a Hammond was very stingy in giving his slaves any of his meat. Although he had many hogs and beef cattle, the master of the plantation only allowed his slaves to eat old horsemeat. Consequently, it was not uncommon from time to time, for a ham or a side of beef to disappear from the smoke or cold meat houses. Mas'a Hammond had given up long ago trying to catch and punish the perpetrators. Exasperated, he would simply raise his hands and state to the overseer when he reported the thievery, "Better a few missing hams and sides of beef then discontented chattel bitching in the quarter about having not enough to eat!"

The only reason why Bloodhound Jack ran into Nate's mother in the cold meat storage house was because he was at the same location for the same purpose. He had been examining some of Hammond's fattest hams and was in the process of selecting one that was smoked with oak wood when he heard the door of the cold meat-storage house creek open. Fearing that it might be the overseer, he hid in one of the corners, hoping to escape detection. Although there was no moon, the stars were out and that provided enough light to see inside when the door was left open. As he listened to the intruder step around in the semidarkness, he realized that the late-night visitor was the spouse of his recent victim. Bloodhound Jack became aroused with lust. Ever since he noticed Nate's mother when he brought in the body of her husband, the slave catcher had masturbated every night thinking about her. Now, here in the night, his fantasy had come true.

In the corner where Bloodhound Jack lurked was a pile of neatly folded burlap sacks that were used to cover the hams while they were being smoked. He had stepped into the pile when he retreated to the corner to escape from being seen. As he watched Nate's mother smell and feel the hams, he quietly squatted, snatched up a folded burlap sack that was on top of the pile, and snapped it open. He then slowly sneaked his way behind Nate's mother, holding the burlap sack open with both hands.

When he got to within two feet of her, he threw the bag over her head and covered her mouth. Nate's mother struggled but she was no match for Bloodhound Jack, who pulled her to the ground and wrapped the sack tightly around her head, muffling her cries. The slave catcher placed his right forearm against her throat and whispered, "Don't move! Don't move an' I won't kill you." Fearing that he might make good on his threats and thinking about her little boy, who now had no father, Nate's mother complied with her attacker's demands. While Nate's mother stoically bit her lip and awaited her fate, Bloodhound Jack frantically loosened his belt and pulled down his trousers. Completing this task, he then lifted his victim's skirt and penetrated her with one forceful thrust. As he pigishly thrusted away, Nate's mother remained silent and refused to show any signs of life. She decided that if she was going to be violated, then she would not give her assailant the satisfaction by showing any struggle. "Let de *bastard* fuck a corpse," she thought to herself. The rape did not last long; Bloodhound Jack wanted it over quickly because he feared being caught violating one of Master Hammond's slaves.

When little Nate saw his mother return without a ham from the storage house and noticed that her face was severely flushed, he inquired what had happened. "Neva you mind, boy. Go back to sleep," was the only reply he got.

Nate only found out what had occurred in the storage house when his mother gave birth to a little girl. She had kept her pregnancy a secret from Nate, and with the exception of a few trusted girlfriends, hid her state from the slave community. Only on the day she gave birth with the assistance of her friends did Nate find out.

The mistress of the plantation, Mrs. Hammond, was told that Nate's mother had just given birth to a half-white baby. Mrs. Hammond strongly disapproved of any commingling of the flesh among the races. "Not on my plantation," she vowed. Therefore she decided, without her husband's knowledge, and after she had secured the overseers' silence in the matter, to send the bastard half-breed child to Savannah, Georgia, where she could be used as a house servant for some friends of hers. Nate's mother did not protest. She loathed the seed that she had carried and wanted to be rid of the child because she did not wish to be reminded that the father was such a wretched individual.

Nate knew in his heart that the man responsible for his half white, half black sister was Bloodhound Jack. He remembered that lustful gaze that the slave catcher gave his mother when he brought back his father's body, and it was well established that neither the overseer nor Mas'a Hammond engaged in sexual interaction with the slaves.

The whole affair left Nate with mixed emotions. On the one hand he was glad that his half-sister had disappeared, but he kept thinking that she was the only family member he had left, and there were moments he had a deep longing to find and embrace his half-sister.

Outside, on the right-hand side of Jean le Fou's cabin, stood a cistern elevated on short stilts and fed by rain water. A wooden gutter ran the length of the roof of the front porch and carried the water into the tower. While Nate was lying in bed thinking about his sister, his thoughts suddenly turned to the desire to quench his thirst due to the previous evening's alcoholic debauchery. He felt very dehydrated and had a burning thirst. His throat and tongue were parched and his lips felt completely dry and tight. He felt as arid as if he had marched in the desert, and all he could think about was turning on the spigot and satisfying his craving.

Nate decided to jump from his corner of the cabin where he had his bedding and pull on a pair of pants that Jean le Fou had given him. He walked out the door and onto the front porch, briefly pausing at the edge of the stairs that led to the dock where the *perogue* was tied, and stretched his body. His arm was healing nicely and Nate was glad that he would be able to take off the bandages in a few days. He gingerly descended the stairs and turned toward the side of the cabin where the water tower was located. The spigot protruded from the bottom of the water tower, and Nate decided that he would simply lie down beneath it, drench his head, and gulp as much water as he could. He placed his head right over the opening and turned on the wooden knob; cold water came rushing out and poured over his head and shoulders. He felt instantly better. Opening his mouth wide, he gulped down sweet water as if he were Moses returning from the desert.

Nate was rubbing his neck and head with his hands as the cold water poured over him. Abruptly, the water stopped pouring; he felt the sharp edge of a blade pressed against his throat and heard a familiar voice that brought dread to his heart.

"Now I gots you. You black *bastard!* You move a muscle an' I'll cut you from ear to ear, *you understand me, boy?*"

Bloodhound Jack was sitting on top of Nate's stomach and using his left hand to keep his prey's arm pinned to the ground. Like a neighborhood bully cornering a weaker and younger boy in some alley, the slave catcher felt triumphant.

Nate's eyes were bulging while his body remained motionless. He could smell Jack's vile breath and see his tobacco-stained, rotting teeth only inches away as his malicious smirk on his pale and gaunt face gave him the appearance of evil incarnate. Bloodhound Jack had planned to take Nate out of sight and hog-tie him, where he looked forward to engaging in a few hours of leisurely torture. He was eager to use his bowie knife in cutting his quarry's flesh and muscle on his chest, legs, and buttocks, and watch him bleed to death.

"I'm goin' cut you to pieces, nigger an' feed your privates to my pups."

While Jack was boasting, Nate's mind was racing. He decided that he would stand a better chance fighting his pursuer right now rather than risk being bound and taken away, where his chances for freedom would vanish. Nate still had his left arm free. His attacker had assumed that with a blade pressed against his throat, Nate would not risk any sudden movement. As Nate's eyes were transfixed on Bloodhound Jack's face, he suddenly shifted his gaze to the right as if he saw something move. This distracted Jack long enough for Nate to seize the moment. He slammed his right knee into his attacker's backside with such force that Jack was propelled into the air as if he was just kicked by unruly horse. Nate sprang to his feet and prepared to take his enemy head-on.

Although surprised, Bloodhound Jack quickly rolled on the ground and rose to his feet with his bowie knife pointed at Nate. He started to lunge at him, taking fast, wide swings with the knife at Nate's throat, pushing him back toward the edge of the water. Nate wanted to stay clear of the big blade, so he kept moving backward toward the edge of the marsh, trying to avoid Bloodhound Jack's lunges. As he retreated, Nate's left foot tripped over the little woodpile that was at the edge of the bank, and he fell backward into the bayou. Jack now thought Nate was at his mercy.

"Pity niggers can't swim," he said with a grin, showing his rotting teeth. "I'm goin' to finish you off right here and now."

Fortunately, the water was not very deep in that particular spot, so Nate was in no danger of drowning. He decided to kneel in the mud of the bayou and splash the water with his hands, imitating a helpless child. This trick lured his nemesis into the water thinking that he would dispatch his prey without any real effort or danger to himself. As Jack swung at Nate's neck and head with the knife, he bolted from the water, grabbed his attacker's head with both hands, and gave him a head butt that sent him reeling back into the water. Nate then seized Jack's right hand and forced the bowie from his grip.

Nate sensed that his enemy had lost the initiative. Bloodhound Jack panicked and turned away from Nate, who now possessed the bowie knife, and started to make for higher ground. He waded as fast as he could but the mud at the bottom of the bayou was soft, making it difficult for him to move quickly. He finally managed to reach the bank and was almost on dry ground when he felt an unbelievable sharp pain in the center of his back. His blood hot with adrenaline, and without really thinking, Nate had thrown the big knife at Jack's back. The blade sunk deeply into the slave catcher's flesh and muscle and split open his lungs, forcing a river of blood from his mouth as his knees buckled and collapsed to the ground.

Nate waded through the knee-deep water and stood next to his tormentor's body, which was twitching slightly on the ground. His legs were submerged in the water of the bayou and Nate thought he resembled a fish out of water. As the dying man choked, gagged, and gasped for air, Jean le Fou emerged from the cabin in his long johns to investigate all the commotion. "*Eh bien. Ah, ah, ah.* Looks like de predator became de prey," quipped the Cajun, bemused by the scene.

"I got to get rid of de body," replied Nate, his chest heaving from the excitement of the fight.

"*Non! Attend!*" commanded Jean le Fou as he raised his arm and thrusted the palm of his right hand forward. He started to smile, and Nate could not understand why the crafty Cajun had a big grin on his face. "Watch." He pointed to some ripples in the water of the lagoon. "He . . . gator bait."

Nate turned toward the bayou and noticed the red eyes of an alligator moving quickly in the direction of Bloodhound Jack's submerged legs. Within an instant, the gator dived and Nate watched the body being violently snatched from the bank. The alligator had seized Bloodhound Jack's legs and was heading down the bayou to get away from the other gators because he did not want to share his breakfast.

Nate's chest was still heaving with exhaustion and emotion. He was glad that his lifelong antagonist had finally been dispatched and that justice was done on behalf of his mother, but felt at the same time uneasy that he had killed his half-sister's father.

Four

The Ninth Cavalry regiment was three days out of Goliad, marching along the San Antonio River. The outfit had halted for the night near an adjacent stream, and the troopers had completed feeding and checking their mounts and equipment before tattoo was sounded.

Pvts. Isaac Moore, Archie Vaughn, and Percy-Ray Pridgeon were conducting a clandestine meeting a few hundred yards from where the regiment was bivouacked. The three enlisted men were sitting on the ground among a cluster of oak trees, passing a bottle of tequila that Percy-Ray had purchased from a Mexican cantina owner in Goliad. He had originally sneaked out of camp and gone into the town to buy a bottle and find a woman to sexually abuse. When he saw several olive-skinned Mexican girls standing by the bar, he became like a child in a candy store. His sexual appetite aroused, he wanted to "fuck everything in skirts."

The colorful patterns that decorated the young Mexican women's loose-fitting clothes and the way they wore their long, raven-black hair over their bare shoulders caught Percy-Ray's attention. He was instantly attracted to the manner in which their jewelry complimented their slender necks and wrists. What aroused his impulses the most, however, was the perfume that these women used on their bodies. When he was able to get close enough to smell them, his senses became alive. It was something about the aroma of the perfume, mixed with their perspiration, that gave off a sexual fragrance. He was so overwhelmed by so many beautiful and sensual women in the cantina that he was unable to decide which wench to go after, and since he spoke no Spanish and all of the senoritas ignored him when he tried to talk to them, he left the cantina frustrated and drunk.

He then sneaked back to camp, awoke Archie Vaughn and Isaac Moore, and demanded that they share the bottle with him. After they had gone down to the river and passed the bottle around several times, Percy-Ray started to boast to them how he could have had his way with any of those Mexican "bitches" in the cantina, if he only had money. This belief was partially fueled by the mouth of Isaac Moore, who was spreading unfounded rumors that the "white troops were being paid mo'." Consequently, Percy-Ray had become bitter that the army was paying black soldiers only thirteen dollars a month.

Pvt. Isaac Moore, always looking for an opportunity to gain influence among the men, listened to Percy-Ray very intently. He waited until his drinking companion finished his little tirade, and then interjected in a philosophical tone, "There will be nev' any justice, my broder, as long as de white man owns ev'ry ting and the black man owns nothing. We must pray to the spirit of Makandal to destroy de whites."

"Fuck prayin', we need to fight for our rights, hear an' now," retorted Percy-Ray as he pulled on the tequila bottle, forcing the worm at the bottom to come close to the neck of the bottle.

"That's right, P-R; that's right," fawned Archie Vaughn.

Lt. Zachary Hennessy had just saddled his big gray gelding and was double-checking his saddlebags when Lt. Donald Smith approached him with a stern look in his face. The outfit had finished breakfast and their morning duties in grooming, feeding, and watering the horses. The noncoms were busy screaming at the green troopers to form up into their respective companies.

"Have you heard?" inquired Smith with an anxious expression on his face.

"Heard what?" responded Hennessy as he adjusted the cinch on his custom-made McClellan saddle.

"Two troopers from A company deserted last night with their horses and equipment," whispered Lieutenant Smith to Hennessy, as if he was informing his friend of a death in the family. "Colonel Hatch wants to keep this quiet, Zach. He can't spare any men to go after them."

"Not go after them? Hell, I'll take Gordon and a squad of men and I'll find 'em in no time . . ."

"No, Zach," interrupted Smith as he waved his hand in front of his chest. "Hatch believes that the outfit must keep moving. He's concerned that we have insufficient officers in the regiment as it is, and that some of the noncoms are questionable. The old man has decided that under these circumstances, it's best to let them go and keep the regiment moving as quickly as we can until we reach San Antonio."

"But doesn't he realize that if the rest of the men find out, it will only encourage others to follow suit?" scoffed Hennessy in disbelief.

"They're long gone, Zach." Lieutenant Smith wanted to end the conversation and return to his company. "It will take too much effort and time to run them down and leave the regiment with less officers to control the men." He placed his hand on Hennessy's shoulder and smiled. "Now let's mount up and get this column moving toward San Antonio."

Nate was conducting a spot check on some of the enlisted men's horse equipment. He would move down the line while the troopers were standing by their horses holding the bridles of their mounts in their left hands. He would tighten cinches on saddles that required adjustments, while berating some of the troopers for overtightening theirs.

"How would you like it if someone tightened your belt like you have done to this horse?" roared Nate at one trooper. The luckless enlisted man gazed at his sergeant major with glossy eyes, fearing being smacked. Nate wanted to make a point that would stick with this green cavalryman. "Do you know how this horse feels, fool, when the cinch is too tight? It feels like this." Without moving his eyes, which were staring right in the trooper's face, Nate kneed the trooper right in the stomach. The man moaned loudly and collapsed to his knees, holding his gut. He did, however, hold on to the reins of his horse. Nate helped him up and reassured him. "Now, son, no harm done. Good thing you held on to the reins. Might mean life or death to ya someday."

Another trooper who was laughing at his companion's plight was caught by Nate. "What you laughin' at? Stand up straight when I'm talkin' to your black ass." Although at times Nate was physically brutal with green troopers, he also could be fatherly. He discovered that using a combination of pain and pleasure with discipline was very effective in training recruits. Most noncoms were consistently brutal and tyrannical in controlling their men. Nate chose to be harsh when the situation really warranted it. He preferred to blend fatherly or brotherly compassion with physical and verbal sanction. He helped the panting trooper who was still holding his stomach from his kneeling position, and in his baritone voice that was loud enough for all the other recruits to hear in the column, lectured them.

"You boys, listen up. If you don't treat your horses like your life depended on them, some red young buck is goin' lift your hair out there on de plains. Never, never overtighten the cinch of your horse!"

Pvts. Percy-Ray Pridgeon and Isaac Moore were observing Nate discipline the star-crossed trooper. Private Moore, always seeking an opportunity to egg on anyone who might be lured into doing his bidding and be a potential convert, whispered into Percy-Ray's ear.

"You see now how dat sergeant does de white man's bidding? See how dat man was brutalized? Where is justice?"

"Shit, there's no justice!" exclaimed Percy-Ray. "The white officers and the sagents are the same as de mas'as and the overseer." He paused for a moment and then his mouth developed his familiar malicious smirk. "And I ain't goin' be driven as a slave no mo'."

"You are learning my broder, you are learning." Isaac Moore then added, "We must now free ourselves from de oppressor."

The regiment was preparing to move out. The ten companies formed a column of fours and awaited orders from their company captains to mount up. First and second lieutenants were posted in front of their respective commands, while the troopers were standing at attention in a perfectly straight column, holding the reins of their horses in their right hands, and resting their left arms along the yellow piping seams of their cavalry trousers. All noncommissioned officers were positioned at various intervals at the ends of each company so they could keep a sharp eye out on their men.

Nate was talking with Lieutenant Hennessy a short distance away from the men of company K. The sun, a big ball of yellow light, was rising in the west. Their horses were allowed to graze while the two men conversed about details that might have been overlooked before taking their positions in the column. Hennessy, always the consummate optimist, remarked to Nate how well he thought the regiment was holding up in its march toward San Antonio.

"Everything in order, Sergeant?"

"Yes, sir, all the men have their saddlebags properly secured to their McClellans and I have checked that the horses' bits and cinches are properly adjusted."

Hennessy smiled and glanced at the men of his company. "I think that you have done splendidly in your efforts to get the men into looking like U.S. Cavalry troopers, Sergeant Major."

"Yes, sir, thank you, sir, but I feel that . . ." Nate changed his mind in what he was going to say. Hennessy, however, noticed his noncom's reluctance.

"Yes, Sergeant? Is there something more you would like to add? If so, speak up, man." Hennessy searched Nate's face for any expression that might give him some kind of indication on what his sergeant major had on his mind.

"Lieutenant, we still have some problems. The men's accoutrements might look like all spit and polish, but most of the men's shell jackets are either too tight or too wide . . . and many of the Jefferson boots that were issued are of the poorest quality and are fallin' apart at the seams. Fact is, Lieutenant, men who lose faith in there uniforms lose faith in themselves and the regiment."

"I realize that, Sergeant. That is why we must reach San Antonio as soon as possible to properly refit the regiment."

Nate pressed on, "What 'bout de Spencers, sir? De men wants to know why de white troops have been issued carbines and we haven't."

"Colonel Hatch and Lieutenant Colonel Merritt believe that the men are not yet ready to be issued carbines or colts. That is precisely the reason why we have not issued Spencers to the men until they master the basics of horsemanship and become familiar with the use of sabers."

Nate experienced a brief flashback to the Battle of Prestonburg. When that "damn fool" shavetail Lieutenant ordered "draw sabers and charge" and led the frontal assault on the Confederate breastworks, Nate knew it was a mistake. He appreciated that the weapon provided a sense of military pride to green enlisted men by conducting saber exercises that entailed cutting and thrashing through the air, and that under certain circumstances a saber charge can be effective, but he also knew that most seasoned officers preferred rapid firing revolvers at a running gallop to overwhelm their foes. That reckless saber charge at Prestonburg against entrenched breastworks and canister nearly killed half the men in the attack, so with the exception of maybe chasing wild Indians, Nate had come to believe that the saber was for show and not for mass killing.

As Nate and Lieutenant Hennessy were conversing, the order finally came from the senior officers to get the column on the road.

"*Companies . . . prepare to mount.*" The men turned to their horses and switched the reins from their right hands to their left.

"*Mount.*" In perfect unison, the troopers placed their left boots into the stirrup hoods of the worn McClellan saddles and swung into the seats. Some of the men winced with pain, as most of the saddles were leftovers from the war so most of the rawhide was completely worn through, or split along the inside rims of the upper side of the saddle tree. This exposed wood that rubbed against the rider's inner thighs like a sharp blade, causing painful blisters and sores.

"*Companies—by columns of fours—all squadrons forty paces interval.*"

The first sergeants moved aggressively to make sure that the men in their charge obeyed quickly, barking out orders to ensure that the troopers' mounts were perfectly straight in each squad. Lieutenant Hennessy gave the order for the color bearer to unfurl the red-and-white company guidon.

"*Companies—unfurl guidons.*"

The flag was made of silk and was indented in the middle, resembling a swallow's tail. The upper half of the flag was red and the bottom half was white. The letter K was in white in the red field, and the number 9 was in red in the white field. Although the Ninth had no official standard yet, as was required by military regulations and much to the dismay of several of the officers, and to Lieutenant Hennessy in particular, the Ninth Cavalry carried several two feet by two and a half feet stars and stripes forked guidons at the head of each company command.

As the companies awaited orders to advance, the recruits remained silent. Nate was at Lieutenant Hennessy's side at the head of the company. Both men rose themselves from their saddles by standing in their stirrups and turned back to look at the column. With the exception of some troopers shifting in their McClellans and adjusting their dragoon saber belts, the only sounds and movements in the column were made by the horses. Some of the greener mounts were chomping on their brass curb bits and digging their hooves into the dirt, while the nags swung their heads and tails to shake off the nasty flies that tormented them, especially when they remained still.

With obvious pride in his eyes, Hennessy sat back in his saddle and tugged firmly on the ends of his brand-new custom-made yellow gauntlets.

"I think the regiment is slowly shaping up," he stated gleefully with an air of confidence. Nate did not respond, and after a brief moment of awkward silence, Hennessy pressed him further. "Don't you think, Sergeant Major?"

Nate could not escape his commanding officer's long gaze, his face and eyes searching for approval.

"Yes, sir, I believe we have commenced to whup these men into United States Cavalry men." Nate's horse was a three-year-old gelding and barely broke. The animal refused to stand still, and Nate had to concentrate on disciplining the beast by keeping a tight rein and talking to him. After a brief pause in his answer to gain control of his animal, he continued in a lower voice.

"I'm jest prayin' that we don't have no mo' desertions, Lieutenant. It's like a poison on de men's minds. Mos' of de boys are willin' to learn an' be good soldiers. Wid mo' drillin' and ridin' experience, they be as good—maybe better—than de colored cavalry in the war 'gainst de Secesh."

As the men talked, the order finally came from the head of the column to move out: "*Companies . . . forward . . . ho.*"

The troopers dug their spurs into their horses' flanks, and the silence that reigned just a few seconds before was suddenly broken by the sounds of mounted troops on the move. Some of the men would urge their mounts forward by making childish clicking noises by pressing their tongues against the inside walls of their cheeks, while others would simply shout "ho" or "yeahhh!" The column moved forward at a walk. Equipment, such as canteens and tin cups, dangled from their saddles, while sabers rattled in their scabbards. The squeaking noise of leather from the saddles, rifle slings, and saber belts resounded in the air and became part of the rhythm of the sounds of the horses' nostrils, shod hooves, and swaying tails.

By the end of March, the Ninth had reached La Bahia Mission on the San Antonio River. The regiment was still one hundred miles from San Antonio, and the company commanders were discussing whether they should cut their daily march from twenty-five miles a day to fifteen due to the continuing deterioration of the horses. It was about an hour before the bugler was to sound tattoo on his trumpet, signaling the regiment to retire for the night. Colonel Hatch, Lieutenant Colonel Merritt, and Lieutenants Hennessy and Smith were sitting on folding chairs at a small table, having coffee beneath their commanding officer's canvas canopy, which was stretched between two palmetto trees. The horses were brought in view of the camp to graze for the night, and pickets were posted around the perimeter of the camp.

"With all due respect, sir, I think that pushing the troops at our current rate of travel will further wear down the horses, and the men will be walking all the time rather than at specified intervals," protested Hennessy, slightly agitated as he crossed his legs and stared at his custom-made boots, which made him look like a dandy.

Hatch had inquired if his company was in a position to continue the pace of twenty-five miles a day. The commanding officer wanted to maintain the existing pace in order to reach San Antonio as soon as possible. He feared that by slowing down the march, potential deserters would seize the opportunity to leave the regiment. Hennessy's friend and commander of company A, Lt. Donald Smith, also agreed with Hatch in this matter.

"I think the best course to adopt, sir, is to continue our current marching pace, but increase the rest periods during the march. If we increase the nooning period from thirty to forty-five minutes, we can give the horses more time to recover from the morning march. In addition, sir, if we divide the lead time into two periods of thirty minutes each, instead of having the regiment lead for forty-five minutes only once in the afternoon, it would greatly relieve the horses and men."

"I concur with Lieutenant Smith," confirmed Merritt. "I think that is the best compromise under the circumstances, sir."

Colonel Hatch was combing his thick, graying mustache with his fingers as he reflected on what to do. He had taken off his frock coat before dinner and placed it around the backrest of his camp chair, revealing his dark blue wool vest with brass buttons. The other officers however, kept their frock coats on and buttoned to the collar.

"I agree with you, Merritt," responded Hatch at last. "Although this would mean that the outfit would bivouac for the night much later than usual, I am of the opinion that maintaining our current march of twenty-five miles a day, while giving the horses more time to rest, is the best consideration." Hatch paused for a moment, then wiped his mouth with his linen napkin and got up from his chair. This signaled the end of dinner and the conversation. Merritt and the two junior officers were about to leave the table but before they could fully rise from their seats, Hatch added with an air of concern, "I suppose it is for the best. The men will be more tired, less inclined to either desert or cause mischief."

Privates Percy-Ray and Archie Vaughn, along with three other enlisted men from companies A and K, were busy polishing off a bottle of tequila about a quarter-mile down the San Antonio River from where the regiment was bivouacked. Unlike the officers and most of the non-coms, the enlisted men did not dine on small game that they had hunted and killed on the Texas open grass plains for their dinner. Their supper consisted of dipping moldy hardtack into a plate of beans. The hard-tack, as most of the equipment and horses, was leftover from the war, and the men had to eat rotten biscuits from boxes that were stamped 1864. The crackers were riddled with tiny holes caused by weevils, who filled them with their webs to incubate eggs.

"That gawddamn meal wasn't fit fo' hogs," scoffed Percy-Ray as he polished off the bottle of tequila and threw it in the river. All the men were completely intoxicated. Percy-Ray had earlier thrown his plate of beans and rotten hardtack on the ground, grabbed his bottle, and headed for the river. Being a good bootlicker, Archie Vaughn also threw his plate on the ground and followed Percy-Ray. Some of the enlisted men who knew that Percy-Ray always kept a bottle of something alcoholic hidden in his saddlebags also had followed after they had finished their putrescent supper. They had sneaked out of camp and found Percy-Ray and Archie Vaughn about a half hour later, hiding among some tall grass, and helped polish off the bottle. Considering that the men were tired and hungry, some troopers really had not eaten enough to satisfy their bellies for days, so it did not take much for Percy-Ray and his drinking cronies to get drunk quickly on virtually empty stomachs.

"Them white officers treat us like we still slaves," said one of the drinking troopers angrily.

"Shit," replied another enlisted man as he rolled a cigarette. "When I was a squirt, runnin' 'round the plantation with nuthin' but an old shirttail, my mistress used to put buttermilk in a trough and we drink with our mouths, jest like the hogs." The trooper completed rolling his cigarette, placed it in his mouth, and struck a match with his thumbnail, igniting the stick into a tiny ball of flame. "I was a wet-nose brat back then and a slave. I didn't knows an' better." He lit the cigarette and took a deep draw from the stogie. As he slowly let out the blue smoke he quietly said in an intense tone, "If she would do that now, I'd kill her." The man pulled on his stogie again, and the tip of the cigarette glowed, briefly lighting up his angry eyes.

Not wishing to be outdone by his comrades, Pvt. Archie Vaughn stepped into the conversation with much bravado. "When, when, when are *we* goin' git them white officers and them nigger drivers—Isaac Moore say we must rise up and take our rightful place as mas'ers of *our* own destiny."

"The *hell* with dat ol' conjure man and his hoodooism, bewitchin' kinda talk," scoffed Percy-Ray as he pulled on the tequila bottle.

The troopers were now engaged in heavy, belligerent drunk talk. Each statement that was made by one of the men, was challenged or acknowledged by the others. The combination of bad food, aching backs and legs from the long march to San Antonio, and the resentment that these men harbored for their superiors fueled the conversation.

"I ain't goin' take no mo' of this shit," Percy-Ray bragged. He paused for a moment, then took a deep breath and heaved his chest and nostrils as if he was a prize bull. *"I'm goin' hurt somebody 'fore this is over!"* he yelled as he charged off in the direction of the camp. Archie Vaughn and the other men followed suit, feeding off one another's animosity.

Sergeant Gordon, Jesse Randolph, and Corporal Mathias were sitting around a campfire. Nate was smoking his briarwood pipe and was still wearing his dragoon saber belt with his Walker-Colt revolver. Jesse was more relaxed. He had removed his blouse and was in his white undershirt, whittling a stick with his pocket knife. Mathias was squinting his eyes by the dimming light of the campfire, reading a copy of *Cook's Cavalry Tactics*. The glass of the delicate wired spectacles anchored to his small nose reflected the red glow of the dying fire. Nate was about to announce that they should see that the men were preparing themselves to bed down for the night, and check the pickets guarding the horses and the perimeter of the camp, when Percy-Ray and his little band of drunk companions appeared. Percy-Ray started to walk over to where Nate was sitting and pointed his finger at him.

"I hates your nigger-driver ass. You think youz better then the rest of us. You're a nigger jest like us and jest 'cause you spend time with

the whites, don't make you no mo' better." Percy-Ray was belligerent and slurring his words as he reeked of tequila.

"Yeah, that's right," added Archie Vaughn.

While Percy-Ray blurted out insults, Nate remained seated, holding his pipe in his mouth while maintaining his icy gaze at Percy-Ray. Mathias had dropped his *Cook's Cavalry Tactics*; his mouth opened as if he was a child in awe of some new discovery. Jesse rose from his sitting position, quickly dropped the stick that he had been shaving, and quietly placed his knife back in the pocket of his trousers. He then lowered his arms, smiled, and clenched his fists as if he was preparing to come to blows.

Although there were five intoxicated, angry men confronting them, Nate remained seated in his camp chair, stone-faced, without uttering a sound. While Percy-Ray shouted insults, Nate's right hand moved slowly toward his holster's flap button. Percy-Ray became increasingly infuriated that he was not getting the reaction that he sought from Nate. Angry and frustrated, he pressed his forefinger against the middle of Nate's chest and started raving like a madman.

"You bastard. I know your kind. You ain't nothin' but an Uncle Tom."

By now Nate had unflapped his holster flap and placed his right hand on the pommel of his Walker-Colt.

The other men in this mutinous little band spread out and surrounded Nate, Jesse, and Mathias. Jesse was waiting for some kind of signal from Nate to move in on the drunk troopers, but for the moment Nate said nothing, so Jesse concentrated on staring down the tall, mutinous private who had a burning cigarette sagging from the corner of his mouth. The two men eyeballed each other as if they were two roosters preparing to fight. Meanwhile Percy-Ray, with Archie Vaughn right behind him, was continuing his tirade in an effort to affront Nate and provoke the sergeant major to make the first move. He momentarily, however, shifted his gaze from Nate to Mathias and smiled as if he were the town tough preparing to beat the crap out of the new kid.

"After I kills you," Percy-Ray pointed to Mathias contemptuously. "I'm goin' squash that toad you-all call a corporal, like a mosquito . . ."

Nate saw his opportunity. All he needed was for Percy-Ray to look away for an instant, and it would be all over for him. Instinctively, he yanked out his Walker-Colt from its holster and whipped the barrel across Percy-Ray's face, splitting both lips and breaking blood vessels in the nose. As Percy-Ray reeled and hollered as if he were a stuck pig, he held his nose with both hands, while the tall enlisted man with the burning cigarette lunged at Jesse while the other two drunk troopers charged Nate while his back was turned.

Jesse punched the trooper with the live cigarette in the face, forcing the stogie back into his kisser and burning his right cheek. Jesse then plunged his fists into the man's stomach, punching him until he fell on his knees, gasping for breath. Meanwhile, Nate was fighting off the two men that had jumped him after he had pistol-whipped Percy-Ray. One trooper climbed on Nate's back and tried to seize the Walker-Colt, while his companion seized Nate's legs.

"Pull 'em down, pull 'em down," yelled the trooper to his companion who was on top of Nate's back.

During all this turmoil, Cpl. Mathias Pryor remained standing, numbed by fear and confusion. His mind was a blank. He had never been in a real fight before, and did not know how to react to this situation. He decided to go back to his tent and fetch his Colt revolver which was only a dozen or so feet away from his bedroll. He dashed to the Sibley, seized his dragoon belt and frantically un-flapped the holster. He then pulled-out his army Colt .44 revolver and ran back outside.

By now Sergeant Randolph had pulled off the man who was on Nate's back, and was trying to restrain him while throwing punches at two other mutinous assailants that had charged into the fight. Mathias returned to the fight and placed himself in the center of the fray and cocked back the hammer on his Colt with both hands. He then raised the revolver above his head, the barrel pointing toward the sky, and discharged the weapon.

The deafening crack of the Colt .44 awoke the camp. The officer of the night and the sentries were immediately alerted, and rushed to the location where they heard the gunshot sound. Lieutenants Smith and Hennessy were not yet asleep when they heard the shot. They were conversing about cavalry tactics when they became stunned by the noise of the gun. Both men stared at each other and instinctively grabbed their service revolvers, and ran out of their tent in the direction where they had heard the report of the firearm. Although both officers still had not removed their boots and trousers, they had taken off their shell jackets earlier, revealing their white undershirts. When Lieutenants Smith and Hennessy arrived on the scene, the first image they saw was Corporal Mathias and Sgt. Maj. Nate Gordon waving their Colts in the air and barking orders to the sentries.

"Report, Sergeant Major," demanded Hennessy, who looked disoriented as he stared at the sentries who were holding the mutineers.

Nate came to attention and saluted. "Sir, I've placed these men under arrest fo' mutiny, sir."

"*Mutiny?*" exclaimed Hennessy in disbelief.

"Yes sir, Lieutenant, *mutiny*. These men attacked us but were restrained," explained Nate as he pointed to the mutineers.

"Hell! I'm not surprised," sneered Lieutenant Smith. "I smelled that this was going to occur," he further added, revealing his inner delight that his prophesy had finally come true.

"Very well, Sergeant Major. I want a full report tomorrow after reveille," responded Lt. Hennessy as he lowered back the hammer on his revolver into the safety position. He wanted to take charge and put an end to this incident as quickly as possible. Most importantly, however, he did not want to listen to Lieutenant Smith's comments and remarks that started off with, "I told you that this was going to happen . . ."

"Yes, sir. Permission to place these men under guard?" inquired Nate as he pointed to the mutineers who gave off hostile stares at the white officers.

"Permission granted, Sergeant Major," confirmed Hennessy loudly. "And see that all the men are back in their bedrolls . . . check the horses, and double the guard for the rest of the night."

"Aye, aye, sir," saluted Nate as he directed the sentries to hauloff the mutineers.

The five prisoners were kept under guard in a Sibley tent near the horse picket line. Some time during the night they heard the lone guard snoring outside their tent and made their escape. They stole the guard's army Colt and carbine and hastily saddled five horses and rode off into the night heading due west.

At dawn, Nate was informed that they had escaped, stolen horses and the sentry's weapons and other government property.

"Damn that Percy-Ray and his boys!" he exclaimed to Jesse, incensed that they had not only escaped, but had taken valuable government property. He was determined to go after them and appealed to Lieutenant Hennessy.

"Sir! We can't let them go like we done the other deserters. These men are guilty of assaultin' noncommissioned officers and have absconded with hosses, saddles, bridles, weapons . . ."

"Yes, yes, I know," interrupted Hennessy. "Lieutenant Smith and I have decided that you should go after them. The horse tracks lead west, and from what I understand, the fugitives are heading straight for Commanche country. But the trail is fresh an' if you get started now, you have a good chance of catching them quickly. Unless of course, the Commanches find them first." Hennessy placed his hand on Nate's shoulder which surprised him. "Sergeant Major Gordon. I can't give you any men."

"Sir! I don't need any help."

"That is exactly what I expected you to say, *Sergeant Major*."

Nate was following the trail at a trot. He had immediately saddled his horse, checked his Spencer and Walker-Colt and had set out into the Western brushy plains where the landscape was dotted by yucca plants that Nate thought looked like giant immobile porcupines, and other thorny vegetation such as catclaw and huisache plants and spiny mesquite trees.

The horse tracks started off showing that the fugitives were pushing their mounts hard in the direction of the Nueces River where Nate suspected they would hope to lose any of their pursuers. As Nate followed the tracks, he noticed that the shod horses were beginning to tire because the imprints were becoming closer together, indicating fatigue. About twenty miles into the search, Nate halted his mount to pick up a horseshoe. He suspected that it came from one of Percy-Ray's little band, but he wanted to make sure. As he turned the U-shaped metal plate in his hands, he became satisfied that the horse had thrown the shoe very recently because there was no rust and the metal still remained bright. "They be slowin' down now," he commented to himself as he looked at the merciless sun in the sky while shading his eyes from its strong rays. He remounted and continued to follow the trail at a trot, confident that time was now on his side.

Percy-Ray Pridgeon, Archie Vaughn, and the three other deserters were now walking their dog-tired mounts single file. The spirit of last evening's alcoholic binge had worn off and the deserters had a burning thirst and felt sick. The horses were stumbling and had become impervious to any encouragement from their riders to move faster. After one horse had thrown a shoe, the luckless rider abandoned his mount and had to double up with a companion which further slowed the advance of the fugitives. By early afternoon, the party had halted near a water hole that had a grove of mesquite trees and watered their thirsty mounts as well as themselves. Tired, dirty, and hungry, the deserters started quarreling.

"What the hell are we goin' do now? We only got four horses and suppose that Sergeant Major is right behind us?" complained one trooper.

"That nigger driver won't follow us," replied Archie Vaughn, looking at Percy-Ray for support but who remained conspicuously silent.

"The hell he won't!" barked back the trooper looking nervously at the horizon. "That man is like a dog with a bone."

"I hongry," complained another deserter who had lost his horse. "Maybe we oughta turn back and go back to the regiment."

"You stupid *fool*," shouted Percy-Ray. "You go back on foot if you wants to. Archie and me are headin' for Mexico."

"Mexico?!" exclaimed the three troopers in astonishment. "We don't wants to go to ol' Mexico. We want to look for gold."

"You all can go anywheres you all damn please, but me and Archie are keepin' the weapons," responded Percy-Ray defiantly as he pulled out the army Colt that he had taken from the guard and pointed the weapon menacingly at the three rebellious deserters.

Archie Vaughn was about to raise the carbine and imitate his mentor when the trooper who had lost his horse was struck by an arrow in the neck. The arrowhead had penetrated the back and emerged in front just below the chin. Blood started to spurt from the fatal wound as if a spigot had just been turned on, and the victim's eyes bulged as he fell to his knees while hideous gurgling sounds emerged from his mouth. The fugitives were stunned and frightened as they gawked in horror at the dying man. An ear-piercing war cry went out a short distance away and the remaining deserters turned their gaze toward a nearby incline where they saw a half dozen mounted Commanche warriors galloping straight for them with very long lances.

"*Holy shit,*" blurted out Archie Vaughn, who aimed the carbine and shot wildly at the Comanches with the sole result that his shot spooked their mounts into taking flight. The warriors and their beautiful, graceful, compact horses were covered with matching war paint and feathers. They raced toward the deserters and the fugitives saw that man and horse were one animal, resembling a moving mass of death enveloped in a cloud of dust.

While Percy-Ray and Archie Vaughn took cover behind the spiny mesquite trees near the water hole, the two remaining troopers ran off to catch their mounts in the expectation of catching them and taking flight. One trooper, who managed to catch his horse and had his right foot in the stirrup, was about to mount his horse when a screaming Comanche, whose braids were wrapped in mink, thrust his long lance through the trooper's torso. Hearing his companion's howls while viewing his body being spiked, the other trooper started to run back to where Percy-Ray and Archie Vaughn were cowering behind the mesquite trees. He ran about twenty paces looking fearfully behind his shoulder as another howling warrior was closing in on him. He was wearing an unbuttoned old dragoon shell jacket with saber guard epaulets. Archie Vaughn and Percy-Ray fired at the warrior, but their hands were shaking with so much fear that their aim was poor and the Comanche simply rode down the hapless trooper with little effort and started circling him in tighter and tighter rings while his wildly painted face made the trooper cover his face in horror to await his fate. When the Comanche's mount could get no closer to the victim, the warrior gave his horse the command to rise on its hind quarters while he cocked back the long lance to skewer the cowering deserter. He gave a great yell of triumph and lanced his prey in the back, pinning him to the ground.

Nate had found the army horse that had thrown the shoe. He found the animal limping on the side of the trail, grazing. Nate dismounted and approached the horse talking soothingly to it. The horse still had its bridle and McClellan saddle. Nate patted the animal on the neck and then examined the hoof that had the missing shoe. Satisfied that this was the horse that was abandoned by the deserters, Nate removed the bridle, saddle, and horse blanket to make the animal more at ease and placed the items neatly in a pile on the side of the trail. He made a mental note of the location and decided that he would retrieve the accoutrements on his way back, and if the horse was still in the area, he would bring the animal back as well. He was about to remount when his attention was seized by successive gunshots that seemed to be originating from in front of him. He quickly mounted and spurred his horse in the direction of the sounds of gunfire.

As Nate galloped toward the sounds of combat, he recognized that the gunfire came from an army Colt and a lone carbine. He patted his horse's neck in anticipation of ordering his mount to prepare for danger and spoke to him. "Looks like de Comanches found de *fools*." He cantered for a mile or so and came close enough to identify what was occurring by the water hole. The Comanches were circling their agile horses around and around Percy-Ray and Archie Vaughn by lowering their bodies on the side of their horses at the precise moment when they passed them. Nate had never seen riders such as these. He watched them in amazement as they would suddenly disappear behind the side of their beautiful horses at a full gallop with only a heel hanging over the animal's back while wrapping the other around the belly. This not only provided cover for the rider but made them invisible as they shot arrow after arrow from below the horse's neck or throw their long and thick lances at Percy-Ray and Archie Vaughn.

Nate calmly watched the Comanches galloping around the deserters as they shot arrows at them. "Them sons of bitches sure knows how to ride!" he exclaimed admiringly, as he attempted to ascertain how many there really were, but with huge swirling clouds of dust that covered the area, it was difficult to determine their number. Squinting his eyes to see through the haze, Nate decided that there could not be more then a half dozen of them, but that was just too many to enter the fray without any help. Certainly not for the likes of Percy-Ray Pridgeon and Archie Vaughn.

Looking at the fine dust clouds that shrouded the conflict at the water hole gave Nate an idea. He dismounted and unrolled his horse picket line and tied the opposite end of the rope to one of his McClellan saddle hooks with the iron picket pin stretched on the ground behind his horse. He then remounted and cocked his Spencer carbine repeater. "*Yeah!*" He dug his brass spurs into his mount's flanks and charged toward the water hole fight as the picket pin dragged and bounced on the ground, creating a cloud of debris. Nate encouraged his horse to go as fast as possible because he wanted to kick up as much dirt and vegetation into the air in order to screen his advance and confuse the Comanches as to how many riders were coming their way. He hoped that when the Comanches spotted him they would think that he was leading a charge of riders willing to engage them in battle. While his horse galloped at great speed, Nate raised himself in the saddle and maneuvered the rifle sling into position to bring the stock of the Spencer to his shoulder. He took aim at one of the Comanches and fired, but the warrior slipped behind his mount's side and the bullet passed over the horse's back harmlessly. Nate fired again at the Comanches and kept firing until he had exhausted his seven shots but failed to hit any of them. Undeterred, and still galloping toward the center of the fight, he moved the Spencer back to his right side, sat back down in the McClellan, and pulled his Walker-Colt. The dust cloud was becoming larger and larger as the picket pin leaped and rebounded on the ground to his rear. The Commanche with the dragoon shell jacket decided to give up the attack on Percy-Ray and Archie Vaughn and charge Nate. He raised the bloody lance in the air that he had retrieved from his previous kill, and yelled a challenge, his horse galloping enthusiastically toward Nate.

Nate and the Comanche warrior were charging each other as if they were set in deliberately creating a violent collision. The warrior, his dragoon shell jacket flowing in the wind as he pointed his great lance forward, screamed as if he was a wild animal, while Nate, his Walker-Colt held at the ready, coolly waited for the right moment. The other Comanches who had been preoccupied with trying to kill Percy-Ray and Archie Vaughn now turned their attention to their companion who was attacking a fearless bluecoat and assumed, because of the large dust cloud behind him, that he was at the head of reinforcements. They decided to withdraw their attack on the two deserters and watch their companion kill the leading bluecoat. As they cheered him on by raising their shields and lances while their horses danced, pranced, and side-stepped at their command, Nate and his adversary were about twenty feet away from each other when they heard the loud crack of the Walker-Colt. They became astonished when they saw their companion, who only seconds before was about to lance the charging bluecoat, fall back over his horse's rump and collapse to the ground.

After killing the charging Comanche with one shot from the Walker-Colt, Nate steered his mount toward the remaining Comanches while aiming the pistol and firing several more rounds that landed near the hooves of the Comanches' horses. Seeing their companion quickly dispatched and fearing that the bluecoat was at the head of a body of soldiers, convinced the remaining warriors that it was time to escape. They commanded their mounts to turn and galloped with all haste in the opposite direction.

Nate was relieved that his luck had held. He had killed one Co-manche and had intimidated the others into fleeing. He slowed his horse to a trot and then to a walk and directed the animal toward the cowering fugitives who were still hiding behind the mesquite trees.

"You deserters can come out now," hollered Nate as he reloaded the Walker-Colt. "De big bad Indians are gone."

Archie Vaughn peeked his little head from behind the spiny mesquite tree followed by Percy-Ray who was holding the army Colt.

"Drop de pistol!" ordered Nate as he pointed his Walker-Colt at the two deserters.

"Don't shoot, don't shoot!" begged Archie Vaughn. "Wez don't got no mo' bullets."

"Shutz your mouth!" yelled Percy-Ray, who thought he could bluff Nate into making him believe that the gun was still loaded.

"Percy-Ray! Either you throw that weapon to de ground, *now*, or I'll blow your fool head right off," demanded Nate sternly.

Percy-Ray hesitated for a moment, but then complied, casting the army Colt contemptuously to the ground.

"Too bad the Comanches ran off with your horses, 'cause it's a *long* way back on foot," said Nate as he dismounted. He made the two fugitives lie on the ground and then reeled in his picket line. He had a new use for the rope now.

Five

Nate was writing in his journal some of the observations he had made regarding conditions on the South Texas Plains. The regiment was a two day's ride from San Antonio and he wanted to keep a record of what he had read in the newspapers and been told by Merritt, Hennessy, and Smith.

As the Ninth Cavalry approaches San Antonio, the morale of the troops has surged. The men believe that their arrival will be welcomed by the citizens of San Antonio and in East Texas in particular. Merritt told me that when federal troops were ordered out of the state to join the Union armies that were forming in the East in 1861, the Texas frontier became wide open again for Commanche and Kiowa raiding parties. Since then, hundreds of settlers have lost their lives and dozens of women and children have suffered the horrors of capture and enslavement. The newspapers are full of stories about dozens of farms and ranches that were burned to the ground and the tens of thousands of cattle and thousands of horses that were stolen or driven off by the Comanche and Kiowa. I am distressed to learn that innocent settlers are being butchered while plowing fields or herding stock, and when I told Jesse and Mathias about how their bodies would be discovered days later, by their friends or neighbors, often mutilated beyond recognition or discovered partially burned in open fires, Jesse's face went pale and Mathias gagged in disgust.

Therefore, our men are naturally optimistic that they will be greeted by the good people of San Antonio with much fanfare and jubilation since we are being sent here to protect the whites from blood-thirsty Commanches and Kiowas.

I am proud that both Mathias and Jesse are learning the basic lessons of cavalry horsemanship. I am particularly proud that Mathias has learned so quickly, and shows great promise in becoming an expert rider. Mathias came through during that nasty melee between us and Percy-Ray's band and proved that he deserved those corporal stripes. I admit, at first I was skeptical. He is timid, slightly built, and one of the shortest men in the regiment. But he has performed well in drill and saber practice and managed to pass every physical challenge while the regiment was training in Greenville.

His two greatest abilities are his literary skills and a desire to always volunteer for special duties. During the cholera epidemic, he was the first to step forward and volunteer for such hazardous duties as assisting in changing bedpans, burning clothes, rags, and bedding, and volunteering for burial detail. I am impressed and proud that he was promoted to corporal at my recommendation, and proved worthy of the double yellow stripes on his tunic's sleeves.

The little corporal's greatest attribute, however, was that he could read and write. I consider him most intelligent when it comes to book knowledge and citing classical verse. He has proved invaluable in helping me with reports. This has given me more time to spend with the green recruits in drill training. I am even a little jealous that Mathias is always reading. One day I found him crouched over a campfire reading passages aloud from Hawthorne. A week later, he asked me questions that he had concerning my personal experiences during the war, and how they related to the theoretical practices that former secretary of war, J. R. Pointsett, wrote about in his 1841 cavalry tactics, or better known as "Pointsett Tactics." Jesse commented that if Mathias would not have joined the army, he would

*certainly have made an excellent preacher, dispelling the gospel
to his brethren in fine rhetorical fashion.*

The column was a day's ride out of San Antonio and Nate was riding
at the head of the company behind Hennessy. The day was hot and
there was no breeze. Both men and horses were plagued by thousands
of flies that pestered the regiment mercilessly causing the troopers to
complain with profanities and respond by frequently swatting the insects off their faces or killing them on their mounts' necks and rumps.
As he was watching Hennessy's horse's tail swing back and forth trying
to flick flies from its flanks, he heard Mathias' big mare approach him
at a rapid trot. "Gawd, I hope de boy doesn't have mo' questions on
cavalry tactics and what not.... I ain't in de mood," Nate whispered
to himself with dread.

"I expect at least two welcoming bands and to be invited to ten
dances," said Mathias Pryor as he pulled up alongside of Nate. His big
chestnut was over seventeen hands, and dwarfed Mathias whenever he
sat on the big beast's back or when he stood next to his mount. Nate
was bemused that the little corporal had named her "Betsy."

"You think so?" replied Nate sarcastically as he watched Mathias
maneuver his horse into position alongside his gray gelding. Mathias
wanted to make sure that his horse was parallel with Nate's. He had
a fetish that every task must be performed perfectly. It was a trait that
he had inherited from his father when he controlled all the affairs of
his master's household.

"I wouldn't get too excited 'bout being greeted with marchin' bands
and being invited to any fandangos," responded Nate finally to Mathias'
enthusiasm. Nate bowed his head and added in a low and melancholy
voice, "No pretty women in flowin' skirts goin' be throwin' flowers at
black men, Mathias." Mathias became suddenly quiet, and the exuber-
ant smile on his face had vanished. Nate raised his head and sighed.
"Most every white person we seen so far in this country had scorn on
their faces." Nate's horse sneezed several times, and the animal's head
jerked downward. He adjusted the reins and continued, "I also knows

that Texas is filled wid ex-Confederate soldiers and a lot of planters who escaped from the ol' South to Texas after they lost their slaves and land to the Yankees. *No sir*. Them white folks ain't goin' be happy to see niggers in blue suits ridin' in to *their* town."

Mathias found this hard to believe. He refused to consider that the white citizens would not greet them with open arms, considering that the Ninth was sent to protect them from "blood-thirsty savages." Mathias shrugged off what Nate had said, and redirected the conversation toward Privates Percy-Ray Pridgeon, Archie Vaughn, and the three other mutineers.

"What's the colonel goin' do to with the men under arrest?"

"Merritt tol' me that de ol' man is goin' try 'em for mutiny and assault, once de regiment reaches San Antonio."

Nate paused to reel in his horse. The animal suddenly shifted his gait, and was out of step with the other horses in the column. The regiment usually started the daily march at a walk and gently increased the pace by trotting for several hours. It was late morning and the column traveled at a fast walk, but Nate's muscular gelding wanted to canter. He had to slap the horse on the side of his face, to remind him that the rider was the boss. He then turned his head toward Mathias after gaining full control of his mount.

"During the war I see many men shot for doin' less than what them boys tried to do. Way I see it, their only defense is that they were drunk. But I doubt it'll help them much."

Lt. Zachary Hennessy was leading his horse at the head of company A when Lt. Donald Smith of company K, walked toward him, leading his mount. The regiment was about fifteen miles from San Antonio when the order was given by Hatch to dismount and lead the horses for an extra thirty minutes before entering the town. Hatch and Merritt wanted the regiment to look its best upon reaching San Antonio, and that required that the horses look as rested as possible.

They knew that the population, in all probability, would be hostile to the arrival of federal troops. Both senior officers were aware that the press had reported that the Ninth Colored Cavalry would be stationed in San Antonio for training and deployment at garrisons in west Texas. The town was a hot bed of secession before and during the war, and recently hundreds of ex-Confederate soldiers and embittered impoverished refuges from the old Southern states crowded the small community.

"Hey, Smith, your horse seems to be about down out." Hennessy enjoyed teasing Lieutenant Smith when he saw an opportunity. Usually, he was the brunt of his friend's banter; consequently, Hennessy rarely missed an occasion to return the favor.

"My horse might look down and out, mister, but yours looks like it's not going to make it another mile. You'll either have to walk in or ride in the rear on a pack mule," laughed Smith as he turned his mount parallel with Hennessy's.

"Have you heard? The old man is going to court-martial those two mutineers once we get to San Antonio," stated Lieutenant Smith, eager to reveal that his gossip was fresher than Hennessy's.

"'Bout time, if you ask me. The regiment has had too many deserters as it is. If we don't punish these two mutineers, it will mean the demise of all discipline in the command," responded Hennessy, as he kicked up dust in the road with the heel of his boot while holding the reins of his horse. "Thank God that the troublemakers were placed under guard in one of the supply wagons in the rear."

Both officers walked for a few minutes in silence. The sun was slowly descending in the western Texas sky, and the air was dry and cool. As the troopers walked, leading their mounts in columns of four, the sounds of shod horses, rattling sabers, and bivouac equipment dangling from their saddle hooks filled the air.

"I was impressed with Sergeant Major Nate Gordon." Lieutenant Smith removed his kepi and scratched his head. "Did you read his report regarding his fight with the Comanches?"

"Yes, I did," responded Hennessy. "I am proud of his actions. The man showed ingenuity and great courage."

"The way he took on that Comanche and bullshitted the others . . . Hell! He's the best man in your company, Zach."

"Best man in the whole damn regiment, Donny," replied Hennessy, trying to match his friend's bravado and profanity.

"Too bad he'll never be an officer," added Smith with an air of sorrow.

"Don't be too sure. The war department might leave that door open if the colored regiments continue to experience acute shortages in recruiting officers...."

"Not in this man's army!" interrupted Smith.

San Antonio, in the spring of 1867, was a dilapidated community. Nate had read that it was once a seat of New Spain's colonial government, and that the frontier town was an oasis of greenery and Catholic civilization in the middle of the Texas prairie. He looked forward to seeing the grand churches, missions, and Spanish colonial homes that were nestled on the banks of the San Antonio River. On the march to the town, he noticed that the ground was fertile with vegetation such as banana trees drooping with fruit, while grapes, flowers, and lush plantings of crape myrtle, hibiscus, and ferns, abounded.

When Nate had mentioned to Merritt that San Antonio must be a jewel of a town, the lieutenant colonel retorted that the economic consequences of the war had left the town's quaint Spanish colonial architecture, built with adobe bricks and finished off with stucco, in a state of physical decay. Merritt explained that most of the buildings had surely become dilapidated due to a lack of money for upkeep, and that soaring property taxes had destroyed real estate values. It surprised Nate when Merritt stated that, with the exception of those galvanized Yankees who supplied the Union army, and the proprietors of cantina's, saloons, and brothels, commercial activity was anemic, and employment opportunities nonexistent.

Merritt also cautioned Nate that he had heard that the community was not only financially ruined, but an open sewer as well. He expressed concern that cholera, typhoid fever, and malaria seemed to thrive within the city, and that putrid piles of garbage and rotting grain became feeding centers for thousands of rodents and millions of flies.

Compounding these problems, Merritt had informed Nate, were

the changes that San Antonio had undergone during and after the war. Nate had not realized that thousands of immigrants from the deep South had arrived with their wagons loaded with as much of their worldly possessions as possible, some even escaping with their slaves in the false hope that emancipation would not reach Texas. Merritt had explained that these immigrants had either fled the onslaught of federal troops in Louisiana and Sherman's march to the sea, or had abandoned their ruined plantations for a new beginning in Texas after they returned from the battles in the East. He reminded Nate that most of these individuals were bitter and resentful that they had lost their slaves and land holdings. After learning about these facts, Nate concluded with much anxiety that surely the now impoverished population of San Antonio must regard the deployment of black troops to garrison posts in the city and in West Texas as the equivalent of pouring salt in open wounds.

During the war, a committee of vigilantes was formed to conduct "necktie parties" where horse thieves, desperadoes, surly Mexicans, blacks, and Union men were frequently strung up from an oak tree on Military Plaza, the center of San Antonio. When the last of the Confederate troops had surrendered in Texas, certain members of the committee of vigilantes decided to became part of the newly formed Klu Klux Klan. Made up largely of Confederate veterans and disgruntled whites, these night riders worked closely with local law enforcement officials and believed that the emancipation of the black man was the work of the devil, posing a threat to their way of life.

One of these individuals was a former Confederate who had returned from the war disgruntled and bitter named James Moody, formerly a major with Nathan Bedford Forrest's cavalry in western Tennessee. He took part in the assault on Fort Pillow which was garrisoned by five hundred Negro troops and two hundred and fifty whites. Moody hated blacks. At Fort Pillow he had murdered, in cold blood, several Negro soldiers after they had surrendered. Although he never owned slaves and was a simple owner of a dry goods store located on the north side of Main Plaza, he enjoyed kicking and slapping blacks around when they used to come into his store to fulfill orders for their masters.

When he returned to San Antonio after Bedford Forrest had disbanded his forces, James Moody came back to a town that he did not recognize. His business was on the verge of bankruptcy because he could not secure credit, and hundreds of freed blacks roamed the streets. He thought his whole way of life had changed for the worst. The South had lost the war, the Negroes were free, and his town was about to be occupied by federal black troops. Dejected, and wallowing in his belief that his status was diminished, James Moody joined the Klan and rose quickly as one of the organization's key leaders. When he read in the newspaper that the Ninth Colored Cavalry was coming to town, he swore an oath in front of his cronies that he was going hang a few, "blue-belly niggers from the highest oak tree in the county."

It was nearly sunset, and the regiment was ordered to form columns of twos in preparation for entering the town. Nate and Jesse had made sure that the men paid special attention during the nooning period to grooming their horses, brushing off trail dust from their uniforms, and shining the brass on their spurs, buttons, and buckles. Nate and the officers were pleased that most of the troopers were taking pride in their new status as United States cavalrymen.

As the regiment marched into town on East Commerce Street toward Alamo Plaza, where the army had converted the old mission into a military depot, the cavalrymen were surprised that there were only a few people on the streets. A dozen mangy dogs, milling around on East Commerce on the northwest corner of Main Plaza, started to bark incessantly at the troopers as they passed by. Nate was appalled by the trash and stench that permeated the dirt streets, and plazas that had become quagmires of human waste and mud due to the recent heavy rains. Dogs, chickens, goats, pigs, and donkeys wandered about aimlessly and scrounged at garbage piles, which were kept in people's backyards. The worst part was the flies. The troopers had to fight off swarms of mosquitoes and other insects from their faces and necks, while their horses vigorously swung their heads in a frantic attempt to dislodge hordes of flies that covered their eyes and ears.

When the column finally reached Alamo Plaza at the far end of town, a group of about fifty individuals had gathered in the middle of the square to greet the black troopers and their white officers with rotten fruit and eggs. Earlier, the small mob had collected putrid produce from garbage piles. One enterprising individual brought up an oxcart filled with old melons that he had procured at Market Plaza. He pulled up the cart on the north side of Alamo Plaza where the crowd had gathered, and encouraged people to help themselves. Old men, veterans, women, and children started jeering, yelling insults and expletives at the troops.

"We don't want your kind here, you black bastards!" bellowed an elderly man, pointing his cane at the column. He was wearing an old black frock coat and stovetop hat. A yellowed silk vest that was too tight protruded around his enormous belly.

"I'd rather have the Commanches then you damn Yankee darkies," shouted a young woman who was cradling a fat baby in her arms. She shook her fist and hollered at the troopers while the infant kept suckling on her nipple.

A half dozen young hoodlums who had gathered around an oxcart started to hurl pieces of rotten melon at the black troops. As a result, and much to the amusement of the adults who were jeering and making obscene gestures, several of the cavalrymen had difficulty controlling their horses while they were being pelted.

Meanwhile, Colonel Hatch had ordered Lieutenant Colonel Merritt to take a small detachment of men to the Vance building which was located on the corner of Houston and St. Mary's Streets. The building was used by the U.S. Army before the war to house senior officers, and Hatch wanted his second in command to inspect the premises and make sure that all was in order. The rest of the command would bivouac at the Alamo for several days, where the U.S. Army maintained a military depot since the state joined the union. At the Alamo the Ninth was to be refitted, draw supplies, and then establish a permanent camp for the regiment on the outskirts of town where they would conduct further training.

Colonel Hatch became furious when he saw some of the civilians throwing rotten eggs and fruit at his troops. His face had turned red with anger and his bushy mustache curved inward as his lips tightened. Only his training as an officer and the hard lessons he had learned while commanding cavalry in the war prevented him from losing his temper and casting patience to the wind. Although he expected a cold welcome and even verbal abuse from civilians and local authorities, he was caught mentally unprepared to handle a potential mob bent on harming his soldiers. He decided that the best immediate course of action would be to ignore the rabble and maintain discipline among his troops while placing them in a defensive position.

He turned to Lt. Zachary Hennessy who was riding parallel to him on his right, and with a crisp and confident voice, ordered the lieutenant to have the troops prepare to form three skirmish lines in front of Alamo Mission. He ordered that each line should be comprised of three companies, or about two hundred men per row. Lieutenant Hennessy saluted his superior officer, and ordered Sgt. Maj. Nate Gordon to pass on the instructions to all company commanders. Nate saluted, and spurred his horse into a canter to report down the line. After waiting a few moments to give the men time to move into position, Lieutenant Hennessy stood up in his stirrups and bellowed the order that Colonel Hatch gave him to execute.

"*Companies*. Prepare to form skirmish lines."

The troop, still somewhat inexperienced with handling their mounts, struggled to maneuver their horses into position. Nate and the other noncommissioned officers sprang into action by encouraging, and at times shouting at their men to control their animals, by reining them into line to await orders to dismount. When the column finally formed three lines in front of Alamo Mission, the regiment radiated a towering appearance. The crowd became stunned by the sight of tall, burly black men starring stoned-faced and standing erect in their saddles. The flapping of the regiment's stars and bars guidon in the late evening breeze added to their disbelief. The hostile mob suddenly ceased pelting the troops with rotten fruit, and all verbal insults and anger venting stopped as quickly as it came.

"Prepare to dismount," Hennessy bellowed. He wanted to make sure that he was heard over the noise of the crowd. The order was then echoed throughout the regiment by company commanders. When

Hennessy was satisfied that all the companies were in position, he ordered the regiment to dismount.

"Ninth Cavalry . . . dismount."

In one sweeping move, the panoramic sight and sounds of eight hundred men dressed in blue, dismounting in perfect unison, was a dramatic event for the citizens of San Antonio. As the troopers lifted themselves from their McClellan saddles, the sounds of sabers rattling, leather squeaking, and shuffling cavalry boots while their horses snorted and stomped, served to remind the local citizenry that the federal army had arrived among them, and there was not a thing they could do about it. The days of the Confederacy were truly gone.

James Moody, along with some of his friends, was observing the proceedings a few hundred yards away from the doorway of a cantina on the west side of Alamo Plaza.

Moody was big man, over six feet and weighing over two hundred pounds. He had a thick red beard which he incessantly combed with his fingers. He was nursing a warm beer and stared at the black troops in the plaza.

"Them Goddamn darkies sure look cute in them blue duds, don't they, Levi?" Moody downed the last of the beer in his glass mug and marched off to the bar to order another brew.

"Why don't we take a pot shot at dem," quipped Levi. "Maybe we get lucky and kill one of them niggers," he added.

"That would be stupid, Levi. Patience my boy, patience. All things come to those who wait." Moody paused and took a large gulp from his beer mug. "You know the Bible, Levi. Didn't yo'r pa read ya passages from de good book?" Moody paused again, waiting for Levi to say something. *"Oh that's right.* You Heebs don't read the good book, do ya?" Moody started to laugh very loudly, and the rest of the cantina's patrons followed his example. It was best to laugh when Moody laughed if you didn't want any trouble with his people. The only person who was not laughing was Levi, but he didn't care. Living as a loner made him hard.

Although Levi was a small man, only five feet, six inches tall, he had a barrel chest, and his hands were very large. He was known in town by his friends as Levi the Heeb. He was the black sheep of a Jewish family that had settled in Beaumont in the 1850's. His father owned a successful tailoring shop where his two other brothers and sister worked. When his mother died on the trail en route to Beaumont, little Levi became devastated and his disposition changed. He became unruly, rebellious, and rejected his father and his faith in the teachings of Judaism. He blamed his father for bringing the family out West, causing the premature death of his mother whom he loved more than anything in the world. He left home one night when was barely thirteen without saying good-bye, and got work at a cattle ranch outside of San Antonio. Through hard work he gained the respect of his cowboy peers, who told him that they considered him one of them and not some "money grubbin' Jew."

When the war broke out, he joined the Ninth Texas Cavalry. Unfortunately for him, he became sick with typhoid fever and was left behind when the regiment moved out. He spent the rest of the war feeling sorry for himself until he was asked to join San Antonio's "necktie party" gang. Longing to be part of the group, he joined the gang where he became one of the leaders. After the war, he joined, like most of the members of the remaining band, the newly organized Klu Klux Klan.

While the Ninth Cavalry remained at Alamo Mission for several days refitting, the men were allowed leave for the first time since the formation of the regiment. Sgt. Maj. Nate Gordon and 1st Sgt. Jesse Randolph became anxious when they were ordered to assist in organizing a rotating system that would allow the men leave in town. Both Nate and Jesse, as well as most of the noncom's, felt that if the men were released in town they would get themselves into trouble with not only the law, but with private citizens who harbored grudges and racial prejudice.

Colonel Hatch and Lt. Col. Wesley Merritt thought otherwise, however. They believed that the men deserved to have some free time after the long march from Greenville, Louisiana to San Antonio, and that it would be a mistake to keep a low profile considering that the Ninth was sent to protect the Texans from Indian depravations.

"Well, they will just have to accept the fact that the Ninth is here. And if they don't accept my men; black, or white, I really could care less. We have our orders. Old glory will fly over the Alamo, and the blue uniform of these Unites States will be respected," replied Hatch, when Nate argued that it was too soon to give the men permission to roam around San Antonio's saloons, cantinas, and whorehouses. He attempted to persuade Merritt that it would be best to pursue further drills and concentrate on discipline and horsemanship exercises, rather than let the men loose in town and provide an excuse for the local population to provoke and race-bait the troopers.

Although most of the regiment bivouacked a few miles west of town, it did not take very long for friction and violence to develop between the local citizens backed by the police and the black troopers. The men would arrive in town after being paid their monthly thirteen dollars and go hog wild all over San Antonio. The cavalrymen were eager to spend their money on having a good time, and looked forward to releasing pent up anger, sexual frustration, and military routine on liquor, women, and gambling.

Nate, Jesse, and Cpl. Mathias Pryor were patrolling some of the back streets near Alamo Plaza where many of San Antonio's licentious establishments were located. Clashes with local law authorities were becoming a daily occurrence. Over the past several days, as the men were allowed leave in town, verbal, and on several occasions, physical friction developed between the colored troopers and deputy sheriffs. Nate and the other noncommissioned officers had been instructed by Hatch and Merritt to be extra vigilant in preventing any conflicts that might develop between the local citizenry and the cavalrymen. Late Sunday afternoon, Nate, Jesse, and Mathias were riding back from where the three of them had spent several hours watching cockfights across San Pedro Creek, a favorite location for Mexicans for engaging in spirited conversation, cockfighting, gambling, drinking tequila, eating spicy foods, wenching, and playing music. Although they didn't place any bets on the warring cocks as dozens of Mexicans were recklessly doing, Nate and Jesse enjoyed watching the carnage between screeching fight birds slicing each other to ribbons. All the cocks had long, sharp, curved *sisshers* attached to the back of their feet that enabled them to slash their opponent with lethal effect. Nate noticed that this was the only big difference between cockfights in San Antonio and Louisiana. He decided that the Mexican contribution to this blood sport was rooted in the owners' obvious fondness for attaching these three-inch, slightly curved double-edged blades to their hapless cocks' legs to add to the carnage. As feathers, blood, and skin pieces flew into the air, the Mexicans would increase their wagers and become more excited as bottles of mescal were passed around.

Mathias became sick. After watching the first fight in which the loser was so badly slashed that the owner had to use a shovel to scoop up all of the bird's carcass parts, Mathias' stomach revolted. He desperately placed his hand against his mouth to prevent the chili that he had for lunch from surfacing, but it was to no avail. Nate and Jesse watched with bemused interest as Mathias' cheeks ballooned—they could not help but laugh. Realizing that he was going to lose the battle, Mathias ran out of the adobe and threw up in a nearby irrigation ditch. He decided that he had never seen anything so barbaric, and preferred to wait for Nate and Jesse at a safe distance, away from the adobe and the bloody cacophony.

The pandemonium of the cockfight reminded Nate of the days of slavery when some of the male slaves would get together on Sunday afternoons and pitch their favorite rooster against each other. Mas'a Hammond had over two thousand chickens, so he didn't mind if some of his roosters would get beat up, or even sometimes killed. He felt that this rather bloody and primitive activity kept his blacks content, so he never interfered as long as they stayed away from Old Messiah, Mas'a Hammond's favorite and most prolific rooster. Jesse had seen a few cockfights in New Orleans and he always enjoyed betting a little money, although he never won. On this particular occasion, he refrained from making any wagers on this fight out of concern that Nate might not approve. Jesse thought that Nate exercised too much patristic behavior at times, so he decided to hold onto his money rather than get into an argument with Nate over how he was just throwing away his money.

Nate enjoyed watching the birds of combat attack and slash at each other by maneuvering their legs with their wings to cut and peck until one of them was too badly gashed or blinded by the long deadly blades. Nate found it refreshing to be among men wearing big sombreros and speaking a different language. He liked the sharp pronunciation on the Spanish words that the Mexicans used such as *atacalo, matalo,* and *acabalo,* when they were cheering their favorite bird, or frantically placing last minute bets.

After about an hour watching the cockfights, the three noncommissioned officers slowly made their way toward Main Plaza on Soledad Street, making sure that there were no stray enlisted men stumbling around drunk and getting into fights. Nate wanted to check Jack Harris' Saloon, one of San Antonio's favorite watering holes and entertainment establishments. Several enlisted men had been physically ejected from the saloon after getting drunk and fighting with civilians. As a result, Hatch had ordered that Harris' was to be off-limits to all enlisted personnel, and that the men were to report back to camp by no later than five o'clock in the afternoon. The regiment's commander recognized that tensions were building between the residents of San Antonio, who were backed by local peace officers, and his black troopers, and ordered the leave time cut so none of the men would be in town after dark.

Nate wanted to make sure that there were no inebriated stray troopers at Harris', and told Jesse and Mathias to ride with him to investigate. As the three men entered Main Plaza, southward, on Soledad Street, they heard loud voices and sharp language that seemed to be coming in the direction of the saloon. Nate immediately recognized one of the voices. It was Pvt. Martin Jackson from his company. As the three men came into view of Harris', they could see that Private Jackson was fighting off three white men.

"Get 'im in a choke hold, Levi!" Moody shouted as he waved a nearly empty glass beer mug.

Although Private Jackson was in a state of drunkenness, he was putting up stiff resistance against his attackers. He had spent the afternoon becoming intoxicated with a few of his company companions in the streets of San Antonio. When his friends tried to persuade him to return to camp, he refused; claiming that he was not drunk enough, and wanted to drink some more. Stumbling, his head spinning, he wandered into Harris' where James Moody and Levi were playing cards. He went straight to the bar and started to pound his fists on the wooden surface of the bar counter and demanded mescal. "*I want that stuff with the worm,*" he clamored belligerently.

When the barman told him to leave, Private Jackson became combative. That was all the excuse Moody needed to put down his cards and slowly rise from the chair. His eyes flashing with anger, he marched over to Private Jackson and yelled: "Didn't you hear what the man told you, midnight?" Private Jackson was as black as coal. Even among his

212

companions, he was frequently teased because they considered him the blackest man in the regiment. He was also known for his stubbornness and strength, and when he became drunk, Pvt. Martin Jackson liked to fight.

"I can stay here as long as I likes," he responded defiantly.

"*You black swine*. How dare you speak to me like that!" He lifted the glass beer mug and smacked Private Jackson on the side of his face, causing his head to tilt toward the bar. Dazed, but remaining on his feet, Jackson simply shook his head as if he was a huge steer that had just rammed the side of a barn. He tried to focus. When he finally managed to concentrate, all he could see was Moody's enormous belly. Instinctively, he rushed at Moody's gut and pushed the big fat man all the way back to the table where Levi was still sitting. When Moody's right spur caught one of the legs of Levi's chair, Moody was sent crashing toward the floor and Levi was sent backward as he held his beer mug, spilling its contents on his new shirt.

Enraged, Levi leaped up from the floor while Moody was moaning in pain, holding his huge gut. Levi pulled out his Smith & Wesson No. 2 Army Revolver that was stuffed in the front of his pants and pulled back the hammer into the firing position. He took quick aim at Pvt. Martin Jackson's head, and fired. The room vibrated and echoed with the deafening crack made by the pistol, and Private Jackson yelled as the bullet grazed his left cheek. Levi recocked the pistol and was about to fire again when the barman yelled: "*I don't want anymore nigger blood on my floor*. Go on outside an' finish him off in de street, fer Christssakes!"

At the same time, a deputy sheriff walked into the bar. He was walking on Commerce making his rounds when he heard the shot, and ran to investigate.

"What the hell is goin' on here?" he bellowed. He saw Levi pointing his gun at this black blue-belly man who was bleeding from his left cheek and James Moody lying on the floor. "*Levi!* Put that damn iron back in your pants," he commanded.

"This nigger came in here to make trouble, what are you going to do about it?" Levi answered back. He down-cocked his revolver and stuffed the weapon back in his trousers.

Pvt. Martin Jackson was pressing the palm of his right hand on his cheek to stop the wound from bleeding. Although temporarily disoriented, he remained defiant. He was breathing heavily, and his limbs were flowing with adrenaline while his hands were closed, forming fists clenched with rage that resembled small cannon balls.

The deputy, who was young and cocky, was for a moment hesitant in how to cope with this unusual situation. By law, he should arrest Levi for shooting a man, especially if he was unarmed. On the other hand, the man who was shot was black and supposedly making trouble and being insolent. Complicating matters was that the black man was wearing a federal uniform. He decided that the nigger had no business being at Harris' and made up his mind that he would arrest him and let the sheriff handle the situation with the U.S. military.

"All right, boy, I'm takin' you in. I got a nice warm cell waitin' for your black ass."

He started to reach for Private Jackson's arm to escort him out of the saloon when his prisoner drew back and yelled, "I'm not goin' with no white man 'less he's an officer in de United States Army!" He shouted, and like a horse spooked by a flying object, Private Jackson bolted past the deputy and Levi and ran through the door into Main Plaza.

Wide-eyed, and with his mouth wide open, the deputy was stunned. He had never seen a man run away so fast. James Moody was back on his feet standing near a window. Concerned that the man would escape, he ordered Levi to go after Private Jackson.

"Well? What the hell are you waitin' for, Levi? Don't let the nigger get away. Go after him, by Jesus!"

Levi bolted for the door and ran after Private Jackson. The deputy and James Moody quickly followed him outside. Private Jackson, who had stumbled on the sidewalk and landed on his right knee, was about to get up and run, when Levi jumped on top of him and tried pinning him to the ground. The private, however, threw him off as if he was a small sack of potatoes.

Nate, Jesse, and Mathias arrived in front of Harris', just when Private Jackson had managed to get up on his feet and was trying to outpace Levi, who was now pursuing him.

The moment Nate saw what was happening, he dug his spurs into his mount and yelled—"*Yaah!*" He galloped his horse in between Levi and Private Jackson, almost knocking over Levi in the process. Nate pulled hard on his reins to stop his gelding, causing the horse's mouth and neck to strain. The gelding became excited, and reared up as Levi attempted to cut past the animal on his left flank. Nate instinctively reversed his mount and blocked Levi's path.

"Hold on there. Everyone jest stop," yelled Nate as he stretched out his arm and showed his palm as a sign of pacification.

Jesse and Mathias moved their horses next Nate's, so all three non-com's formed an impregnable line that divided the two white men from Private Jackson.

"You all are interferin' with a deputy in the performance of his duty," roared the young deputy, waving his fully cocked Griswold & Gunnison .36-caliber revolver in the air. Although he recognized Nate's prominent sergeant major stripes on his sleeves, the deputy deliberately refused to honor his rank.

"*Get de hell out of the way, you black bastard,*" demanded James Moody, who used the nearly empty beer mug as a prop in gesticulating to Nate to move his horse as his frame filled the doorway of Harris'.

"You do not have the right to talk to the sergeant major that way, sir," retorted Mathias, surprising Nate who thought Mathias would be too timid to express such a provocative statement.

Stunned, by Mathias' articulate tone of voice, Moody paused for a split second and walked into the street and scoffed sarcastically,

"*Well, well, well?* What do we have hare?" He paused again and continued as his voice became more sardonic.

"We got us an educated nigger!"

"And wearing spectacles, to boot," added Levi.

For a moment, the three white men had entirely forgotten all about Private Jackson. They never heard a black man speak English as if he had attended a university. Levi was briefly reminded that this man talked a little bit like his father who was also learned. Initially taken aback, he then quickly reminded himself that he loathed his father, and that he hated this little darkie who spoke better than he.

"Now, now, mister. We don't want no trouble with you all. This man will be dealt with by military authorities, sir," said Nate to the deputy, while he was also shifting his gaze from Moody and Levi.

"You're not fixin' to let dat nigger go wid dem . . . are you deputy?" complained Moody, as he pointed at Nate, Jesse, and Mathias.

"Now Moody, I'm the law here, and I will decide." The deputy didn't want any citizen telling him how to do his job, especially in front of blue-belly niggers.

Sensing that this was an extremely volatile situation, Nate decided that he better find a way that would satisfy the deputy while ensuring Private Jackson's safety until he could notify Lieutenant Hennessy.

"Mr. Deputy. Let me send a man to fetch my commanding officer, so we can resolve this matter in a legal way."

Uncertain of how to handle this problem, the deputy thought for a moment, and decided that the matter should involve the sheriff.

"I'll agree to that, but I will have to take this man into custody."

"That will be fine, sir, but Sergeant Randolph and I must accompany you. You see, sir—I have to fulfill my responsibility toward this enlisted man. I can't allow this man outta my sight considerin' that he disobeyed orders by frequenting this saloon."

The deputy sheriff thought for a moment as he scratched his forehead. "Very well," he responded as he down-cocked his Griswold & Gunnison revolver. You can follow me to the sheriff's office, but keep downwind from me, ya hear?!"

Nate ordered Corporal Mathias to ride back to where the Ninth was garrisoned on the western part of town and inform Lieutenant Hennessy that Pvt. Martin Jackson was being held at the sheriff's office, and that Sgt. Maj. Nate Gordon and 1st Sgt. Jesse Randolph were waiting for him. The sun was almost level with the horizon and Mathias did not want to be caught on the road after dark.

He cantered Betsy out of town toward the open road that led to the bivouac area until his mare's right leg suddenly started to limp. Mathias got off his horse and examined Betsy's hoof.

What he discovered dismayed him completely. "Damn, girl, you have lost your right shoe." Nevertheless, Mathias decided to push on.

The regiment was only a couple of miles out of town, and if he walked the animal as fast as possible, he could make it in less than an hour. Still inexperienced and ignorant when it came to horses, Mathias remounted his mare, not fully realizing that he risked injuring the animal by riding with only three shoes. He did not realize that it would be better for the horse if he walked alongside the animal, rather than remounting and forcing the horse to carry more weight.

As his horse hobbled down the road, he became very conscious of his loneliness. Only the sky, and what appeared to him to be countless of bright dots peering endlessly from horizon to horizon filled the great empty landscape. The millions of stars created enough light for Mathias to see the road and the shadows of the oak and willow trees that broke the otherwise monotonous terrain.

As he pondered the beauty of the vast Texas night, breathing the fresh air, he thought how this was such a refreshing change from all those months drilling in the stagnant environment of Louisiana. He began to hum a little nursery rhyme that his mother had taught him when he was a little boy in Charleston, South Carolina. Suddenly, he felt his big mare's muscular body tense up, and her usual calm demeanor became erratic. The mare's ears began to twitch backward and forward, signaling to Mathias that the animal sensed danger, and might, at any moment, bolt. Mathias tightened his grip on the reins and attempted to speak softly to the big beast in order to regain control.

"Easy girl, don't get spooked. Not way out here . . . in the dark."

As he was stroking the mare's neck, a loud voice pierced the stillness of the night, and startled Mathias.

"Havin' problems controlling your horse, Jethro?" jeered the rider, as he lit a torch that was soaked in rags and oil, revealing the appearance of two riders directly in front of Mathias in the middle of the road. Mathias was cut off, leaving him no room to advance. A few seconds later, four more riders brusquely appeared from behind an oak tree and sealed off his retreat. Dressed in white robes that covered their entire bodies, all the riders had large pentagram markings painted in black and red on their chests. The riders' heads were completely covered in tight exaggerated pointed hoods with two silver-dollar-size holes where the eyes appeared. There was no opening for the mouth. When one of the riders spoke, the cloth of the hood around the mouth area would move as if they were sock puppets.

Their horses' heads were also covered in hoods which made their pointed ears resemble satanic figures riding from the depths of Hades. The long, flowing white sheets that stretched from the crest of their horses' neck all the way to the hip joint and drooped to the ground, reminded Mathias of a drawing he once saw in a book in his former master's library that showed knights in armor mounted on war horses.

The lead rider, a big fat man, was wearing a black cape that moved in the wind as if they were the wings of a crow ready to fly off its perch. He was mounted on a huge black stallion that snorted and stomped the ground nervously with his hooves. The fat man carried a sawed-off shotgun in his right hand, his index finger on both triggers. The twin hammers were fully cocked. His voice, cynical and boisterous, repeated, "Like I said Jethro—havin' problems with your horse? . . . Haw, haw, haw . . ." Moody stood up in his stirrups and positioned himself as if he was about to make some important announcement. "Boys. This hare . . . is the *educated nigger*, I tol' yawl 'bout."

The rear man, the smallest rider in the group, pulled out a match from inside his robe and lit another oil-soaked rag mounted on a long stick. As he fired the torch, the light of the flame reflected off Mathias' spectacles.

"Maybe we should give the blue-belly darkie a lesson in riding horses," said the man with the long torch, as he raised it high above his head, marking the spot where Mathias was boxed in by the riders.

"The Klux!" Mathias whispered to himself, finally realizing who these men really were. Although he felt his heart racing in his chest, his body remained frozen in the saddle, and his small hands gripped the reins tightly.

He had heard horrible stories in the freed men's camps in the Carolinas, how white men, mostly ex-Confederate veterans, would dress up in robes with hoods, and ride in the middle of the night. Mounted, and moving stealthily, they would swoop down on Negro camps and travelers and use the lash and lariat to instill fear, feed superstition, intimidate, terrorize, inflict beatings, and murder helpless blacks who dared to exercise their newly won rights and freedoms.

Mathias' heart thumped uncontrollably, while he continued to struggle to control his horse. Although lame, he sensed that Betsy wanted to take off and get away from the robes that flapped in the breeze. Mathias realized that if he did not do something drastic and immediate, he would be either tortured or murdered by these men.

"What's the matter? Cat got your tongue?" laughed Levi, as he in turn lit his torch.

This sent a cold shiver down Mathias' spine. As he looked about, he realized that he was completely surrounded. He knew that time was running out if he wanted to try and escape this predicament. Finally, he cleared his throat which had suddenly become unbelievably parched, and tried to speak. "I, I, I'm just going down the road, sir, back to camp. Please, sir, your horse is blocking my way."

The night riders were temporarily stunned by Mathias' appearance of calmness, and the way he spoke.

"*Whoweee*. You were right, Colonel! This nigger *sure* is aducated. And surly too," roared the rider next to Moody.

"You mean you *were*, goin' down dis road, *Jethro*! Your learin' black ass belongs to me now!" bellowed Moody, raising his sawed-off shotgun at Mathias' head.

Mathias' eyes were shifting from rider to rider. He wished that Nate had not ordered him to ride back to camp and fetch Lieutenant Hennessy. Although he was carrying his army Colt .44 percussion revolver, he knew that if he made a move to unflap the holster, his face would be blown off by Moody's shotgun.

Mathias' mind was now preoccupied with escape. He thought that if he could force Betsy past Moody fast enough, Moody would not shoot because he might hit one of his own men. He knew that his mare, by throwing a shoe, could not outrun Moody's stallion and his Klux rabble, but if he could somehow break free, and put some distance between the KKK and himself, he stood a small chance of escaping. He decided to make a break. With a high pitched yell that startled the night riders, he jammed his spurs into Betsy's flanks. The huge beast bucked, hitting Levi's horse squarely in the face, temporarily stunning the animal. Then, in a state of wild panic, Mathias' big mare reared on her hind legs and leaped in between Moody and the other rider's horse, and jumped past them as if the mare were a Mexican jumping bean. The shock of the impact by Mathias' big mare forced Moody to drop his sawed-off shotgun as he struggled to retain control of his now-spooked stallion.

Mathias became exhilarated by his sudden flight. Although lame, Betsy rose to the occasion, forcing herself to gallop down the road toward where the Ninth was bivouacked. Leaning forward as if he were a professional jockey, Mathias wrapped his arms around Betsy's neck and closed his eyes.

He did not get very far, however. As he heard the report of a carbine, the next thing he felt was his horse's weight shift forward as her front knees buckled, plunging the mare's body, head first, into the dirt of the road.

"*Goddamn it,*" shouted Levi, holding a .50-caliber Sharps. "*I missed the nigger but shot the horse.*"

Mathias' face was badly cut up from the fall. He had been projected from his mount as if he were a pebble being launched by a slingshot. As Betsy lay on the ground mortally wounded after collapsing in the middle of the road, Mathias attempted to lift his bruised body from the ground, but felt dazed and disoriented. The fall had knocked the wind out of his lungs, and his spectacles dangled comically from his left ear.

The night riders, having recovered from their initial befuddlement when Mathias abruptly rode out of the cirle, caught up with their quarry and now moved in on him with glee. The burning torches illuminated the area and the long flames flickered erratically, giving the riders' appearance a phantomlike quality as the cloth of their robed horses slightly swayed in the warm Texas night breeze.

"Levi! Get that new lariat I bought this afternoon. I'm goin' give it a good stretchin,'" boasted Moody. Anticipating his plans for Cpl. Mathias Pryor, Moody's eyes were flashing, wild with excitement.

Mathias was still on his knees. Although his face and hair were caked in dust, he managed to put his spectacles back on his face. The left lens, however, was smashed, so he could only properly see with his right one. As he attempted to stand up, he suddenly felt the tightening jerk of a rope around his waist. He then felt his body plunge backward, slamming against the ground. The rider who had roped Mathias spurred his mount to walk backwards, and the slack in the lariat tightened as he wrapped it around the pommel of his saddle. He then turned his horse around and without saying a word, glanced at his leader, waiting for the signal. James Moody nodded in approval, raised his left arm in the air, and the riders formed a straight line as if preparing for a race. Satisfied that all was going according to plan, Moody sharply lowered his arm and jabbed his Mexican spurs into his black stallion. The rest of the men followed, galloping off into the night with Mathias screaming his head off, his body twisting and turning on the rocky ground.

Seven

Nate was becoming impatient. He was pacing back and forth in front of the sheriff's office, dragging his spurs in the dirt as a way to pass time. The deputy had prohibited Nate and Jesse to enter the jailhouse and wait.

"Y'all can wait outside," he ordered. "The sheriff don't allow no Africans in de jail 'cept as convicts."

It had been hours since he sent off Cpl. Mathias Pryor to inform Lieutenant Hennessy regarding Pvt. Martin Jackson's infractions at Harris' and that he was in civilian custody.

Sergeant Jesse Randolph was more relaxed. He had been given a chair by a pretty señorita who felt sorry for him standing in the street. Jesse sat in the chair and tipped it so the rim of the back was leaning against the wall. He removed his kepi and placed it over his face, and folded his arms against his chest. He wanted to get some sleep, but Nate's pacing and the noise that his brass spurs made in the hard ground kept waking him up.

"Stop your pacin'; can't you see that I'm trying to sleep?" said Jesse as he lowered the chair's front legs to the ground.

"I knows something happened to that boy. I can feel it!" Nate was convinced that Mathias did not make it back to camp.

"Damn fool probably got lost," replied Jesse, attempting to solicit humor.

"No, no. Mathias is a good boy. He's in trouble; I can smell it."

"You smell the dung and garbage piles 'round town," laughed Jesse.

Tired of waiting and concerned that it was now almost dawn, and still no word, Nate decided to investigate.

"Jesse, you wait here till I get back. I'm goin' find out what the hell happened to Mathias."

Without so much as a look at Jesse, he quickly untied his gelding's tether and mounted his McClellan without using the aid of the stirrup. He pressed his thighs and knees tightly against his horse's flanks and the beast broke into a canter at a rapid clip. Nate headed west, toward camp.

It did not take long for Nate to find Mathias' dead mare. Buzzards were circling on the horizon and Nate spurred his mount to gain more speed. When he located Betsy's corpse, several buzzards were already feeding on the carcass. He tried shouting them away but one stubborn buzzard kept pulling out entrails from the horse's stomach and ignored him. The scavenger kept eagerly sticking his smooth curved head and beak into Betsy's soft underbelly to pull out pieces of entrails and devour them as if they were a delicacy. Nate finally had to kick the goulish and obstinate bird away with his right boot. *"Get the hell outta here— you bastard!"* he screamed at the top of his lungs as he sent the scavenger flying, leaving buzzard feathers in its wake. Although Nate was no stranger to dead horses being devoured by buzzards, the fact that it was Mathias' mare made him lose his composure.

Betsy was buckled forward on collapsed knees and was leaning toward the right. The animal's big head and long neck hung in the dirt as the horse's long tongue lay hideously exposed and twisted with millions of flies hovering about. Nate examined the bullet hole where the slug entered the mare's hip joint, and its exit point in the breast, where a pool of blood had formed. The animal had been entirely stripped of all its equipment and with the sole exception of the "U.S." brand on its hip, there was no evidence that the animal had once belonged to the army.

As Nate searched the horizon for any sign of where Mathias might have disappeared to, he felt deep anxiety.

Leading his horse, Nate walked around the perimeter of Mathias' dead mount. He had a little trouble calming his horse when the gelding smelled Betsy's pool of blood. He noticed that there were many hoofprints of shod horses in the vicinity, indicating that riders had been present. A few yards away toward the north, he found Mathias' broken and smashed spectacles. He pushed back his Kepi and sighed deeply.

"The boy prob'ly dead," he said to himself softly with an air of hopeless resignation.

After a few more seconds of investigating the ground, Nate noticed that the horse tracks led south. He decided to follow them but in his heart he knew he would find Mathias at the end of the trail, and dreaded the prospect of what he would eventually discover.

Nate took his time by walking his horse and leaning forward in the saddle while keeping his head bowed toward the ground. His eyes were transfixed on the horse tracks, and looking for clues. Earlier, Nate had noticed what appeared to be a log that seemed to have been dragged on the earth. At first he was a little puzzled but the wide scrapings in the ground went on and on, so he followed the tracks. He thought the markings might have been made by Indians or some animal dragging a carcass or even someone covering up horse tracks. As he continued to follow the trail though, he decided that they were made by the same riders he was tracking.

By now, the sun was fully up in the sky, resembling a large yellow disk that had suddenly appeared over the horizon. In the distance, Nate noticed a grove of tall cottonwoods near the banks of the San Antonio River. What caught his attention however, were several buzzards circling near the tops of the trees. He immediately spurred his gelding and galloped in the direction of the cottonwood grove. When he arrived at the center of the grove, his eyes caught the figure of a man completely naked and suspended on a rope with his neck through a noose from one of the tree's lower branches. The head leaned toward the right and Nate had difficulty making out the color of the man's skin because so many buzzards were feeding on his body. Nate felt deep disgust as he stared at the corpse and became appalled when he noticed that one big bird was tugging at the corpse's scrotum with its sleek, long beak.

Nate yanked on the reins of his horse, causing the animal's mouth to be brusquely stretched by the bit.

"Jeez Crist! My Gawd . . . Mathias!"

Although Nate was nauseated by the sight, he quickly drew his

Walker-Colt and started firing wildly into the air to scare off the scavengers who were so busy helping themselves to Mathias' flesh that they did not notice his arrival.

"Flesh eaters! I'll kill all of you."

The rapid fire startled the birds and they flew off the corpse to retreat to other branches in the cottonwood grove to lurk. Although shaken by the lurid sight of Mathias' dangling and broken body, he calmly led his nervous horse to where his friend was suspended. He halted the gelding and propped up his knees on the seat of the saddle so he would be able to stand on top of the McClellan and reach the rope with his knife. Standing erect on the seat, feet close together, he pulled the bowie knife from its sheath, and with one clean sweep, cut down his friend's tortured corpse and watched the grisly body collapse to the ground. Nate then jumped from the McClellan and landed with both feet on the ground, a practice that he had done hundreds of times when he was a boy on the plantation. Looking at Mathias' naked body that had been beaten, whipped, and ravaged by the buzzards, Nate collapsed to his knees and started to cry as if he were a lost child.

I brought Mathias' broken body into camp today. I would have preferred to have buried him out there on the plains, but army regulations required me to bring in the body. His body was horribly mutilated by the buzzards and the beating he got at the hands of those bastards. His right hand was missing. It appears that it was cut right off with a knife.

Nate was feeling awful. It was painful for him to make this entry into his journal. During the war he had to make many sad entries concerning death. But those entries were about men who had either died in battle or from wounds or from disease. Mathias' violent senseless death had struck intense outrage which he had not experienced since the days when he was a slave.

Colonel Hatch has ordered an investigation into the murder of Corporal Mathias Pryor. He instructed Lieutenant Colonel

*Merritt to "find the culprits and bring them to justice." I don't
believe that the investigation will get anywhere. The night riders have disappeared while the local law remains obstinate in
providing any cooperation in locating Mathias' killers. The
whole regiment is disgusted with Mathias' death, and I am
personally appalled that the general population blames the U.S.
Army for the abduction and murder of Mathias because he was
a man of color who wore the uniform of the United States
Army. My experience as a slave, and then as a runaway, has
taught me to expect no quarter in the hands of those whites
who view my brethren as nothing more than stupid cattle. Even
during the war, I had seen many black soldiers robbed of their
wages by corrupt white officers, while an indifferent war department regarded the plight of the colored soldier in the Union
army as nothing more than a nuisance. Although I am bitter
and very upset about Mathias' gruesome murder, my duty as
noncommissioned officer is to use my influence and position of
authority to calm their growing anxieties and anger among the
men toward whites and the army. Many of the men wanted to
"gwine to town an' kill whites to pay back whut dey done to
Corp'ral Mathias!"*

*Private Martin Jackson was released into the custody of
Lieutenant Hennessy and placed in the guard house along with
Privates Percy-Ray Pridgeon and Archie Vaughn. All three of
them will face court martial charges. I fear that the combination of Mathias' death and the imprisonment of these individuals will be a tempest in a teapot.*

Spearheading the wave of revenge and retribution was Pvt. Isaac
Moore. He had ceased his hoodoism but remained discreetly active in
spreading the gospel of offering spiritual protection against whites and
talking about how it was the responsibility of every black man to seek
salvation through the power of Touissant Overture, the great leader
who threw out the French from Santo Domingo. Pvt. Isaac Moore
would draw large audiences at night when he would talk about Touissant Overture's exploits against Napoleon's army. He would re-

count how thousands of French soldiers and planters had their throats cut and the hordes of black warriors that drove the whites into the sea and gained their freedom from their cruel white oppressors.

Pvt. Isaac Moore also spread rumors regarding the incarceration of Privates Percy-Ray Pridgeon and Archie Vaughn. He would spread gossip that the prisoners were being fed nothing but rotten bread and putrid water, and that their hands and feet were shackled, "like in slav'ry times." Isaac Moore also predicted that the men would not live to face their court martial. "The white officers will kill them. There will be no justice for them, and dere will be no justice for Corp'ral Mathias."

The brutal murder of Cpl. Mathias Pryor by the Klan and the hostile reception that the Ninth Cavalry received in San Antonio by the white population, stirred passions of resentment, and many of the enlisted men felt that their officers did not care about their welfare.

Several days later, Sgt. Maj. Nate Gordon and First Sgt. Jesse Randolph were patrolling the perimeter of the camp. The bugler had sounded tattoo about an hour before, and the two noncoms were ordered by Lieutenant Hennessy, the duty officer for the night, to verify that the men were all in their tents, and that the pickets were keeping a clear eye. It had been drizzling all day with intermittent cloud bursts of pouring rain, and although Nate and Jesse were wearing ponchos, they felt cold and wet. It was the ninth of April, and the regiment had been in San Antonio since the beginning of the month.

"Let's go and check on Private Isaac Moore," said Nate, turning to Jesse. Nate's kepi was soaked, and the brim poured water down the right side of his chest. The night was dark and misty, but Jesse noticed a glitter in his friend's eye when he suggested that they go and see what Private Moore was up to.

"I think that man gots to be arrested, before he spreads mo' rumor." Jesse could not understand why Private Isaac Moore was allowed to talk to the men about seeking revenge and killing some of the officers.

"We got to catch him in the act, Jess. So far, it's jest barn and drink talk. That's why I want to keep a sharp eye and watch that bad boy."

Private Isaac Moore was stripped to the waist and standing in the middle of his worn Sibley tent with about a dozen enlisted men from A, E, and K companies. The soldiers were packed in the canvas shelter as if they were steers in a railroad freight car. Several candles were burning in small glass containers and were positioned in the center of the tent where a small makeshift altar was erected. Standing near the candles was Isaac Moore. He was wearing a silk *nkisi* charm around his neck that was commonly known as a *pacquet-congo*. As he twisted and toyed with the charm that resembled a long penis in his delicate fingers, Isaac Moore preached about his powers in communicating with the dead.

"*Bisimbi*: my broders . . . represents de spirits of de dead who make de *pacquets-congo*. T'rough dis charm, I summon de forces from de spirit world dat will protect us frum de evils of de white man."

"*Give us the power!*" cried one trooper with great enthusiasm who seemed to be in a trance. He took another big gulp from the mescal bottle and bellowed again. "*Give us the power.*" He then passed the bottle to a companion, who took a deep gulp of the hooch and joined in the chanting. Most of the mutinous soldiers were squatting on the ground, fueled by strong drink and swelling confidence because their numbers were growing; other devotees in the tent started to cry out in rhythmic form.

"*Yeah. Give us the power, soz we can revenge Corporal Mathias.*"

Isaac Moore was delighted at the response he was getting from this small crowd of enlisted men. Events were going to plan. He was proud of his ability to excite the passions of the men so they would follow him and do his bidding. Isaac Moore decided that the time had come to rise up and destroy their enemies.

"Tonight. We strike my broders. We will free Percy-Ray and Archie Vaughn who are in bondage at the Alamo, and kill all the whites."

"What 'bout the sergeants who will not follow us?" blurted out a concerned soldier.

The tent suddenly fell silent. Isaac Moore was prepared for this line of inquiry. He knew some of the men might resist seeking confrontation with some of the black noncommissioned officers, especially if Sgt. Maj. Nate Gordon decided to take any action against them.

"Does who oppose us, must also die. Black men who do the bidding of de white enemy, is poison to us." Issac Moore stretched out his arm and made a quick horizontal sweep. "And must be destroyed."

The room again fell silent, but Isaac Moore was prepared to seize the moment by reassuring his followers.

"My broders. Men like Sergeant Major Nate Gordon are a threat to us, an' our success." His eyes suddenly lit up and his face became so contorted that it struck fear among some of the men who were closest to him. Staring at his followers as if he was going to strike one of them with his long bony hands, he calmly and slowly explained, "I will personally see to his destruction . . . if he interferes in our efforts."

First Lieutenant Zachary Hennessy was at his camp desk writing his mother in Woodstock, Vermont. He wanted to express to her his sense of jubilation that he was an essential part of the Ninth Cavalry, and that he really believed that he was making a difference in advancing the rights and education of his men. Hennessy had not felt this happy since he was with the First Vermont Cavalry at Appomattox when the Vermonters were ordered by Gen. George Custer to advance against the last battle line that Bobby Lee had thrown against Sheridan's mass cavalry. Sitting on his camp cot near Hennessy was Lt. Donald Smith who was cleaning his Starr revolver. Earlier, he had disassembled the weapon and placed the cylinder, nipples, screws, and small parts into a tin cup that was filled with boiling water, and placed it on the floor. He then scrubbed all the parts including the barrel and frame with a hog's bristle brush.

"Donald. Do you mind not getting any of that dirty water on my bedroll while you use that foul brush?" Hennessy was irritated that his companion's scrubbing was splattering dirty water on his personal effects.

"Frightened that I might soil your clean boots, Hennessy?" retorted

Smith as he dropped the cylinder of the army Colt in the bucket of warm water because he thought the part needed to soak some more. Hennessy smirked as some of the drops of the dirty warm water sprayed his bedroll. He wanted to explain to his mother how although the regiment had many problems, he felt confident that the Ninth would distinguish itself once given the opportunity. He would often mention Sgt. Maj. Nate Gordon to his mother, and how he considered Nate indispensable in assisting him in not only the tedious task of paperwork, but in training the regiment and keeping the men in line.

Lt. Donald Smith was in the process of reassembling his Starr revolver when 1st Sgt. Jesse Randolph entered the tent. He was breathing heavily and spoke rapidly.

"*Sirs*. Beg to report..." Jesse saluted. "Some of the men are plannin' mutiny, and Sergeant Major Gordon is in grave danger of being kilt..."

"At ease, Sergeant, at ease," replied Hennessy, trying to clam down his company's first sergeant. "Now what is going on?"

Jesse took a deep breath. "Sir, some of the men from companies A, E, and K are plottin' to ride to town and revenge the death of Corporal Mathias. Then ride to Vance House and kill Colonel Hatch and Lieutenant Colonel Merritt."

Lt. Donald Smith was not surprised. He had anticipated that the troops would mutiny, and now there was nothing left to do but squash this insolent behavior with brute force. Smith knew that the incident outside of San Antonio with a few rebellious troopers was not the end, but only a prelude to what really was to come. He quickly finished reassembling his Starr revolver and started to load the weapon with ball and cap.

"Where is Sergeant Major Gordon?" Hennessy inquired anxiously.

"He's standin' by sir. He instructed me to fetch officers and men to stop the mutineers 'fore they kill somebody."

Lieutenant Smith finished placing percussion caps on the nipples of the Starr and half-cocked the revolver. Hennessy grabbed his saber belt and unflapped the revolver cover and pulled the revolver. He rotated the barrel to verify that each chamber was loaded, and properly capped. He hoped that if he needed to use the weapon, it would not misfire as the weapon was prone to do in damp weather.

"*Sergeant*. Assemble an armed detail as fast as you can and meet us where company K is bivouacked."

"Sirs? Should we not proceed together with an armed detail?" Jesse did not like the idea that these two white officers were going on ahead. He thought to himself, "Don't these white fools know what they are up against?"

"There's no time, Sergeant," snapped Lieutenant Smith. "We've got to stop this rabble before they steal the horses. Now move, Sergeant, move! Go get the detail."

Nate was standing near the Sibley tent where inside, Isaac Moore and his little band of mutineers were being worked up into a frenzy by their leader. They were chanting; "*Death to whites and long live Toussant Ouverture*. Nate could see the flickering flames of several candles behind the tent's canvas and noticed that three drunk troopers were dancing wildly in the middle of the Sibley and hooted and bellowed as if they were animals. Nate debated whether he should enter the tent and arrest Pvt. Isaac Moore right then and there. If he waited for reinforcements it might be too late to curtail the mutineers' plans. Impatient and nervous that the growing passions of the mob might be let loose at any moment at the command of that voodoo priest, Isaac Moore, he drew his Walker-Colt and cocked the hammer on the four and a half pound horse pistol and was about to barge into the tent when he had second thoughts. He suddenly considered the possibility that he might be overpowered by the angry mutineers, some of them he knew were carrying their service revolvers, while all of them had knives. No, he said to himself, I better wait for Hennessy.

All of a sudden, the mutineers in the tent started to pour out of the Sibley en masse, as if they were angry ants surfacing from the hole of their hill. Nate was stunned, he had not anticipated that they might emerge from the tent so quickly.

"*There's the Uncle Tom!*" shouted one mutineer, as he waved a butcher knife at Nate.

Isaac Moore was the last to emerge from the tent. He was completely naked except for a shanty loin cloth draped around the middle of his body, and was still stroking his neck charm that resembled a penis with his bony fingers.

"*Hold it, right there Moore.*" Nate pointed the Walker-Colt right at Isaac Moore's head. "*Don't move a muscle, Private.*" Nate's eyes were intense and every muscle in his face stiffened while his body flowed with adrenaline. Moore starred at the huge barrel of the Walker-Colt and stopped. Nate then added with his commanding baritone voice, "Don't move . . . any of yeah."

Although the mutineers froze at the sight of Nate's big horse pistol, some of them had their army Colts in their hands and pointing the revolvers at Nate, while others brandished menacing skinning knives. It was a stand-off. The mob fell silent, waiting for some kind of signal on what do to next.

"*Y'all under arrest fo' mutiny. Put down your weapons, now!*" Nate was prepared to stand his ground. He was not going to let these bastards go any farther, and was particularly outraged that most of the mutineers belonged to his troop, company A.

"You're not goin' to arrest anyone," scorned Isaac Moore as if he were in a trance. He raised his arm and pointed his long finger at Nate and spoke in a low voice as if he was putting a curse on the man. "*You* will get out of *our* way."

The air was thick with the intensity of the moment, and Nate decided to fully pull back the hammer on the Walker-Colt and keep a light finger on the trigger. He was about to fire and blow away Isaac Moore's head and take his chances with the other men when he felt a hard blow at the back of his neck. He staggered, then dropped his revolver and collapsed, face first to the ground. One of Isaac Moore's followers had circled back around the Sibley and crawled to where Nate was standing. He managed to grab a cast iron skillet that rested on a stump near the campfire and used it to whack Nate. The mutineers became jubilant at the sight of Nate's body lying on the ground. Isaac Moore grinned and raised his arm into the air.

"*The horses. To the horses, my broders,*" he commanded as the mutineers cheered in wild triumphant jubilation. The rabble was not only inebriated, but intoxicated with the notion that their day of reckoning had arrived.

Lieutenants Hennessy and Smith found Nate on the ground bucked and tied. Isaac Moore had instructed one of his followers to gag Nate with his own bandanna and ordered that he be tied up. Hennessy immediately cut the ropes that had tied Nate's hands and feet and noticed that he was badly cut at the back of the head and dazed by the blow.

"Sergeant Major . . . Sergeant Major?" Zach Hennessy pulled his linen handkerchief from his shirt and folded it to form a head bandage that he was going to wrap around Nate's wound.

"Don't . . . don't . . ." Nate was groggy and his head felt as if he was kicked my a mule. "Nev', neva, mind' 'bout me sir." Nate paused for a moment and felt the back of his head. The open wound felt tender and the blood dripped over the collar and back of his shell jacket which irritated him more than the blow itself. After a few moments, he managed to collect his thoughts.

"Private Isaac Moore and men from companys A, E, and K are stealin' mounts to go to town on a killin' spree. They's got to be stopped, sir."

"*We'll stop them, by God,*" replied Lieutenant Donald Smith, defiantly. He was itching for a fight, and wanted to kill the mutineers and be rid of the bad apples in the regiment, once and for all.

"They probably have already stolen mounts, and are on their way into town, Donald," replied Hennessy, matter-of-factly.

"*Goddamn it. I knew this shit would happen.* Where in the hell is Sergeant Randolph and those men?" Lieutenant Smith was becoming impatient. He was eager to pursue the culprits and hunt them down as if they were rabid dogs that needed to be exterminated immediately.

"Right here, Lieutenant." Jesse Randolph was running with a squad of six men. He was in front, holding his Colt while the other troopers held Spencer repeaters at the ready.

"Sergeant Randolph reporting, sir." He gave a crisp salute to Hennessy and Smith.

"About time, Sergeant!" replied Smith furiously.

"We have no time to waste. If we mount up now and ride like hell, we might be able to intercept them at the Alamo," said Hennessy calmly. He was behaving with greater composure than Lieutenant Smith. Although Zach Hennessy was emotional, and at times, passionate in his beliefs, he was always rational and clear thinking when under pressure. He was convinced that it served no purpose expending energy needlessly, when rational thought usually attains greater results. He believed that this philosophy saved his life many times during the war.

Pvts. Percy-Ray Pridgeon, Archie Vaughn, and Martin Jackson were sitting on crude wooden stools in the guard house at the Alamo where they had been kept since their arrest. The United States Army had used the Alamo Mission at various times for a military depot since Texas joined the Union. The guard house was located in front of Alamo Mission in one of the old Indian-quarter adobe huts near the south gate.

The prisoners were incarcerated in a single room and had grown very restless waiting for their court martial proceedings to commence. They still remained defiant, and all of the jailees harbored deep resentment toward their white officers and especially toward those noncommissioned officers that sided with them.

The sergeant of the guard became very concerned that the prisoners might escape. The adobe hut was old, its walls had deep cracks, and the roof leaked. It would not take very much effort to break out. Percy-Ray got up from his stool and stared out the window. The window opening had some wrought-iron bars and whenever the guards were not paying attention, he had been diligently working to loosen them with a spoon.

"I know I can get these bars out . . . I can feel them give way," he said hopefully.

"And then what, P-R? Wez goners an'ways," derided Archie Vaughn who was despondent that he was facing a court-martial. He saw no hope of escaping. They were strangers in this immense country, and even if they would escape they would surely be hunted down. Blacks were killed by whites in Texas as if they were Kiowa or Commanche.

"*Nigger* . . . you can stays here and rot, fo' all ah cares. Once I pry this bar out, I'm goin' ske'dadle." Percy-Ray was scraping away at the base of the bar he was trying to pull out, when the sergeant of the guard's face appeared through the small window in the center of the oak door.

"*What de hell is goin' on in there?*" he roared.

Startled, Percy-Ray nearly dropped his spoon. He had depended on Archie Vaughn to watch for the sergeant of the guard, but his companion became too preoccupied with his gloomy prospects to pay much attention to the guards. There was a long awkward silence among the prisoners in the room and the surprised sergeant continued to gawk through the little window. As Percy-Ray started to turn around, he heard a loud thump against the oak door and what sounded like flesh and muscle being hacked by a butcher. The sergeant of the guard's body became suddenly rigid while his eyes and mouth popped wide open in amazement. He gave a loud gasp and like a balloon being deflated, the prisoners could hear the air escaping from his mouth.

The jailees were initially dumbfounded and confused. It was only when they saw the blood pouring out of the sergeant's mouth and nose that they realized what had happened.

"I thinks he's stuck to the door," exclaimed Pvt. Martin Jackson, as he rubbed his eyes and yawned. He had been napping and awakened when he heard the sergeant of the guard shouting.

"Get the keys, get the keys," commanded a voice from outside the door. Within a moment, the door swung open with the body of the sergeant of the guard impaled to the door by a saber.

"*Jes' Crist! You sticked him like a hog!*" exclaimed Archie Vaughn, aghast.

Standing in the frame of the doorway as if he were a prince, was Isaac Moore. He was still stroking the charm around his neck while his eyes flashed. "Dis bad black man will no long be yo'r jailer my broders," he assured them. He then raised his right hand in the air and spoke as if he were some kind of messiah. "*We have come to free you, my broders.*" The prisoners were astonished and dumbstruck. Issac Moore paused, then opened his arms like a charlatan preacher seeking to embrace potential converts. "Join us in our struggle. Help us avenge de death of our broder Mathias," he commanded in his trancelike voice.

"*Whowee!* What are wez standin' here fo'? Les go!" clamored Percy-Ray. He then ran and embraced Isaac Moore as if he were a long lost companion. Feeling equally exhilarated, the other prisoners started shouting chants of retribution while a bottle of mescal was passed to them by one of their deliverers. Pvts. Percy-Ray Pridgeon, Archie Vaughn, and Martin Jackson had joined the mutiny.

Percy-Ray and Martin Jackson were handed Colt revolvers that had been taken from the sergeant of the guard and the sentry who was overpowered in the brief melee when Isaac Moore and his followers stormed the guard house. As Privates Percy-Ray, Archie Vaughn, and Martin Jackson filed out of the cell, the fugitives almost slipped and fell on the pool of warm blood that poured from the wound where the sergeant of the guard had been impaled on the oak door. The dead man still had his face wedged in the little window frame of the door and was standing on his toes. (A position he shifted to when he became impaled.) Percy-Ray thought that the dead sergeant of the guard looked rather comical with his bulging eyes and mouth wide open as the face remained motionless. He became amused that his jailer was pinned to the door and laughed heartily as he watched the corpse swing back and forth with the door as if he was a great coat on a hook.

"That nigger sure got his!" laughed Pvt. Martin Jackson, as he walked past the dead sergeant. The other mutineers also laughed and one of them slapped the back of the victim's head just for good measure, causing more laughter among the mutineers.

"*Silence,*" Isaac Moore commanded. He did not want to lose control of the mob, and he knew time was running out to fulfill his plan to kill the senior officers who were quartered at Vance House, and attack the town before the regiment could mobilize and pursue them.

"Follow me my broders . . . *Kill the white officers.*"

A great cheer went up among the rebellious soldiers. They felt confident and strong. With Pvt. Isaac Moore leading the way, they set off in the direction of Vance House to kill Colonel Hatch and Lt. Col. Wesley Merritt.

Lieutenants Hennessy and Smith were galloping ahead of the column heading for Vance House, located on the corner of Houston and St. Mary's streets. Although his head was pounding with pain, Sergeant Major Nate Gordon insisted that he accompany the armed squad into San Antonio and intercept the mutineers. The officers and Nate, however, were not aware that Isaac Moore had stormed the guard house and liberated Percy-Ray and his little band who had now joined the bulk of the mutineers.

First Sergeant Jesse Randolph was ridding next to Nate and was concerned that his friend might make the wound worse by riding a horse. He kept looking at Nate's bandage that Lieutenant Hennessy had wrapped around his head to stop the bleeding.

"How's your head, Nate?"

"Like shit! I feel like shit." He paused for a moment then turned to Jesse, his face contorted with anger. "But I'm going to feel a hell of a lot better once I take care of those bastards."

Hennessy's mind was racing. He was contemplating how to handle the situation once the squad arrived at Vance House. Turning to Lieutenant Smith, he yelled so his voice could be overheard over the galloping horses' shod hooves. "I think that we should deploy the men in a skirmish line in front of the building."

"Suppose the mutineers have already penetrated the building?" asked Lieutenant Smith, as he pulled his kepi down farther over his forehead so the hat would not fly off.

"Then we will have no choice but to go in after them," Hennessy quickly retorted. He dug his spurs into his mount and took the point in the column.

The small detachment arrived at Vance House. There was a slight drizzle that made visibility poor, and with the exception of the flickering gas lights seeping through the closed plantation shutters on the second floor, Vance House and the corner of Houston and St. Mary's was dark, and the streets were deep with mud due to the recent heavy rains.

Lieutenant Hennessy and Smith quickly dismounted and reconnoitered the perimeter of the building. After they were satisfied that there were no signs of any unusual activity, they met in front of the hotel.

"They're not here? Where in the hell could they be?" asked Smith, disappointed.

Lieutenant Hennessy was about to say something when Nate moved his horse close to the officers. "Sirs. Beg to report."

"Yes, Sergeant? Report." Hennessy allowed Nate to interrupt him.

"Sir, I believe that the mutineers might have gone to the Alamo an' freed the prisoners. I suggest that we deploy the men in the front of the building and on the second floor balcony. I 'spect that Private Moore an' his rabble be here shortly." Nate then smiled. "And we can be waitin' for them."

Hennessy stared at Nate's head wound and thought for a moment. "Very well, Sergeant Major. Deploy the men. Lieutenant Smith and I will inform Colonel Hatch and Lieutenant Colonel Wesley Merritt of the situation."

They found the main door locked so the two officers pounded on the door and demanded to be let in. A fat elderly Mexican woman finally opened the door but before she could say a word, Hennessy and Smith barged past her and made for the stairs to the second floor where Hatch and Merritt had their rooms.

As Nate and Jesse were barking orders to the troopers, Isaac Moore and his mutineers appeared out of the dark. The voodoo man was out in front with Percy-Ray and Archie Vaughn and were mounted on horses they had stolen from the regiment. The rabble possessed all the attributes of intoxicated men gone wild with anger motivated by revenge. The dozen or so rogue troopers were bunched up in the middle of Houston Street, screaming insults and threats while brandishing revolvers and knives as their horses pranced, snorted, jerked, and behaved nervously because their demented riders had worked the animals into a wild state.

Nate was standing near the main entrance to Vance House with two troopers. Sergeant Jesse Randolph had gone inside and was in the process of placing his men on the balcony, when Isaac Moore moved forward on his horse and faced Nate. Nate immediately noticed that the voodoo man was surprised to see him standing. He knew that Moore had thought that the blow to his head should have removed him as an obstacle to his plans, and render him immobilized because he had him bucked and tied. Now, however, Nate knew that the rebel leader would have to back up the bold words that he had boasted earlier in the tent to his devotees.

Nate had already pulled his Walker-Colt from the holster when he was ordered by Hennessy to deploy the men, and waited calmly. When he heard the mutineer's horses galloping toward him, he placed the weapon behind his back so it would be out of view.

"You are in our way, Step aside an' we will not hurt you," commanded Issac Moore, trying to bluff Nate.

"Get down from your horse, *Private*. You're under arrest." Nate's eyes stared at his enemy like a hawk about to pounce on a rabbit. Although the Walker-Colt still remained hidden behind his back, Nate adroitly maneuvered his thumb to fully cock the hammer.

"Then go to your white God!" Issac Moore pulled his revolver that was tucked into his loin cloth, cocked the weapon while using both hands, and fired wildly at Nate.

The shot missed its target but spooked the horses of the mutineers into a bucking and rearing frenzy. Four of the rogue troopers lost control of their mounts and immediately fell to the ground, while several others fired their pistols at Nate and the two sentries.

Nate quickly drew the Walker-Colt from behind his back and plunged to the ground on his belly when the first shot rang out. He firmly held the pommel of the horse pistol with his right hand while his left supported his right hand's wrist, and dug his elbows into the mud. Although there was much pandemonium in between neighing horses, cursing and screaming mutineers, and gunfire, Nate watched carefully for the opportunity to get a good shot at Isaac Moore or Percy-Ray by moving the Walker-Colt back and forth in a horizontal motion.

Fortunately, both Colonel Hatch and Lieutenant Colonel Merritt were out of the building having dinner with some prominent local citizens at a hacienda a few miles out of town. When Lieutenants Hennessy and Smith heard the report of gunfire in front of Vance House, they sprinted down the stairs and out of the building right into the fight.

The corner of Houston and St. Mary's had now become a chaotic mix of yelling, black powder smoke, whining and colliding horses, and flashes of gunfire that illuminated the street as if it were a lightning storm. Lieutenant Hennessy stepped out onto Houston Street searching for Sgt. Maj. Nate Gordon. The lieutenant called out for him, trying to shout above the morass of confusion. He clamored for Nate's rank's first, then by name several times in an attempt to locate him.

Nate heard Hennessy's voice and saw his commanding officer standing a few feet away from one of the entranceways of Vance House. He was about to respond, when a .52-caliber bullet from a Spencer repeating carbine penetrated the lieutenant's forehead. The shot blew the back off his head, splattering brain, bone, flesh, and hair on the exterior wall. Hennessy's body stumbled backward and landed on his buttocks on the pavement, his back propped up against the stone wall of Vance House.

"*Ah got Hen'sse! Ah got Hen'sse.*" exclaimed Percy-Ray jubilantly.

Nate howled out of rage when he saw Hennessy's brains spattered and his body collapse to the ground. Furious, he charged Percy-Ray who was on horseback. Percy-Ray frantically pulled the lever forward and back again on his Spencer, took quick aim and fired again. *Click.* The carbine was empty, and Nate was moving toward his target with great speed and agility. As he drew closer to Percy-Ray, he steadied his big horse pistol and pointed the weapon squarely at his target's chest and placed the index finger firmly on the trigger.

"*You're goin' to hell, boy,*" bellowed Nate as he fired the Walker-Colt at Percy-Ray at point blank range. The heavy lead ball pierced his chest with such force that he was blown off his saddle and across the rump of his horse. Percy-Ray seized his chest and coughed up blood as he gasped and choked for air while he lay on the ground. He died within a few seconds, chest pumping blood all over his white under-shirt.

Lt. Don Smith also witnessed the death of his comrade, Lt. Zachery Hennessy and Nate's subsequent shooting of Private Percy-Ray Pridgeon. He was kneeling on the sidewalk at the corner of St. Mary's and Houston streets with three other troopers. They formed a disciplined skirmish line and remained calm as they fired into the crowd of mutineers who were now dispersing out of fear and confusion. Several of them were seriously wounded and lay on the ground moaning in agony and pleading for water.

First Sergeant Jesse Randolph's squad of troopers were taking their time aiming and firing their Spencers at the rebellious soldiers from their positions on the second-story balcony at Vance House. Jesse walked back and forth behind the shooters, encouraging them to pick their targets carefully. Jesse was not aware that Lieutenant Hennessy was dead, but did see Nate charge Percy-Ray and blast him off the saddle. He also noticed that both Pvts. Archie Vaughn and Martin Jackson were wounded. Jackson was withering on the ground with a painful stomach wound, while Archie Vaughn was screaming his head off and clutching his knee that had been shattered by carbine fire.

Pvt. Isaac Moore and two of his toadies were dismounted and firing their pistols at Vance House from behind a wagon they turned over at the other end of Houston Street. Nate had fallen back to where Lieutenant Smith and the three troopers were positioned, and resumed firing.

"*Sergeant*. Stay here and continue to draw their fire, I'll circle 'round and cut them off," ordered Smith, who had just finished reloading his Starr revolver.

"Aye sir," replied Nate.

Pvt. Isaac Moore started to have second thoughts about his revolt. Most of his men had scattered off when Nate charged Percy-Ray and shot him, and several were badly wounded. Out of ammunition, he decided to break off the attack and disappear among San Antonio's winding dark streets. Without saying a word to his two remaining followers, he bolted from his concealed position behind the overturned wagon and ran down St. Mary's Street with great haste. He did not get very far, however. Emerging from an alley that fed into St. Mary's, Lt. Don Smith nearly bumped into the voodoo man. Both men were startled but Smith was more prepared to deal with the unexpected.

Isaac Moore froze and threw his hands in the air. He then started to plead, "You can't shoot an unarmed man," he said with a smirk. "I know de law . . . I will have to stand a court-martial."

Lieutenant Smith was unmoved by Isaac Moore's pathetic legal plea. He had been anticipating this moment for a long time. He smiled at the voodoo man and calmly shoved the barrel of his Starr in Moore's face and pulled the trigger. A spark emanated from one of the nipples on a cylinder chamber, causing the weapon to misfire. "Damn it to hell! roared Smith, frustrated that all his efforts to keep his revolver in perfect working order had been in vain.

Taking advantage of this bit of good fortune, Moore turned and bolted in the opposite direction, running as fast as he could. Lieutenant Smith regained his composure and concentrated. He calmly and methodically recocked his Starr, so the cylinder would revolve to another chamber and took aim at Moore's back. Although he could barely make out his target due to the darkness of the night, he could hear him fleeing down the alley and quickly estimated the distance and height of his target, and fired twice. The blasts briefly illuminated the area and Smith saw Moore's body skid and roll over in the mud as if he had been thrown from the back of a wagon.

Nate ran in the direction of where he heard the gunshots. He arrived upon the scene with a torch that one of the mutineers had discarded when the shooting started. He found Lieutenant Smith standing over Isaac Moore's almost naked body, examining the two gunshot wounds. One of the slugs had penetrated his body through the lower back, and had exited through his neck, causing blood to ooze all over his neck charm. Nate calmly put his Walker-Colt in its oversized holster and bent over Moore's body.

"Your hoodoo preachin' ghost tales are over, voodoo man. No mo' disturbin' dead folks." He then removed his gauntlet and with his naked hand, seized Isaac Moore's bloody neck charm. He stared at it for a moment, then spat at the item and threw the charm in the filthy gutter as if it were a piece of dog dung he had found under his boot.

Eight

Colonel Hatch, Lieutenant Colonel Merritt, and Cpt. C. W. Balbert, who had been appointed to lead the investigation into the reasons for the recent riot, were reviewing the captain's findings.

"Just as I had expected," confirmed Colonel Hatch loudly. "Your report sustains my original beliefs that one of the main reasons why this outrageous incident took place was due to a lack of enough officers. By God, the regiment only had fourteen officers at the time of the mutiny while we needed at least twenty and Washington doesn't give a damn." Hatch paused briefly and stroked his mustache. "I made it quite clear that if the Ninth Cavalry is going to be an effective military force, they should send me more line officers or disband the unit . . . Nothing can be expected of us under the present circumstances."

"Begging the colonel's pardon, sir," pleaded Captain Balbert. "The investigating officer was considered a very efficient officer with an eye for detail."

"Yes, Captain, I realize that," replied Hatch as he continued to stroke his mustache.

"Yes, sir. I also pointed out in my report that many of the recruits proved to be too light, too young, and possessed weak constitutions. . . ."

"Because the recruiters were overzealous, and indifferent!" interrupted Merritt. "Those officers responsible for recruiting the riff-raff that caused this mutiny should be court-martialed for dereliction to duty." Merritt was furious that the riot broke out in his regiment. He had gone through the entire war without any comparable incident. For this to happen now, after four years of bloody civil war, was an unpardonable blemish on his otherwise spotless record of military service.

Captain Balbert attempted to reassure Hatch and Merritt.

"Be what it may be, I believe that the war department will act very quickly on my recommendations to speed up the recruitment of officers for service in the Ninth."

"I remind you Captain, that Lieutenant Colonel Merritt and I have written the war department ad nauseum regarding the gross shortage of officers in the Ninth." Hatch sighed and looked at the ceiling. "In hindsight, the regiment should never have left New Orleans without a full complement of officers. Let us hope that we have a second chance to rebuild what I believe will be a fine cavalry regiment."

Nate was making an entry into his journal when a sentry appeared at the entrance of the Sibley tent. The sentry was with the sheriff's deputy of San Antonio. The same deputy that had arrested Private Jackson at Harris'. Nate rested his quill pen on the camp desk and looked up at the deputy who appeared to be nervous.

"Very well, Private. Return to your post," Nate ordered, as he shifted his sitting position in the camp chair to face his unexpected visitor. He crossed his legs and folded his arms against his chest. "What can I do for you . . . Deputy?"

"I got a message for you," replied the deputy as he reached into his vest pocket and removed a folded handkerchief. He then took a few steps forward into the Sibley and placed the article on the camp desk next to Nate's journal.

"What's this?"

"It's from Moody. He wanted you to have a little souvenir," replied the deputy surly. "He wanted to make sure."

"Sure of *what*?" retorted Nate, who was becoming irritated with the arrogant deputy.

"That Moody is the one responsible for your little souvenir. Go ahead . . . look inside, you'll know what I mean, *black man*." The deputy then turned on his heels and walked out of the Sibley and disappeared, leaving Nate alone with the folded handkerchief.

Nate stared at the article, dreading what he would find inside. He slowly unfolded the handkerchief and became aghast when he saw a small dark shriveled hand. "Mathias!" he whispered to himself.

Nate spent the night thinking about Mathias and how he would phrase the letter to his dead companion's sister. A few hours before reveille, he finally put quill to paper. He struggled with the words but kept the letter on an official level while writing that Mathias was not only a good soldier, but a friend. Nate decided not to tell her the cause of Mathias' death but simply wrote that he had died in the service of the United States Army. After he had written to Mathias' sister, he entered a few paragraphs into his journal as a means to vent his melancholy.

> *I have finally written to Mathias' sister in Charleston, South Carolina. It was the most difficult letter that I have ever written. Of course, I did not let her know the details of his death. As for my personal feelings, my heart remains bitter and I seek revenge. I told Merritt that we now have proof that Moody was responsible for Mathias' death, but he told me that local law officials are not willing to help us and the army remains powerless to proceed without their cooperation. He also told me that I must not seek revenge, and that the time and place for justice will come in due time. I agree! I will one day return and avenge Mathias' murder.*
>
> *Since the mutiny, the Ninth Cavalry has undergone major changes. Although the regiment's honor is stained by the mutiny, the melee was a blessing in disguise in that at least all the bad apples that plagued the Ninth have been eliminated. The regiment is finally able to report that all ten companies have sufficient officers, and as a result, morale and discipline have improved. The flow of supplies and equipment have been accelerated, and the Ninth is able to get down to the serious business of drilling and teaching the troop's cavalry tactics and procedures.*
>
> *I asked Colonel Hatch about the future deployment of the regiment. He told me that after the men are rigorously drilled*

and fully equipped, his outfit would be broken up with different companies assigned to various post on the western and southern Texas frontier protecting the settlers from Commanches, Apaches, and Kiowas.

Am I pleased with the work that I have done with the Ninth? Did I make a difference in shaping these men into a body of fighting soldiers?

Nate paused for a moment and gently placed his quill on the table. He puffed on his pipe and stared intensely at the soft light of the oil lamp, his mind deep in reflection. He took a deep pull on the pipe and picked up his quill and wrote one sentence in his journal.

The results are not good enough!

Then as an afterthought and perhaps as a way of seeking redemption for his feelings of inadequacy in his efforts regarding the Ninth, he added:

Maybe sometime in the future, I will have an opportunity to come back and make up for what I have failed to do with these men.

I am returning to my old regiment, the Tenth Cavalry, located at Fort Leavenworth. My former outfit is now in the process of going through the same problems that the Ninth has experienced, and my former commanding officer, Colonel Benjamin Grierson, had written Hatch, his old comrade-in-arms, requesting that I return to assist him in training the Tenth for duty on the plains. So help me! I will not have the same results with the Tenth that I experienced with the Ninth. I will be ever more vigilant!

Nate's pipe needed a refill. As he taped the bowl against the leg of his table and emptied the ashes, he thought about Lieutenant Hennessy. He decided that he must write something about the unfortunate death of that good man.

248

Although I feel the loss of Lieutenant Hennessy, I do not feel deep remorse. During the war, I often lost friends and saw men blown to pieces by canister and grape shot. Over time, I have conditioned himself not to feel human loss, and pride myself to do the best I can for my men and teach them how to survive.

When I told First Sergeant Jesse Randolph that I was returning to my former regiment, he wanted to transfer to the Tenth as well. With my assistance, I have asked Wesley Merritt to give it high priority, and Jesse's request for transfer papers was quickly processed. We both leave for Fort Leavenworth at the end of May.

Part Three

FIGHTING THE CHEYENNES

One

FORT LEAVENWORTH, KANSAS, JUNE, 1867

Sgt. Maj. Nate Gordon and 1st Sgt. Jesse Randolph arrived at Fort Leavenworth after a lengthy trip by steamboat up the Mississippi River from New Orleans. They changed steamers at St. Louis, and proceeded west on the Missouri in a small paddle wheel until they arrived at the fort's docking facilities. As the paddle wheel prepared to berth, Nate and Jesse heard the sounds of a bugler calling reveille.

Nate was ecstatic. For the first time in months, he felt relaxed and a rare smile appeared on his face. Jesse was standing near him by the railing on the port bow and noticed his friend's usual quiet demeanor disappear upon sighting the vast rolling Kansas hills. Although the air felt hot and dry, the aroma of blooming flowers permeated the air and the plains were green from all the water melted from the winter snows. The sky was completely cloudless and brilliantly blue, making the early morning sun seem brighter than anywhere else on earth. Nate removed his pipe from the corner of his mouth and looked at Jesse as if he were about to tell him some great secret.

"We're home, Jess. Home. Smell that sweet air and see them heavenly hills reachin' beyond creation?" Nate took a deep breath as if he were some coal miner that had spent too much time in the hole.

"Yes, sir!" acknowledged Jesse. "Sure diffrent than the South." His hands were leaning on the railing while Nate moved quickly to be the first in line to get off the steamer. He couldn't wait to get off the boat and plow into the multitude of human activity taking place on the waterfront.

Nate thought about how Fort Leavenworth, since 1829, was the military gateway to the West and how during much of the three decades preceding the war, and immediately after the conflict, the post was the most important military hub on the central plains. "Yes sir . . . de permanent Indian frontier," he whispered to himself. He pondered how this overly-extended line of defense was designed to protect thousands of immigrants that were traveling on the Oregon and Santa Fe Trails.

Nate tried to explain to Jesse the history of the post, but his companion was only mildly interested. He started to lecture him on how the post was the jumping off point for the "Army of the West" that conquered New Mexico. He also talked about how the post was a focal point for numerous military expeditions that were led by such notable men as Captain Bennett Riley, who provided the first military escort of caravans over the Sante Fe Trail in 1829, and by Captain Henry Dodge, who marched up the Platte River to the Rocky Mountains. "And now what will the fort be doin'?" asked Jesse, trying to be obliging to Nate's explanations.

"Well, de post is now an ord'ance ars'nal for all military encampments west of de Missouri, and now . . ." Nate had a huge grin on his face, "Fort Leavenworth will be the trainin' site fo' the Tenth."

Jesse was amazed that Nate's behavior became almost boyish the moment the steamer prepared to dock. For the sergeant major, born a slave and who toiled for the first twenty years of his life in the stifling southern Louisiana sun under the shadow of the lash, the sights and sounds of the docks of Fort Leavenworth invigorated him. Nate Gordon had returned to his true element.

Nate was not only familiar with the post, the river docks, and the town, but delighted in inhaling the aromas that filled the air and listening to the sounds of human energy that made the fort the epitome of the American frontier. He felt totally at ease walking among the Indians, trappers, prospectors, teamsters, mule skinners, tradesmen, scouts, and newly freed blacks and half-breeds that thronged in the dusty streets and riverfront. He even smiled at some of the drunks who staggered and bellowed—after all, this was the frontier, and it was still open country for all.

He loved watching immigrant families in their overloaded covered wagons heading West. He noticed that the faces of the men and children were full of excitement with the prospect of adventure in a new land, while the older women looked apprehensive. The variety of people who stopped at Fort Leavenworth on their way West possessed vigor and a sense of purpose that impressed him. Whether they were mule skinners spitting huge wads of spent tobacco in the dirt as they told lewd jokes, or burly freighters tightening ropes on their huge bull trains, or wagon masters screaming at greenhorn immigrants to get their wagons in line, Nate felt a sense of comradeship with these people.

As the two noncoms made their way toward the post, they passed two scouts who were dismounted from their big mules and talking loudly between themselves. Nate liked the look of the mules. They were big and healthy-looking animals. When he was a slave he enjoyed working with the mules that were on the plantation. He found them more intelligent and durable than horses. Mas'a Hammond used them to haul heavy loads in his wagons and Nate, being the best man on the plantation in handling horses and mules, was always assigned the responsibility of overseeing and driving the mules. Nate whispered to Jesse that he wanted to eavesdrop on the two plainsmen's conversation. With the exception of half-breeds and Indians, he knew that scouts always had the latest information on events occurring on the frontier.

Nate had seen many burly scouts when he was previously at Fort Leavenworth, but somehow he thought that these two men seemed different. They appeared to have a genuine quality of frontier seasoning that made them stand out even in such a diverse place as the river docks of Fort Leavenworth. Nate could not help but notice how these two scouts were dressed and the manner in which they talked as they stood next to their well-behaved mules. Their accoutrements, designed for living on the frontier, were equally impressive. Their long rifles, side arms, knives, and saddles were all visible, and one of the scouts had a panting, mangy dog sitting quietly at his side as his long tongue hung from his mouth.

This particular scout was over six feet, well-proportioned, and had a dark full beard and mustache that covered his entire face below his nose. He was also filthy. His long, brown, curly hair drooped over his shoulders and it became clear to Nate that this man had not seen a comb or a bar of soap in months. He was cradling a .58-caliber converted 1865 breech loading Springfield rifle and Nate noticed that his coat, which was casually draped over the altered McClellan saddle, was of U.S. Army issue because of the color, length, and circular cape. He was wearing long boots and buckskin paints, and Nate particularly liked the plainsman's blouse which had short fringes on the back and front of his shoulders and underarms. His well-worn sombrero was slightly cocked to the left and he was puffing on a briarwood pipe at full blast while he listened to his equally tall companion.

"I know fer sure, California. It was Roman Nose an' his thievin' Cheyenne Dog Soldier raidin' party dat stole the stage stock at Pond Creek Station," exclaimed William, "Medicine Bill" Comstock.

I 'gree," responded California Joe, still blasting on his pipe. "I believe dem savages are gettin' bolder all the time. The Seventh Cavalry got men kilt and wounded in full view of Fort Wallace!"

"And the dead fell into the hands of the Cheyennes," interrupted Medicine Bill. "You should have seen how the troopers looked af'er them Injuns got through carvin' them up."

Nate had heard about the formidable scout, William "Medicine Bill" Comstock. He knew that he was chief of scouts for Custer's Seventh Cavalry. Nate noticed that like California Joe, he also wore a wide hat, but the front brim was creased backward, fully revealing his dark wavy mustache. Unlike California Joe however, Nate observed that Medicine Bill was dressed cleanly and appeared to be a man of strong fiber. Nate had read in the newspapers that Medicine Bill was considered a professional, who did not drink on the job as his friend, California Joe, always did. Nate liked Comstock's black velvet suit and the way his unbuttoned coat hung on his shoulders and how his trousers were thrust into well-worn polished black boots. Nate remembered reading a quote from Custer in which the boy-general considered him the best scout on the plains, and that the plainsman was not only familiar with every strip of timber, water-course and divide for hundreds of miles, but a superb horseman and hunter. Custer called him fearless in the face of danger and an excellent tracker who knew the customs and languages of all the Central Plains Indian tribes.

"That's what happens to green troopers, Comstock." California Joe paused to take a pull on his pipe, then with a glee in his eye, smiled and winked at Medicine Bill.

"Poor Custer. I think the pretty boy-general is slowly figurin' out that Injuns don't fight like whites."

"An' de plains ain't Virginie!" added Comstock.

"An't dat a dead mortal sin," jested California Joe, laughing.

While the men laughed, Nate knew that they had caught the attention of California Joe when the dirty scout's boozed-laden eyes met Nate's. California was bemused by the sight of this coal black Yankee dressed in blue wool in the June heat. He felt like saying something insulting but restrained himself and pulled on his pipe so intensely that Nate could not help but see the red glow of burning tobacco in the bowl. For a moment, there was tension in the air as the four men starred at each other in silence.

"You boys lookin' fer dat tar baby cav'ry reg'ment at the post?" blurted California Joe, chuckling. The curved stem of his briarwood pipe was lodged in between his front teeth, and whenever he opened his mouth, one could see his yellow stained teeth due to his incessant habit of smoking "tabacky."

Nate moved closer to the two scouts and gave them a casual salute. Although both Comstock and California Joe were about six feet tall, Nate towered slightly over the both of them.

"No, sir! I know de fort." Nate paused, then grinned. "And I know de commanding officer of de Tenth Cavalry Regiment."

"An' you're a mighty fancy sergeant," joked California Joe as he stared at Nate's uniform and wide chevrons. "You boys think you're up to fightin' de Cheyenne, Arapaho? Or dem bastards, de Sioux?"

"We will be! Soon enough," said Jesse as he stepped next to Nate and faced the two scouts. Jesse was also taller than the two plainsmen. "As long as we're givin' the opportunity to fight," he added, looking straight down into Medicine Bill's eyes.

There was again a moment of awkward silence among the men until Comstock pointed his braided rawhide quirt at Nate and Jesse.

"You boys are all right," said Comstock as he nodded his head. "But bein' newcomers here, I hope dat you'll be smarter dan dat *green* Lootenint Kidder."

Nate did not understand what Comstock meant. Who was Lieutenant Kidder?

"Beggin' your pardon, sir, who is Lieutenant Kidder?" asked Nate, perplexed.

"You mean who *was* Lootenint Kidder?" laughed California Joe while his pipe remained wedged in between his front teeth.

Nate could smell the foulness of the scout's body odor. In addition, California Joe's breath reeked from tobacco and whiskey. He stank so much that Nate had to exert considerable effort not to reveal his disgust. He placed his hand over his nose and started to breathe from his mouth.

Comstock was only too eager to elaborate on the fate of Lieutenant Kidder and his company.

"Well, twelve green troopers were massa-creed next to Fort Wallace trail. Dey were ordered to deliver dispatches to de fort when Pawnee-Killer and his band rattlesnaked de twelve men and de lootenint. I was with General Custer when we found the remains."

"What happened?" inquired Jesse as if he were a little boy asking his grandfather to tell him the rest of the story.

"Lootenint Kidder was jest a boy. This was his first scoutin' an' his men were all green an' young. The way I figure . . . dem boys never had a chance. We found the bodies in a circle . . . all stripped of clothing and hacked as if dey were hogs. The corpses were so badly mutilated that we couldn't even identify the lootenint!" Jesse's eyes became huge and his smile turned into a frown as he became more and more repelled by Medicine Bill's narration of the Kidder Massacre. Although intrigued, Nate's face showed no signs of expression as he listened. Comstock noticed that his narrative interested the two willing listeners and started to depict the scene more graphically. "Each man was scalped, an' thar heads were bashed in with their noses hacked off."

Comstock noticed that his story was scaring Jesse, so he delighted in continuing with the details of the massacre, but before he could continue, California Joe looked at Jesse and blurted out laughing. "Why, you look like you're turnin' white, Sergeant!"

"Dare more to tell . . ." interrupted Comstock. "Many of the troopers in Kidder's command were in piles of ashes . . . *Burnt alive!*" Comstock enjoyed emphasizing the last two words as if he were trying to scare a bunch of children. By now, Nate had noticed that Jesse started to look sick and seemed to experience difficulties keeping his morning coffee from rising to his mouth. Comstock took advantage of this and pressed on.

"Each butchered trooper had twixt twenty to fifty arrows shot into their bodies... Why, they looked like a bunch of giant *porcupines!*" California Joe laughed at Comstock's last description and slapped the flanks of his mule as his dog barked several times in approval. Medicine Bill waited for his grisly friend to stop laughing before he continued. "What's more, we found hands, private parts, and brains on top of rocks and in the tall grass...."

"*Ouwe*," hooted California Joe. "*Shit... if I's didn't know better, jist listin' to ya, Comstock, would make my asshole twitch like a beaver trap.*"

Jesse started to gag. He pressed his right fist over his lips and tried to hold back what was fast rising from his stomach. He bolted from the group and darted down behind a nearby building to take care of the problem. Nate was bemused that Jesse was revolted by the description of the corpses' condition while he was not really bothered by these graphic details. During the war, he saw men ripped in half by canister or blown to pieces by gunfire. He also knew all to well how cruel a fellow human being be to another, especially if he or she is of a different race. It would take a lot more than just a good story by this scout to make him lose his coffee.

"Did the men put up a fight?" Nate asked solemnly as he crossed his arms against his chest.

"Oh, we found a whole bunch of spent rim fire shells all 'round de circle whare the boys died," Comstock replied matter-of-factly. "I expect that they did put up a fight... probably till the very end."

"Dey might have put up a fight, Comstock, but I doubt that they kilt any Injuns. Dem green troopers probably panicked an' de fight didn't last longer dan a man havin' a shot a rye at de saloon," ridiculed California Joe as he pulled a pint of whiskey from one of his saddlebags. He feared that the thrill of his intoxication was wearing off, so he uncorked the bottle and took a big gulp of the whiskey.

Comstock ignored California Joe's last statement. Instead, he turned to Nate—Medicine Bill wanted to teach Nate and Jesse a lesson.

"What you boys have to learn out hare is dat, never be took alive by Injuns if you know dat de situation is hopeless. Better to keep de last bullet for yourself, or you might find yourself burnt alive like dem poor cav'ry troopers. An' another piece of advice I am goin' give you sergeant, is that if I know anything, it's Injuns. I know jest how they'll do anything and when they'll take to it. You see, Injun huntin' and Injun fightin' is a trade all by itself, and like any other business, a man has to know what he's about, or ef he don't, he can't make a livin' at it. My experience with you army folks has always been that the youngsters among ye think they know the most, an' you couldn't tell them nothin'. Half of 'em can't tell the difference twixt a trail made by a huntin' party or made by a war party to save their necks! What's more, they can't tell the difference twixt a buck ridin' a pony or if it might be a squaw. Out hare, either you larn quick or you're dead!"

Col. Benjamim H. Grierson was running his index finger along the scar that ran down his right cheek. His face was heavily bearded so only the very tip of the old injury which was caused when a pony kicked him in the face was visible. The kick left a nasty disfigurement that earned him the nickname "Scar Face"

Colonel Grierson became a hero during the war. He was a small-town music teacher in Illinois when the Confederacy opened fire on Fort Sumter. An ardent admirer of Abe Lincoln, and firm abolitionist, he immediately volunteered his services to the Union. Much to his surprise, he was offered a commission as a major of the Sixth Illinois Cavalry, and rose to be a brevet major general of volunteers by the time General Lee had surrendered at Appomattox.

Although skittish of horses, his name became a household word throughout the north after his daring military raid into the heartland of Mississippi and Louisiana. With three hundred men, Grierson and his elite cavalry traveled six hundred miles in sixteen days eluding Confederate cavalry while disrupting rebel supply lines and forcing them to divert hundreds of men from the defense of Vicksburg. His raid facilitated Grant to capture the Gibraltar of the South and both Sherman and Grant commented that Grierson's raid was the most brilliant cavalry expedition of the war. The South had dashing Jeb Stuart, but the Yankees had Scar Face Ben Grierson.

When the Tenth Cavalry Regiment was formed, both Grant and Sherman thought that the best man to train and lead this new regiment was none other than Col. Benjamin Grierson. He accepted the commission and became determined to make the Tenth Negro Cavalry one of the best outfits in the United States Army. Being an abolitionist, he held a burning conviction that his role was to help the black race attain their full potential. He believed they could be completely assimilated within American society as equal citizens. Grierson believed that the army was an excellent avenue in achieving these goals. He would place a high priority in promoting literacy and religion among his men, and insisted that his junior officers would treat the men as United States soldiers and nothing less.

By the time Nate and Jesse arrived at the garrison, most of the soldiers were in the process of completing their breakfast and were streaming out of the mess hall toward their morning duties. At the northwest corner of the parade ground, several infantry and cavalry companies were wearing dress uniforms and preparing to pass on review in front of Fort Leavenworth's commander, Gen. William Hoffman and his staff.

Sgt. Jesse Randolph was amazed at the sight of the fort's size, the tidiness of its parade ground, and solid wooden construction of the garrison's buildings. As the two noncoms walked briskly on the east side of the parade ground where the handsomely built dragoon barracks with their deep verandahs and inviting porches were neatly lined up in a long row, Jesse became suddenly enthusiastic.

"Is the regiment quartered in these kinds of houses?" inquired Jesse hopefully.

"Boy . . . how man' times I've gots to tell you that the black soldiers ain't gonna be treated like the whites. Last I heard, the men of the Tenth were quartered in the worst part on the post."

———

Nate was thinking about the commander of Fort Leavenworth and how he had ordered that the Tenth Cavalry be lodged on the most inhospitable spot at the fort. The ground was on the lowest part of the post where conditions resembled a swamp that resulted in many of the recruits becoming infected with pneumonia. Nate reflected how the garrison's commander, General Hoffman, an ardent and fiery racist, did everything in his power to make Colonel Grierson's mission impossible. Only a few nights before on the paddle wheel steamer, Nate had written in his journal his impressions of Hoffman the last time he was at Leavenworth.

A master of the petty, and void of all human compassion, the general prided himself in his frugality and total obedience to the "book."

During the last year of the war, he was superintendent of Elmira Prison in western New York, where he ruled with an iron fist. The prisoner-of-war camp became one of the deadliest places for captured Confederate soldiers to spend their captivity. By the end of the war, nearly three thousand Rebs had perished due to horrendous sanitation conditions, lack of shelter, clothing, and no medical attention. The man prided himself in returning most of the money to the federal government that was allocated to him to run the prison. Now ... I have no love for those men I fought against during the war, but they were real fighters and they did not deserve to be treated like animals! Hoffman had boasted loudly that he had saved the government a needless financial burden at the expense of his internees. Never met a man like Hoffman, who feels absolutely no remorse.

The commander of Fort Leavenworth has even more contempt for my race than he has for Southerners, and especially Negroes who want to become soldiers in the United States Army. He considers Colonel Grierson along with those white officers who volunteered to train and lead the Tenth as unworthy, and felt a deep disdain toward them. He insisted that Colonel Grierson keep his "niggers" at least fifteen yards away from his white troops, and denied permission for the regiment to parade. Hoffman persistently badgered Grierson with complaints about improper training procedures and interfered with the commander in his attempts to provide good horses and equipment for the regiment.

Vindictive and hateful, General Hoffman is the antithesis of Colonel Grierson in every way. The former, who never led men in the field, was an individual who obsessively followed the book of military regulations, and took pleasure engaging in contemptible trivial warfare with colleagues who he envied. The latter, (Grierson) a national hero, is a philosopher-warrior who gained respect by his actions as an able field commander and believes in the inherent goodness of all mankind.

What I have learned and thus concluded, is that the daily friction between Grierson and Hoffman symbolizes the characteristics of turmoil that the army is experiencing since the war. Officers such as Hoffman were typical of the army before the war where a small, narrow-minded officer corps existed and practiced a chivalric code of behavior. During the war, I remember a captain explaining to me that the works of Sir Walter Raleigh influenced the thinking among these officers, and an entrenched "we-take-care-of-our-own" esprit-de-corps developed that resisted change, or any alteration in tradition that would threaten the status quo.

The war radically transformed this officer corps. Unlike General Hoffman, tens of thousands of men from all kinds of different backgrounds and origins rose through the ranks based on merit in the field of battle. Although social transformation and the horrific realities of the war destroyed the "knightly ideal" that I was told about, senior officers, and especially those who saw no action and spent most of the war behind a desk, such as Hoffman did, resisted any change that would alter the military as they knew it before the war.

As Nate and Jesse were on their way to report to Colonel Grierson at regimental headquarters, they came upon the parade ground and noticed that various infantry and cavalry regiments were attired in full dress uniform and preparing to pass on review in front of Fort Leavenworth's commander. General Hoffman and his staff were seated in the reviewing stand waiting for the proceeding to commence. In the southeast corner of the parade ground, Nate noticed several companies of black troopers standing by their mounts.

"Over there Jess," said Nate as he pointed in the direction where the black cavalrymen were assembled. "Troopers of the Tenth Cavalry preparin' to pass on review."

They decided to make their way toward the southeast corner of the parade ground when Colonel Grierson and his staff appeared dressed in full dress uniform. Nate marched up to his commanding officer and saluted. He was finally with his regiment and he was ready to serve it.

"Sergeant Major Gordon and First Sergeant Randolph reportin' for duty, *sir*."

"Very well, Sergeant Major," said Grierson returning the salute. "At ease." Although Grierson looked pleased to see Nate, his mind seemed completely preoccupied with other matters. Grierson looked at Jesse and then smiled. "I have anticipated your arrival, First Sergeant. Sergeant Major Gordon has written me about you, and I can assure you that your services will be needed in this regiment."

"Yes sir," replied Jesse, standing at attention. "I will do my duty, sir."

"That's all I ask from my men, Sergeant," replied the colonel as he slipped on his dress gauntlets. He then took a deep breath and spoke in a concerned voice. "The commander of the post has denied us permission to parade with the other regiments. I am determined that he will not deny us that right today."

Gen. William Hoffman was sitting in the middle of the reviewing stand with his staff. His adjutant, a young lieutenant fresh out of West Point climbed the few steps up to the reviewing stand and approached Hoffman.

"Sir, beg to report."

"At ease, Lieutenant; what is it now?" responded the general, rather bored.

"The Tenth Cavalry is preparing to march in the dress parade, contrary to your explicit orders, sir."

Hoffman slapped his spotless white gauntlets which he had been holding in his right hand and cuffed them against his knee as his face became red with rage.

"Blast that upstart colonel of that nigger regiment!" cursed Hoffman, startling some of his staff and junior officers. "Lieutenant, tell him to report to me at once."

"Sir," replied the young adjutant. He saluted and marched off the reviewing stand and walked rigidly across the parade ground as if he were a toy soldier. He halted when he arrived in Grierson's presence and repeated what his commanding officer told him.

"Very well Lieutenant, lead on." Grierson knew that this day would come. As he marched across the field, he thought about Hoffman's deliberate policy of denying his troopers equal treatment with white regiments and circumventing horses, equipment, and supplies from his men. His behavior not only jeopardized his mission and goals for the regiment, but was entirely against what the United States Congress, the president, and Generals Sherman and Grant had approved. Grierson was determined that his men were going to march in this in this dress parade, and he was prepared to confront the senior commanding officer of Fort Leavenworth.

From General Hoffman's point of view, Colonel Grierson and his regiment of darkies were a disgrace. Grierson was a simple music teacher who did not go to West Point, and his men, subhuman. They represented an affront to the purity of the of the United States Army, and he was resolved to do everything in his power to see that Grierson and his black troopers failed. He was not going to be a part of the destruction and debasement of the army that he had known before 1861, and who had won the war.

As Grierson approached the viewing stand, Hoffman was eyeing him. He turned to his staff and slyly commented, "I am going to take this brevet major general of volunteers down a peg or two. This is the regular army now, by God, and I'll be damned if this man will run roughshod over my orders."

"You requested my presence, sir?" Grierson came to attention and saluted.

Hoffman grudgingly returned the salute and immediately commenced to lay into Grierson. "How many times do I have to tell you that I want your niggers at least fifteen yards away from my soldiers, and preferably downwind, *mister!*" Hoffamn's face was becoming a deep crimson like the face of an old drunk. "And why are your men gathered in parade dress? I hope you are not contemplating that you will march in the parade..."

Grierson was quick to cut him off. "General, with all due respect, I have every right to march my men in front of this reviewing stand. I will not be denied that right. My men have earned this privilege in spite of your meddling..."

"Meddling, Colonel? As senior commanding officer of this post, I have the power to run this fort as I see fit," retorted Hoffman, almost getting up from his comfortable chair.

"No, sir! You do not have the right to circumvent what the United States Congress and the president of the United States has signed into law. The Tenth Cavalry is a legitimate regiment and is hereby entitled to the same privileges and honors of any other outfit in the United States Army."

"*Entitled? Privileges? Honor?*" scoffed Hoffman, as he leaned his head forward as if he were a toad preparing to croak. "You mean to tell me that these monkeys who have come down from the trees, are soldiers?" Some of the staff officers started to chuckle, but Grierson remained unfazed.

"Unlike you, sir, who spent the war riding a chair and starving Confederate prisoners, some of these so-called *monkeys*, served their country in the war with honor and distinction and thousands of them paid the ultimate price. General, you are the commander of Fort Leavenworth, not Elmira Prison!"

Some of the staff officers who had been chuckling now coughed with nervousness upon hearing Grierson's retort. This infuriated Hoffman. He knew he could lose the respect of his junior officers unless he reversed this verbal confrontation in his favor.

"It was my duty to kill as many of the enemy while I was superintendent of Elmira as it was your duty to kill Secesh on the field. Although I, sir, was much more effective! And as for your darkies, Colonel, the parade field is not at your disposal if I order it so." Hoffman finally got up from his chair and peered down at Grierson from the railing of the viewing stand as if he were the schoolmaster and Grierson the unruly student that needed to be disciplined. "And I order that your troops remain at parade dress and that is final, Colonel."

Grierson had enough. He realized that trying to reason with Hoffman was a waste of time, and he disliked senseless verbal confrontation. He decided that his efforts were better spent elsewhere rather than reasoning with this philistine. Grierson gave the general a hard stare and gently shook his head as if he pitied the man for his ignorance and pettiness. He turned on his heels and reversed face without saluting, a breech in military procedure, and returned to his men taking his time walking off the field.

Nate and Jesse were ordered to get some breakfast and then report to regimental headquarters. The mess area was covered by a patchwork of different discarded army wagon canvases and tents that leaked when it rained and became very hot during the day. When Colonel Grierson asked General Hoffman for a decent building at the fort that could be converted into a mess hall for his men, the general simply replied in an astonished manner, "Why do you want a building for your Africans? They spent their whole lives barefoot and sleeping outside, so why should I make available a structure for your niggers when white troops need them more?"

Nevertheless, the men of the Tenth did the best they could under the circumstances. They repaired and made mess furniture, so they would be comfortably seated, and Grierson managed to acquire decent food most of the time and the black cooks were far superior and imaginative in making do with what they had than their white counterparts.

This particular morning, the men were enjoying a bonanza of culinary delight. Fresh biscuits soaked in molasses served with ham and eggs. One of the sergeants had purchased a boar past his prime from a pig man in town and smuggled the swine back to the regiment where the cooks promptly slaughtered it. They hooked the large hams and hung them from the top of large oak barrels and slowly smoked them for a couple of days.

While Nate was smoking his pipe after eating his breakfast, Jesse was on his third helping. As a consequence of losing his breakfast in the dirt while Comstock was recounting the ghoulish details of the Kidder Massacre, his stomach was empty and when he smelled the hams, his appetite returned.

As Jesse was wolfing down his third helping of biscuits, Nate noticed that a perfectly well-dressed private had entered the mess area and looked as if he was searching for someone. Nate rose from his chair and shouted at the private,

"Lookin' for me, Private?"

The enlisted man slowly turned to Nate and made his way through the tables and chairs. When he came close enough, he stood at attention.

"Sergeant Major, Colonel Grierson sent me to brin' you and de first sergeant to regimental headquarters." The private looked at Jesse, who was still eating in a ravenous manner and then added, "As soon as you're finished eatin'."

"What's your name, Private?" inquired Nate, a little intrigued by this enlisted man's demeanor.

"Private Reuben Waller, Sergeant Major." He spoke in a loud, clear, confident voice that impressed Nate. His uniform was a perfect fit, not that that in itself was anything unusual for black soldiers. Nate knew through much experience, that most of the uniforms that negro troops received, as was the case during the war, were of the worst quality and fitted the men poorly. The black soldiers however, were so proud of the fact they were part of the United States Army, that they went to great lengths to tailor their uniforms so they would fit perfectly. As a result, Nate thought that many black regiments looked more professional than the white ones. What got Nate's attention however, was the way this private wore his blouse, trousers, forage cap, and leather accoutrements. His boots were of good quality and polished to a high gloss finish. They were not military-issue. His forage cap fit him well and most noticeable was the manner in which he wore his uniform. He seemed completely at ease, as if he might have been in the army for a long time or familiar with military dress and procedure. If this was the case, why was he just a private and not perhaps, at least a corporal?

"Been in the army long, Private Waller?" Nate sat back down in his chair, still puffing on his briarwood pipe.

"Not in this army, Sergeant Major." For a moment, Nate looked a little puzzled, then he thought he knew what Reuben Waller meant.

"You were in the Union army as an infantry man durin' the war, is that what you mean, Private?".

"No Sergeant Major, I wasn't in the Union army durin' the war."

Again Nate became puzzled. He fixed his gaze on Private Waller and puffed on his pipe more vigorously. Jesse meanwhile was still wolfing down the remaining biscuits on his plate while remaining oblivious to the conversation.

"Where you from boy?" Nate inquired in an authoritative tone.

"I's born in Ten'see."

"You were a free man 'fore the war, Private Waller?"

"No, Sergeant Major, I's a slave durin' the war, but I 'companied my master who was a Confederate general in Bedford Forrest's outfit."

Jesse immediately stopped eating and Nate nearly choked on the smoke from his pipe upon hearing the name of Bedford Forrest. Seizing the moment, Reuben Waller continued.

"Yes, Sergeant Major, I served my master faithfully durin' the war. I was with him for ov'r thirty engagements and I saw what happened at Fort Pillow . . . when our men ov'ran the fort."

"You fought for the slavers 'gainst our own people?" inquired Jesse as he put down his fork with complete astonishment.

"I served my master who was a general in the Confederate army." Reuben Waller paused, then said softly, "He was a good man, and he always done right by me. While I served him, I became fond of the horse soldiers, so when the war ended, I decided to enlist in the Tenth."

"What do you mean when you said *our men* ov'ran Fort Pillow?"

Jesse was trying to understand why Reuben Waller would put himself in the same camp as the Confederates. Hundreds of black Union soldiers were shot and bayoneted after they had surrendered, so Jesse was bordering on outrage.

Nate was impressed that Pvt. Reuben Waller remained composed and at attention. Private Waller paused for a moment, contemplating how best to respond to Jesse's query.

"Like I said, Sergeant. My master was good to me. He always talked 'bout us an' we and *them* meanin' the Yankees, and how the war was not 'bout slavery, but 'bout Yankee aggression 'gainst free states and that we are family, and gots to stick together, and that afta the war, he was goin' give me my freedom . . ."

"Well. We'll never know, will we, Private?" interrupted Nate as he continued puffing on his pipe.

"What you mean, Sergeant Major?" responded Reuben Waller, a little confounded.

"He's means, your *mas'a, boy!*" bellowed Jesse. "The sergeant major means that we'll never find out if that Secesh mas'a general of yours would have *ever* given you your freedom, 'cause *we* won the war, and not the slave states," added Jesse firmly, as he pointed at himself and then at Nate.

There was a moment of awkward silence. Nate noticed the tension rising in his friend's body, so he tapped the bowl of his briarwood pipe on the heel of his right boot that was crossed over his left and emptied his pipe. "Well Private, what you waitin' fo'? Can't keep the colonel waiting."

Col. Benjamin Grierson and Cpt. Louis Carpenter were conversing at regimental headquarters. Grierson, still reeling from the verbal confrontation he had earlier with General Hoffman, was trying to make sense of what happened and decide what to do next in getting the Tenth equipped and trained in order to move out of Fort Leavenworth.

"I am at my wit's end, Louis. That officer . . ." Grierson paused for

270

a moment as if he were enjoying this brief moment of silent contempt for the commander of Fort Leavenworth. "Hoffman is making it completely impossible for me to accomplish our mission. I have written department headquarters, but I sense that they will not render us much assistance."

"I am afraid that we are on our own, Ben. We will just have to make do for now. But, in the end, we will prevail," assured Captain Carpenter, as he crossed his legs and shifted in his chair while sitting across from Grierson's desk.

Cpt. Louis H. Carpenter, line officer for the Tenth Cavalry, had joined the regiment in September, 1866. Like Benjamin Grierson, he was a born leader and possessed qualities that made him an excellent cavalry officer without the benefit of attending West Point. These kinds of men, along with Wesley Merritt and George Custer, gained their rank and won their medals through merit, courage, and audacity. Louis Carpenter, originally from New Jersey, enlisted as a private in the army when the war broke out. He rose through the ranks to become a lieutenant colonel in the Fifth Cavalry and received brevets for gallantry at Gettysburg and Winchester.

"We are not getting the support necessary to equip and train the regiment. Our horses are *third rate*, and we still lack Spencers and Sharps carbines and other essentials to equip the regiment for service on the frontier." Grierson paused for a moment and nodded his head as if someone had just told him some disturbing news. "Louis, do you sense that we are abandoned?"

"Perhaps abandoned is not the most accurate description in deciphering the current state of affairs," responded Carpenter in a hopeful tone of voice. He realized that Grierson was tired of the shenanigans that were being played on him and the Tenth, but Carpenter remained optimistic that the future for the regiment would be bright and that current circumstances were just temporary.

"Ben, this regiment, along with the Ninth Cavalry and the four Negro infantry regiments that were established by congress with the full support of Generals Grant and Sherman, will not be defeated by the likes of General Hoffman and his anachronistic beliefs."

"What about the West Pointers?" retorted Grierson. "Do you really think that they believe in our cause of elevating the black man to full citizenship?"

"Sherman and Grant are West Pointers," responded Carpenter, reminding Grierson that not all West Pointers were entrenched in a past that no longer exists.

"Nevertheless, I am now determined to get the regiment out of Fort Leavenworth double-quick even if some of the companies are not fully equipped." Grierson snapped out of his melancholy mood and seized the pen from its ink jar and started to write on a fresh sheet of paper. "In addition, Louis, I am now going to issue orders that will bring an end to the racial descriptions and characterizations made by my officers in reference to the men. From this day forward, no officer in the Tenth Cavalry will refer to their men other than as soldiers of the United States Army."

"Are you referring to the terms colored and Negro?" inquired Carpenter, knowing full well what Grierson's answer would be.

"I mean that my men will no longer be referred to as Africans, darkies, tar babies, niggers, colored, blacks, or even Negroes." Grierson paused for a moment and confided to Carpenter, "Even I at times am guilty of this practice. When I write my wife, I use the term colored to describe my men." Grierson took a deep breath. "And I will have to change as well."

As Grierson signed the orders, Pvt. Reuben Waller knocked on the door. "Enter," said Grierson with expectation. He knew that Nate and First Sergeant Jesse Randolph were on their way.

The three soldiers entered, saluted, and stood at attention. Grierson raised himself from the writing table and told them to be at ease while he dismissed Private Waller.

"I presume that you observed this morning's events on the parade ground, so I think you have a good idea what we are facing here. In short, nothing less than impossible conditions. You, Sergeant Major, most of all," Grierson pointed to Nate, "are familiar with the problems that the Tenth and Ninth Regiments have encountered in acquiring horses and equipment. I have just received instructions from General Sherman that I have the discretion to deploy the troops to the frontier when I decide which companies are ready for active service. I will be assigning companies, D, E, and L to Indian Territory and the rest of the regiment will be stationed at various posts along the Smoking Hill Road to protect the workers who are building the Kansas Pacific Railroad and the settlers who are traveling West. You, Sergeant Major Gordon and you, First Sergeant Randolph will be transferred to Fort Hays and serve in company F." Grierson stood up from his chair and straightened his frock coat. "Are there any questions?"

Jesse felt a sense of anxiety overcome him. "Colonel, sir. We've . . . heard reports . . .'bout Indians attackin' settlers and spreadin' holy terror fo' hundreds of miles . . ."

"That is correct, First Sergeant Randolph," interrupted Grierson, matter-of-factly. He scratched his beard near where his scar was located and sat back down in his chair.

"When war broke out between the North and the South, the federal government pulled out most of the troops in the West. As a consequence, the situation on the Central Plains has deteriorated to the point of chaos. Thousands of horses and stock have been run off or stolen by hostile bands of Sioux, Cheyenne, and Arapaho and hundreds of settlers have been killed. Dozens of women and children have been captured and are held by these hostile bands under repugnant conditions. Railroad workers, surveyor teams, and military patrols have been ambushed and murdered, farms burnt to the ground, and the military along with local militia, has been powerless to reverse these events. Therefore, the situation is grave and the longer we wait to act, the greater the chances that Indian depravations will continue." Grierson paused and then inquired, "Now, are there any more questions?"

"Colonel, sir, this means that the Tenth will see action?" Nate was concerned that the regiment would be used for fatigue duty as this was frequently the situation for so many black soldiers during the war. He wanted to fight and not dig latrine ditches for white troops, or be relegated to minor duties unfit for fighting men.

"May I answer, sir?" Cpt. Louis Carpenter had remained a silent spectator during Grierson's briefing. The Civil War veteran now wanted to comment.

"Sergeant Major, the officers in this command will do everything in their power to be part of any military action against the hostile tribes. The frontier is vast and the military is overextended. In addition, congress is in a penny-pinching mood so we can expect very little help from even our own government. However . . ." Carpenter's face became tense and his eyes seemed to pierce the air like a bird of prey. "Make no mistake! Every able-bodied man will be needed if we are to force the hostiles back to their reservations and compel them to halt their attacks. I assure you, there will be enough glory for all."

Carpenter's little speech stirred Nate. It was exactly what he wanted to hear.

"Yes, sir. We'll be ready." For the second time during this day, Nate smiled.

Two

OTTOWA COUNTY, NORTH CENTRAL
KANSAS, SUMMER 1867

Mrs. Shaw was filling her pail with water from a creek that was a tributary of the Solomon River. The creek flowed near the crude sod house that Mrs. Shaw and her husband had constructed when they first arrived on the prairie a few years ago. Her younger sister, Mrs. Foster, was trying to light a fire in the hearth to start breakfast. She was seven months pregnant and had not been feeling well. This morning in particular she felt more nauseous and fatigued than usual and her ankles were so swollen that her shoes did not fit, forcing her to go barefoot. She was hoping that a little coffee would revive her.

Both sisters' husbands were on a hunting trip in the Blue Hills to kill game in order to provide their families with fresh meat in preparation for the long winter months that were only weeks away. Although Cheyenne depravations against whites had cost hundreds of lives ever since federal troops evacuated their garrisons in the spring of 1861 to fight the Rebs back East, the Shaw and Foster families, as was the situation with many settlers, had little choice but to remain on the prairie. Where would they go? They left the East after selling their farms at cut-rate prices and came West with just enough supplies for a few years at best. They lived on a subsistence level and one or two failed crops would mean complete ruination and homelessness. To abandon their struggling farms now after all the sacrifice and work and return East would be unthinkable even if there were problems with the Indians.

As she dipped her second bucket in the creek and watched the pail fill with water, she thought about her spouse who had been gone now for over two weeks with her sister's husband. All sorts of terrible thoughts traveled through her mind as she pondered various tragic possibilities. Had he become sick? Had his horse, Big Jim, become lame? Or were the two men simply lost? Maybe the mule that they had brought with them as a pack animal had died and they were experiencing problems bringing back the fresh meat. Mrs. Shaw was always concerned that her husband would have an accident with his hunting rifle. His older brother had fatally shot himself on the trip out West because his revolver accidentally discharged when the weapon was tucked in his pants fully cocked. She feared that her husband, who was also careless with guns, might have met the same fate and was bleeding to death somewhere in the hill country. The worst concern that Mrs. Shaw had was that her husband might have been ambushed by Indians. This terrified her the most. Every time the prospect of this occurring entered her mind however, she quickly shrugged her head and dismissed the possibility that her husband might have met some fiendish end at the hands of the "savages."

Cougar Eyes and his Cheyenne Dog Soldiers, the *Hotame-Ho' nehe* raiding party, were hiding about a quarter of a mile away in a deep ravine observing Mrs. Shaw and reconnoitering the area around the sod house. Like his namesake, Cougar Eyes was crouched behind a ravine as if he were a big cat stalking prey and stared patiently and intensely at his quarry, watching every movement. His face was entirely colored. The top half from the nose to his hairline was painted a deep black, while the bottom part was chalk white. Cougar Eyes' long hair was wrapped into two tight braids that hung against his chest, and he was dressed in a red-colored tunic with German silver armbands. His long black-and-white stripped breechclout was made from stroud cloth and his feet were adorned with beautiful white quilted moccasins. His war pony's head, a swift mustang with a white face, had a Mexican silver bridle and the animal's rump was painted with many coup markings.

The thirty-member-strong raiding party had a very good month ravaging the tiny settlements along the Solomon River Valley. For most of the summer, Cougar Eyes and his band spent their days killing settlers and immigrants. Whole families were wiped out and women folk, regardless of age, were swept away by the warriors into captivity which in most cases was worse for the fair-skinned white women and children than death. Kansas railroad workers a and surveyors were cut down as if they were jackrabbits or sage hens. The Cheyenne warriors particularly enjoyed running off stock, burning homesteads, and engaging in brutal, mass rapine. By mid-August, the raiding party had decided that one last good binge of stealing, burning, and killing along the Solomon River Valley before returning to camp in the Republican River Country of North West Kansas, would quench their thirst for the season.

Cougar Eyes possessed no remorse in his heart for the heinous activities he and his raiding Dog Soldiers had inflicted on whites. He was the leader of his particular warrior society and a survivor of the Sand Creek Massacre. Cougar Eyes' heart burned with revenge as his mind and spirit thought about the atrocities that were committed by the whites. He was just becoming a man when Colonel Chivington and his drunken cutthroat "Hundred Daysers" who made up the Colorado Volunteers, descended on his village, the encampment of Black Kettle's peaceful Northern Cheyennes. Although the tribe's chief, Black Kettle, was under the protection of the United States Army, the volunteers, thirsting for revenge against any Indian, peaceful or hostile that they held responsible for recent depredations, slaughtered hundreds of women and children. Their scalps, noses, ears, tongues, and fingers were sold on the streets of Denver along with Cheyenne private body parts such as breasts—converted into tit bags and scrotums stretched into humidors.

Cougar Eyes lost both sisters and he saw his baby nephew thrown up into the air by a blue coat and bayoneted as he came down. He also had witnessed his mother's stomach slashed open by a saber and her breasts slit off by several militia volunteers. One of his sisters was shot in the face while the other had her head blown off when Chivington ordered the howitzers to open fire on the village.

Cougar Eyes often felt a deep sense of guilt that he was unable to defend his family from the atrocities committed by the white men.

During the attack, he was told to leave the village along with some older braves to organize a pocket of resistance farther up the creek in order to draw away the attacking troops from the Cheyenne camp. The maneuver proved to be ineffectual and failed to halt the murder of women and children.

Ever since the Sand Creek Massacre, Cougar Eyes had sought revenge against the whites for what they did to his family and village. He was inducted into the Dog Soldiers' *Hotame-Ho' nehe* warrior society when he turned fifteen, and experienced the traditional ritual of initiation. This entailed having a dog rope which was eight feet long and made from a strip of tanned buffalo hide decorated with porcupine quills and eagle feathers, tied around his neck with the other end fastened to a stake which was firmly planted in the ground. This ritual was to test a warrior's abilities and to demonstrate his unflinching bravery in the face of the enemy by defending the small perimeter that extended as far as the dog rope would allow him to maneuver. He would give no ground, and die in the process if necessary. He earned his right to be a Dog Soldier when he participated in a raid against a Pawnee village. While his fellow Cheyenne braves were stealing the horses, Cougar Eyes planted his stake into the edge of the Pawnee camp and taunted his enemies to come out of their lodges and fight him like men rather than cower as if they were frightened squaws.

One young Pawnee warrior with an unusually high roach and long flowing scalp lock, and who was older than Cougar Eyes, took up the challenge and charged at him wielding a tomahawk while yelling at the top of his lungs, determined to split his enemy's head wide open. Cougar Eyes however, had trained for this very moment for months. His face was painted red and his head was adorned with a red and yellow fringed turbanlike headdress. He wore a hairpipe breastplate and a red breechclout made from stroud cloth. He was prepared to meet his attacker and defend his ground to the death. When the young Pawnee brave came within a few feet of the perimeter, Cougar Eyes grabbed the pommel of his hunting knife that was tucked in the back of his breechclout belt. The Pawnee youth swung at Cougar Eyes' head but the Cheyenne was able to duck and avoid the blow. He then plunged the knife into the hapless Pawnee's stomach and twisted the blade from left to right, ensuring that his victim would not recover from such a fatal wound. Cougar Eyes yelled in triumphant jubilation and raised his bloody knife in the air when a fellow Dog Man rode up on his war pony and pulled the stake that pinned the dog rope and drove him away with his quirt. Cheyenne tradition demanded that the only way Cougar Eyes could be excused from his dog rope ritual of meeting certain death was to be beaten back by a companion. He had now passed the supreme test for bravery and he became a *Hotame-Ho' nehe*, a Dog Soldier. Over the years, he distinguished himself in battle with the blue coats many times and he became the leader of his own warrior society. Now, he did not want to kill Pawnee, the *Ho' nehetane'es,* as much as he thirsted for white man's blood and property.

Mrs. Shaw finished filling the two pails of water and walked back with some difficulty to her small crudely built sod hut. She could smell the coffee slowly brewing and it pleased her to see the sliver of white smoke pouring out of the slightly crooked chimney. She was worried however, that in a week or so, the family would exhaust their supply of coffee beans and would also run out of meat. She started to think about her husband again.

"It's going to be another beautiful day," she said, smiling to her sister as she removed the faded red bonnet from her head, revealing a sunburned and heavily lined face. Both sisters seemed to have aged a decade after only a few years on the frontier. When they had first come West, their skin was milk white and their blond, almost golden hair, had not yet developed streaks of gray. After Mrs. Shaw had laid the pails down on the dirt floor, she ran her fingers through her thick blond hair, and made sure that her hair bun was secure and tight, otherwise insects who also lived in the ceiling and walls of the sod house would venture into her hair and attempt to take up residency. She sat down at the kitchen table near her sister who was looking more nauseous and anxious than usual.

"I remember when Mom gave you that bonnet," said Mrs. Foster wearily, with a slight smile on her face. Her pregnancy had not been easy. She had developed problems such as persistent vomiting and diarrhea.

"Yes," replied Mrs. Shaw as she stared at the bonnet which was lying on the table. "Mom was so concerned that I might ruin my fair complexion and that the sun would bake my head out here." Both women stared at each other and simultaneously chuckled as if they were innocent little girls again, but several years of harsh frontier existence had wiped out any illusion of any short-term relief from the burdens of living on the Central Plains. Both sisters knew that they were aging fast, and that their complexion as well as their backs, hands, and feet were being slowly deformed while any exposed skin was slowly being dried out by the back-breaking work of homesteading in a harsh climate where everything had to be made or grown on the place, or do without. They felt that their only prime consolation was the prospect of making as many babies as possible before they became barren. Then their offspring would hopefully, if some of the children survived, take care of them during their twilight years.

"You really should get some fresh air for yourself and the youngin' your carryin', Sis!" Mrs. Shaw was concerned for her younger sister. She really wanted her to have a successful birthing considering that she had already had two miscarriages.

"I know, I know," snapped Mrs. Foster in an irritated tone. "I . . . just don't feel like doin' anything." She paused for a moment and covered her mouth with her right hand as if she were going to throw up. After a few desperate moments, she managed to bring the nausea under control and speak. "I just feel sick and weary all the time, and whatever strength I can muster . . . has to be for doin' chores. . . ."

"I told you I can take care of things around here until our husbands get back so you'll have a smooth birthin' and get well again," interrupted Mrs. Shaw as she placed her heavily calloused left hand on her younger sister's shoulder in an attempt to lift her spirits.

"You goin' to have a healthy child," she insisted, in a tone that sounded as if she had some power to predict the future.

The pregnant sister nodded as she put down her chipped porcelain cup on the table. The coffee was so watered down and weak that it tasted as if it were something else.

"Then you must stay strong and save your strength for the birthin' which can be any day now," begged Mrs. Shaw, and her sister responded by meekly nodding and forcing a crooked smile on her sunburnt face.

When Cougar Eyes saw Mrs. Shaw enter the sod hut, he signaled the other Dog Soldiers that it was time to move on their objective. He leaped on his mustang and held his green shafted lance in the air and waited a few moments for his fellow braves to leap on top of their war ponies. He then gave the signal with his lance to advance on the farm. He dug his white moccasins into his mount's ribs and the beast lunged forward. The raiding party charged down the ravine toward the Shaw-Foster homestead.

The two sisters didn't hear the approaching Dog Soldiers. Not that it would have made any difference if they had, for the Cheyennes moved swiftly and appeared in the front yard within a minute.

Mrs. Foster was sipping her coffee when she saw a figure pass in front of the tiny sole window that was located on the south side of the sod hut. She froze and her eyebrows twitched in astonishment. She was still holding her chipped porcelain cup in her hand and was about to tell her sister that she thought she saw something move across the window when Cougar Eyes and three other Dog Soldiers burst through the door and entered the room. The abrupt intrusion by wildly painted and attired warriors with haunting headdresses, bearing tomahawks, war clubs, knives, and pistols, while very unnerving, was far exceeded by the loathsome staring of the Dog Men's cold eyes. Realizing that their worst fears had just materialized, and powerless to defend themselves, the two homestead women stopped breathing. They knew that there was nothing they could do except await eventual doom. While two Dog Soldiers started to roam around the room and rummage through the hut for food and search for articles that might interest them, the sisters seized each other and locked themselves in a tight, desperate embrace and held each other as if they were little children who thought they were going to be devoured by some monster.

Two big bucks, one with a green feather tucked in his hair in the back of his skull and wearing a silver pipe breastplate, and another whose face was painted red and who had initially entered the hut with Cougar Eyes, found the flour bin and started to devour its contents as if they had not eaten for several days. Within a few moments their torsos, faces, arms, and hands were covered in flour and the scarce substance scattered all over the cabin. After the warriors had enough flour, they started to seek other amusements. The brave with the green feather looked at Mrs. Foster. He gave her an intense stare as he licked the flour from his fingers and moved closer to where the sisters were sitting.

Cougar Eyes watched his companions rummage and loot the contents of the sod hut from the doorway. He did not participate in petty theft, especially when it came to whites. To kill the *Ve' ho' e* (whites), was entirely different than stealing items made by them. Cougar Eyes believed that he would be contaminated and lose his strong medicine if he used articles that came from the *Ve' ho' e* culture. He did however, enjoy stealing the horses of the *Ve' ho' e* and kidnapping their women and children to use them as slaves.

The Dog Soldier who was wearing the silver breastplate was now joined by his comrade who was wearing the green feather, and the two warriors started to pry Mrs. Foster loose from her older sister's arms. The white women started to scream hysterically as the two braves attempted to wrench the women apart. At first, they were not successful. They pulled at their skirts and arms, but the women only held each other more tightly. Finally, the two Dog Men managed to separate Mrs. Foster from her sister when the warrior with the green feather started to repeatedly strike Mrs. Shaw's arm with his long coup stick, forcing her to briefly release her grip and allowing them to drag her younger sister away from the table. Nevertheless, Mrs. Shaw lunged at her younger sister and managed to grab her forearm, preventing the two Dog Men from dragging Mrs. Foster outside. Cougar Eyes had had enough of this nonsense. This was taking entirely too long. He seized Mrs. Shaw's neck and pulled her up from the floor. He choked her until she released her hold on her sister and then started to whip her face with his quirt. After a few moments of this treatment, he slammed her back down into the kitchen chair and pulled out his war knife and placed the blade to her throat while he pulled her hair, forcing the head backward. As her chest heaved rapidly in fear and her body trembled, Mrs. Shaw realized that her neck would be slashed wide open if she did not remain still.

While Cougar Eyes held the blade of his skinning knife to Mrs. Shaw's throat, his two companions were dragging Mrs. Foster from the sod hut. As she screamed and sobbed, one brave held her arms while the other struggled with her legs and feet as she kicked wildly in an attempt to break free from her assailants. She kept pleading, "Please! I'm pregnant. Please, I'm going to have a baby!" Cougar Eyes was still pulling Mrs. Shaw's hair with such force that she feared that he was going to rip her entire scalp off. He then made her lie down and forced her face into the dirt near the door way as he placed his white beaded moccasin on her back. After Mrs. Foster was dragged outside, seven other warriors who were near their war ponies decided that they wanted to participate. They pulled out their skinning knives and began cutting away at her dress and undergarments as if they were removing a hide from a deer. Mrs. Shaw could hear her sister's screams and incessant pleas to the warriors to stop. She started to weep as she heard the horrifying sounds of her sister's clothing being ripped from her body and the hollering cries of joy and amusement from the Cheyenne Dog Men who were slapping her pink white flesh as if she were a plucked prairie chicken.

With the exception of Cougar Eyes, one by one, all of the thirty warriors in the raiding party took their turn raping and sodomizing the pregnant white woman over a four hour period. While two Dog Men restrained her, each brave decided to sexually abuse her in his own fashion. One Dog Soldier would mount her as if he were a dog mounting a bitch while another preferred to have her standing erect while he gleefully ravaged the hapless woman. One imaginative brave instructed four of his companions to suspend Mrs. Foster horizontally and spread eagle about four feet from the ground with her face facing the sun. He then dropped his crimson colored breechclout, revealing his huge organ and proceeded to merrily pump away with a huge grin on his face. After about an hour, her screams ceased, although her tormentors continued to sexually abuse her and whip her breasts and buttocks with their horse quirts, coup sticks, and bow lances, while her flesh slowly roasted in the hot Kansas sun. After about three hours, she found the strength to beg for water. Her pitiful requests were scoffed at by the Dog Soldiers and the rapine continued until she finally fell unconscious.

Some of the warriors who did not get an opportunity to ejaculate however, were not satisfied and they were disappointed that Mrs. Foster had passed out. They then turned to Cougar Eyes demanding that he give up Mrs. Shaw. Having no interest in this particular activity, Cougar Eyes obliged them. He wanted his fellow braves to satiate their lust for revenge toward the *Ve' ho' e* as those blue coats did when they murdered his family at Sand Creek. For a moment, he remembered the peaceful Cheyenne camp at Sand Creek and the tall lodge pole that flew the American flag. His chief, Black Kettle, was given the flag as a token of friendship and to serve as a guarantee that his village would never be attacked by the white man. He remembered how his mother screamed at the top of her lungs while pointing to the flag before her stomach was slashed open with a saber by a young drunk trooper. So why not give his brother warriors what they wanted? They all had relatives who were butchered by the *Ve' ho' e* at Sand Creek, so for the Dog Soldiers, this was simply revenge.

Cougar Eyes coerced Mrs. Shaw outside and tethered her to a hitching post. He forced her to lie on her elbows and knees as if she were a ewe or a sow. The rope was so tightly fastened around her neck that she thought she was going to choke. As she gagged and struggled to breathe, the bucks repeated the ritual of cutting her clothes off and taking turns mounting her. The Dog Soldiers would squat on the ground in a circle eating the food that they had stolen from the sod hut and patiently await their turn. One fat buck, who was wearing an open 1858 infantry frock coat with brass buttons and captain bars, was taking a long time to ejaculate. He made hideous grunts and his voice heaved with effort as he thrust his thighs forward and backward to move his penis back and forth and back and forth as if his organ was a well-oiled steam pump. Finally, the fat buck ejaculated and as he sighed in relief, let out a big fart that sounded like a duck call. This caused much laughter and amusement among the squatting Dog Soldiers and even Cougar Eyes chuckled.

Before Cougar Eyes and his band decided to retire from the home-stead and go home, he removed a carbine from above the hearth in the sod house that he had noticed earlier. As he was making his way toward the door, he saw a blue beaded necklace lying on the dirt floor. When the Dog Men first invaded the home they emptied every drawer and turned over every piece of furniture in search for items they deemed desirable. Consequently the surface of the floor was littered with flour, clothing, kitchen utensils, plates, spilled food, and personal items such as pictures and the blue necklace. The inexpensive piece of jewelry had been a gift from Mr. Shaw to his wife when he announced that the family was going to migrate to the Kansas frontier. Cougar Eyes hes-itated for a moment because he did not like to take items that were fabricated by whites. He thought for a moment and decided that maybe the necklace might have been made by non-whites, so he picked up the article and attached it around his neck. He then casually strutted outside and went up to Mrs. Shaw and pulled back her long bloody hair, looked into her face and empty eyes, and smiled as he pointed to the blue-beaded necklace.

As the sun slowly descended in the West, the evening sky lit up in bright scarlet, the Dog Men trotted their ponies loaded with booty and departed as quietly as they had arrived. They had left Mrs. Shaw sobbing, still tied to the post while her younger sister, Mrs. Foster, remained spread-eagle on the ground, wrists and ankles bound tightly by leather strips—unconscious.

Nate and Jesse were off the main trail toward Fort Hays from Leav-enworth. They had decided to make a slight detour north of the trail near the Solomon River to see if they could locate buffalo herds. Nate had only seen a few of them on his last stay at Leavenworth and after he explained to Jesse how he found them to be swift noble beasts his companion kept badgering him to wander off the trail to see if any of them could be located. Nate finally acquiesced and the two noncoms found themselves near the Shaw-Foster Homestead. Nate noticed that they were near people when he spotted a line of white smoke rising from a distant ravine climbing into the blue horizon.

"Let's go see if we can get some buttermilk at that farm," suggested Nate.

"Now, how do you know that line of smoke is a farm?" retorted Jesse. "Fo' all we knows, there could be hostiles makin' camp."

"Hostiles don't make fires in the open. Only non-Indians are foolish enough to make a fire where you can spot it fo' miles. I expect that there's a homestead beyond that last ravine 'cause it's near a creek, and that de folks have a cow."

Jesse smiled at the prospect of sipping fresh buttermilk and getting down from his horse for a little while. "*I'll race ya,*" he dug his spurs into his mount's flanks and charged in the direction of the line of smoke. Nate followed closely behind but he did not push his horse.

Mrs. Shaw was still tethered to the post and sobbing uncontrollably while her sister had completely passed out. The sun was slowly going down so the intensity of the heat and strong rays of light of the day were dissipating. When Jesse's horse galloped down the ravine and trotted into the front yard of the Shaw-Foster homestead, his thoughts about cool buttermilk disappeared. His first thought when he saw Mrs. Foster tied spread-eagle and Mrs. Shaw tethered like a dog was that they were not human bodies but slaughtered livestock because their white flesh was so burned and lacerated with cuts and bruises. He commanded his mount to halt and pushed back the visor on his kepi and squinted his eyes. When he finally realized that these two women were tied, stripped naked, and that one was at least eight months pregnant, his mouth opened in abhorrence.

When Nate trotted into the front yard he noticed Jesse sitting erect in his saddle, perfectly frozen as if he were a statue. "What's the matter, boy? Scare off the homesteaders with your ugly face?"

When Nate pulled up next to Jesse he heard loud sobbing coming from the post where Mrs. Shaw was tied. His eyes popped open in shock and he exclaimed, "Gawd al'mighty, Gawd al'mighty! What the hell?" Although horrified at the ghastly sight, Nate did not remain motionless in the saddle as Jesse was still doing. "*Come on. Help me, Jess,*" Nate ordered, as he leapt from his mount and proceeded to untie the bed blanket from the rear of his McClellan. "*Get the woman that's*

tied to the post. Cut her loose and . . . and use your bedroll to cover her up.
I'll get the one who is pregnant."

Jesse obeyed and removed his bedroll and took out his knife from
its sheath and quickly marched up to a sobbing Mrs. Shaw. He cut her
loose from the post and unfurled the wool blanket and gently placed
the article on her back. He saw that she was severely sunburned, and
that she had sustained hundreds of cuts and bruises all over her body.

While Jesse remained busy attending to Mrs. Shaw, Nate had cut
loose the four leather strips that were attached to stakes that had bound
Mrs. Foster to the ground spread-eagle. She also had suffered severe
sunburn on her face, neck, breasts, stomach, thighs, legs, and feet, and
Nate lovingly placed the blanket on her ravaged body. He noticed that
her lips were cracked from thirst and her hair looked like the tail of a
donkey that had just relieved itself. Nate ran back to his horse to fetch
his canteen and saw that Jesse was busy removing the tight leather
strips on Mrs. Shaw's hands. "How's her condition?"

"Can't get her to stop sobbin'," responded Jesse, frustrated that the
hysterical woman would not cease her wailing.

"Get your canteen and give her some water."

Nate returned to Mrs. Foster who remained unconscious and
started to try and revive her with water. He took out his bandanna and
poured some water out of the canteen on the article. He then took the
moist bandanna and started to touch Mrs. Foster's lips. While he was
trying to rejuvenate her, Nate heard Jesse yelling, "*No, ma'm . . . please
no.*" Nate turned around and saw that Mrs. Shaw had seized Jesse's
army Colt and had pulled back the hammer of the weapon. Jesse stood
back a few paces in front of her, hesitating to grab the weapon for fear
that the revolver might go off in his direction. Mrs. Shaw sobbed and
placed the barrel of the army Colt to her right temple. Jesse kept pleading, "Please, Ma'am, please. Don't do that . . . Put down the weapon."

The moment that Nate saw what was happening, he raced toward
Mrs. Shaw from her right side and hoped that it would give him
enough time to seize the revolver from her hands. Mrs. Shaw had her
index finger on the trigger and slowly squeezed it. The thunderous
crack of .44-caliber shot rang out just as Nate grabbed Mrs. Shaw's

wrist and turned the barrel of the army Colt toward the sky. Frustrated that her attempt at suicide had failed, the woman started to wail hysterically even louder than before demanding that she be allowed to kill herself because she had been violated and felt that her soul was permanently defiled. Mrs. Foster struggled with Nate in an attempt to break free, but he did not want to waste words. Nate opened the palm of his right hand and slapped the women with such force that she stopped crying and became still. Nate had never done this before, but when he was a boy on the plantation he saw a man slap a hysterical woman and the women had ceased wailing. He realized it was a questionable move, but under the circumstances he felt that he had no choice.

"Let's get these women into de soddie and keep them warm. The sun must have gotten to them and they been without water. They both comin' down with the fever."

Nate and Jesse spent the night nursemaiding the two hapless women in the soddie. Jesse made a large fire in the hearth and had taken care of the horses. Although Mrs. Shaw remained in a state of partial shock, she kept mumbling over and over again, "My blue necklace, my blue necklace, my blue necklace..." Her sister's condition however, remained grave. Mrs. Foster had regained consciousness in the middle of the night but her body was so burned by the sun that Nate kept thinking she looked like the boiled crawfish that he had devoured at Jean le Fou's cabin. She was shaking with a high fever and her face, breasts, and buttocks were raw. Nate felt helpless as the women kept repeating, "My baby? My baby!?"

"We gotta leave by first light and get these women to Hays," decided Nate as he turned to Jesse. They were standing near the hearth listening to the deep breathing of the two sisters who had finally gone to sleep, and Nate and Jesse were relieved.

"You think they can make it?" queried Jesse as he stared at the dying embers in the hearth.

"No choice. Can't stay here and play nursemaid. We got orders to report," Nate took a deep hit off of his pipe and reflected aloud. " 'Sides, they'll have a better chance at the fort. We will have to double-up on de horses and when de mounts become tired, dismount and walk while they remain in de saddle. With luck, we can be at Hays in two, three, days."

Early on in the second day on the trail toward Hays, they found Mrs. Shaw's husband wandering about aimlessly near the banks of the Solomon. Nate was the first to spot him. He was walking as if he was completely intoxicated while clutching his bloody left hand that was wrapped in a handkerchief. Half of his fingers on the hand had been shot off and the bottom of his right ear was blown off from a passing bullet which also slit open the side of his neck. The blood from that wound covered his right neck, shoulders, and side, rendering him a pathetic figure. He and his brother-in-law had been ambushed by a roaming band of renegade Pawnee, and Mrs. Foster's husband and been shot through the head at close range with a pistol. Mrs. Shaw's husband had managed to outrun the war party with his fast horse as bullets buzzed by him, but his brother-in-law had hesitated to let go of the mule that carried the meat that they had hunted and killed in the Blue Hills. As a result, the Pawnees rode up to him and shot the man out of his saddle. Mr. Shaw's horse sustained several wounds that caused the animal to expire within an hour after the ambush, so Mr. Shaw had spent three days hiding while trying to make his way back home.

"Hel . . . help, me!" he blurted out as he stumbled into Nate's horse as if he were a seasick passenger seizing the rail of a ship being tossed at sea. Nate dismounted and grabbed his canteen.

"Easy man, easy. Sit down an' let me look at your hand." After Mr. Shaw took a gulp of water from the canteen, Nate unfurled the makeshift bandage and saw that three of the wounded man's fingers were bloody stumps. As he was examining Mr. Shaw's wound, Mrs. Shaw, who had sat motionless and silently in the saddle, suddenly noticed that it was her husband standing before her and started to weep with joy. She leaped from the McClellan and embarrassed her wounded and disoriented husband while gently caressing his dirty and blood-crusted hair. "Oh, thank you God! Oh, thank you Lord for bringing him back to me!" she sobbed over and over again, as Nate and Jesse looked on awkwardly but with a sense of shared jubilation.

Three

JULY 1867, FORT HAYS AND HAYS CITY, KANSAS

About a quarter mile from Hays City, Nate and Jesse heard the sounds of revolver fire. It was dusk and they had been following the trail along the Smoky Hill River that led to Fort Hays when their horses, green animals that still needed to be fully broken into cavalry mounts, slightly bolted at the sounds of rapid shooting. Nate and Jesse, along with the two sisters and the wounded husband were a sorry sight as they entered Hays City. The women were riding while the two noncoms walked and led their horses. Nate had constructed a primitive travois to transport Mr. Shaw by cutting two branches of cottonwood along the banks of the Solomon and used Jesse's and his horse's picket lines to fasten the poles together and create a back by zigzagging the rope between the two poles for the wounded Shaw to lie on.

Nate was thinking that he had to take care of these traumatized civilians before he could report, as ordered, to Captain Armes, Company F Tenth Cavalry. As they got closer to the edge of town they could discern other sounds such as music playing on a piano and loud female laughter accompanied by more gunfire.

"Sounds like this is some wild place," said Jesse as he tightened the reins to better control his horse. He was concerned that his gelding might bolt if he became spooked by sudden unfamiliar sounds.

"Yeah, I heard 'bout this place. Some of the officers back at Fort Riley tol' me that Hays is the Sodom and Gomorrah of the West," explained Nate.

"Sodom and what?" inquired Jesse, puzzled.

Nate took a deep breath and patted his horse, calming the big gelding's nervousness. "My mother tol' me that it's a place of evil and sin, Jess. Kinda like what we experienced with Issac Moore an' his hoodooism back in N'Aulins."

Nate had heard and read how Hays City was just being established and how the makeshift town preyed on the railroad workers who were constructing the Union Pacific railway and on enlisted men from the Seventh Cavalry who came into town from nearby Fort Hays. Nate had anticipated that Hays City would be typical of most western settlements that had sprung up following the army or the railroad or had been hurriedly established because gold was found nearby. The town, because of its utmost proximity to the advancing Union Pacific, became a mecca for every pimp, whore, con artist, loan shark, gambler, booze peddler, and thief on the prairie. Nate knew that other walks of life were also represented in large numbers such as buffalo hunters, scouts, teamsters, visiting Europeans who wanted to experience the West, prospectors, bitter and destitute former Confederate soldiers, and fugitives who were trying to stay one step ahead of the law.

Back at Leavenworth, he overhead a conversation between officers of the Seventh Cavalry that the town's main attractions such as the saloons, brothels, and gambling parlors, were a plague on the men from Fort Hays who would desert the post at night and visit these establishments to spend all of their money on "soiled doves" and drink overpriced, watered-down liquor until they fell down drunk. The hapless soldiers would then be subsequently robbed of any valuables that they might have carried on their person and thrown out onto the street. The officers talked about shootings occurring constantly, day and night, and fueled by liquor and lawlessness, men would invariably argue over money in a card game or for the attentions of a woman or on a point of honor and start shooting. The situation became so bad supposedly, that it was dangerous to use the only hotel in town, the Gibson House, because bullets from the street would whiz right through the quarter-inch timber boards, wounding or killing its occupants who were usually horny and inebriated soldiers and buffalo hunters trying to enjoy a whore.

During this time, Hays City had only one street, South and North

Main. When Nate and Jesse approached the Gibson House on South Main Street, the sun was falling behind the horizon and resembled a big ball of fire. Nate wanted to get to the fort before dark if possible and hand over the civilians to the surgeon at the hospital but he was uncertain where the post was located. He decided that he would inquire as to its location if he saw someone who might look helpful. The town had quieted down for a few moments and the night riffraff and suckers were still to making their appearance at the saloons and brothels. There were some drunk buffalo hunters milling around passing an enormous jug of shine in front of the Gibson House. One of them, a small young man who looked like he had lost all of his teeth and was so filthy that it appeared that he had not taken a bath since he was born, was shooting off his Sharps .50-caliber at a can down North Main. Down the street, some Mexican drivers were squatting in a circle near their mule teams eating chili. Their wagons were full of freight and they dared not leave them unattended if they wished to keep their inventory safe from thieves.

Nate was about to ask the Mexicans if they knew which direction the fort was located when a tall man dressed in a Prince Albert frock coat emerged from the front door of the Gibson House. He took a few steps forward and struck a match with his thumb. He then slowly placed the burning matchstick close to the tip of his cigar that was centered in his mouth. He slowly turned the stogie to make sure that the entire circumference of the cigar was evenly lit. This action distracted Nate and he turned his attention away from the Mexicans. The man was about six foot three inches tall, muscular, broad shouldered with a slim waist. He wore custom-made top boots with riding breeches and his coat was open revealing a dark green silk vest. His shirt was white linen and an elegant red cravat was tied neatly around his neck. Beneath his sweeping black hat that crowned his head perfectly, shoulder length dirty blond hair fell all the way past his shoulders and a long mustache that was well groomed drooped past his jaws. As Nate and Jesse slowly directed their horses in his direction and came closer, they noticed a wide red sash around the man's waist where a pair of pearl-handled Navy Colt .36-caliber pistols were stuffed, one on each side, butt forward for easy withdrawal.

The man's hawklike gray eyes stared right at Nate. "You boys need any help?" he asked in a courteous but not overly concerned manner.

"We just rode in and we lookin' for the fort. We got wounded civilians," responded Jesse desperately. Nate flinched a little. He wanted to do all the talking. He had more experience in communicating with white people. He did not feel that Jesse used the right tact in trying to get information from whites.

"You two are part of the Tenth, ain't ya?" inquired the tall man as he puffed on his cigar while turning the stogie in his slender fingers. Nate was looking at the man's clothes. Not since he left the plantation had he seen a white man look so good. In addition, he seemed very cool and self-assured as if nothing could touch him or he would fear any man.

"Yes, sir, we part of the Tenth," said Jesse eagerly, "and we are here to fight Injuns."

"Oh, you'll find them soon enough," quipped the tall man, still puffing on the cigar while his riveting eyes searched Nate's face.

"My name is Sergeant Major Nate Gordon and this is First Sergeant Jesse Randolph." Nate saluted and then continued, "I be much oblige if you could point the way to Fort Hays."

"The fort is about sixteen miles southeast of here. You'll find the Seventh and Tenth Cavalry bivouacked by Beaver Creek." The tall man paused, removed his cigar and slowly blew out the smoke from his mouth, savoring the tobacco. "I think these civilians would be better off here in town then at that tent camp the army calls a fort."

Nate thought for a moment about the man's suggestion, but after all he had heard about Hays City, he decided that his civilian charges would be better off in the care of the army. "No thank you, sir. These people are under my care an' I'll let the army handle this."

"If you can wait for moment I'll have my horse saddled up and I'll take you to the fort," replied the man.

"Thank you, sir, but that will not be necessary," responded Nate. "Beggin' your pardon, sir. My name is Sergeant Major Nate Gordon. Who do I have the privilege of addressing?"

The well-dressed man smiled and Nate thought that he resembled a cat because of his long whiskers. "Fact is, I'm the best paid scout for General Custer. Maybe you've heard of me? Name's James Butler Hickok, but my friends call me ... 'Wild Bill.'" He drew on his cigar again and waited for their reaction as if he were an actor on-stage waiting for the audience to respond.

Nate and Jesse remained silent. Jesse never heard of Wild Bill Hickok, but Nate remembered reading about this man who was making newspaper headlines as a shooter.

"Yes, sir, I've heard 'bout you," replied Nate calmly.

"Did you also know that I was involved in the underground railroad before the war?" boasted Wild Bill as he took another puff from his cigar. James Butler Hickok enjoyed recounting his exploits, real or invented. In this particular case, he wanted to show how "progressive" his views were toward blacks.

"No, sir." Nate was surprised and confused. How could this dude, dressed as a dandy and carrying twin pearl handle revolvers that were stuffed in a red sash, have assisted escaped slaves find their way north?

Hickok noticed the puzzlement in Nate's face.

"Maybe you can come by the Gibson House some evening. I'm usually playin' a little poker with some friends of mine. We can talk 'bout the old days."

"Yes, sir, much 'bliged," responded Nate eagerly. "I jest might do that."

As Nate and Jesse walked next to their mounts on their way out of Hays City, several large wagons drawn by mules slowly approached them from the opposite direction. At first, Nate noticed that there was nothing unusual about this caravan, but as the wagons came closer, it became clear that the drivers were heavily powdered women dressed in bright gaudy clothes that were more in keeping with the attire of whores than mule drivers. The lead wagon was partially covered by a canvas in the front while the back remained open. Two people sat in front. The driver, a plump woman past her prime, was chewing and spitting wet wads of tobacco as she held the reins in her long black gloved hands. The passenger who sat next to her was a fat dark man who was smoking a cigar and wearing a gray plantation hat accentuated with a wide crimson band around the crown. Nate thought that the fat man was dressed just as vulgar as his charges. He was clad in tight bright-green satin trousers and his linen ruffled shirt was a deep lavender while his taut red brocaded silk vest held his enormous paunch as if it served as a girdle.

"Gawddamn pimp and his hoes," commented Jesse.

"You right 'bout that," acknowledged Nate, as he twitched his nose in disgust as a vapor of cheap perfume engulfed the air.

The first wagon passed them by in a cloud of dust. The second vehicle, which was also driven by a trollop, transported the group's furniture items such as beds, headboards, chairs, mirrors, vanity sets, carpets, and vulgar oil paintings also passed them with relatively little observance. When the third wagon passed, an old Rucker-pattern military ambulance, Nate took more notice then he had shown with the two preceding ones because it carried a half dozen painted harlots driven by a stunning, petite half-breed young woman with long shiny raven hair that glistened in the early twilight. She was wearing a colorful patterned wool poncho and a well-worn straw sombrero hung from her upper back. Nate at first caught only a brief glimpse of the young woman, but her natural beauty and demeanor made her so different from the conspicuous whores, he felt compelled to turn his head again and gape intensely at her. The half-breed also turned around to look at Nate, and met his eyes for a brief moment before the right front wheel of the wagon suddenly pitched itself into a deep ditch ejecting her from the driver's seat. She screamed as she tumbled onto the road and Nate feared that the rear wheel might crush her as the wagon now had no driver to control the mules. His mind flashed into the past, when he witnessed that green lieutenant's head being crushed by a runaway wagon at the battle of Prestonburg.

Nate released the reins of his mount and rushed to where he saw the young woman fall. Fortunately, the wagon had halted but the two front vehicles kept moving as they were unaware of what had occurred. Nate found her face down in the dust. She seemed to be unconscious and feared that she might be seriously injured. He slowly bent over and seized her tiny arms that were stretched out in the dirt as if she were an abandoned puppet. He started to pick her up when he heard her moan. "*Que me pasó?*" She placed the palms of her delicate hands over her forehead and bowed her head as if she were trying to gain her sense of orientation.

"You all right, ma'am?" inquired Nate, his voice expressing concern regarding her condition. He became captivated by her beauty as he held her in his arms and kept staring deeply into her round brown face. Her eyelids were flickering as if they were the delicate wings of butterflies and Nate could feel her heartbeat rapidly as a result of the shock she received from the abrupt fall.

"*Sí, Sí, señor! Muchas gracias.*" She looked into Nate's eyes and felt self-conscious of being in a state of helplessness. She quickly stabilized herself and pulled away from Nate and stared at his wide yellow chevrons. "*Gracias, Sargento Mayor.*"

"Glad to assist, ma'am," replied Nate as he touched the visor of his kepi.

The young half-breed woman smiled gently and nodded as she climbed back into the wagon seat and retook hold of the reins. She then slapped them smartly against the backside of the mules and yelled, "*Andale!*"

Nate watched as the wagon rolled forward to catch up with the others. His body and mind felt peculiar. He had never felt this way before interacting with a woman. He discovered that he was drawn to her and that he felt a kinship with her because she was a half-breed and that reminded him of his sister.

Four

Cpt. George Armes, the commander for F Company, Tenth Cavalry, was agitated. As he sat in his Sibley tent reading reports that the Cheyennes had attacked Campbell's Camp, a Union Pacific Railway workers station located a little more than a dozen miles from Fort Hays, he fretted about not having enough resources to protect railway laborers, settlers, or any civilian who ventured a few miles from the fort.

Captain Armes, as was the case with most of the line officers on the frontier in the immediate post-war period, considered the army's senior quartermasters in Washington and especially the war department, as a collection of uncooperative, often corrupt, and incompetent fools. Although both white and black troops suffered the consequences of poor diet and mediocre medical attention, Negro regiments were harder pressed because they were the lowest priority on the supply line.

The commander of F Company had already lost seven men due to cholera and he feared that his company would further be decimated if things did not change. Armes was relieved however, that at least his men were just issued new Spencer repeating rifles and that although his troopers were green, morale was high. In addition, it gave him some satisfaction knowing that at the Tenth Cavalry, as opposed to the vainglorious Custer's Seventh Cavalry, desertions were almost nonexistent, and his men did not go into Hays City to get drunk and die in barroom brawls.

Armes was a competent, brave officer who often preferred to rely on his instincts rather than following orders from superiors if he thought he knew better. A veteran of the war, he rose to become a brevet colonel of volunteers and although he had only recently joined the Tenth in June, he felt close to his men and confident that they would perform well under fire.

A corporal shouted from outside his tent that two noncommissioned officers were here to report.

"By God, send them in," Armes shouted back.

Nate entered the tent first, then Jesse. They saluted and stood at attention. They were tired, hungry, and their uniforms were caked with splattered mud from the long ride.

"I have been expecting you two for over a day now!" Although Armes was irritated that Nate and Jesse were overdue, he was relieved that they had finally arrived.

"Yes, sir. Beggin' the Captain's pardon...We were detained by transportin' wounded civilians that we found on the trail."

Armes did not want to waste words discussing the reasons. He had already been told by the officer of the day that civilians had been brought to the hospital. Armes rose from his chair and ran his fingers through his short, cropped wavy beard, "I recognize that you did your duty, Sergeant Major. Your care and attention to those civilians who had suffered much from Indian deprevation is duly noted." Armes then sat back down in his chair and placed his elbows on the table and folded his hands as if in prayer. "Your arrival at this hour is fortunate, as I am short of noncommissioned officers, and especially good ones." He paused for a moment and looked into Nate's eyes. "Colonel Grierson informed me that you can read and write." Armes was struck by Nate's Herculean appearance and although he was a noncommissioned officer, Armes could not help notice that the cut of this Sergeant Major's uniform was exceptional and would have made some of the officers in any regiment blush with embarrassment and envy.

"Yes, sir, I can read and write." Nate always felt proud when he could say those five words, especially to a white man in front of other blacks. He felt that he had honored his mother's request that he must, "'mount to something" while serving as an example to his brethren. He also knew that many whites could not read or write, so he cherished his abilities as proof that the black man could achieve intellectual equality, and even superiority over the white man.

"Good, good . . ." exclaimed Armes. "We are desperate for those qualities. Up until now, I have been doing all the paperwork and I need clerical assistance." Captain Armes' facial expression, which up until now was rather relaxed, suddenly became more serious. The lines in his forehead stiffened and became more accentuated while his normally soft, droopy eyes became very focused and penetrating.

"Sergeant Major. Company F will to take the field tomorrow, at dawn, to pursue and engage the Cheyennes. A Dog Soldiers' raiding band has murdered seven railway laborers at Campbell's Camp within the last twenty-four hours!" Armes spoke as if he were a Shakespearean actor speaking from the stage.

Nate and Jesse were stunned. They had hoped that they would see action with the hostiles soon, but they never suspected that they would be possibly thrown into a fight with the Cheyennes upon their immediate arrival at the fort.

"Yes, I know Sergeant Major, you and the First Sergeant are tired from your ride from Leavenworth and you don't even know the men in my company." Armes paused and stroked his beard a little more vigorously than before. "Nevertheless, I have a strong feeling that you will do your duty and prepare the men for a fight with the hostiles."

"Beggin' the Colonel's pardon, sir," said Jesse in an apprehensive tone of voice. "Is the company well equipped?"

"That's a very good question, First Sergeant." Armes shifted his stare from Nate to Jesse, who, up until now, he had ignored. "The men are equipped with brand new Spencer Repeaters and have been issued Army Colt forty-fives. As for the horses, they are, alas, pretty much windblown relics of the late war, but they will have to do for now."

"How many rounds am-munition for each trooper, sir? And will we be issued sabers?" inquired Nate anxiously. His mind was racing. There was so much to do before dawn. He was totally unacquainted with the men who made up F Company, their training, discipline, condition of their equipment, morale, marksmanship, etc . . . He was therefore determined to spend the rest of the night preparing the troop.

"The men will be issued twenty-five rounds for their Colts, and make sure that all of the tubes of their Blakeslee quick-loaders are filled to capacity. As for sabers . . ." Armes took a deep breath and sighed as if he were an impatient schoolmaster losing patience with a pupil. "The first thing you learn when you fight Indians is that stealth is one of the few advantages we have. And when we lose that element of surprise by carring sabers that are rattling like the devil, the cavalry becomes useless because we can never find the Indians. Now, we do not have much time, so I suggest that we ready the company for a fight. You are dismissed."

"Aye, aye, sir," said Nate and Jesse simultaneously as they saluted and marched out of the room to get F Company prepared for action. Nate was a little disappointed that the men would not be carrying sabers. *Ain't nothin' like a saber,* he thought to himself. A razor sharp long knife gives a man courage. Nate had to agree, however, that Armes' observation was correct in stating that the rattling of the weapons does sacrifice the element of surprise. But . . . the weapon sure puts fear into the enemy if they see that the long blade coming straight for them. Yes, sir, nothin' like cuttin' down a man with a saber. He then thought of Mrs. Shaw and Mrs. Foster. He wanted to check on them at the hospital but there was no time. He decided they would have to wait until his return. Besides, he decided, he felt that his energies should be concentrated in getting the company prepared for the immediate task at hand, and that was to punish the hostiles that committed such atrocities on civilians.

Five

Nate and Jesse, again, did not sleep very much during the night. Company F, composed of a strength of thirty-four men, was camped along the banks of the Saline River. They had left Fort Hays the day before and picked up the Cheyenne raiding party trail at Campbell's Camp. Captain Armes followed the pony tracks, northeasterly, along the Saline, anticipating "catching up with the hostiles and punishing the savages for their atrocities," as he had told Nate the night before.

When the small command reached the river at the end of the day, Armes ordered the troopers to camp for the night as they could not follow the trail in the dark. He ordered Nate and Jesse to make sure that the men and horses rested as much as possible, for he intended to march the column before dawn, and follow the pony tracks and catch up with the Dog Soldiers.

The first night that Nate and Jesse spent at Hays, the two noncoms used the time to become acquainted with the men of Company F, and inspect equipment. Nate examined each Sharp and Spencer carbine and every 1860 Army Colt revolver to verify that the weapons were in perfect working condition, and that the ammunition was of good quality. Horses, saddles, bridles, blankets, packs, boots, rifle sling straps, and even the brass spurs, were scrupulously examined. Nate made several troopers re-clean their carbines and Jesse had to admonish three enlisted men for dirty boots and wearing unbrushed shell jackets.

Dawn was about an hour away and Nate and Jesse were going around the camp ensuring that the troopers were saddling their mounts properly and in silence. Nate loved being awake during the predawn hours. Even when he was a slave on Mas'a Hammond's plantation in St. Charles Parish, he loved to get up before anyone else so he could be alone and enjoy the few moments of peace and listen to the sounds of birds and insects before the overseers started yelling, "All niggers git to work!"

As he examined each hoof on every mount to make sure that none of the horses would throw a shoe and go lame, he whispered to the troopers how important it was to take care of their mounts if they were to survive in hostile Indian country.

Captain Armes had ordered that no campfires be made to avoid possible detection from Cheyenne scouts, so the men were only allowed to bite into hardtack biscuits before going to bed the night before. Now in the dark, as they groped to pack up their accoutrements and saddle their horses, some of the men felt cranky because they were not allowed to make coffee. Nevertheless, all of them were excited at the prospect of catching up with the Cheyennes and having the opportunity to fight. They felt they were going to have the jump on them, and if they rode hard and with a little luck, they would be on top of their quarry by midday.

As soon as the sky cracked from the light of the dawn sun, the troopers were riding in columns of fours and were following the trail at a fast trot. Armes and Nate were up front while Jesse was near the rear watching for stragglers and making sure that the men kept quiet. As the column moved along the banks of the Saline, the only noise made by the troopers were the faint sounds of shod horses, clanging tin cups and canteens, creaking leather, and the occasional grunt by some of the men urging their mounts forward. There was a strong breeze coming from the north so the regimental guidon flapped in the wind and the standard bearer had to keep a strong hand on the staff so it would remain vertical.

Nate and another sergeant, William Christy, were riding near Armes. Sergeant Christy and Nate knew each other before Nate was sent to Louisiana to help organize the Ninth Cavalry. Sergeant William Christy was a former farmer from Pennsylvania and had joined the Tenth at the same time as Nate did when the regiment was being formed at Fort Leavenworth. He was a resourceful individual and enjoyed talking about his dream of settling down on a large farm in the West after he retired from the cavalry and have some livestock and horses. Nate liked talking to him because he was a free man before the war and came from the North. William Christy had never experienced the hardships of slavery and was a black man who knew the value of freedom and the sense of dignity of owning his own land.

Cougar Eyes and about thirty Dog Soldiers were hiding behind some big cottonwood and willow trees and in the tall grass that grew along the banks of the Saline while another war party of equal size waited in complete seclusion behind a ravine that was located about a hundred yards northwest from the river. The Cheyenne Dog Soldiers were painted and dressed for war. Some braves carried colored lances decorated with human hair and eagle feathers, while others carried an assortment of repeating rifles such as Starr and Smith carbines, as well as revolvers stolen from their victims during their many raids and fights. Most of the warriors, however, carried the favorite bow lance. This was a long bow of recurved design with a lance head at one end. The weapon not only served as a powerful bow but could be used to lance an enemy as well. In addition, the bow lance indicated membership in a Dog Soldier society by their color and decoration. Other Dog Men carried rawhide shields rimmed with cloth and eagle feathers with painted symbols such as birds, bears, and butterflies, and held powerful bows in which their strings were made from bear gut. Their quivers were stuffed with arrows and dangled from their sides while their ponies were also painted in wild colors and symbols that represented the warrior's personality, coup history, and medicine that would ensure them of invincibility against an enemy.

Cougar Eyes preferred to carry a war club that had several spikes protruding from the tip of the large weapon on the strike side. He intended to kill the blue coats up close as they had when they murdered his family. He enjoyed clubbing his enemies while staring into their eyes and watching for any signs of fear or the desire to beg for mercy. Which of course he never gave. At Sand Creek, his mother begged for mercy but was murdered nevertheless. He was splendidly dressed in war regalia. His head was crowned with a red and yellow turbanlike headdress and his powerful chest was covered with a string of silver hair plates, and huge dentalium-shell eardrops drooped from his ears. His biceps were decorated with German silver armbands that he had traded for, and he wore a red-and-white-striped vest that closely matched his red-striped leggings with a dark stroud-cloth breechclout. His feet were decorated in yellow-beaded moccasins. In addition to carrying his war club, Cougar Eyes was armed with a single-shot Smith carbine that he had stole from the Shaw-Foster homestead.

As Colonel Armes saw the big clops of cottonwood trees in the distance he halted the command and waited for the flankers to scout the area before advancing any farther. The two front flankers were not only green soldiers, but inexperienced in watching for Indian signs. Rather than shifting their gaze from the ground in order to pick up tracks, to sweeping the area in front and sides as they were supposed to, their eyes concentrated on staring at the horizon. As a consequence, the two flankers where taken completely by surprise when Cougar Eyes screamed from the top of his lungs and charged out from the clops of cottonwood trees and tall grass at a gallop wielding his huge war club. As he charged in the direction of the flankers, he was immediately followed by the other thirty Dog Men that had waited with him until the moment of ambush was ripe.

The warriors emerged from the cottonwood trees as if they were angry ants pouring out of their nest. They howled blood-chilling war whoops and blew on their war whistles which completely stunned both flankers. One flanker reeled his big gelding around and spurred the beast toward the column as if he were being pursued by demons, while the remaining one sat paralyzed in the saddle and became so horrified at the sight of the oncoming horde of Dog Soldiers that he was unable to think and react. As he sat in the saddle, his gaze transfixed at Cougar Eyes' approach, he felt a sudden warmth in his crotch and inner thigh area and then a sudden coldness as the liquid ran down his legs.

"*Jesus Christ.* I jist pissed in my new trousers!"

As he looked down at his crotch and saw the dark stain on his sky-blue wool pants, Cougar Eye swung his war club against the hapless flanker's forehead as his pony swept past him. The trooper was hit with such force that his head snapped back, lifting his torso from the saddle and forcing the rest of his body to be projected over his mount's haunches onto the ground. His neck was broken and his forehead shattered as if it were a crushed egg.

The surviving frontal flanker reached the column hollering, "*Injuns! Injuns. Hundreds of Injuns are right behind me!*" As he was bellowing, Nate stood up in the saddle and saw that about fifty or sixty Cheyenne warriors spread out in a long straight line heading straight for the command. Some of the troopers' horses were becoming excited and unruly, forcing several cavalrymen to fall out from the main column. Nate and Sergeant William Christy glanced at Colonel Armes.

"Orders sir?" said Nate calmly, in a tone of voice that was better suited for inquiring if the Colonel desired more coffee in his cup rather than waiting for the command to swing into action.

"Sergeant Major!" said Armes finally. "Tell the bugler to sound dismount and have the men form a skirmish line."

"Aye, aye, sir. *Bugler. Sound Dismount.*"

By now, the other Dog Soldiers who were hiding behind the ravine decided to surge forward from their place of seclusion and formed a second wave of attacking Cheyennes. Altogether, about seventy to eighty warriors were descending at full speed toward Colonel Armes and Company F.

The bugler, a young man who was only nineteen years old eagerly placed the trumpet against his lips. Upon seeing the onrush of howling Dog Soldiers however, his mouth and tongue became so dry that he was unable to produce a sound from his horn.

"*Spit boy. Spit,*" yelled Nate desperately. The bugler tried again but failed to work up enough moisture in his mouth to blow into his instrument.

"*Gawddamn it, boy!*" bemoaned Nate. Without waiting for the bugler to sound Dismount, he instinctively turned his bay gelding on its hindquarters and spurred the animal into a gallop down the length of the column barking orders to the troopers to dismount and form a skirmish line with every fourth man holding four horses in the rear.

The men of F company obeyed instantly. They jumped from their horses, holding their carbines in their right hands while handing over the reins of their mounts to every fourth man in the column. Within fifteen seconds, a skirmish line was established with twenty-seven men waiting for orders to commence firing with Spencers and Sharps carbines against an onslaught of about eighty Cheyenne Dog Men.

Nate was standing next to Colonel Armes in the middle of the skirmish line while Sergeant William Christy was at the western end and Jesse was at the far eastern point of the line. Colonel Armes wanted the attacking warriors to come as close as possible to the skirmish line to achieve maximum firepower effect. Both Nate and Armes, as well as Sergeant Christy and Jesse, were standing with their Colts cocked and ready while the enlisted men were instructed to fall into a kneeling position with their Spencers and Sharps carbines shouldered and fingers on the triggers.

A galloping horde of screaming painted warriors and war ponies dressed in battle regalia was an unnerving prospect for green soldiers on the frontier. The Dog Men had very little respect for the way white men fought, and believed the pony soldiers to be weak and cowardly men who, when faced with the warrior prowess of a Dog Soldier, would usually cut and run. The Dog Men considered their tactics superior to the pony soldiers and believed that they were stronger on an individual basis. While the army relied on fire power, the Dog Men preferred stealth, terror, and individual courage to place fear in the hearts of the soldiers. The highest honor for a Dog Man was to humiliate his opponents by counting coup, and most importantly, they preferred to fight on terrain of their own choosing, and if outnumbered, they would scatter to the four winds at great speeds, making pursuit extremely difficult.

Cougar Eyes, dressed in a magnificent red-and-yellow turban, had tied matching trade cloth bows on his mustang's mane and tail, and was in front of the charge, while his companions urged their ponies forward as they screamed epithets and war cries at the cavalrymen and blew on bone whistles. Many of the warriors pointed their long lances with glee at the blue coats, anticipating the kill, while others waved their shields and fired their rifles at the troopers.

Colonel Armes held his Colt in the air but continued to withhold the order to fire as his penetrating hawklike gaze stared intensely at the oncoming Cheyennes without moving a muscle in his face. His body remained perfectly motionless in the pistol standing position and his right hand's index finger was lightly pressed against the trigger. Some of the shots fired by the charging Cheyennes were hitting the ground around the Colonel, spurting dirt and sod into the air and splattering some of the troopers' uniforms and faces. Armes however, remained completely unfazed. As a Civil War veteran, this was nothing compared to a disciplined volley fired by Confederate infantry. The horses were less tranquil. Some of the animals that were being held by the horse handlers were becoming excited by the screams and smells of the Dog Men and the aroma of charging Indian ponies.

"Sergeant Major. Get those horses further back to the rear," bellowed Armes, as he continued to stare at the approaching Dog Men while arrows and bullets struck the ground or whizzed by as if they were swarming bees. Armes could make out the colors of some of the Dog Men's faces, and he especially took notice that Cougar Eyes and several other braves had their faces painted completely red, while others drew black or yellow stripes down their checks or around their mouths.

Nate also held his weapon, the trusty Walker-Colt in the air, fully cocked, but he was taking aim at the charging horde while Armes' barrel was pointed toward the sky. The sergeant major was totally in his element. He was cool and prepared for a fight. His training, experience, and temperament suited him perfectly for moments such as this upcoming battle. He moved his eyes up and down the skirmish line to watch for any breech in discipline while also keeping one eye on the horses. The horses must be safe at all costs, he kept repeating to himself in a low tone of voice. He was not concerned with the onslaught of the charging Dog Men, for now, that was the officer's responsibility. His duty was to ensure that the boys remain cool and take careful aim at their targets, and above all, not waste ammunition. He remembered that during the war, at the Battle of Prestonberg, the Confederate defenders held their fire until the charging black troopers of the Fifth Cavalry were within almost spitting range. The results were devastating for the first wave. Over a quarter of the men were cut down within a few feet of the Confederate defensive line. He knew that Armes was going to employ the same tactic.

Some of the troopers on the skirmish line were becoming nervous and gave anxious glances toward Nate and Armes. Adding to the tension, several of the horses in the rear started to become very unruly by refusing to remain still. Some of them started to rear and behave in a crazed manner while others neighed loudly and snorted as they tried to break loose from their handlers.

"Keep your eyes forward boys, get ready to fire, an' don't waste your bullets," said Nate sternly, as he caught one trooper glancing at him. "Aim for the horses, boys, put dem damn bastards on dere asses." Nate knew that the chances of these green troopers hitting the riders were much slimmer than if they would shoot the ponies. Accomplishing this, an Indian on foot in front of a disciplined skirmish line was easily killed, if there was natural cover. The Dog Men were about fifteen yards away when Armes, finally, decided that it was the right moment to blunt the attack. He lowered his Colt and aimed the weapon right at Cougar Eyes. In a strong and clear voice, he commanded, "*Ready . . . Aim . . . Fire.*" Although Armes missed hitting Cougar Eyes' head by a hair, the sudden deafening sound of carbine and revolver fire stunned the Cheyennes. As a sheet of gunfire rang out from the skirmish line drowning the war cries of the Dog Soldiers and horse neighing, a cloud of blue smoke moved along the firing line as if it were an early morning fog moving close to the ground. "*Fire at will, fire at will,*" ordered Armes as he pulled the trigger on his Army Colt and cocked back the hammer and fired again. He worked the revolver as if the weapon was his only link to staying alive. Troopers equipped with Spencer repeaters were firing and furiously pulling back on the levers and hammers while Nate was calmly firing his Walker-Colt with deadly accuracy at the Cheyennes.

The Dog Soldiers were not expecting to be met by a hail of bullets from repeating rifles. They had anticipated to terrify the blue coats and cut them down as if they were panicked buffalo.

The first volley of fire wounded or killed a dozen warriors' ponies. Some of the neighing beasts collapsed in mid-gallop, headfirst into the ground as a result of being struck by multiple gunshots while others staggered, unable to advance. Although many of the riders were thrown into the air as if they were paper dolls which rendered them momentarily disoriented, the fallen warriors remained defiant, and several of them, after recovering from being ejected from their ponies, continued to rush at the skirmish line with war clubs, tomahawks, and knives.

Nate aimed his Walker-Colt at one of the charging Dog Men who was on foot and running toward Colonel Armes with a long lance that was painted half yellow and half black with a scalp of human hair dangling from its shaft. The warrior's face was painted red and he was ready to plunge the lance tip into Armes' face. Nate fully pulled back the hammer and squeezed the trigger as if he was firing at a practice target rather than at a howling, painted brave that was only a few feet away from his commanding officer. The shot struck the Dog Soldier through the middle of his chest, forcing him to release his grip on the lance while thrown from his feet and landing on his back, clutching the wound while he wiggled in the grass mortally wounded.

The remaining Cheyennes who were on foot were also cut down by Spencer repeaters from the skirmish line, killing several of them and wounding some others. The field was now littered with wounded and dead Cheyennes and their war ponies. Scattered articles such as feathers, war bonnets, shields, lances, arrows, and horse blankets covered the terrain in front of the skirmish line. Some of the ponies that were slowly dying were breathing heavily as they bled to death on the ground while others tried pathetically to get up, but were too exhausted and injured to lift up their broken limbs from the grass.

Realizing that the blue coats were not going to waver and that they had already suffered casualties, Cougar Eyes decided to halt the attack and retreat to the rear. He reined in his pony and raised his lance and war shield in the air and commanded the Dog Men to retreat behind a deep ravine that was about a hundred and fifty yards north of the Saline.

The initial Dog Soldier attack had failed to weaken the skirmish line, and as the Cheyennes retreated, Armes gave the order to Nate to cease firing. The bugler sounded the command and Armes turned to Nate.

"Sergeant Major! Report," said Armes as he emptied the cylinder from his army Colt. After the spent shells fell to the ground he reached into his cartridge box and replaced the empty chambers with new cartridges. He then dipped into his cap pouch and started to rapidly replace each nipple with a fresh cap. Nate was also reloading his weapon as he walked down the skirmish line encouraging the troopers to reload their carbines and seeing if there were any casualties.

"We, we, sure . . . sure put them bastards on their asses, Sarge," laughed one enlisted man as he rammed another Blakeslee tube in the butt of his Spencer.

"Yeah, them devils be walkin' home before we through," commented another trooper as he wiped his face with his sleeve.

"No talkin', boys. Keep your mouths shut and reload your weapons," commanded Nate.

"Any wounded or dead, Jesse?" Nate was calm even though his blood was hot with excitement from the fight. He had not fired his weapon in anger since the riot in San Antonio and was gratified that he was finally shooting at the real enemy. He was also pleased that the boys behaved well and that they demonstrated coolness under fire against superior odds and did not yield any ground to the enemy.

"No cas'alties here." Jesse paused for a moment to gaze at the sky and remove his forage cap to wipe his head with his bandanna. The day was becoming hotter by the minute and most of the men were already soaked with perspiration while their mouths, lips, and tongues were dry and caked with dust. The sky was void of any clouds and worst of all, there was no breeze in the air and the flies were beginning to pester the men and horses. "I thought de boys done good," said Jesse approvingly.

"Yeah, I thought so too!" replied Nate proudly. "Jess, make sure that the men who carry Spencers are fully loaded with new Blakeslee tubes."

One trooper, whose throat, tongue, and lips were so parched that he had trouble speaking, begged Nate for permission to go to his mount and retrieve his canteen. "Permission denied, Private! Stay on the line," was Nate's sharp retort.

"How's Christy's part of the line? Any wounded or dead?" inquired Jesse as he made his way toward the rear to check on the horses.

"No, don't think so. I gots to report back to Colonel Armes." Nate rushed back to his commanding officer's side and reported that there were no casualties among the men.

"What about the horses? Have any of them been shot or injured?" asked Armes, anxiously.

"First Sergeant Randolph is inspecting de mounts now, sir, but besides a few arrows in the saddles . . ."

"The red bastards will be back," interrupted Armes as his eyes squinted toward the ravines where the Dog Soldiers had secluded themselves. "They will try at least one more charge."

"The boys will hold them, sir. I know we have our backs to the river, but we gots water and as long as the ammunition holds out, sir, we'll be aw right."

Just as Nate was talking to Armes, about twenty more Dog Men reached Cougar Eyes' band behind the ravine. The sounds of *hi, hi, hi* and other similar calls could be heard from their place of concealment. The Cheyennes were now emboldened with these additional reinforcements and Cougar Eyes decided to immediately launch another attack.

"Here they come again!" shouted Sergeant William Christy as he cocked back the hammer of his Army Colt. Colonel Armes ordered Nate to divide the company into two different firing positions. Those with Spencer repeaters would continue to kneel while those who carried Sharps carbines were ordered to stand.

"Every man with a Sharps fall into a standin' firing position, now!" barked Nate. Thirteen cavalrymen out of the troop stood up and placed their carbines at the ready. Colonel Armes noticed that most of the men with Sharps were concentrated on the left flank which left the skirmish line unbalanced in terms of maximizing firepower evenly along the line.

"Sergeant Major!" clamored Armes, the Cheyennes again fast approaching the line and time running out. "Have those troopers with the Sharps spread out evenly throughout the line?"

"Aye, aye, sir." Nate ran up to several troopers who were using Sharps carbines and placed his hand on their shoulders and led them to their firing positions on the line. He would then tell them to "make every shot count."

The Dog Soldiers were coming fast and Armes wanted the line

ready to fire before the command would be overrun. The skirmish line was reformed again within a few seconds and Armes gave the order to prepare to fire. The cavalrymen placed their rifles against their shoulders and pressed their right cheeks on the stocks while gently placing their index fingers on the triggers. Some of the men were breathing heavily and sweating profusely while others tried to control their shaking hands and fingers.

Cougar Eyes was again in the front of the Cheyennes' charge and was armed with the carbine that he had stolen from the Shaw-Foster homestead. He did not carry the weapon in the initial charge against the soldiers, preferring to club his hated enemy to death and to preserve his strong medicine by not using any tools the white men made. He was however still wearing the blue necklace that Mr. Shaw had given to his wife. He thought the article added to his war regalia. The *ho' nehe* (soldiers) initial firepower however, was much greater than that of the Dog Soldiers, so he made up his mind to retrieve the carbine. He decided that he would kill the *ve' ho' e* invaders by shooting the gun from his pony, then when he became close enough to club his enemy, he would discard the rifle and start smashing heads.

When the Cheyennes were fifty yards away, Colonel Armes instructed Nate to tell the troopers who were using Sharps carbines to prepare themselves.

"*Sharp shooters, prepare to fire,*" commanded Nate as the sounds of war whoops, bone whistles, gunfire, and galloping unshod horses came closer and closer.

"*Fire.*" The distinctive report of multiple .50-caliber Sharps carbine fire rang out a deafening sound that sent several ponies and their riders again tumbling to the ground. Armes then ordered the Spencers to open up.

Colonel Armes fired his revolver again at Cougar Eyes whom he had recognized from the earlier attack because the warrior rode a mustang with a white face that was painted a pale yellow with dozens of tiny round black spots. His first shot missed him, so he adjusted his aim and pointed the weapon carefully at Cougar Eyes' upper torso just as the Dog Man raised his carbine to his shoulder and fired at the colonel, hitting Armes in the hip. The commander of company F grunted loudly then collapsed on his knees as if he was a wooden marionette in a Punch and Judy puppet show. He immediately clutched the wound with his left hand which was now pumping blood and the liquid was slowly soaking his wool trousers and oozing through the fingers of his yellow gauntlet. His right hand still held the Army Colt, but the wound preoccupied Armes so much that he was not in a condition to use the weapon, unless directly confronted. He became obsessed in retrieving the white linen handkerchief that rested in between his shirt and frock coat, and became frustrated that he could not unflap the two central brass buttons to reach the article. Armes was not panicked, but he needed the handkerchief to slow down the bleeding, so he struggled to maneuver the fingers on his bloodied left gauntleted hand to unbutton his coat, while he cursed and gritted his teeth.

Nate noticed immediately that the colonel was shot. He saw him collapse to the ground and clutch his hip. As the skirmish line continued to hold firm and the men continued to pour a controlled fire on the Dog Men, Nate ran to his commanding officer's assistance, and kneeled in front of him. Several rounds fell close to the two men, but only managed to spray dirt and sod on their uniforms and faces. Nate noticed that Armes was trying to unflap his buttons to get to his handkerchief. He placed his Walker-Colt on the ground and with both his hands, unflapped the colonel's central buttons. He pulled the white garment from inside the frock coat and gave it to his commanding officer. Then, without waiting for any instructions, Nate decided to seize Armes underneath his armpits and pull him away from the skirmish line.

"You've got to get to the rear, sir," Nate yelled, as he snatched Armes' body and started to drag him toward the rear where the horses were located.

"Keep up the fire, Sergeant Major, watch the flanks." Armes was clutching his wound with his white linen handkerchief which was already soaked in blood while Nate ran backward dragging his commanding officer's heels through the short grass. Nate finally rested his colonel's body against a big cottonwood tree near the horses.

"Sir, you goin' be aw right?"

"I'll be all right, damnit!" replied Armes, breathing heavily, as he pressed on his linen handkerchief against the wound. "Now get back to the line where you are needed."

"Aye, aye, sir!" Nate raced back to the line.

The troopers on the skirmish line had again managed to blunt the attacking Cheyenne's charge. Several more warriors fell to the ground and about a dozen horses were severely wounded, rendering them useless to their riders. Unlike the first attack however, the Cheyenne organized themselves into two attacking waves. This surprised the troopers but Sergeants Christy and Randolph calmly ordered the men to reload and fire their weapons. With the exception of several men suffering from superficial wounds from arrows and gunshots, there were no fatal casualties and the skirmish line held.

Nate was now in charge. Armes was in too much pain from his hip wound to lucidly command the troop while the Cheyenne were pressing their attack. The Dog Men had retreated once again behind the ravine, allowing the men on the line some respite. Nate immediately called Sergeant Christy and Jesse to a brief conference.

"The colonel is wounded and is not able to command the boys in this fight."

"He hurt bad?" inquired Sergeant William Christy.

"The colonel be aw right," said Nate with confidence, as he waved his hand in the air. There was a brief moment of silence between the noncoms that was only broken when Nate added, "If we kin git outta hare 'fore he bleeds to death." His voice became more grave and guarded. He wanted to impress upon Christy and Jesse that although the troopers repelled two Cheyenne Dog Soldier charges, they were still very much outnumbered and their backs were against the river. It was his way of instilling fortitude among his men and making them realize that to be cocky usually leads to disaster.

"Think they goin' make another charge?" inquired Sergeant Christy ominously.

"Believe so," replied Nate calmly, as he placed fresh caps on the nipples of his cartridge cylinder.

"The boys are running low on ammunition, Nate! If they charge us again, we..."

"I've given that some thought, Jess! If they do charge again, we'll stop them again and when they retreat, we'll saddle up and ride outta here."

Jesse and Sergeant. William Christy looked stunned. "What 'bout the colonel? Can he ride?" asked Jesse, confused. "And won't them Indians chase after us? We'll be cut down like sugar cane durin' harvest time!"

"The colonel can ride," replied Nate assuredly, although he was not totally convinced that he could. He did know, however, that was the only choice Armes had if they were to avoid being boxed in. "I intend to fall back defensively and usin' maximum firepower to cover our asses," added Nate. "There will be no panic among the men! You boys gotta see to that. 'Sides," Nate's face cracked a big smile. "The hostiles' ponies will be all tuckered out if they charge us again, so we'll have time to gits a head start."

Cougar Eyes was examining his mustang for any gunshot wounds. Unlike many of his fellow Dog Men, his mount had not suffered any harm during the attack against the blue coats. He was impressed by the heavy gunfire coming from the soldiers that forced the warriors to break off their attacks. Normally, the blue coats would fire a volley and by the time they reloaded their rifles, the Dog Men would have slaughtered or counted coup on many of them. He was also perplexed by the new weapons the soldiers used that fired round after round without reloading. During other engagements, the blue coats would only carry singleshot carbines, so when they fired a volley, the Dog Soldiers would seize this opportunity to run them down. The disciplined volleys from the soldiers was disturbing, but what really bewildered Cougar Eyes was that the men in the blue uniforms were black, *Mo' ohtae*. He kept wondering and asking himself, who were these *Mo' ohtae-Ve' ho' e*— black and white men? Cougar Eyes knew that he had shot and seriously wounded the leader of the soldiers. He had identified him because he was out in front and gave the orders. He thought that shooting the leader would throw the blue coats into disarray, giving the warriors a crucial advantage. He also deduced that considering the leader was white, the *Mo' ohtae-Ve' ho' e* black-and-white men who were surely inferior to the white man, would panic after seeing their leader and superior fall.

But that had not happened. The *Mo' ohatae-Ve' ho' e* pony soldiers with their fast firing rifles held their ground and inflicted casualties on his war party. This presented a dilemma for the warriors. The Dog Men were faced with the prospect of losing honor if they allowed this small band of soldiers to escape without taking any horses, killing them, or counting coup. They had charged twice, yet they were unsuccessful in routing the enemy who were fighting on foot while their ponies were becoming tired and shot-up. Worse of all, some of their fellow braves were killed or lying wounded on the ground and they were becoming concerned that they would not be able to retrieve them, as was the strict custom.

Some of the Dog Men started to question their medicine. They debated whether this was a good day or not to do battle against the blue coats. Sensing growing discord and anxiety among the braves, Cougar Eyes decided to mount his horse and shame the other warriers into one more final charge against the hated *Ve' ho' e* invaders. He believed that his medicine was good because he had prepared himself properly for battle. He had trained his body and mind to become a Cheyenne warrior and proved that he was worthy of being a leader of his Dog Soldier society through his prowess as a killer of Pawnees when he barely attained manhood, and a killer of whites, when he reached full manhood.

After all, today was a good day for Cougar Eyes. He had shot the leader of the black and white men, and his pony had charged the blue coats twice and escaped unharmed. Feeling confident and sensing victory, he was determined that his Dog Men society was not to be shamed. As the braves argued, Cougar Eyes leaped on his war pony and brandished his lance while admonishing the warriors to join him. He reminded them that they were many, and the soldiers few, and that these thieves were trespassing on Cheyenne land while they sat arguing like old squaws rather than fighting as Dog Soldiers. This shamed most of the other Dog Men to mount their ponies and prepare for another attack on the *Mo' ohtae-Ve' ho' e*, black and white men.

Nate was examining the horses to make sure the animals were in good enough condition for a breakout. With the exception of some superficial arrow wounds, the command was fortunate that none of their mounts were seriously wounded or had been killed. Although in great pain, Colonel Armes was mad as hell, and in a way, this kept his mind from thinking about the throbbing pain in his wound. Nate and Jesse had bandaged Armes' hip as best as they could and were satisfied that they had at least slowed down the bleeding.

"The bastards are going to charge again, Sergeant Major," cursed Armes. "But this time," Armes winced in agony as he grabbed the trunk of the cottonwood tree and pulled himself up in order to stand on both feet. Nate offered to help, but Armes, trying to save face, refused his sergeant's help. "They will try and out-flank us and sweep our position." The makeshift bandage was soaked in blood and Nate blinked as he looked at the colonel's hip wound. He became concerned that he might not be in a condition to ride.

"Sir, we runnin' out of ammunition, if the hostiles continue to press their attack, we be in a fix 'fore nightfall. I suggest that we break-out when we stop their next attack and make a runnin' fight back to the fort." Nate spoke quickly but then his voice became calmer when he directly addressed Colonel Armes. "Sir. Can you ride?"

"I can ride damn it!" bellowed Armes, again wincing in pain. "Just put me on my horse." He waited until the pain subsided somewhat before finishing what he had to say. "I, I, don't think the boys are up for a running fight against these red bastards..."

"*Here they come again!*" yelled Jesse. Nate ran back to the center of the line and cocked his Walker-Colt. "Hold back your fire, boys. Wait till they come in *real close*," he commanded, as he positioned himself on the skirmish line. The Cheyennes were charging all together now and their war whoops, taunts, and the thud of galloping, excited horses filled the air once again.

Nate placed himself next to the guidon and checked to make sure the shaft was solidly placed into the ground. "The flag will not waver," he whispered to himself. He watched the approaching Dog Men for any sign that they might try and split their force to overwhelm the skirmish line's flanks. By now, most of the men had unbuttoned their shell jackets to allow some air to pass through their bodies. The heat kept increasing throughout the day, and now, the flies were really bothering the men and horses as the insects became drawn to the smell of sweat, blood, and strong odors.

"*Hold boys, hold . . . wait,*" commanded Nate calmly but firmly. Several of the men cocked their weapons and prepared to shoot, while others wiped the perspiration off of their faces with their gauntlets, or ran their tongues along their lips to relieve the dryness and dust that caked their faces. "Wait . . . ," repeated Nate as the warriors kept coming closer and closer. The encroaching horde were now about fifty feet away when suddenly the Dog Men sharply divided their force to attack the skirmish line's flanks. "*Fire at will at the flanks,*" Nate bellowed, as he fired the Walker-Colt in rapid-fire succession, evenly shifting his shots from the western flank to the eastern end until the cylinder was empty. Gunfire, blue smoke, screams and yelling, filled the air after the troops led out volley after volley. Since it was a windless day, the stench of sulfur burned eyes and nostrils, and both cavalrymen and Cheyenne had to shoot at each other through a cloud of dust and gun smoke.

Cougar Eyes led the charge on the western end where Sergeant Christy anchored the line. The Dog Soldiers were within a few feet of the blue coats and firing their guns at the soldiers. Nate saw that the western end of the skirmish line might be breached so he yelled at Jesse to hold his position and raced to aid Sergeant Christy. As he ran toward him, Nate noticed one Dog Man who was carrying a carbine and riding a fine horse with notched ears and clusters of eagle feathers that were tied together with red cloth on the animal's mane and tail. The Dog Soldier was tall and wore an otter-skin turban topped with a single eagle feather. His powerful war horse, bowing its head and neck in a charge position, was approaching with great, speed. The warrior lifted the carbine to his shoulder and pointed the barrel at Christy's head as his war horse snorted loudly and pulled back its ears. Christy saw that he was about to be run down by the Dog Man's horse, but before he could react, the Dog Soldier fired the weapon into the sergeant's face.

Nate saw the bright red flash that emerged from the barrel and the spattering of bone, tissue, blood, and flesh that sprayed the air from Christy's head. The little sergeant who was once a farmer in Pennsylvania stumbled momentarily, then fell forward as if he were a tree felled by an ax. The warrior, waving his rifle high above his head in triumph, shouted a loud victory call, as blood slowly oozed from Sgt. William Christy's head and formed a pool that slowly soaked the prairie grass.

"Shit-to-hell!" yelled Nate, as he ran toward Christy and almost stumbled in the process because his spur caught a cop of grass. He was to late to save Sergeant Christy's life but was determined to stabilize the western end of the skirmish line. Cougar Eyes saw Nate rushing toward the end of the line. His rifle was empty so he threw the weapon away and grabbed his huge war club from his belt. He screamed at the top of his lungs and with his body, commanded his mustang to charge the big *Mo' ohtae-Ve' ho' e* man.

Nate stopped, raised his revolver, and took aim at Cougar Eyes' upper torso. He closed his left eye and pulled the trigger when the warrior was only twenty feet away. As Nate fired, Cougar Eyes, anticipating this move, lowered his frame along the right side of his mustang's neck, just as the sergeant major pulled the trigger. Nate missed, but recocked and fired the Walker-Colt again, but the hammer fell on an empty chamber. The piece was empty, and by now, Cougar Eyes had raised his huge war club, aiming the spikes of the weapon at Nate's head. The big *Mo' ohtae-Ve' ho' e* man however, ducked the blow and thrust his shoulders and heaved his massive body into the warrior's mustang's chest and grabbed the animal's right leg and bent it back. Both beast and rider toppled to the ground.

Cougar Eyes was taken by surprise by this action and required a few moments to catch his breath. Nate drew his bowie knife from its sheath and rushed at the Dog Man who was now standing and had recovered his war club from the ground. Nate was about twice the size in height and weighed a hundred pounds more than his Cheyenne opponent. He was about to pounce on Cougar Eyes when he noticed a blue necklace around his enemy's neck. As the blue beads of the piece of jewelry shined brightly in the afternoon sun and almost blinded him,

Nate thought about Mrs. Shaw and her lamenting the loss of a blue necklace. Holding the huge bowie knife above Cougar Eyes' head, Nate was about to plunge the wide blade into the Cheyenne Dog Man's throat when another Cheyenne warrior who was carrying a yellow-striped lance with a long flock of human hair attached near the lance tip, noticed that his companion was about to be overwhelmed by the big black-and-white man. As he yelled blood curdling war whoops, he skillfully maneuvered his pony to swipe Nate's left side, knocking him to the ground. The Dog Man then tried to stick Nate in the face with his lance while Cougar Eyes used this opportune moment to leap onto his comrade's mount. Nate parried the warrior's persistent lance thrusts with his bowie knife while trying to get up on his feet, but the mounted brave kept urging his pony forward into Nate, pinning the sergeant major to the ground. Nate kept rolling on the ground to escape the hooves of the horse and thrashed at the lance thrusts with his bowie knife every time the tip came close to his chest and face. After a while, the brave became frustrated that he was unable to stick the blue coat with his yellow-stripped lance. The black-and-white pony soldier was very fast and the warrior knew that Nate knew how to handle a knife by the way he parried each one of his thrusts. Finally, at Cougar Eyes' urging, after he saw that his fellow Dog Soldiers were retreating from the battle site, did he give up trying to stick Nate.

Although the western end of the skirmish line was breached by the attacking Dog Men, the troopers of Company F remained calm and had refused to give ground. Their disciplined gunfire prevented the warriors from sweeping down the line while inflicting casualties on the Cheyennes. Their horses exhausted, and the charge blunted, the Dog Men retreated. As they departed however, scattering out of range, they remained defiant and bellowed war whoop cries while brandishing their weapons and shields in the air. Nate felt exhausted. As he reloaded his Walker-Colt he noticed the blue necklace on the debris-strewn ground. He stared at the article for a moment and stooped to pick it up. He smiled and unbuttoned the central brass button on his tunic and placed the piece of jewelry inside the shell jacket.

This last attack was costly for the cavalrymen. As Nate and Jesse assessed the situation they realized that their position was growing more untenable with every charge. Sgt. William Christy had been killed, and their commanding officer was wounded and losing a lot of blood, while several of the enlisted men suffered wounds inflicted by arrows and gunshots. What most concerned Nate however, was that several horses had been hit by gunshots and arrows during this last attack, and if the animals started to get killed, some troopers might have to ride double, thus slowing down the retreat. In addition, the men were running out of ammunition. Therefore, it was clear to Nate that they had to try and break out of the encirlement.

"Gawd am I thirsty!" said Jesse, his voice parched, his face crusted with dust and gun smoke mixed with perspiration. He struggled to lick his dry lips with his tongue as he unfastened his canteen from his McClellan saddle hook. The men had fought for over three hours with barely enough time to rest or drink any water because the canteens were with the horses and Nate had refused to give permission for any trooper to leave the skirmish line. The day was very hot and the air smelled of acrid smoke and along with the dust, soiled the men's faces and uniforms. In addition, the heat of the searing sun made the troopers sweat so much that stains made by salt crystals covered the area around some of the men's armpits and backs. Some of the men had perspired so profusely that they experienced difficulties lining up their sights because of the rivers of sweat that streamed down their faces, flooding their eyes.

"I think it's time to organize a withdrawal and make fo' the fort," said Nate as he recapped the nipples of his Walker-Colt cylinder.

"Yeah, I think you're right," replied Jesse. "You goin' tell the colonel?"

"Get the men ready to mount up and prepare the company to move out," Nate told Jesse, as he walked over to the cottonwood tree where Colonel Armes rested.

Colonel Armes had already made up his mind. He saw Sergeant Christy, a man who he had known and relied on for several months, get shot in the face and collapse in the grass. He also realized that the men might endure another charge but that in all likelihood, the Dog

Men would prefer to lay siege to the command from the nearby ravines. If that happened, the troop would be boxed in and it might be days before any rescue could be anticipated while the shortage of ammunition would place the troop at a long-term disadvantage. Armes reasoned that to remain in this location would invite possible annihilation. Therefore, an organized running fight would be their only hope to escape the Dog Men.

"Sir! I think . . ."

"I already know, Sergeant Major!" interrupted Armes in a voice that revealed his irritation over the fact that he had not only been wounded, but that he was led into an ambush like some shave-tail lieutenant fresh out of the Point. As he reached for the reins of his horse, he signaled his orderly to help him mount his mare who became very excited from all the sounds and smells of battle. The animal started to rear and turn in circles as the orderly begged the horse to calm down long enough for Armes to place his boot in the stirrup and mount the frightened beast.

"Prepare the command for a break out," he instructed, as he finally managed to place his backside into the McClellan. The bleeding from his hip wound had temporarily stopped but the colonel's makeshift bandage was soaked in dried blood and flies started to congregate and crawl over the bandage. "Have two squads cover our retreat!" Armes' voice was strained but his will remained strong.

"Aye, aye, sir," saluted Nate.

Jesse had already ordered the troopers to mount up in columns of four and instructed the flankers to remain in view of the column. The cavalrymen were checking the cinches and other horse equipment when Nate mounted his horse.

"Jesse," said Nate, as he pulled the lever down on his Spencer. "Take care of de colonel. I'm goin' be with de boys in de rear."

"Goin' cover our asses, big brother?" jested Jesse, smiling.

"Don't I always?" retorted Nate, as he motioned two squads to follow him to the rear.

———

Although the Dog Men had almost turned the west flank of the blue coats' skirmish line, their horses were in poor condition for pursuit. Cougar Eyes noticed that the soldiers were organizing a breakout, so he ordered several of his braves to snipe at the column with rifle fire while he prepared the warriors for another mounted charge.

Colonel Armes and the column had already galloped out of the encirclement, retracing their march toward Campbell's Camp, leaving Nate and twelve men alone to face the Cheyennes. The two squads were mounted and formed a straight line while holding their Spencers in their right hands while the butt of the carbines rested on their right hips. Their duty was to ensure the escape of the column by delaying pursuit by the enemy.

Seeing the tiny size of the remaining force, Cougar Eyes mounted another pony and encouraged the warriors to follow him again. "We will kill them all!" he boasted, as he dug his heels into his mustang's flanks and squeezed his thighs to direct his mount toward Nate and the two squads.

" 'Member boys, wait till I gives de order to fire, and aim fo' de horses," reminded Nate, as he stared at the approaching Cheyennes.

The Dog Men were galloping their mounts as if they were prepared to ride right through Nate and the twelve troopers. Cougar Eyes and his fellow braves were feeling confident and a sense of exhilaration that was intoxicating, overwhelmed them. He believed that these few *Mo' ohtae-Ve' ho' e* men would flee like antelope or be killed where they stood.

Rather than wait for the Cheyennes to come in close before opening fire, Nate ordered the troopers to fix their front sights for long range firing in order to execute several volleys before the Dog Men came close enough to encircle his squad. Nate raised his right arm and waited for a few seconds before giving the order to fire. The warriors were howling expletives, blowing on their bone whistles, and shouting *hi, hi, hi* . . .

"At one hundred yards . . . fire." A sheet of flame rang out the moment Nate lowered his arm. The carbine fire was in complete unison, resulting in the deadly effect of sending several mortally wounded ponies into the ground and ejecting their riders.

"At seventy-five yards . . . fire." Again, the same effect was achieved by tearing holes into the charging Cheyennes, and Nate ordered one more volley at fifty yards before he barked, *"Fall back, boys . . . Run like hell."*

The last volley blunted the charge long enough for Nate to order his men to reverse their mounts and spur the animals toward the main column. Nate waited until all of his troopers had departed and then emptied his Spencer at the Cheyennes as fast as he could work the lever, cock back the hammer, and pull the trigger. He trained his field of fire at a 180-degree range, hence hitting targets from left to right. The Dog Men were already reeling from the shock of rapid and accurate gunfire from the blue coats which convinced them to hold back their ponies. Now, this *Mo' ohtae-Ve' ho' e* man was still firing his weapon and creating pandemonium among the braves. Cougar Eyes, who had not been in front of this charge because his mount was slower than his mustang who had run off the battlefield after he was de-horsed by Nate, again exhorted his warriors, and berated them that they were behaving not like formidable *Hotame-Ho' nehe*, but rather like frightened children.

Nate spurred his mount as fast as the beast could run. He finally caught up with the two squads and urged the men to ride as if they had Lucifer breathing down their backs. The Dog Men, now sufficiently humiliated by Cougar Eyes' belittling, were about a half mile behind and closing.

Nate and the rear guard galloped their horses for about three miles when he ordered the two squads to halt and reform a mounted skirmish line. The troopers obeyed instantly, and were once again prepared to fire additional volleys.

"Rapid fire boys fire rapid fire," he commanded as he pulled out his Walker-Colt and took aim and fired the piece into the Dog Soldiers. The Cheyennes, this time however, did not ride close together and when they saw that the blue coats were reforming their skirmish line, they fanned out as if they were a scattering flock of birds. The cavalrymen emptied the four remaining cartridges in their Blakeslee tubes when Nate gave the order to again fall back.

"Make for the column," he roared as he spurred his horse and pressed down on the visor of his kepi so the hat would not blow off his head.

The main column by now was about three miles away and also moving at a rapid gait. Colonel Armes was in front while Jesse was in the rear making sure that there were no stragglers. Jesse kept looking backward for any signs of Nate who he knew was fighting a rear action and from the sounds of rapid and repeated carbine fire, was engaged in a hotly contested fight. Jesse decided to ride up and see Colonel Armes.

"Beggin' the colonel's per-mission sir, shouldn't we wait for Sergeant Major Gordon?"

"Not yet, damnit! We gotta move," Armes yelled back. He was extremely uncomfortable in the saddle and experienced pain with every move his horse made.

"But, sir . . ." responded Jesse desperately.

"No, Sergeant. The rear guard is giving us time to make our escape. Now fall back to the rear."

"Sir," replied Jesse as he saluted and reined in his horse to allow the column to pass. As he was about to take his position at the rear, he saw Nate and the twelve troopers emerging at a full gallop from a ravine about a half a mile away.

"Thank Gawd!" Jesse was relieved and was about to inform Armes when he noticed that Nate and his boys were being closely pursued by about fifty Cheyenne warriors and they were all heading in the direction of the column.

"*Colonel.*" Jesse spurred his horse back to where Armes was, and pointed to Nate and the approaching Cheyennes.

Once Armes saw that the rear guard was being chased by the Cheyennes, he forgot about the pain in his hip. "Sergeant, have the men form a mounted skirmish line in a V formation."

Jesse organized the troopers to form a V formation to face the attack while providing cover for Nate. The V formation also had the advantage of making it difficult for an enemy to outflank their opponent. As Nate and the two squads approached the command, Jesse instructed two troopers to get out of the way to allow Nate and the fleeing rear guard within the V formation. When they poured through the gap that was made for them, their horses were galloping so fast that it took the men several dozen yards of ground to rein in their mounts. They then maneuvered their heavily breathing and lathered-up horses into the V formation and Nate ordered the men to reload.

"Back already, Sergeant Major?" scoffed Colonel Armes. The commanding officer was feeling the throbbing pain in his hip again, and was becoming impatient.

"Sir. We did de best we could, but de ground is not favorable for defensive action, sir . . ."

"It's *shit* ground, Goddamnit!" interrupted Armes, as he again winced in agony from the wound because his horse bolted slightly to the left. He slapped the beast with his right hand and cursed the animal. Armes' mount was not the only horse in the command that was becoming unruly, several of the men were experiencing difficulties keeping them stationary, while they steadied their carbines.

When the Cheyennes saw that the blue coats were in a stationary position with their weapons ready, rather than fleeing in disorganized panic, they reined in their ponies. Those warriors who possessed rifles and bows started to shoot at the troopers while others with lances and bows yelled insults and taunted them with vulgar gestures, in an attempt to provoke the pony soldiers into chasing them.

"Hold fast boys, don't let the bastards intimidate ya," yelled Nate as the ground around him was being pelted by bullets and arrows.

The Dog Men decided not to engage the pony soldiers in another frontal attack. They resolved themselves to shoot at the troopers from behind a coulee and inflict sufficient casualties so they would panic and run. Then the warriors would chase down their prey one by one, as if they were on a hunting expedition.

After a few minutes of being shot at, Colonel Armes decided that he preferred to resume the organized retreat maneuver rather than remain in the open and provide targets for the sniping hostiles. He summoned Nate and instructed that the V defensive formation prepare to reverse itself and proceed at a rapid gait toward Campbell's Camp.

"Troop, about face, forward ho," ordered Nate. The V formation reversed itself, and proceeded at a rapid gait.

The Dog Soldiers did not pursue them. The fight had lasted over six hours in the searing heat and the warriors and their ponies were exhausted. In addition, several of the braves in the war party were wounded, and there were only a few hours of light left in the day to retrieve their comrades who had fallen and who either needed burial or assistance. The Cheyennes also realized that these black and white soldiers possessed powerful medicine, and although the Dog Men did manage to kill one of them and wound their chief, they were impressed by their tenacity and decided that it would be better to let them go, and fight them another day.

Cougar Eyes was not satisfied, however. He felt that his fellow *Hotame Ho' nehe* could have done better, but realized that the element of surprise had not yielded the projected results. He decided to charge his mustang up a tall ravine and halted the big beast in sight of the retreating column. He stood erect on the back of his mustang using his calves to project his height and started to howl. "*Ne'aahtove!*" (Listen to me.)

Nate heard the warrior bellow and turned around. Jesse and Armes as well as the rest of the battered command were too preoccupied in pushing their mounts forward to look back. Nate fell out of the column and pointed his mount in the direction of where Cougar Eyes had halted his mustang and with equal defiance, yelled back as he thought about Sergeant Christy. "We'll meet again, you bastard!"

When Nate and the command returned to Fort Hays, he decided to pay his respects to the Shaws and see how Mrs. Foster was doing. When he inquired about their whereabouts, he was informed that they were still at the hospital. He brushed off his uniform and polished his hightop boots and walked through the maze of tents that made up the fort. He found them sitting side-by-side on camp chairs outside a large and airy tent that served as a convalescence station. Mrs. Shaw was wearing a simple, out-of-fashion dark dress that one of the post's officer's wives gave her. Her long blond hair was wrapped in a tight bun and a straw hat shielded her blistered face from the sun. Mr. Shaw, Nate thought, looked much more pitiful than his recently ravaged wife. The top half of his head was wrapped in a white a bandage that was so tight that

Nate saw that the right side of Mr. Shaw's face was smooth because the ear had disappeared. His left hand arm rested in a pathetic-looking sling and the hand was heavily bandaged.

"Glad to see you again, Sergeant," smiled Mrs. Shaw as she clutched her husband's left arm, who in turn nodded his approval. Nate thought that she looked much better, and that her wounds and sunburned skin seemed to be healing well. Mr. Shaw started to get up but Nate saw the pain in his face from the wounds he had sustained and placed his hand on the man's shoulder.

"Please, sir. Please remain seated." Nate felt touched that the wounded and slightly emaciated man wanted to get out of his chair to greet him.

"How are we all doin'?" inquired Nate humbly as he removed his kepi and rotated the brim and visor of the hat with his fingers.

"We'll be fine, thank you," replied Mr. Shaw gratefully.

"And . . . Mrs. Foster?" Nate dreaded asking this question for he knew what the probable answer would be.

Mrs. Shaw's mouth started to twitch and her eyes became glossy and watery. She bowed her head and started to cry.

"She lost the baby and the surgeon told us that she don't eat, sleep, talk, or wanta git out of bed." Mr. Foster also bowed his head. "She . . . she gots no more life in her when you look into her eyes."

A long and awkward silence descended upon the group. Nate felt sad but he wanted to move on. "I . . . gots something fo' you all." He reached into his shell jacket and removed the blue beaded necklace. The moment Mrs. Shaw heard the rattle of the piece of jewelry she looked up. She had recognized the familiar sound that the blue beads made when they rubbed together.

"My blue necklace!" she responded with glee. Her eyes became wide with excitement and she took a handkerchief to dry her face and blow her nose. Nate handed the piece of jewelry to Mrs. Shaw and she gently held them in her hands that still showed signs of healing cuts and bruises. Nate saw that her wrists were still black and blue from the tight leather strips that had slashed her skin.

"No, Sergeant," choked Mrs. Shaw as she fondled the blue beaded necklace. "I . . . would like to give you this." Mrs. Shaw held the article in the air as if she were making a sacrifice for the gods. "For saving our lives. Maybe one day soon you will have a fine woman to love you . . . as my husband and I love each other."

"But, ma'am, I can't accept . . ."

"Please, Sergeant! We are going back East, and since my husband gave me this as a gift for coming West, I don't want it to remind me of what had happened." Nate looked at Mr. Shaw and her husband nodded in approval.

"Thank you, ma'am," Nate was shaking his head in disbelief. This was the first time that someone had given him such a gift. "I will cherish this necklace, with all my strength."

Wild Bill Hickok was playing a leisurely game of solitaire while he sat with his back to the wall in the barroom of the Gibson House in Hays City. The oil lamp lighting in the saloon made his long dirty-blond hair glow brilliantly, as if a halo of gold hovered over his head. Dressed in a dark green custom-made frock coat with wide lapels that was complemented by a black cravat, he flipped cards with his left hand while his right nursed a shot glass of whiskey. Wild Bill always held his cards with his left hand so his right would be free to draw his .36-caliber Navy Colt if he needed to instill manners into any man who dared to insult him or cause any trouble.

Wild Bill was used to such establishments that followed the railroad such as the Gibson saloon, with its crude construction and primitive interior commingling with the stale stench of tobacco, liquor, burning oil lamps, and reeking body odor. Most of the patrons, as was the case in all these places, became drunk on cheap booze, were boisterous, belligerent, lonely, and homesick.

Although the barroom at the Gibson House was packed with customers, Wild Bill couldn't find anyone who wanted to play cards and gamble. His eyes slowly gazed around the room that was filled with hopeful prospectors, greenhorns from back East seeking adventure, fugitives from justice, mule skinners, packers, crude teamsters, hucksters dressed up as dandies, sleazy pimps, gun slingers seeking a reputation, gamblers dressed in silk-embroidered vests, and heavily made-up prostitutes, known as horizontal workers.

As he entered the saloon, Nate was nearly knocked over by two fighting buffalo hunters who were being thrown out onto the street by the bouncer of the Gibson.

"You sons-a-bitches go do your fightin' else w'ere," shouted the bouncer who was even bigger than Nate. He threw the two intoxicated buffalo hunters from the doorway into the muddy street that was mixed with horse and cow manure. Without uttering a sound, Nate quickly moved his big frame just in time to avoid them and walked into the saloon. Although black troopers rarely ventured into town on leave for fear of being shot or lynched, Nate was not bothered by that prospect. On the contrary, he secretly wanted to be provoked. Then the opportunity would be available to demonstrate plainly, to anyone who challenged, or "fucked with him," that they were going to pay a high price. To Nate, this was not the South, but the frontier, and as far as he was concerned, the rule of law was nonexistent and traditional rules of behavioral propriety between blacks and whites were not applicable but were on an equal footing.

The saloon smelled of tobacco and oil smoke, and was poorly lit, but Wild Bill Hickok noticed Nate in the doorway and beckoned him to come over to his table.

"You look almost as good as I do, Sergeant," yelled Wild Bill over the noise of the saloon. As usual, Sgt. Maj. Nate Gordon was characteristically dressed to military regulation. His shell jacket and trousers were brushed, and the gold piping on his collar and sleeves were bright. The military insignia of his rank, bold chevrons, as well as the polished brass buttons, high-top boots, and saber belt, glowed in the oil lamp lighting of the saloon. Nate's kepi was slightly tilted over the right eye and his clean gauntlets were stuffed in the belt. The trusty Walker-Colt, its huge butt protruding from its holster, was cleaned and loaded. Unlike Nate however, who always dressed in perfect military regulation, Wild Bill Hickok enjoyed attiring himself for effect, and for the occasion, and this evening, the plainsman was dressed in his traditional evening attire and looked every inch the gambler. His shoulder length, slightly curly hair was perfectly parted down the middle of his scalp and was well oiled. Wild Bill's mustache, which was lighter than his hair, was carefully combed down the sides of his mouth. He wore a light-gray velvet frock coat with wide lapels that was accentuated by black silk piping. His red-and-silver brocaded vest was buttoned only at the very top, thus revealing a crisp white shirt. Hickok's waist was wrapped in a wide red sash that held a .36-caliber Navy Colt with its butt forward, ready to be drawn. The main centerpiece of this costume however, was his jeweled collar stud that was pinned above his prominent white silk cravat.

"Yes, sir," replied Nate, surprised that Wild Bill beckoned him to come to his table.

"Pull up a chair, the night's been kinda slow for doin' any card playin'," complained Hickok, as he downed what was left in his shot glass. "Guess the word's out that I'm not some push ov'r for cards," he laughed.

"I'm no card playin' man, Mr. Hickok," replied Nate, dryly.

"Didn't think so," snapped back Wild Bill, as he ostentatiously shuffled the deck with great expertise in an attempt to impress Nate with his prowess for handling cards.

Nate pulled out his briarwood pipe and tobacco pouch from his Haversack and started to stuff the bowel.

"Another shot for me," yelled Hickok to the barman. He then turned his elegant head toward Nate and lifted his right eyebrow and raised his shot glass toward the barman. "And one for my friend, Charley!"

"Yes, sir, Mr. Hickok, right away," responded the barman as if he was a private responding to a general's order.

"Nice to have respect," said Nate, a little sarcastically.

"Out here, there is only one way to earn and keep respect," exhorted Hickok, as the corner of his mouth cracked a smile, and his gray eyes sparkled.

Nate placed his pipe in between his teeth and ignited the bowl after he struck the tip of a match underneath the table.

"Well, it won't be forever that the bullet will rule this part of the country," said Nate, matter-of-factly.

"Country's changin' fast," replied Hickok. He was becoming a little impatient because the barman was taking his time with the drinks. Wild Bill disliked poor service. "First the war, then the end of slavery. In twenty years there's goin' be no more buffalo and Indians." He paused, then added in a rather resigned tone of voice, "This whole country will be filled up with people from everywhere pretty soon."

"Country needs law and order 'fore anything," added Nate. He puffed on his pipe and savored the tobacco. There was a moment of awkward silence between the two men, but Nate was curious about this man who was not only famous, but dressed as if he were a prince and spoke with a velvet voice. "From what I hears, you killed a lot a men."

"Just sons-of-bitches that needed killing," replied Wild Bill, matter-of-factly as the barman finally brought the whiskey shot glasses and placed them on the table. He then filled each glass to the brim and left the two men alone.

"Heard you boys got into a hell of a fight with them Dog Soldiers down by the Saline," inquired Hickok as he raised the shot glass to his lips and downed half of its contents. Wild Bill was disappointed that he was not available to accompany Colonel Armes with Company F in his recent pursuit of the Cheyennes. General Custer had demanded his services during the same period, so Hickok had to scout for the Seventh Cavalry. Considering that Wild Bill was employed during the month of July to scout for Colonel Armes, and had been unavailable to accompany him in his pursuit, thus missing the fight, galled the plainsman.

"Hell of a fight!" exclaimed Nate, as he gently placed the shot glass to his lips and sipped the liquor. It had been a long time since Nate tasted any alcohol. He was not a drinking man, but every now and then, depending on the circumstances, he would have a shot or two of whiskey. Although he did not show it, he was flattered that the famous gun fighter had asked him to sit with him. With the exception of the Cajun Jean le Fou, Nate had never drank with a white man.

"Colonel Armes, he's a good man," remarked Hickok, a little embarrassed that he was not in the fight. Wild Bill always wanted to fight Indians. Although he had been engaged as a scout for the army during the past year, he never ran into many Indians. "I wish I could have been at that fight with you boys," remarked Hickok. "But General Custer kept me occupied with scouting duties." He was jealous of Custer, who always seemed to get his name in the newspapers more frequently than he did.

The plainsman suddenly started to reflect on the past. He was feeling the whiskey and Nate had reminded him of his youth. "When I was a young cuss growing up in Illinois," Hickok paused for a moment and looked at Nate with his piercing gray eyes, "my father became an abolitionist and became part of the Underground Railroad." Nate remained silent and continued to puff on his pipe. Feeling a little frustrated that he did not get the reaction he desired, Wild Bill leaned his chair back against the wall. His gray eyes sparkled again, while he elegantly lifted the glass of whiskey to his lips and took another sip. "My pa hid lots of runaways in the house. Sometimes for days on end.

"My pa was a deeply religious man who came from the Lake Champlain region of Vermont. When he moved us to Illinois, he became *impressed* with the moral and righteous activism of the Quakers, who were engaged in helping runaway slaves escape to Canada."

"I was a runaway," said Nate gravely.

"I figured as much." Hickok prided himself in sizing up people. His natural curiosity, confidence, and courage enabled him to be a good judge of people's character and abilities. He considered this a gift which allowed him to escape many perils and earn his living by constantly being on the edge of danger.

"My father hid runaway slaves in the attic and basement of our house." Hickok took another sip from his shot glass. "While preparations were made for them to be escorted North, I would talk to the fugitive slaves. I liked some of them." Hickok wanted to add, "but did not really trust most of them," but thought it might be considered as an insult.

"Ran away from Louis'ana, and kept running, and running, till I came to Kansas and joined the army," informed Nate as he lifted the shot glass and gently sipped the whiskey from the brim. He was beginning to feel melancholy as he recalled the past and the days when he was a slave.

Sensing that Nate was becoming despondent, Hickok decided to change the direction of the conversation.

"One of the runaways that stayed with us, was a gal named Hannah. She stayed with us for a couple years, and was a great help to my mother." Wild Bill chuckled a little and smiled, "I used to confide in

Hannah. When I broke some rule or was caught doin' something bad, an' my pa wanted to thrash me, I'd seek out Hannah . . . for solace and protection." Hickok raised his glass in tribute, and imitating his father added, "Let the good woman's soul rest in peace!" He then polished off the whiskey.

"Heard you were a sharpshooter durin' de war," inquired Nate, wanting to also change the subject to something else. Every time he thought about the days of slavery, he could not help but think about his mother. The woman who worked herself to the bone every day and who still found time for her only son to teach him how to read and write at great personal risk.

"Oh, I was a lot of things during the war." Wild Bill stroked his long mustache that resembled the whiskers of a cat, and started to shuffle the deck of cards again. "Scout, spy, wagon master for ox teams, an' yes, at the Battle of Pea Ridge, I was a sharpshooter." Hickok turned to Nate and smiled, "The war was an exciting time, don't you agree, Sergeant?"

"The war give us freedom, sure 'nough, but the struggle ain't finished." Nate took another sip from his glass.

Two extremely drunk troopers from Custer's Seventh Cavalry were standing by the bar yelling and shouting at each other. They were near enough to be overheard by Wild Bill and Nate, and one of them was complaining bitterly that he was cheated at cards while playing poker with Wild Bill the week before, and now that he was broke and wanted another drink, was becoming increasingly hostile.

"Believe that man is referrin' to you, Mr. Hickok," said Nate dryly as he puffed on his pipe.

"I believe you're right, Sergeant." Wild Bill continued to shuffle his cards while keeping one eye on the two potential troublemakers at the bar.

The troopers were now becoming more belligerent and the one who had the misfortune of losing money to Hickok the week before bellowed. "That fancy-pants cheated me from my money!" His drinking companion also started to direct his gaze on Wild Bill and Nate. "Mr. Fancy-Pants got a nigger drinkin' buddy too," he clamored, laughing as he loosely dangled his beer mug, spilling its contents on the sawdust floor.

The cheated trooper and his companion stumbled over to the poker table, making their way through the throng of saloon activity and barroom smoke, until they reached the table.

"I, I, want de money you ch. . . . ch. . . . eated me out of," blurted the trooper in a drunken haze.

Wild Bill stopped shuffling cards and gave the trooper an icy stare. Then, in a very grave tone of voice, addressed him with complete contempt. "Son, I've kilt men for sayin' less. Now, I know that you're drunk and feelin' lonely, but you lost your money fair and square, so I suggest that you, and your drinkin' companion, leave the premises 'fore I stop being generous for not puttin' a bullet 'tween your eyes."

"You duck-face-dandy, give m'ah friend's money back!" yelled the other trooper as he leaned over the table and placed his palms on the surface to support his weight near Hickok's shot glass.

With the ease, grace, and speed of a cat, Wild Bill reached for his long bowie knife that was stuffed in his sash and drove the blade into the back of the offending trooper's hand, pinning it to the table. The stabbing sounded as if it were a butcher working on a piece of raw meat. The trooper howled with pain so loudly that everyone in the barroom stopped what they were doing to gawk. Hickok then drew one of the Williamson .41-caliber Derringers from his vest pocket and placed the snub-nose piece right into the trooper's face while he pulled out the bowie knife as if disengaging a stubborn piece of steak from his fork.

The wounded man stopped screaming and clutched his bleeding hand while his beady eyes stared at the Derringer as if the weapon was a wasp sitting on his nose. He whimpered like a sick puppy and started to beg Wild Bill not to shoot him.

Nate remained motionless during this whole affair. Instinctively, he wanted to intervene by telling the drunk troopers that they were out of line and that the stripes on his sleeves gave him the authority to throw them in the stockade. Wild Bill however, reacted so quickly, and the dispute seemed to be a personal matter between Hickok and the white soldiers of another regiment, that Nate decided best to stay out of this affair for the time being.

"Nobody calls me duck-face and lives," said Wild Bill in a tone of voice that would cower most men into submission.

"Pl., pl., don't, don't kill me. I, I, ap' poligize," whined the soldier.

"You snot-nose bastards git the hell outta here 'fore I change my mind 'bout lettin' you live." The troopers, by now much sobered by the experience, walked away as if they were two beaten dogs with their tails between their legs.

"Pretty impressive," said Nate as he puffed on his pipe.

"I'm a fighting man, you know, and I'll brook no man to degrade me, I can't stand that, you know." The plainsman then stared into Nate's eyes and commented dryly, "and I think you know what I mean?" He wiped off the blood and bits of flesh from the bowie knife with his handkerchief which he discarded immediately upon the bar-room floor, and placed the blade back into its sheath. He ordered another round of drinks and resumed shuffling the deck of cards as if nothing had ever happened. Only this time the barman was very prompt in delivering the bottle of whiskey to the table.

Seven

August on the western Kansas plains is hot and dry, with the ironic prospect that a short and very long winter is only weeks away. Colonel Armes was waiting for Sergeant Major Nate Gordon to report. He had recovered sufficiently from his hip wound to resume his duties as commander of F Company, and was preparing for another expedition against the Cheyennes. Colonel Armes was instructed to join forces with the Eighteenth Kansas Volunteer Cavalry under the command of Cpt. George Jenness.

General Sherman had ordered the governor of Kansas to raise a volunteer cavalry regiment from the state to assist the army in squashing Cheyenne depredations along the upper Solomon River basin on the High Plains. Although Armes was skeptical about having support from militia, he was somewhat gratified that the addition of ninety plus men to his own company would considerably bolster his strength in facing Cheyenne warriors.

"Yes, enter," replied Armes after he heard the knock on the office door. Nate entered, saluted, and stood at attention.

"Morning, Sergeant Major."

"Mawnin', sir. Glad to see the colonel is at full speed, sir," responded Nate, using the officer's brevet wartime rank. Nate always tried to be careful in addressing officers with the rank that they possessed during the war, but when referring to them in their absence, he would use their current rank.

"At ease, Sergeant Major. Please, have a seat." The colonel motioned with his hand to the old barrack chair that was facing his desk.

Nate sat in the chair and folded his hands in his lap. He had just come from fatigue duty at the stables, supervising the men while they groomed their mounts and cleaned their horse accoutrements. Consequently, his boots were not in their usual spit-and-polish state and he was a little self-conscious of that fact. He wanted to change his uniform before meeting with Colonel Armes, but the orderly was insistent that he report at once.

"I will be to the point, Sergeant Major. I have just received orders that we are to depart tomorrow at first light and seek out the hostiles along the upper Solomon. We will be joined by the Eighteenth Kansas Volunteer Cavalry which will bring up our combined strength to about one hundred and fifty men and officers."

Nate noticed that Armes always felt awkward briefing noncoms and junior officers. He decided that the colonel preferred to be on a horse in the field commanding troops, not behind a desk. But Nate decided that there was another factor as well in this man's personality. He was convinced that although Armes respected, and was proud of the fighting abilities of his Negro troops, he did not feel completely comfortable being with them unless in the thick of a fight. Armes had confessed to him on the way back to Hays from the Saline fight that with the exception of seeing a few free Negroes when he was growing up in New Jersey, he had never had any real contact with people of color. It was only when he was fighting in Virginia that he saw hundreds of slaves fleeing ruined plantations or in the employ of the Union Army. Nate sensed that Armes had difficulties in getting along with people in general, but Nate had recognized that the colonel felt even more distant and aloof with his own black soldiers. After a few moments of silence, Armes coughed, and asked him if he had any questions.

"Will the column be supplied by wagons or mules, sir?"

"Excellent question, Sergeant. The Eighteenth Kansas will be providing supply wagons and teamsters that will be part of the column, but I want you to see that troop F be equipped with enough food for a week, and that the men receive a hundred rounds of ammunition for their carbines, fifty rounds for the army Colts, and enough oats as the feedbags will carry. In other words; full packs." Armes paused for a moment as if he was distracted by something outside his window, but then added, as if he knew what Nate was thinking, "No, Sergeant, the company will be leaving their sabers behind."

"Yes, sir, but beggin' the colonel's pardon, sir, won't the wagons slow us down?"

"I intend to split the column when I deem it necessary and give quick pursuit. And if that is all, Sergeant Major, you are dismissed."

"Aye, aye, sir."

Captain Jenness and Lieutenant Price were discussing the flicker of light in the distant eastern horizon. They were standing near a supply wagon at the tail end of the column that was bivouacked along the banks of Solomon River in the High Plains country. It was a very dark night, and if it were not for the stars and half moon, the men would be in total darkness. The two officers of the Eighteenth Kansas Cavalry had marched out of Fort Hays with Colonel Armes' Tenth Cavalry the day before, and had bivouacked at dusk. The column moved rapidly, traveling seventy miles within forty-eight hours. Armes decided to bivouac the men for the night and ordered no campfires and posted extra pickets around the horses and perimeter. The command was now deep into Cheyenne country and the prospect of ambush was on the minds of all the men. In the High Plains country, where the only real form of natural seclusion were deep ravines, the flicker of even a small campfire at night can be seen for miles. Even during the day, a line of smoke if not properly dispersed, can be detected from great distances.

"What do you think George? Think it might be dem boys from the Seventh?" inquired Lieutenant Price, a little eager to please his commanding officer, Captain Jenness.

"I'm not sure. Could be some of dem patrols from the Seventh Cavalry, but then again, could be Cheyenne," responded Jenness as he scratched the stubble on his face. "Go and git Colonel Armes and tell him about dat light."

Colonel Armes was already asleep in his tent, but quickly rose to his feet when told of the fire on the horizon. Lieutenant Price escorted him back to where Captain Jenness was discussing the matter with some of his noncoms.

"Good evening sir, thought you might want to take a look at that light in the distance." Jenness, a tall man with a very cool demeanor, pointed to the light in the east. "Price, here, thinks it could be Major Moore of the Seventh Cavalry."

"No, I don't think so," responded Armes dryly.

"But sir, beg to differ. Aren't we suppose to meet up with them . . ."

"Mister, the cavalry does not light campfires in enemy country," retorted Armes, cutting off Price whom he considered a shavetail. He then added some sarcasm, as he was often prone to do, "even Custer's men are not that brash."

"So you think they could be Cheyennes?" inquired Jenness, seeking confirmation.

"Maybe, this is their country, you know. And they don't fear us. Or, it could be some damn fool civilian who doesn't know what the hell he's doing," retorted Armes.

"Permission to take half of my command and see, sir," said Jenness, enthusiastically, as if he was an overeager schoolboy.

This took Armes by surprise. He then thought to himself, with some amusement, "My, my, aren't we bright-eyed and bushy-tailed?"

Armes paused for a moment and bowed his head in thought. "Very well, Captain, take forty of your eager volunteers and determine if they are hostiles, and where that campfire is located. Then report back to me by dawn. And if there are hostiles, under no circumstances are you to attack. Is that clear?!"

"Sir," snapped Jenness as he saluted. Armes reluctantly returned the salute, and Jenness motioned to his sergeant to prepare to mount up and move out.

Jesse and Nate were doing their rounds. The routine was always the same. Verifying that the horses were well-tethered on the picket line and the sentries alert was the top priority. Next, spot-check equipment and weaponry. Nate had to tell several troopers to remain silent or they might wake up in the morning without their hair. One trooper mentioned, "Shit, Sergeant, Injuns don't want no curly black hair dat looks like a buffalo hide." Nate knew better. When he was at Fort Riley, he spoke to scouts and half-breeds who told him that Indians will lift any man's hair. He was told bluntly that there was no difference. For a Cheyenne warrior, the ritual of scalping one's enemy or the enemy of their friends was learned and appreciated even before puberty. It did not matter if you were black, red, or white, male, or female, the motivation was the same, and at the very least, an essential part of a warrior's obligations, such as counting coup or stealing horses. Nate was determined to let this young upstart private have an ear full.

"Boy, a warrior could, and *will*, lift your scalp faster than you can swat a bug from your wrist." Nate's face was inches away from the hapless trooper's face. The private could smell the sergeant major's strong body odor which offended his nostrils. "And if your mouth keeps yeapin' like some ol' woman, your black curly hair goin' be on some young buck's *lodge pole* or *coup stick*! Now shut up, and gets some sleep."

"Yes, Sergeant Major," responded the corrected trooper timidly.

As Nate was dressing-down the surly trooper, a corporal appeared from the dark. "Sergeant Major. The colonel wants to see you."

Armes was still in the rear of the column where the supply wagons were. He was staring at the light on the horizon when Nate approached.

"You want to see me, Colonel?" There was what seemed to be a long moment of silence. Except for the cacophony of millions of insects that broke the tranquillity of the Kansas night, there was complete stillness. Nate noticed that Armes seemed to be in a trance as he stared at the flickering light on the horizon. "Sir? Any orders, sir?" inquired Nate, again.

Armes finally broke the silence. "Did you notice that light on the eastern horizon, Sergeant?"

"Yes sir, Sergeant Randolph and me were discussin' it earlier, sir."

"I've sent Captain Jenness and forty of his bright-eyed volunteers to investigate." As Armes kept staring at the distant campfire on the horizon, Nate thought that the light from the bright stars and moon

345

gave Armes' face a ghostlike appearance. His right hand and arm were leaning against the tailgate of one of the supply wagons. Nate noticed that his commander's face revealed his discomfort whenever he was standing. Armes had told him that he still felt sharp pains in his back and leg from the hip wound. "If they have not returned by dawn, we will leave Lieutenant Price with the wagons and the company will proceed northwest, toward the Valley of the Beaver."

"Any special orders, sir?"

"Just have the men ready to move out by six, one way or the other," stated Armes, still transfixed at the flickering light.

Captain Jenness and his forty volunteers only found dying embers at the site of what was a campfire, but that was all. The Cheyennes had left long before his arrival, and now he had trouble finding the trail back to the bivouac area. He decided to camp for the night and rejoin the column at first light.

Nate and Jesse awoke at five, and by five forty-five, they had F troop mounted and ready to move out. It was another typical daybreak morning on the plains. The air was clear and the dew from the grass gave the air an invigorating aroma while the sun rose from the horizon as if it were a giant ball of light that seemed so close you could touch it.

Jesse was in the rear and Nate and Armes were in the vanguard of the column. The colonel was mounted and stood ramrod straight in the saddle which helped alleviate the flashes of pain that shot through his muscles due to his hip wound. He had been holding his pocketwatch in his opened right hand palm for over ten minutes. He gazed at the face of the clock off and on, and finally, after giving the timepiece one more good look, he closed the lid and placed the watch in his vest pocket. It was six o'clock on the dot, and he was not going to wait for Captain Jenness any longer. "Damn fool probably got lost," he whispered loudly to himself. Nate was close enough to hear the colonel's comment and for the first time in two days, smiled. He then thought to himself, "Yeah, I thought them white militia boys might be bitin' on somethin' bigga then they could chew."

"Sergeant Major," exclaimed Colonel Armes, as he stared off toward the horizon that was nothing more than hundreds of miles of rolling ravines and coulees covered by a sea of buffalo grass that moved in the breeze as if they were waves at sea. Nate advanced his horse a few paces toward his commanding officer and saluted. "Orders, sir?"

"Have the column move out, and for the love of God, keep the men quiet."

"Aye, aye, sir."

Roman Nose and Cougar Eyes were holding a conference with some other Dog Soldiers about what to do regarding the presence of the pony soldiers who had invaded the heart of their country.

"They have returned. The *Mo' ohtae-Ve' ho' e* blue coats that I have spoken to you about have come back in greater numbers," said Cougar Eyes. He had just returned from scouting the banks of the upper Solomon and had located the bivouac area of the pony soldiers. He had noticed that about forty white men had departed earlier in the direction of the campfire that he had lit to draw them out, in order to divide their strength. He had also seen Armes and the black and white men leave with troop F at a rapid gait, in the direction of Beaver Creek. Roman Nose laughed, and shook his protective war bonnet to make sure that all the feathers were untangled before placing the article on his head as if he were a prince in a self-crowning ceremony. "Let them come. We will start killing these thieves when the sun is in the middle of the sky."

Roman Nose who was called *Voo' xenehe*, was a giant of a man, the epitome of a Cheyenne brave in every manner. Courageous, self-assured, vain, and a true follower of Cheyenne spiritual medicine and tradition, he had sworn that he would fight the *Ve' ho' e* invader until he was killed, or the enemy driven from Cheyenne land. At a height of over six feet, he towered over most men while his muscular physique would make a Greek god blush with envy.

"We will divide our forces in two. You will attack the *Mo' ohtae-Ve' ho' e* pony soldiers at Beaver Creek, and I will pursue the whites," commanded Roman Nose, as he mounted a beautiful white stallion that

347

kept prancing in little steps while breathing heavily and snorting with excitement. He urged the stallion to a nearby stream where he paused in the middle of the cool running water and plunged his red-striped lance into the bed of the stream. He then slowly opened his arms with his palms facing the rising sun that was slowly creeping over the horizon, and tilted his head. *Voo' xenehe*'s body embraced the warm and bright rays as if he derived all of his strength from the sun. He basked in the warm sunlight while the sounds of the gently rippling water rushed by the legs of his stallion and the lance. As he relaxed his body and filled his lungs with the clean, cool air, he strived to attain spiritual peace and guidance.

Nate was reflecting upon the death of Sgt. William Christy. During the war, he made it a point not to befriend any of the other noncoms and certainly never with any of the enlisted men. It just really was not worth it. When he first joined the army, he made several friends while he was a raw recruit, but within a few months of fighting, they were all killed. So Nate reasoned that it served no purpose to become close with men who died as if they were flies in a killer frost. Sgt. William Christy, however, was different. What was special about his death, was that he became the first casualty of the Tenth Colored Cavalry, and Nate had to ask himself how many more men from Negro regiments must die a lonely death, before the public recognized black soldiers as possessing equal valor with white regiments?

Like all creeks that flowed from the major rivers of the plains, such as the Platte, Solomon, and Republican Rivers, the Valley of the Beaver was a scrubby place. Nate noticed that the soil was covered with tough buffalo grass so he deduced that the land must be a natural and traditional hunting ground for bison for many of the tribes of the plains. It did not bother him that there were no trees or vegetation that grew above five feet, and the only dominating topographical feature in the valley was Beaver Creek, a wide and shallow body of muddy water that meandered through deep ravines crowned by moderately high ridges that overlooked the landscape.

Company F was cantering in columns of four and Colonel Armes had ordered that all flankers were to remain in view of the troop. He wanted to avoid a repeat of what had occurred in the last fight, when one flanker was stupidly killed, and by the time the remaining ones had alerted the column that they were about to be attacked, there was hardly any time to prepare for counter defensive measures. Therefore, Armes reasoned that it was best to keep the men together as much as possible while not compromising the eyes and ears of the column by reigning in the flankers too much.

The men were keeping their mounts in good regimental step, and Nate was content that the troopers, now battle-tested and less anxious regarding the fighting prowess of their enemy, moved relatively silently. With the exception of creaking leather and the monotonous sounds of tin utensils and accoutrements rubbing against the rims of McClellan saddles, the column moved as quietly as possible.

Much to Nate's dismay however, Armes ordered that the company guidon remain unfurled. Nate knew that it made perfect sense that the colonel did not want to wave anything in the air that might be detected by the Cheyennes miles away, hence giving away their position. Although the dust being kicked up by big and heavily-shod army horses could be detected for miles, and the numerous piles of dung made by the troops' oat-fed mounts that were dumped on the trail could easily be sniffed out by any Cheyenne scout. Therefore, Nate wondered what was the point of keeping the guidon unfurled. Especially when they were told to expect units of the Seventh Cavalry who were also hunting for the Cheyennes along the numerous creeks of the upper Solomon and Republican Rivers. They at least, with the usage of a spy glass, would be able to recognize which regiment the column belonged to if F troop were spotted by elements of the Seventh from a distance. Besides, thought Nate, the boys had trained hard and had proved their mettle against the Dog Soldiers. So Nate reasoned that the men merited to ride with the regimental and company guidons unfurled and flapping in the wind.

As company F approached the Valley of the Beaver at a canter, Armes had hoped to intercept either bands of raiding Dog Soldiers with stolen stock and hostages, or find lodges along the sand banks near Beaver Creek. The column briefly galloped over a series of deep ravines as if they were a fast-moving snake maneuvering over large mounds. The ravines were so deep and wide that it was impossible to see anything in the distance if you were at the bottom of one of them. As the front flankers crested one of the ravines, they saw what looked like five hundred mounted Cheyenne warriors suddenly emerging from a distant ravine as if they appeared from nowhere. The mounted warriors formed a straight line about three hundred yards dead ahead of the column.

The flankers reined in their horses as if they were trying to stop their animals from falling off a cliff. One of them, who was a corporal, sharply raised his soiled white gauntlet glove into the air, signaling the column to halt. Nate repeated the arm signal and the troop came to a sudden halt in the middle of the ravine. For a brief moment, the corporal remained too stunned to even say *whoa* to his horse. Armes motioned to Nate and the bugler to accompany him, and the men spurred their mounts to the crest of the ravine to investigate, and they also became immediately startled at what they beheld.

The spectacle of hundreds of mounted warriors forming a straight line mounted on their painted war ponies, with their lance tips pointing in the air, and thousands of feathers twitching in the wind, was much more than what Armes had bargained for. He had not anticipated that he would run into such a large war party who was preparing to charge him, rather than the other way around.

Cougar Eyes, who was at the center of the line, raised his long lance and commanded in a loud and encouraging cry, "*Noheto!*" (Let's go!) The other warriors responded by howling war whoops and blowing on their bone whistles as they directed their war ponies to charge the blue coats while shouting, *hi, hi, hi*.

Not since the war had Nate seen such a sight. Only this time however, the enemy were not a tired, ragged Confederate cavalry, but eager savage warriors, approaching as if they were a tidal wave.

"*Bugler sound Dismount,*" commanded Armes, as he jumped off his horse and handed the reins to his orderly. This time the bugler was able to muster enough spit to blow on his instrument. Armes then turned to Nate, "Sergeant Major! Have the men form a skirmish line on the crest of the ravine."

"Aye *sir*," replied Nate,

Jesse took charge of making sure that all of the horses were kept close together at the bottom of the ravine while the troopers scampered up the sides while maneuvering their rifle slings so their Spencers and Sharp carbines were held with both hands and ready for immediate use when they got into position on the skirmish line by either kneeling or lying down.

The Cheyenne horde were about seventy-five yards away and there was not enough time to wait for all of the men to get into position, so Armes commanded Nate to give the order to fire at will.

The sergeant major did not have to repeat the order twice. The troopers went to work immediately, firing round after round of Spencer, Sharps, and Colt shot into the charging warriors' line. Unlike the troop's first encounter with the Cheyennes, however, the men remained calm and felt confident. Rather than just blasting away blindly at the horses, the cavalrymen took their time aiming at the riders, and slowly squeezed the triggers. This sudden hail of accurate fire sent horses and riders tumbling to the ground as a cloud of gun smoke saturated the air and obscured the vision of both attacker and defender.

All hell had broken loose, and if it was not for the natural cover of the ravine, company F would have been annihilated the same way Lieutenant Kidder and his party met their grisly fate. The braves shot at the troopers with rifles, shotguns, and sent hundreds of arching arrows from their lance-bows into the ravine which wounded many of the horses.

The warriors' line broke after the first few volleys and this forced them to swarm around the ravine in an attempt to outflank the cavalrymen. Anticipating this maneuver, Colonel. Armes ordered Nate to spread out the skirmish line perimeter. Nate yelled for Jesse who was still with the horses, and the two noncoms hurriedly placed troopers on the flanks and rear of the ravine. As Nate was directing a squad to concentrate fire on the left flank, a hail of arrows poured into them from the sky. One cavalryman screamed as an arrow penetrated his left eye. He seized the shaft in horror, and started frantically to yell for help. Nate rushed to assist him, but as he was about to reach the wounded trooper, felt a sharp pain in his right leg just above the boot, causing him to stumble and fall on his left leg. He had also been hit with a Dog Soldier arrow.

"*Damnit to hell,*" he blurted, as he stared at the shaft. The trooper who had the arrow in his eye was now hysterical as he held the shaft of the arrow while blood poured from his eye. He was walking around aimlessly on the crest of the ravine bellowing for someone to help him as cavalrymen and Cheyenne Dog Soldiers continued to shoot at each other.

"Get down, ya damn fool," screamed Nate, trying to be heard over the sounds of neighing horses that were panicked and suffering from arrow wounds, gunfire, shouting soldiers, and howling Indians, but it was no use. As Nate tried to get up and pull down the hysterical trooper to safety, the wounded man was shot twice, one bullet hitting him in the stomach, while another passed through his neck, severing the artery. A jet of blood spurted out from the wound, spraying Nate and several other troopers nearby. The dying trooper collapsed on his knees and then fell to the ground as if he were a sack of grain.

Several of the cavalrymen that had been splattered with the dead soldier's blood were on the verge of panic. One man, after touching his face and seeing the blood on his hand, began to howl, "I'm hit, I'm hit, my Gawd, I'm hit!"

"No, you're not, you moron! That ain't your blood, keep firin' and don't panic," yelled Nate, chastising the trooper.

Fortunately, the arrowhead was not buried deeply into Nate's leg. As the men of Company F kept up their disciplined fire at the now circling Cheyennes, Nate, his back to the ravine, grabbed the arrow shaft. He wanted to see if it could be pulled out without ripping too much muscle and flesh.

Jesse, seeing his friend hit by an arrow and fall, immediately rushed to assist Nate after he barked some orders at the horse handlers. When he got to Nate, his friend was sitting on the buffalo grass tugging at the shaft.

"Are you aw right?" Jesse was concerned. Nate was wounded, and one trooper had already been killed. Another cavalryman had half his face blown off by a Dog Soldier that carried a shotgun. The Dog Man's face was painted red on the sides and white in the front. He was dressed in a dark war shirt that was accentuated by a silver pectoral *Naja*, which was a small crescent-shaped design that resembled a bird soaring to the heavens. He had boldly galloped his pony up to the blue coat as the soldier was reloading his Sharps and tapped the *Mo' ohtae-Ve' ho' e* on top of his head with his long coup stick. He then yelled so loudly and hideously, that the pony soldier and some of his nearby companions were so startled that they failed to react. The warrior then lifted his sawed-off shotgun and at almost point blank range, fired his weapon and blew the trooper's face right off his skull. He then yelled again, and as he turned his war pony around with his knees and galloped off, he quickly rotated his entire body over to the left side of his pony to escape the gunfire from the cavalrymen.

Adding to the confusion, some of the horses and especially the mules, were seriously wounded by deep arrow punctures and bleeding profusely, soaking the surrounding ground with blood. The animals were reeling from pain and fear, making it difficult for the troopers who were holding them to retain control.

"Don't leave the colonel alone, Jess! Get back there, the man needs you. I be aw right. Now go man, go," yelled Nate as he gently but firmly elbowed Jesse away. Jesse paused for an instant, long enough to give Nate a reassuring smile, and was off to join Armes on the skirmish line on the crest of the ravine.

"I can yank this bastard out," Nate whispered to himself. The arrow had not penetrated very deeply into Nate's leg. About three-quarters of the arrowhead had punctured Nate's skin and muscle, but the back part which was shaped like a swallow's tail had not penetrated. He pulled out his red bandanna from in between the dusty central brass buttons of his shell jacket, and placed it where the shaft had entered the leg. With his right hand, he reached for the base of the arrow and took a deep breath as if he were preparing to dive into a pool of water from some great height, and wrenched it out with one great movement. Nate's face became slightly contorted with pain but he remained completely silent. He had decided that he was certainly not going to cry out in front of the men no matter how much pain he felt.

The moment reminded Nate of the time when he was severely

beaten by Mas'a Hammond's stupid overseer. He was twelve years old when he and his best friend sneaked into the smokehouse and stole a fat ham bone. They were caught by the overseer as they were stuffing their mouths full of the juicy ham, and both boys got a brutal thrashing. While Nate's best friend hollered and wept and begged for mercy as the overseer beat him with a large willow stick and kicked him with his boots, Nate took his medicine without uttering a sound.

The wound started to bleed in earnest, and Nate felt his heart pound rapidly against his chest. He quickly wrapped the bandanna around his leg and managed to get back on his feet. He then leaped on his good leg toward Jesse and Colonel Armes.

Captain Jenness and Lieutenant Price of the Eighteenth Kansas were under siege by Roman Nose and hundreds of Cheyenne warriors. Jenness had rejoined Price, the supply wagon, and the other half of the regiment by mid-morning, and had proceeded to link up with Armes when the volunteers were caught by surprise by Roman Nose. As was the case with the Tenth, the volunteers faced overwhelming odds and possible annihilation. Unlike the Tenth however, there was virtually no natural cover to take refuge, so Jenness quickly ordered his fellow Kansans into a thin square and commanded the men to open fire with their Spencer repeaters. This defensive strategy, however, was growing more precarious by the moment, as the Cheyennes responded by circling the white men while firing their weapons into the square, inflicting casualties. Within minutes, men and horses were dropping like flies, and Jenness feared he was going to be overwhelmed.

"We can't stay here too much longer," yelled Lieutenant Price as he held his horse and fired his .44-caliber Remington six shooter into the mass of circling Cheyennes.

"How many wounded?" inquired Jenness, as he worked the lever on his Spencer.

"Eight so far . . ." responded Price glumly.

Jenness cocked the hammer, aimed, and pulled the trigger. He was trying to shoot down a huge Cheyenne warrior who was charging the square on a beautiful white stallion.

Roman Nose was wearing his ceremonial war bonnet and carried a huge lance. The great warrior was completely naked except for his beaded moccasins and a long loincloth. He towered over all of the other braves, and his reputation for courage and strength was at its peak. As he galloped his stallion toward the circle, some of the other men of the Eighteenth Kansas started to take aim and shoot at Roman Nose with their Spencer repeaters. The other braves retreated at a safe distance to watch their leader charge the *Ve' ho' e*, while providing verbal encouragement and by yelling war cries and blowing on war-whistles.

By now, half of the men in the square were aiming and shooting at Roman Nose, as his white stallion approached them with great speed.

"Get that bastard!" cried Jenness, as he was reloading his Spencer. *Voo' xenehe*, however, continued to charge and escape injury as he encouraged his magnificent horse to run through the square. One soldier, who fell out of line with the other men, was run down as if he was hit by a runaway wagon by Roman Nose's stallion, and as the great warrior charged through the square, the Kansans shot at him as fast as they could, but *Voo' xenehe* rode through, unharmed.

The braves, who were watching Roman Nose ride through the Kansans and count coup, marveled at their leader's feat. They raised their lances and shields into the air and clamored in approval. Even the whites were impressed.

"Never seen such a sight," remarked Lieutenant Price to Jenness, as he adjusted his hat.

"Shit, the men must have gotten off fifty rounds. And not one of 'em hittin' that damn red skin," scoffed Jenness, as he kicked the sandy ground in frustration. "We've got to get the hell outta here, Price." The commander of the Eighteenth Kansas was becoming very anxious. The Cheyennes were preparing to charge again, while they still continued to keep up a hot fire, wounding more of his men and horses. Jenness was faced with the strong possibility that his command might be wiped out if they did not find cover or link up with Colonel Armes and the Tenth.

"Have the men prepare to move out, load the wounded on the wagons."

"But the wagons will slow us down," whined Price.

"The wounded get priority, and I am not leaving the wagons behind!" Jenness was becoming irritated with Price. He wanted to move out and link up with the Tenth who he reckoned were not far away toward the northwest. He also realized that he would have to fight every inch of the way.

Nate and Jesse were conversing with Colonel Armes. All three men were on their stomachs while Armes was viewing the nearby ridges for signs of activity with his spy glass, a possession that he had owned since he became an officer in the late war. The Cheyennes had halted their mounted attack on the ravine, preferring to lay siege on the black and white soldiers. Except for a random round fired by an overly enthusiastic warrior, gunfire activity on both sides had more or less subsided. It was dusk, and the horizon and sky were a beautiful warm red that appeared to be painted by an oil brush. The long thin clouds and setting sun made the otherwise stark landscape look majestic.

"Sure is beautiful," marveled Jesse, as he gazed at the sky.

"Beautiful," replied Nate, with equal amazement. It pleased Jesse that although Nate was wounded and the company was surrounded by wild, hostile warriors, Nate smiled at the sky. He thought how different the sky and landscape looked from Louisiana. It reminded him of those glorious sunsets in the bayou when he was on the run from Bloodhound Jack, and those quiet evenings with his friend, Jean le Fou, listening to gator tales.

"Where in the hell is Jenness and the goddamn Eighteenth Kansas!?" exclaimed Armes, finally. As is the case with all officers engaged in battle, nothing is more irritating and nervewracking to them then the element of uncertainty.

"Don't think we goin,' see any signs of them till mornin', sir." Nate knew that it was going to be impossible to make any kind of fire in the ravine that only provided buffalo grass for fuel. A fire would have been helpful though. It would have served as a beacon for the Eighteenth Kansas, making it easier for them to locate Company F.

"Damn fools probably got lost," said Armes sarcastically. He then collapsed the spy glass and turned to Nate. "Well, there's nothing more we can do tonight, 'cept see to the wounded and horses."

"Aye, aye, sir," replied Nate while motioning to Jesse. "Let's go, Jess." As Nate and Jesse quietly descended to the bottom of the ravine, Nate felt the throbbing pain in his leg and although he poured a half a bottle of whiskey that Jesse had fetched for him from his saddlebag on the wound and bandaged it tightly, he was concerned that gangrene might develop. He could still walk, but with difficulty, and he knew that tomorrow the throbbing pain will be worse and walking would be increasingly difficult.

"Jess. Soon as we take care of the boys and the horses, I'm goin' stitch up this wound." Nate paused for a moment and in an embarrassing tone of voice asked Jesse, "Might need your help for this."

"First time you asked me fo' anything," smiled Jesse, as he placed his hand on his friend's shoulder.

"Come out of hole and fight, you sons-of-bitches!" yelled a Cheyenne brave from a nearby ridge who spoke some English. The Cheyennes were frustrated that the *Mo' ohtae-Ve' ho' e* soldiers with their *Ve' ho' e* officers would not come out of the ravine and face them. Some of the braves decided to taunt their enemies by shouting insults and decrying their manhood.

Cougar Eyes was sitting on a blanket near his pony discussing with Roman Nose and a few other Dog Men what to do about the blue coats that were hiding in the ravine.

"They fight well these *Mo'otoae-Ve' ho' e* pony soldiers," stated Cougar Eyes.

"They are cowards," interrupted Roman Nose contemptuously. The great Cheyenne warrior leader had a very good day. He had ridden through the pony soldiers without being injured and had counted coup in front of all his followers. The braves were also successful in cutting off two soldiers from the rest of the regiment as the Kansans fled. The hapless white men were lanced and shot full of arrows and then scalped. Their bodies were then mutilated and left to rot in the buffalo grass where the wolves would complete the grisly episode.

"Still, many of our brothers are wounded and some have been

killed," insisted Cougar Eyes. "Now we must crawl on our bellies to bring back their bodies before dawn."

"We will kill them tomorrow," responded Roman Nose with an air of supreme confidence.

"And if they don't come out of the ravine?" inquired Cougar Eyes.

"Then I will go and find other *Ve' ho' e* to kill. I will not waste my time here," stated Roman Nose, as he wrapped a blanket around his torso.

Captain Jenness was brooding as he listened to the cries of the wounded and their moaning for water. He dreaded listening most of all to the hideous sounds of dying and wounded horses and mules. The Kansans were spending a miserable night in the ravine, and although Jenness had managed to extricate his fellow Kansans from the ambush site by retreating to a gorge, where, like Armes and Company F, they were now holed-up like trapped animals, surrounded by hundreds of Cheyenne. He was upset, that he had already seen three men killed—two of them falling into the hands of the *savages*. He felt helpless as he watched two hapless volunteers fail to keep in step with the square while reloading their Spencers. Ten warriors descended upon the two stragglers and dragged them off their feet. As Jenness watched in consternation, the Dog Soldiers ran off on their galloping ponies yelling in great delight. He buried his face in his hands in disgrace and mortification. He realized that this shameful loss of two of their companions to the *red skins* had horrified and demoralized the Kansans. "Poor bastards!" he whispered to himself as he sat alone at the bottom of the ravine contemplating the harrowing fact the two men were being tortured. After he had prayed that they would meet a quick death, he decided to break out at dawn from the ravine and follow the trail made by Company F, and link up with Armes.

Nate's leg wound kept him up all night. The pain throbbed throughout his leg and felt at times as if it were on fire. To keep his mind off the agony, he concentrated to remain vigilant and encouraged the troopers to get as much sleep as possible while he watched for any signs of hostile activity. Both Nate and Jesse also used the quiet of the night to check equipment, weapons, and the horses. Nate was particularly disturbed that many of the animals were suffering from arrow and gunshot wounds. It pained him more to see horses and mules suffering than men because animals are unwilling victims while men fight knowing full well that they might get killed. He thought about the war and the hundreds of gruesome mangled corpses of horses, mules, and donkeys that he had seen butchered by grape shot, artillery fire, and close-range gunfire. Nate sighed heavily, then fetched his canteen and used what precious water that he had to clean some of the wounds and cool down the wounded animals. Nate also talked to them and whispered in their ears that everything was going to be all right, and that they were going to make it.

It was a few hours after dawn had broken over the horizon and the sun was beginning to shed its warm glow over the bleak High Plains landscape, when the sniping and insults from the Cheyennes resumed. Although tired, filthy, thirsty and hungry, the troopers did not complain and remained relatively quiet and awaited at their posts. A few of them would whisper to each other and Nate overheard some of them making jokes and laugh.

"*Come out of hole and fight*... Mo' ohtae *bastards*," yelled the brave who spoke a little English from a nearby ridge.

"*Fuck yourself, bitch,*" yelled back one wounded trooper who was fed up with being taunted.

"*Private*, shut your mouth! You in de U-nited States cavalry. And not some fieldhand screamin' at odder niggers cross the way!" Nate always became angry and irritated when enlisted men would speak in loud profanities.

"But Sarge, them tham red skins..." pleaded the wounded cavalryman.

"Don't care, boy. Soldier gotta remain in control and keep a cool head at all times."

Jesse came up to Nate and tapped him on the arm. "The colonel wants to see you."

Nate crept to where Armes was lying on his stomach. He was

anxiously surveying the ridges with his spy glass, searching for Jenness and watching for any movement the hostiles might make.

"How's the leg, Sergeant Major?" inquired Armes, still training his spy glass over the horizon. It was several hours past dawn and Armes was still hoping to see Jenness and his command through the spy glass.

"I'll make it, sir," he responded confidently.

"Good, good." Armes collapsed the glass and turned to Nate, "Can't have my best noncom laid up."

"Yes, sir," replied Nate, somewhat gratified that the commanding officer would show any concern. His leg was throbbing with pain again. The ache was tolerable while he remained motionless, but every time Nate would move around, the discomfort from the recent arrow would would bother him.

"How the men holding up?" asked Armes, expecting the worst.

"Morale is high sir, and de wounded can travel."

Colonel Armes nodded in approval and stroked his beard. "If Jenness is not here within a few hours, I intend to break out from this Godforsaken ravine." Armes searched Nate's face for any signs of emotion or feedback.

"Sir, we are greatly outnumbered," said Nate calmly while remaining stone-faced.

"I believe that some of the Cheyennes have left the area. Earlier, I noticed several hundred warriors leave, led by a brave on a splendid white horse."

"Think they goin' after de Kansas Volunteers, sir?" inquired Nate, a little surprised that Armes did not call for him when he noticed that some of the Cheyennes were leaving.

"Maybe. Then again, maybe the whole thing is a ruse to draw us out," explained Armes calmly.

"But if they are waitin' fo' us . . ."

"We can't stay here. The water is runnin' out and the horses won't last too much longer," interrupted Armes.

"Riders in the distance, sir. Looks like they be comin' straight fo' us," announced a corporal, who was on his belly on the crest of the ravine at the southeast corner.

The faint sounds of gunshots were beginning to become discernible to the men of company F, and all the troopers' eyes were now concentrated on the cloud of dust in the distance. Armes aimed his spy glass in the direction of the riders while the reports of rifle and pistol fire were becoming louder.

"It's Jenness and the Eighteenth Kansas in a running fight," exclaimed Armes, as he removed the glass from his eye. "The greenhorns are trying to link up with us."

Captain Jenness and his fellow Kansans were in a fight for their lives. The volunteers had pulled out from their own ravine before dawn, and had traveled a few miles unmolested, when Roman Nose and his war party appeared again. The Cheyennes kept up a hot fire on the Eighteenth Kansas for miles, inflicting more casualties on the whites, and Jenness had a hell of a time keeping his men together and maintaining discipline. Ever since the Kansans had abandoned the protection of the ravine, they had advanced more in a skeddadled mode than an organized advance toward Armes. Now, as his men cursed and shot back at the attacking Cheyennes while struggling to control their wounded or panicked mounts amid whirling dust and smoke, gun fire, raining arrows, and lances, Jenness saw in the distance the guidon of the Tenth Negro Cavalry flapping in the breeze on top of a ravine. His lips were too dry, and his tongue too parched to speak, but in his mind, he prayed that he, and his embattled command, would make it to where the guidon of the Tenth Cavalry was planted.

"Sergeant Major!" cried Armes. The colonel felt rejuvenated. He was tired of being holed up like a rat while his men were being taunted and shot at by hidden Cheyenne snipers. "Prepare the men to mount-up, draw pistols," he commanded. His otherwise stern face, cracked a smile. "Let's show those volunteers what real cavalry can do."

"Aye, aye, sir." Nate saluted enthusiastically and yelled for Jesse. He was glad that they were going to break out. He had also grown tired and irritated at the taunts and looked forward to obliging those savages with a forceful charge. He knew his boys were eager for a little tit-for-tat with the red skins. The bugler sounded the order for the company to mount up, and for the next few minutes, the troopers scrambled for their horses and adjusted their accoutrements in preparation for a charge.

Jenness had again become surrounded by hordes of mounted warriors yelling war whoops while shooting hundreds of arrows and bullets into the Kansans who were forced to form into a hollow square on foot with most of the surviving horses and wounded men in the middle. Cougar Eyes and the Dog Men had intensified their attack on the volunteers when they realized that they might affect a link up with the pony soldiers in the ravine.

"Company, prepare to charge," commanded Armes as he raised his well-worn right gauntleted hand into the air and pulled on the reins with his left to control his mount, who wanted to bolt forward. The troopers had mounted and gathered at the top of the crest of the ravine and formed a straight line, their army Colt revolvers at the ready. Although some of the horses were becoming excited as they stood in the line, and the troopers had to endure sniper fire from the ridges, the cavalrymen remained calm and eager to teach their tormentors a lesson.

"*Bugler. Sound the charge.*" The bugler had taken a sip of water from his canteen before mounting his horse, so he was prepared for this order. Unlike the first fight, he was determined never to be caught again in the humiliating position of not having enough saliva to blow on his horn. He took a deep breath and placed his lips on the mouthpiece. His cheeks bloated outward, and the sound of music came forth, as if it were Gabriel blowing on his trumpet.

"*Charge,*" commanded Armes, as he lifted his body from the saddle and abruptly lowered his right hand forward. He then spurred his sorrel and was the first one down the slope of the ravine, followed by Nate and the rest of the company, all hollering as if they were laughing and defying death.

Cougar Eyes and his *Hotame-No' nehe* were taken by surprise. They had been preoccupied with trying to overwhelm Jenness and the Kansans in the open, and had not anticipated that the pony soldiers would come out of the ravine and attack them. Although the Cheyennes were superior in numbers, the dramatic effect of a company of pony soldiers galloping in a straight line, threw the hostiles off guard. Cougar Eyes and his Dog Soldiers decided to regroup behind the safety of the ridges.

Armes however, was not going to let the warriors off that easy. He pushed his company for several miles chasing the Dog Soldiers while his men fired their .44-caliber Colts at the fleeing braves. The troopers felt exhilarated. Finally, they had the chance to pursue the Dog Soldiers who had sniped, taunted, and insulted them for hours.

Although the charge drew off the attacking Cheyennes away from Jenness and the embattled Kansans, Cougar Eyes and his Dog Soldiers had managed to scatter in small groups with their swift ponies, and within a few minutes, the warriors had disappeared among the ravines, ridges, and coulees in the Valley of the Beaver.

When it became clear that the troopers were not going to catch the fleeing Dog Soldiers, Armes halted the charge and ordered Nate to reform the company into columns of fours, and return to where Jenness and the Eighteenth were located.

Captain Jenness had already taken cover in the deep ravine where F Company had been holed up. His men and animals were exhausted, and were greatly relieved that they had succeeded in rejoining Armes and Company F of the Tenth Cavalry.

"It was grand to see those men charge those red skins," said Lieutenant Price admirably.

"Black soldiers chargin' Injuns. Now I've seen everything," replied Jenness, as he took a swig of water from his canteen.

Eight

Although the charge that was made by Colonel Armes and F Company against the Dog Soldiers was a courageous act and I believe earned a certain degree of respect among the Cheyenne warriors, I am convinced that the braves only left the Valley of the Beaver after they thought it was not within their immediate interest to lay siege to a now reinforced detachment armed with Spencer repeaters. We were fortunate though, that by evening, the Cheyennes had drawn down their rifle and arrow sniping sufficiently for Armes and the Eighteenth Kansas to return to Fort Hays. Had they laid seige, they would have inflicted more casualties

Nate was sitting in a camp chair at the tent hospital at Hays and writing in his journal regarding the recent battle but was having trouble concentrating because the huge crimson sun was setting in the horizon and he became mesmerized by its beauty. Jesse had managed to find an old patch quilt and placed the article behind his friend's back while his bandaged leg rested on a crude stool.

For Company F, Tenth Cavalry, thirteen men were wounded, and one man was killed. For Jenness and the Eighteenth Kansas Volunteers however, sixteen men had been wounded, three dead . . . two of his men fell into the hands of the Cheyennes. I'd rather not ponder on the fiendish circumstances of their demise. In addition, the Kansans lost their

supply wagon and many of their surviving horses were wounded
and if it was not for our *generosity, many of the wounded*
would not have made the trip back to Hays. For the men of
F Company, the battle at Beaver Creek proved that they were
now an established disciplined unit within the Tenth Cavalry.
Colonel Armes is proud of his men. His troopers had fought
the Cheyennes to a standstill while inflicting what he estimated
was about fifty casualties on the enemy.

I know that Armes is secretly satisfied with the fact that
his men had performed better on the field than the Kansans,
and that if it were not for his troop, the volunteers probably
would have suffered greater casualties, or possible annihilation.

Nate's leg wound was healing well thanks to his foresight in drenching the wound with whiskey immediately after he had yanked the arrow out and with Jesse's assistance, stitched the slit in his flesh under a star-filled Kansas sky. When the company returned to Hays, Armes had ordered Nate to report to the hospital and have the post's surgeon examine the wound. Nate dreaded receiving any medical attention when he knew he could probably take better care of himself. He kept pondering in his mind how during the war he saw countless men, black and white, Yankee and Secesh, struggling to walk, as if they were crippled insects, after the butchers who the white men call *surgeons* got through with them.

Fort Hays' surgeon, Dr. Miles Bellows, was a portly, medium sized man with thinning red hair and beard. He came from the Champlain valley in Vermont where his family ran a large dairy and livestock business. Raised by sound abolitionists, the usual taciturn man became awed by Nate's warrior physique and sharp, handsome facial features. He also noticed that while other wounded men would limp into the hospital whining and looking downtrodden, Nate, although limping, was dressed to perfection and was wearing his kneetop cavalry boots as if he just wandered in from a Parade Dress Review. His patient's physique and gladiatorlike appearance instantly reminded the doctor of one of his favorite heroes when he was studying Roman history at

Dartmouth College. *"Spartacus,"* he whispered loudly to himself but Nate overheard him anyway.

Nate immediately saw the sudden expression of astonishment in the doctor's face.

"Spart . . . who?" inquired Nate, calmly.

"Spartacus," responded the doctor, equally calmly as he checked Nate's wound. "SPARTACUS Spartacus . . . Have you ever heard of him?"

Nate thought for a moment and replied, "No sir, never heard of the man."

"He was an escaped slave who organized a revolt of thousands of slaves against their Roman masters, and at one point, threatened the economic power of the Roman Empire," explained the doctor as he removed the bandage on Nate's leg to check the wound. Nate felt ignorant, and Nate loathed that feeling. He made a mental note to find out more about this man, Spartacus.

"You have done a rather good job stitching the puncture in your calf," complimented Dr. Bellows as he turned the limb in his delicate hands. Nate felt awkward when the surgeon touched his skin and gently pressed his fingers near the wound. Other than experiencing the lash or the back of a hand in his face from the overseer, or enemy, Nate had never felt a gentle white man's hand on his body. "Yes, yes, the stitching is tight and even. Very good!" observed the surgeon approvingly. "Tell me, Sergeant Major, have you had much experience in stitching wounds?"

Nate took a deep breath and rolled up his right arm sleeve on his shell jacket and pointed to the old scar on his right arm. "This scar was from a bull gator in de Louisiana swamp! I stitched this arm up my'sef in the dead of night when only the owls of the bayou were my witnesses." For an instant, Nate thought about Jean le Fou. He remembered how although he had stitched the wound himself in the dead of night in the swamp, the wound had become infected, and had it not been for the Cajun's swamp remedies, he might have lost his arm.

———

Nate and Jesse were out riding a few miles from the main trail that led into Fort Hays from Hays City. They enjoyed exercising their mounts every evening an hour or two, before the trumpeter sounded Stable Call. The two noncoms enjoyed the solitude and sense of freedom they received while they sat on their McClellan saddles and watched the sun set over the plains as hundreds of jackrabbits leaped all around them. He always smoked his briarwood pipe and Jesse would do all of the talking while Nate half-listened, hummed approval at whatever his friend said, while preferring to gaze at the magnificent red dusk sky.

As they leisurely made their way down the trail toward Hays City, because Nate was always interested in locating troopers who might be absent without leave looking for liquor and whores, a cloud of dust appeared a mile on the far end of the trail heading straight toward them.

"Riders comin' in a hurry," Jesse remarked.

Nate removed the pipe from his mouth and stared down the road, squinting his eyes.

"Looks like a gen'ral and his staff," he replied with assurance.

"How can you tell that?" mocked Jesse, a little bemused.

Nate was not surprised that Jesse couldn't tell. It takes experience in war to develop the aptitude for survival. By searching for clues that will render enough information to develop a picture of what is to come, one can become better prepared to meet the unexpected.

"Can't you see the personalized standard a-flappin' in the wind?"

Jesse squinted and finally noticed the regimental standard fluttering slightly above the cloud of dust that was being kicked up by army horses. Suddenly, several dogs appeared running in front of the group.

"*What the hell?*" exclaimed Jesse, as he stared in amazement at several stag hounds. They were the biggest dogs he had ever seen. The long-legged sleek hounds playfully circled Nate and Jesse, as their tongues drooped from the sides of their mouths and panted heavily.

Gen. George Armstrong Custer was cantering his horse ahead of his orderly, who was carrying his personal regimental banner, and the general's favorite scout "Medicine Bill" Comstock. The boy general was returning to Fort Hays from Fort Riley, and had traveled a hundred a fifty miles in less than sixty hours. He had had been ordered by his superiors to return to his command and await orders regarding a general court-martial. Although he was the protégé of Generals' Sherman and Sheridan, the boy general had gotten himself into trouble by shooting deserters without a trial and was also charged for being absent without leave, and the unauthorized use of a military ambulance. Custer was in turn, furious that he had been denied to visit his wife, Libbie, and was convinced that the congress wanted to find scapegoats for the costly failure of the Hancock campaign of the past year.

"Brunettes!" derided Custer to himself, when he became close enough to determine the color of Nate and Jesse's skin. Custer had every intention of riding past Nate and Jesse, when "Medicine Bill" Comstock who was accompanying the general, noticed Nate and reined in his big mule.

"Howdy, Sergeant Major." With the exception of his dark mustache, Comstock was clean-shaven and his long thick raven hair was greased backward under his straw sombrero.

Nate was stunned. He had not recognized Comstock. His face was covered in dust and bronzed from the sun and his boots and clothes were splattered with mud. "Yes sir, Mr. Comstock." Nate saluted him as if he were an English constable responding to a civilian inquiry.

Medicine Bill stretched his arm and offered his hand. Nate responded by clasping the plainsman's huge right hand, and the two men smiled at each other.

"The Injuns told me that you boys had quite a fight with the Eighteenth Kansas in the Valley of the Beaver," inquired the plainsman with a smile on his face. His carbine rested easily on his saddle and although Comstock let go of the reins, Nate noticed that the mule did not lower his head to graze, demonstrating the animal's disciplined nature.

By now Custer had realized that Comstock had halted to talk to the two black cavalrymen. The general reined in his gelding and turned the animal around, while his orderly who was carrying the banner, followed suite. Curious why his favorite scout was talking with a pair of *"brunettes,"* Custer urged his horse toward where the three men were conversing.

When Custer pulled up his gelding next to Comstock while his orderly bearing his commander's banner maneuvered his mount right behind the general, Nate and Jesse became flabbergasted. Here he was in the flesh! Nate thought to himself. The famed boy general. The youngest man in the history of the United States Army to make brigadier general, the hero of Yellow Tavern where he defeated Jeb Stuart, and a witness to Robert E. Lee's surrender at Appomattox. In addition he was the personal friend of Generals Sheridan and Sherman. Custer stood perfectly erect in the saddle, and placed his left hand on his hip as if he were preparing to be photographed while the broad brim on the general's white hat gently moved in the breeze.

Both Nate and Jesse came to immediate attention in their saddles and saluted. Nate was glad that he was suitably dressed for this unexpected meeting with Custer who was attired in his customary ostentatious manner. Nate noticed every detail. White gauntlets, hightop boots, wide brim planter's hat, sky blue cavalry breeches with yellow seams, and a dark blue bib shirt with white piping. A scarlet cravat was elegantly knotted around his neck that highlighted his long wavy blond hair and mustache.

"At ease," said Custer lamely, returning the salute. He then quickly turned to his scout and remarked, "Friends of yours, Comstock?"

"The sergeant an' I have met before, Gen'ral. He was jest 'bout to tell me 'bout the big fight they had with the Cheyennes up on the valley of the Beaver."

Custer became intrigued. He had heard how Armes and the Eighteenth Kansas had quite a little battle near Beaver Creek.

"You were there, Sergeant?" Custer asked Nate, sharply.

"Oh yes, sir," interrupted Jesse enthusiastically, eager to show off.

Nate cringed and thought to himself, there he goes 'gain, shootin' off his big mouth. But this time, to the boy general! "That's right General. Company F of the Tenth fought off 'bout a thousand Cheyennes," reported Nate.

Custer sneered in irritation. "A *thousand* you say, Sergeant Major? I find that *hard* to believe."

"Oh, I believe it, Gen'ral," riposted Medicine Bill. "I've heard that dem Dog Soldiers under Roman Nose . . . are thicker on the upper Republican dan a soddie droppin' fleas in de spring."

"Did you say that they were Dog Soldiers?" inquired Custer, as he stroked his thick dirty-blond mustache with his right index finger.

"Sure were, Gen'ral! Never seen a bunch a warriors that looked so colorful and hollerin' so loudly, that even the devil would run!" responded Nate with great confidence as he remained ramrod straight in the saddle. He was in the presence of a national hero whose name evoked reverence among men who followed him during the war, and Nate wanted to be at his best.

Custer was impressed that both Nate and Jesse were dressed to perfection, and that the bridles, saddles, and general condition of their mounts were up to snuff. It was obvious that these noncoms from the Tenth had tailored their shell jackets and took extra care of their equipment to look as military as possible. Custer thought for a moment about his troubles with his own regiment. The numerous desertions, equipment problems, and the failure with locating and engaging the hostiles, had frustrated the hero of Yellow Tavern. He recalled how he had been offered the command of the Tenth Cavalry but had refused because he did not want to lead black men. He thought it was ironic that the *"brunettes"* were seeing more action than his beloved Seventh.

"How many casualties did you inflict on the Cheyennes?" Custer stared at the big sergeant major with his blue eyes, and Nate was amazed how young *"dis white boy"* looked. Although the boy general's light skin was tan from the strong plains' sun, Nate could still see the freckles on his boyish cheeks.

"We determined that we must have inflicted 'bout fifty killed and wounded upon the hostiles, Gen'ral." Nate paused for a moment, than added, "But then again sir, the hostiles removed all of their dead during the night makin' it difficult fo' us to make an accurate count."

Custer's gelding, a big chestnut with a long mane and an elegant tail that almost touched the ground, started to prance with his hooves and snort. Like his master, he was becoming restless, and wanted to move on.

"*Fifty?* Those numbers seem exaggerated, Sergeant Major!" responded Custer skeptically. The general had barely seen fifty Indians all summer long, never mind killing that many. Nate noticed that he was becoming irritated and his mind appeared to be preoccupied with other matters. Before Nate and Jesse could salute, the general had abruptly turned his mount and spurred the animal toward Fort Hays with his orderly and hounds following closely behind.

"Ain't he something?" said Medicine Bill Comstock.

"I have to admit, I can see why men would follow him," remarked Nate, as he watched the boy general canter down the trail with his banner flying behind him.

"I hear you! But then again, you can see why some men *can't stand him,*" replied Comstock, cracking a cynical smile.

Nine

Nate and Jesse were on stable call. They had completed breakfast about a half hour ago and were now busy inspecting how the troopers were grooming their mounts, removing the dung piles, and making sure that the animals were well watered and fed before they were turned out from the picket line to graze with a herd guard. All the men, including the officer of the day, was dressed in white stable frocks. A fatigue outfit, if not washed frequently, would reek to high heaven.

For the horses, this was their favorite part of the day. Nothing was more interesting for a horse than receiving their morning portion of grain and the animals enjoyed the attention that the troopers gave in using the curry-comb and brushes on their "pets." The sharp morning air was invigorating, and although the horses were well-lashed to the picket line, the animals responded by nipping at each other's noses, while others challenged their neighbors with a look of a sparkling, provocative eye, or by snapping and squealing at each other across the line. Some of the more aggressive mounts would rear, buck, or plunge in wild delight in anticipation of going out.

One trooper who was having problems keeping his horse still while he brushed him started to punch the horse in the head with a clenched fist.

"Gawddamn it, Private! What de hell do ya think *you're doin'*?" shouted Nate, furious that one of his men would do such a thing.

"But, Sarge, mah mare wont stay put," complained the trooper.

"Suppose I bash your little head every time your sorry ass misbehaves?" retorted Nate, as he approached the trooper as if he were a

373

bull charging a matador. "When a horse acts up on de line, take de animal and *walk him* for a spell away from de other horses," explained Nate, as he pulled the knot on the lead rope and proceeded to walk the nervous horse away from the picket line.

Jesse was examining a cracked hoof on a horse when Colonel Armes, dressed in his stable frock outfit, told him to go and get Nate because he had some orders. While he waited, he also looked at the horse's cracked hoof, and pondered what would be the best treatment. He decided that the hoof would have to be bound tightly and the animal kept isolated.

"Colonel, you wanted to see me?"

"Yes, Sergeant Major," replied Armes as he wiped off the dirt on his hands by slapping them together. "I want you and Sergeant Randolph to take a squad of men from Company G and follow the railroad tracks for forty-five miles until you reach the railroad camp and provide protection to the laborers who are working on the line."

"G Troop, sir?" Nate was a little puzzled.

"They are the only men that are available for this duty and all of the company's noncoms are at the hospital, sick with either cholera or acute gastritis." Armes paused for a moment, trying to find the right words. "Sergeant, I'm depending on your experience here, you know we are still short on line officers so this is your chance to perform the duties of an officer." Armes searched into Nate's face for any reaction.

"No problem, Colonel, we'll handle it." Nate was relieved. The cholera epidemic that had broken out several weeks before had stricken dozens of men at Fort Hays because of the bad water in the streams that were used by the soldiers as their primary source for drinking and cooking. So Nate had been hoping to get an assignment that would take him away from the debilitating disease and the best way to avoid becoming infected was to go on duty far from Hays.

Nate and Jesse, with eight other troopers, made the forty-five mile journey to the railroad camp in a day. Nate did not want to push the horses any faster for fear of wearing them down because the terrain was uneven and the day was hot. They arrived at the railroad camp just as the sun was setting.

Nate thought that the railroad camp was a pathetic sight. The workers, when not toiling long hours laying track, lived in squalid old tents, temporary shacks that were built with rough lumber, and dugouts that would flood in a downpour. Their meals were cooked outside in open fires, while at night, they would be plagued by millions of fleas and ticks.

Nate observed that the laborers were either mostly fresh immigrants from Europe who spoke very little English, or former soldiers from both armies, who were down on their luck, thus compelled to work for very low wages under dangerous conditions.

The next morning Nate found Jesse enjoying a hearty breakfast with the men near the picket line away from the stench of the camp. Nate noticed that the troopers were eating beef hash, eggs, dry bread, and coffee. When he inquired where they had gotten the food, Jesse told him that some of the European laborers who had expressed gratitude for the protection that they were providing had been generous. Jesse also told Nate, however, that he had overheard some of the other civilians, mainly ex-Confederates and low lifes, making contemptuous comments and criticized the army for "sendin' a few no good niggers."

Jesse knew that something was on his friend's mind. He seemed irritated and preoccupied. "Prob'em?"

Nate did not answer immediately, his face still showed signs of weariness. "Jess," he finally said with apprehension, "two civilians wanna go huntin'. The railroad foreman tol' me that de camp needs fresh meat fo' de laborers and de man insists on an escort. Jess, I gotta send you to 'company them. I need de rest of de men here, to protect the camp."

"When do I go?" inquired Jesse, happy to leave the stench of the camp and go for a quiet morning ride.

"Soon as you're mounted, my man," replied Nate, concerned that his friend might run into trouble somewhere in the Smoky Hill country.

The two civilians who Jesse was accompanying told him that they were from Ohio. He thought that they appeared to be decent enough young gentlemen and that they were young, eager, and a little arrogant.

"What made you gent'men come West?" inquired Jesse as the three of them leisurely walked their horses together among some of the low ravines about five miles out of camp. The morning light was soft and the air fresh. Their horses snorted and sneezed as they bobbed their heads and flicked their tales from flank to flank to keep the flies away.

"Money and adventure!" answered one of the young men confidently, as he loosened the color on his tight red bib shirt.

"Yeah. We figure that we work the railroad for a spell, make enough money and move on to better prospects," replied his companion as he adjusted his hat which was too big for him and kept slipping down his forehead.

"Sounds promising," responded Jesse, trying to sound optimistic but remaining unimpressed. If there is one thing that he felt he understood about the frontier, it was that the West was full of cavalier people with lofty ideas how to strike it rich.

"Tell me, Sergeant. Are there many Negroes in the army?" asked the man with the red bib shirt, unabashedly.

"Oh, yes sir! Hundreds of us are wearin' the blue uniform of the United States Army," responded Jesse proudly as he straightened his tall frame in the saddle.

"Really? That many," replied the man skeptically whose hat was too large for his head.

"Ever seen any Indians?" inquired the man in the red shirt.

Jesse thought for a moment and reined in his mount, forcing the two railroad workers to do the same. "I've seen more Cheyenne Dog Soldiers this past year then maggots eatin' a carcass." Jesse knew that he had made an impression when he noticed that the two young men's faces grimaced in disgust.

"We have not seen one damn Indian since we came here," responded the man in the red shirt with an air of disappointment in his voice.

"Well sir, maybe today, we'll get lucky."

"I certainly hope so. I'd love to shoot me a damn redskin," retorted the man with the oversized hat.

Jesse was about to respond to the young man's arrogant boast when a small herd of mule deer appeared over the horizon. Sensing the thrill of the hunt, the two impetuous young men decided to give chase. Jesse preached caution, but the two men ignored him, and encouraged their mounts forward with all haste ahead of their one man escort.

Jesse noticed how the herd of mule deer started to bolt before the civilians started to go after the deer. At first he found this peculiar but thought nothing of it. Then it struck him. Dog Soldiers must be in the immediate vicinity to have spooked the herd of mule deer.

It was too late to warn the young civilians. They had galloped about a quarter mile when seventy Cheyennes charged from the cover of a ravine. Within a fraction of a minute, the two civilians, who moments before had been chatting away with not a care in the world, were overwhelmed by the Dog Soldiers before they were able to fire a single shot from their carbines. The warriors proceeded to gleefully slaughter the two white men by lancing and shooting multiple arrows from their bow lances. While a few braves stayed behind to scalp and strip the bodies, the bulk of the Dog Soldiers started to pursue Jesse.

Jesse immediately turned his mount around and drove his spurs deeply into the horse's flanks and made for the railroad camp. He urged the big mare forward with his whole body, squeezing his knees against the saddle and slapping the horse's rump with his rifle barrel as he yelled, "Yaa, yaa, yaa, run girl, run!"

Jesse was galloping for dear life. Although his horse was moving fast, the Dog Soldiers were closing in on him fast, yelling war whoops and shrieks as they brandished their lances and carbines into the air. He felt that his pursuers were gaining on him so he looked behind his right shoulder and saw to his horror that the Dog Men were gaining on him with their swift war ponies. Jesse continued to apply pressure on his spurs and encourage the mare to gallop faster, but he knew that time was running out.

Cougar Eyes was leading the chase but decided to halt his pony and take aim at Jesse with his carbine. He wanted to quickly dispatch

Jesse and then go on to the railroad camp where he had planned to slaughter all the workers, loot the camp, and burn the shacks and tents. He squeezed the trigger and by the time Jesse heard the report of the carbine, he felt a sharp pain in his left shoulder that sent him tumbling from the saddle. Wounded and dazed, he managed nevertheless, to quickly get to his feet. He looked around for his horse, but the animal had bolted, and now he was wounded in the shoulder and on foot with a yelling horde of Dog Soldiers fast approaching.

To his great relief, Jesse saw that he was only a few feet away from a hole in a railroad cut. He decided to scamper for the small shaft and seek refuge. As soon as he threw himself into the hole the Dog Men were only a few yards away, and would have killed him if he had not crawled into the shaft.

Cougar Eyes did not want to waste more time trying to root out one frightened pony soldier from a dark hole when he wanted to lead the attack on the railroad camp. Several braves however, dismounted and decided to investigate.

Jesse crawled as far he could in the dark, damp shaft and pulled out his Army Colt and pulled back the hammer. He had a strong feeling that the bullet wound had shattered his shoulder blade, and that he might bleed to death. Sweating, breathing heavily, and in pain, he could hear the Cheyennes conversing outside and wondered what they were going to do. He supported his back by sitting up against the far end wall of the shaft, and started to come to terms with himself that he might not escape. If so, he decided to take as many of those "*red devils*" as he could before he was killed. He thought that the only way he was going to be killed, unless he bled to death first, was that the Dog Men would have to drag him out of the hole, and considering that he was over six feet tall and weighed over two hundred pounds, it was not going to be an easy task.

"*Come in an' git me, you bastards!*" he yelled defiantly.

One Dog Soldier, with a red and yellow turban on his head obliged him and stuck his head into the hole. Jesse quickly shot at his face, grazing the brave's left cheek, causing him to wail in pain. This first surprised, then infuriated the other braves who started to jab their lances wildly into the hole, spearing Jesse as if he were a big fish.

Nate was surveying the northern horizon for any signs of hostile activities. He wished he had a spy glass like Colonel Armes had. He kept repeating to himself in a hushed whisper the words that his commanding officer had told him at the picket line. "My chance to be like an officer." He became determined that he would purchase a spy glass as soon as he saved enough money. Nate was worried about Jesse. He knew his friend was capable enough, but if they ran into a large number of Cheyennes out there on the plains, they would not have much of a chance.

All of a sudden, a thin cloud of dust was beginning to emerge from the northwest and the horses who were grazing with their saddles and bridles on, started to look up toward the same direction and a few of them started to buck and snort. This made the troopers in the squad aware that many riders in the distance were heading in their direction.

"Damn it. They are a-comin'," said Nate, condemning the reality of the situation.

"Who comin?" inquired one trooper looking up at the cloud of dust that was getting closer with every passing second.

"Bad company! De hostiles, boy. *De Dawg Men*." Nate figured that he had about five minutes to prepare the railroad camp for an attack. Very few of the civilians had any weapons, and his squad of seven men could do little in defending such a large perimeter. Therefore, he made up his mind to do the unexpected and hope for the best.

"Mount up boys. Check your cinches and weapons. Prepare to charge." Although Nate's blood was running hot, and his adrenaline flowed, he remained calm and reassuring. He knew his squad was going to be grossly outnumbered, but decided that he had no choice but to defend the railroad camp, and the best way to do that was to assault the enemy before they attacked him.

"We'll charge de hostiles firin' our Colts, and when I give de order to dismount, you'll form a skirmish line and fire at will with your Spencers. Any questions?"

"Who be holdin' the hosses?" asked one trooper.

"You will boy! Ev'ryone will hold their own horses in this fight! We need *ev'ry* man firin' on the line," ordered Nate, as he mounted his horse. He then unflapped his holster flap and pulled out his Walker-Colt. He carefully revolved the cylinder as his men tightened cinches, checked weapons, adjusted their forage caps, and mounted. Satisfied that all the chambers were full in the cylinder and the nipples capped, he cocked back the hammer and turned to his squad of troopers. *"Ready boys?"* The cloud of dust was becoming larger on the horizon and the sounds of *"hi,hi,hi . . . "* could be heard as Cougar Eyes and his band closed in on the railroad camp. Nate noticed that his men were nervous. Their faces and bodies were tense and their hands tightened as they held their reins with their left hands and the Army Colts with their right, and although it was late fall, their faces were sweaty. Some of the men's horses were becoming jittery at the smell and sounds made by the charging Dog Men and their unshod war ponies. Nate wanted to reassure his men so he turned in his saddle and faced them. "Boys! Trust me. We'll be aw right. We have de training, confidence, an' most important, we have de element of surprise." He then raised his Walker-Colt in the air and dug his spurs into his mounts' flanks. "Follow me boys . . . *Charge*."

The troopers' horses needed little prodding. They bolted with zeal toward the Cheyennes as their riders yelled at the top of their lungs, racing to meet the Dog Soldiers.

The troopers fired several rounds from their Army Colts into the mass of Cheyennes at a gallop, wounding several warriors and crippling some of the ponies, but the Dog Soldiers' charge remained intact. Nate was riding in the middle of the charge line firing his Walker-Colt with deadly accuracy. The Dog Soldiers were about a hundred yards away and coming fast, when he decided that the time was right to dismount and form a skirmish line. He threw his hand in the air and reined in his horse.

"Halt! . . . Dismount! . . . form skirmish line!"

The troopers' horses had barely stopped when the men jumped from their saddles as they holstered the Colts. They then maneuvered their rifle slings so the butt of the Spencers would be against their shoulders, while holding the reins with their left hands. The cavalrymen then commenced firing, working the levers and pulling the triggers while remaining calm.

Cougar Eyes and the Dog Soldiers were first taken by surprise by the pony soldiers' pistol firing charge, but were now in awe that the blue coats had dismounted and were firing their repeaters with great accuracy, hitting a number of braves and throwing confusion among the warriors. Fearing that they would suffer additional casualties, the Dog Men halted their charge to regroup and attack again.

"*Reload*," yelled Nate. He was satisfied that his strategy had worked and the boys held fast and remained calm. He knew, however, the Cheyennes would be back momentarily.

Jesse Randolph was in a hell of a predicament. He had been stabbed already five times in his legs, arms, thighs, and face by the lances of the Dog Men who had been wildly jabbing into the railroad cut hole. Jesse was able to parry some of the thrusts by using his Colt to divert the lance tips away from his torso, but the Dog Men managed to continue to cut and puncture Jesse's arms, legs, and face. Each time he was stabbed he would cry out in pain, and the braves outside would shout in delight, inviting more thrusts into the shaft. The hole was dark and dank, which made it hard for Jesse to see the lance tips plunging into the shaft, so every time he would feel a sharp pain on his legs, thighs, face, and groin, he would know that he had been stabbed. He became so furious and frustrated with his tormentors that he wanted to bolt out of the shaft and, knowing that he would be killed, take a few of the "son's-of-bitches with me." He thought that if help did not arrive soon, he would be slowly stabbed to death by the red demons outside the hole.

Cougar Eyes recognized that these blue coats were the *Mo' ohtae-Ve' ho' e* soldiers, and had identified Nate by his bright sergeant major chevrons as the big black soldier who fought him in the fight near by the river. This time however, he was surprised and confused that there were no white officers to lead the black and white pony soldiers. He had thought that these men could not fight without their white leaders, but after he saw them charge while they fired their pistols and then dismount with great speed and open up with the repeaters, he became stunned by such actions.

Nevertheless, Cougar Eyes started to admonish his fellow braves for letting this small group of black and white pony soldiers stop their attack. As he attempted to rally his fellow Dog Soldiers, Nate and his squad started to advance on foot while firing their Spencers. As they led their horses, they poured a hot fire into the Cheyennes, and now it was the Dog Men who were taken by surprise.

Nate had ordered his cavalrymen to advance while firing to keep the warriors off balance while seizing the initiative away from the enemy. Nate's experience as a cavalryman during the war, and the lessons learned at the recent fight at the Saline River and Beaver Creek, had shown him how numerical superior forces could be defeated by smaller ones, if discipline remains strong, and the men keep their cool while firing. This combination would often throw an overconfident enemy into confusion long enough to allow the inferior force to either escape, gain time, or even turn the tide of battle.

The Dog Soldiers were indeed thrown off-guard by these tall black and white pony soldiers advancing as if they were infantry. Many of the braves' ponies were going down with hideous wounds which produced confusion and made it difficult for the Dog Soldiers to regroup. With the element of surprise gone, Cougar Eyes failed to convince his fellow braves to press their attack. Their enthusiasm wavering, and with Nate approaching with his squad as they rapidly fired their repeaters at will, forced the warriors to withdraw.

"*By Gawd, we did it! Thank the Lawd,*" praised Nate, as he raised his right arm that held his Spencer repeater—the barrel, red hot and still bellowing smoke. He raised his head to the sky and opened up his arms as if he were a preacher giving thanks for a miracle. Not since he saw the line of cooking smoke from Jean le Fou's cabin when he was on the run from Bloodhound Jack, had he felt such jubilation. Nate was not a religious man, but the fact that he took the initiative away from the Dog Men, and that the troopers performed splendidly against a force that was at least seven times larger than his own, felt as if it was the second coming.

The troopers' first reaction was to go to their McClellan saddles and reach for the canteens and quench their thirst. Some of them collapsed to the ground from exhaustion and started to unbuckle their tight shell jackets. Nate, forever vigilant, ordered them to their feet and to remain watchful.

"Gotta be mindful, boys. Them Dawg Men might be back. Get on your feet and check your horses."

The cavalrymen of Company G Tenth Cavalry not only saved the railroad camp from a surprise attack by the Dog Soldiers, but had beaten the hostiles off the field of battle. The troopers, however, were too exhausted to celebrate their good fortune. They had fought an intense engagement against a powerful foe, and were just relieved that they were alive and their horses relatively unscathed.

"Can we go back to de railroad camp, Sarge?" inquired one trooper as he checked his mount. The cavalrymen's faces and hands were caked and streaked with dust and gun smoke, mixed with sweat. Their armpits had large circles of salt stains from perspiration, and some of the men's trousers and shell jackets were ripped due to arrows and bullet holes fired by the Dog Men.

"Mount up boys, we goin' look fo' Sergeant Randolph," ordered Nate as he swung into his saddle.

Jesse was still being stabbed by lance tips. In addition to the bullet wound in his shoulder, he now had eleven puncture wounds on his hands, arms, face, neck, torso, and legs above the cavalry boots. Though none of the wounds were life threatening, he was bleeding profusely and his uniform resembled blood soaked rags. Out of frustration, he had fired his army Colt several times toward the opening of the shaft in a vain attempt to scare off his tormentors, or when he thought he saw one of the "red bastard's" painted faces appear in the opening of the hole. He also continued to defy them with his own verbal taunts, daring them to come into the hole one by one.

Nate and the squad were riding at a trot along the railroad works in the direction where Jesse and his two white civilians had gone. Fortunately, the horses were in fair condition and had a good feeding that morning before the attack. After several miles of searching, Nate spotted buzzards circling in the air about a half mile away in the east. He knew exactly what that meant, and his heart sank. He commanded the squad to gallop in the direction where he knew a corpse or two was being picked at by the scavengers of the sky.

The bodies were the two white civilian railroad workers. They were already covered by buzzards, and as soon as the squad came close enough to see the mangled corpses, two of the troopers gagged and threw up. For a moment, Nate was reminded of Mathias, and how he had to chase the buzzards away from that hapless man's lacerated body. Nate dismounted and kicked two of the scavengers off one of the civilians' faces, while the others were driven off when he waved his kepi at the large beady-eyed birds. The railroad workers were scalped, and their thighs and underarms were slit wide open. Their throats were cut so deeply that their heads were nearly severed from their torsos.

As the cavalrymen remained transfixed at the tortured bodies of the luckless civilians, a faint cry could be heard in the distance.

"Sarge, where do you think Sergeant Randolph be?" inquired one trooper. "Maybe he . . ."

"Shut your mouth," said Nate, interrupting the trooper as he placed his big hand next to the rim of his right ear. The men listened, and sure enough they could hear Jesse calling for help from his railroad cut hole.

Nate mounted and touched his spurs to his horse's flanks and directed the big animal toward where he heard the cries for help. The Dog Men who had been jabbing their lances into the shaft had given up on trying to dislodge their quarry from his place of seclusion when they saw the bulk of the warriors gallop away. Within a minute, Nate had located the shaft and was calling Jesse's name.

"In here, I'm in here," responded Jesse, as he struggled to crawl out of the hole. He was a pitiful sight. His uniform was ripped to shreds and he was bleeding from numerous wounds. His face was streaked with blood, sweat, and dirt and he was breathing heavily. Nate jumped from his McClellan and all of the other troopers followed suit without waiting for the command to dismount. They rushed toward Jesse and helped him to his feet.

"Ain't you a sight fo' sore eyes," said Jesse laughing, as he pressed his left hand on his bleeding right shoulder.

"And you're de sorriest sight I ever saw," responded Nate with a smile.

Ten

Dr. Miles Bellows was in the process of sewing up the last puncture wound on Jesse's body when Nate entered the operating tent. The doctor had loaded up Jesse with a strong dose of laudanum and removed the bullet that was lodged in his patient's shoulder. Fortunately, the round did not penetrate too far into his shoulder so Bellows was able to remove it with little trouble. He then spent hours sewing up his patient with hundreds of stitches.

The post hospital at Fort Hays however, was not much of a medical establishment for either white or black soldiers. The Vermont doctor had to attend the sick and injured under camplike conditions, spending much of the day swatting flies that he feared would cause infection. Supplies were not sufficient to deal with the problems of cholera, pneumonia, snake bites, skin rashes and burns; or barely adequate to patch up wounds inflicted by knives, gunshots, hatchets, and horse kicks. The colored soldiers were usually treated then released to rest at their own regimental bivouac area while the white soldiers were allowed to recover in a big tent tended by medical orderlies.

"You are a fortunate man not to have bled to death in that hole," lectured Dr. Bellows as he bandaged Jesse's thick leg.

"I would have if dat man didn't come as soon as he did," replied Jesse, as he pointed at Nate who was now standing by his cot. Nate smiled and gently placed his hand on Jesse's left shoulder, relieved that his friend was going to be all right.

"Not since the war have I seen so many wounds," commented Bellows as he wiped his hands on a clean rag. "We've come a long way since then, though. We know now, we made serious mistakes in treating wounds and amputations by allowing infection to spread." Bellows paused for a moment, exhausted from all of the stitching. He then turned to Nate who reminded him again that this big sergeant major resembled his hero, Spartacus. "I'll be releasing him to you in a couple of days, so I'm making you responsible for his well-being after that, Sergeant Major. Make sure that he gets nothing but rest and avoids all unnecessary movement." The doctor, a little embarrassed, then added, "I'd prefer to keep him here, but as you know, this is impossible. . . ."

"Yes sir, I know. I'll take care of him," replied Nate matter-of-factly. He knew the reason why Jesse was not permitted to recover with the white soldiers in the big airy tent where he would be the most comfortable.

Nate enjoyed keeping Jesse company while he was convalescing. He would visit his friend in the evening after completing his duties and use the time to smoke his pipe while making observations in his journal while Jesse chattered away about how bad the food was.

> *Fighting on the plains has come pretty much to a standstill this fall of 1867, and Colonel Grierson has ordered that all the troops of the Tenth that were scattered throughout the Kansas frontier report to Fort Riley for the winter. I have been told that he had been instructed by his superiors to station a few detachments to different railroad camps to protect laborers who were toiling on the Kansas Pacific Railroad. These detachments will have to leave fairly shortly, before the winter snows would make travel more difficult and endanger the health of the horses.*
>
> *The shortages of line officers however, has forced Grierson to rely on noncoms to command several of these detachments. Considering that we have done so well without line officers in the field, I suspect that he will continue to delegate authority to his most trusted noncoms. I do take pride in the fact that we performed well at the fight at the railroad camp, and for*

the first time in my military experience, I do not miss having white officers giving me orders.

Pvt. Reuben Waller appeared in the doorway, perfectly dressed as usual. His boots were well shined and his kepi was placed squarely on his head. Nate had not seen the soldier since the regiment had been formed at Fort Leavenworth during the past spring. He thought about Waller's stories regarding Fort Pillow and Bedford Forrest, and how he was once the personal servant of a confederate general.

"Colonel Grierson wants to see me, Private?" inquired Nate, cocksure that was the reason for Private Reuben Waller's visit.

"Yes suh," replied Waller, a little stunned that the sergeant major knew in advance that he was sent to fetch him.

"Never call me sir, Private. Call me Sergeant Major."

Colonel Grierson and Captain Louis H. Carpenter were going over regimental reports when Carpenter's orderly, Private Waller, knocked at the door.

"Enter," replied Grierson. "Louis, get me that map we were looking at earlier." Grierson pointed to the map that was lying next to a pile of papers that were neatly stacked at the right corner of his desk.

Private Waller opened the door in a very genteel manner, which made Nate think to himself, "boy must have been a good house Nigra for dat Secesh General."

"Ah, Sergeant Major Gordon." Grierson returned Nate's salute, and motioned for him to sit. He then dismissed Private Waller. The commander of the regiment was delighted to see his favorite noncom. A man who he considered not only instrumental in training the Tenth and Ninth Cavalry, but who had won high praise from his subordinate officer, Col. George Armes, for Nate's actions on the Sabine River and Beaver Creek. Grierson had recommended to the war department that Nate receive the Medal of Honor for his bravery in defending the railroad camp against overwhelming odds, but he knew in his heart, that the medal would probably not be awarded for the simple reason that Nate was not white, and that the Seventh Cavalry was receiving all the attention in the press, while the brave exploits of the colored regiments were ignored. What really disturbed Grierson however, was the only reason why the Seventh received more press coverage and attention, was because of that goldie lock General Custer, who coveted publicity for himself and his overrated regiment. When Grierson examined the facts, the Tenth Colored Cavalry had fewer desertions, and saw an equal amount, or more action than Custer's Seventh, and with less support. The colonel of the Tenth resented that his men were ignored simply because they were black, and that the troublemaking, publicity-seeking, boy general, kept hoarding the headlines with his antics.

Capt. Louis Carpenter was sitting by the potbellied stove. It was mid-October and the signs of a harsh winter were apparent. Carpenter's feet were cold, so he had maneuvered his feet near the stove. A cold rain had been sweeping eastern Kansas for several days and the strong winds were already harsh on the men and horses. Carpenter had seen virtually no action during the past summer as he was primarily occupied with drilling the troopers of H Company at Fort Wallace, but had returned to Fort Hays.

"Sergeant Major, are you familiar with the terms of the Medicine Lodge Treaties?" inquired Grierson, with a serious look on his face.

"I read 'bout it in de papers and there's been a lot talk 'bout it." Nate paused for a moment of reflection. "I believe de gov'ment wants the put de Southern Cheyennes, Arapahoes, Commanches, Kiowas-Apaches on res'vations in return fo' gratuities."

"That's correct," replied Grierson, in that typical school master tone of voice of his. Grierson nevertheless was impressed with Nate's quick answer and his knowledge of the different tribes of the Great Plains. He smiled to himself and thought how this big noncom, a former slave and veteran of the late war, never ceased to surprise him. He then continued as if he were behind in conducting a lesson plan for a student. "There will probably not be much raiding this winter because of the coming snows and the belief among the tribes that the government will be distributing their annuities by next year." Grierson scratched his beard near where his scar was located. He then asked for the map that Louis Carpenter was holding for him. Carpenter walked over to Grierson's desk and spread the chart on his commander's desk. Grierson then beckoned Nate to come and see. "Nevertheless Sergeant Major, I'm going to send you, and the same squad of men that served you so well in your defense of the railroad camp, to spend the months of November, December, January, and February, patrolling and guarding these railroad labor camps as a precaution against marauders." Grierson pointed to various points on the chart, and Nate paid very close attention to his commanding officer's instructions.

Grierson then rose from his chair and walked to the window. As he gazed at the parade ground, he noticed that some of the soldiers were already wearing great coats to fend off the winds swooping down from the plains while the air circled violently with dust and dried grass. He then turned his back to the window and approached the potbellied stove where Captain Carpenter had retaken his seat. He stretched his arms toward the top of the stove and opened up his hands to feel the warmth. He then turned and faced Nate, searching his eyes for any signs of a reaction to his instructions.

This order did come as a surprise to Nate. He had expected to spend the winter at Fort Riley where accommodations were reasonably comfortable. The thought of being in a railroad camp during peak winter months with civilian laborers who did not care much for black troops, was not a very attractive prospect. Nate had heard from Comstock and other scouts how brutal the cold, howling winds, and snows can be on men and animals on the plains. Never mind the tales that he had heard about the loneliness and boredom suffered by individuals who were not strong enough to withstand a long hard winter, and where insanity and alcoholism would visit the vulnerable.

Nate cleared his throat which felt a little dry. "When do I depart, sir?"

"In one week. You must depart before the first snows, and from what I am feeling in the air, this will be soon." Grierson then moved away from the stove and sat back down in his chair behind the desk. "Now, if there are no further questions, you may draw your supplies from the quartermaster for four months and start preparing your men and horses."

"Aye, aye, sir." Nate's mind was racing. He had never experienced a winter on the frontier before. During the war, he had spent the winter months at various army camps that were cold, wet, muddy, and filthy, and where scabies, dysentery, cholera, scurvy, and other maladies thrived among soldiers living closely together, but a winter on the plains was something new and possibly more dangerous. He kept hearing Medicine Bill Comstock's words in his mind, "If ya winter on the plains, keep ya wits 'bout ya."

Eleven

JANUARY 1868

Pvt. Filmore Alexander was on night guard duty where the squad's horses were corralled at the railroad camp. The camp was located about a hundred miles west of Fort Hays and a hundred miles east from Fort Wallace. It was a clear night and the moon was out. Only minutes earlier, he had been awakened from a deep, warm sleep by the sergeant major, who reminded him that he was on guard duty for the second half of the night watch, and that he had five minutes to get out of his bedroll and relieve the guard who protected the horses and mules against predators and thieves. For Private Filmore, this was his nightly nightmare; doing picket duty during the coldest, loneliest, spookiest part of the night, where there were no trees or any thing else that represented signs of warmth or comfort. Just a blanket of snow that crusted the horizon as far as the eye could see. He cursed the wretched climate and longed for the days when he was barefoot in Alabama.

Filmore Alexander hated being at the railroad camp where the white civilians ignored and mocked him, and he abhorred the merciless cold and snow more than anything else. He would do his guard duty shivering, as if he were a doll being violently shaken by some cruel bully who was tormenting some young girl's favorite play item. It did not much matter how many layers of wool clothing he wore, and that he wrapped his head with scarves as if he were a mummy, his fingers, toes, and face would get so cold, that the pain became excruciating. At times, when the temperature dropped to thirty degrees below zero, every single breath he took would burn his lungs.

Nate had told him that the scouts at Hays had cautioned that this winter was going to be as bad or worse than the winter of 1866–1867, where fourteen blizzards dumped so much snow in the West that workers on the Central and Union Pacific Railroads were buried alive in forty foot drifts, and hundreds died of exposure because the competing railroads relentlessly pushed their laborers. As Private Alexander stomped his feet to keep his toes from freezing while staring at the twenty-foot-high snow drifts, he thought about the two troopers who had their feet and some of their fingers frostbitten, and how two of the horses and one mule had died from the cold.

As he shivered, stomped his feet, and tried breathing without feeling the pain in his lungs from the cold dry air, he could hear the cries of a pack of wolves in the distance. This was not unusual, for he had heard them almost every night for two weeks howling to each other. At first he was apprehensive when he heard them, but after a few nights he became accustomed to their cries. Tonight however, he thought that their howling sounded much closer to the camp than usual, but then again, the air was so frigid and the land so void of any obstruction, that sounds carried for miles and it proved difficult to gauge the correct distance from where the noises came from.

Private Alexander was walking back and forth along the length of the corral fence when he thought he saw a shadow move to the left of him. He halted his walk and looked around but noticed nothing. Some of the horses were now snorting and snickering as they moved their ears back and forth. Alexander resumed his monotonous pacing when he saw another shadow near the fence. Now the horses were making more noises and moving about in a panicked state. This time Filmore Alexander halted, and shouted, "*Halt*. Who goes dare?" Nothing, he saw nothing, with the exception of the snickering horses. It was deathly quiet which made him very nervous. For a moment he though that Indians might be lurking about trying to steal food or the horses, when suddenly the lone surviving mule from the squad started to bray loudly while the horses began kicking and moving wildly about in the small corral. "*What the hell?*" Alexander thought some of the horses might be picking on the mule and as a consequence, the animals were becoming excited. He yelled *ho*, a half dozen times to quiet them, but the horses kept galloping around in circles as if they were possessed, and the mule was now braying so loudly that he knew the camp was going to be awakened by all the commotion.

The mule was fighting for his life. Three wolves had attacked his front and back legs, trying to bring their prey down. The hapless beast kicked, brayed, and plunged around in the center of the corral in an attempt to shake his attackers while Private Alexander watched in horror. He lifted his Spencer to his shoulder and struggled to take aim at the biggest wolf but feared that he would miss and hit the mule instead. Finally, he had a clear shot of the big predator when the mule was able to shake the big carnivore off his left leg. Private Alexander squeezed the trigger but it wouldn't move. "*Froze.*" He yelled disgustedly. "Gawd damn trigger froze." Meanwhile, the mule's right front leg was brought down by another wolf and the beast was now close to being finished off unless Private Alexander could chase them off.

He planted the butt of his Spencer in the fresh snow and leaned the barrel of the rifle against the middle rail of the corral fence and proceeded to struggle to unflap the brass button on his holster. His hands were so numb because of the frigid conditions, that he could barely move his fingers even though he was wearing his gauntlets. As he cursed and tugged on the brass button to get at his army Colt, the mule continued to bray furiously and Alexander could hear the growling, yelping, snarling wolves rip and tear at the animal's flesh. Alexander finally managed to unflap his holster and seized the pommel of the Colt. He quickly removed the piece but had to use both his thumbs to fully cock back the hammer because his hands were so numb with cold. He stooped through the middle railings and entered the corral determined to shoot the wolves at close range. All of a sudden, he didn't feel cold anymore, his adrenaline was flowing so fast that he even felt a little warm. He maneuvered among the panicked horses to get where the fallen mule was now being ripped apart by the hungry wolves and took aim at the largest one. He fired, and the wolf yelped and wiggled in the dirty corral snow. He recocked his Colt and was ready to fire at another predator when a fourth wolf leaped at him from behind, forcing him to the ground. Now it was Pvt. Filmore Alexander who was being attacked. One of the vicious animals had seized the trooper's right wrist and was cutting through his flesh, while another one kept biting his face. He started screaming for help as he kicked his legs and feet in a desperate frenzy to throw off the predators, when he heard four shots ring out in rapid succession. The wolf that had been chewing on his face had abruptly stopped, and collapsed on Alexander's chest while the others fled, abandoning their kill. The next thing he knew, Nate was pulling off the dead wolf from his chest and he could see the sergeant major's breath that resembled a cloud of thin fog in the cold night with the light of the moon in the background.

Filmore Alexander's face and right wrist were badly mauled and he was now shivering again. Nate had heard all the commotion, and instinctively pulled on his boots with lightning speed and seized his Spencer. He tore out of the dugout where the squad was quartered, dressed only in his flannel drawers and shirt, and headed toward the corral at a run. He had seen the wolf lunge at Private Alexander and pull him down. He quickly raised his Spencer repeater and started firing in rapid succession, aiming for the wolves who were mauling his trooper's face and wrist. By now, several other soldiers and civilian laborers had emerged from their makeshift cabin-tents and ravine dug-outs armed and demanding what was going on. Nate ordered two of the troopers to help carry Alexander, while a white civilian railroad laborer, with a strong English Cockney accent offered to sew up Private Alexander's badly torn face at his cabin.

"I did a lot of sewin' on men's faces and bodies at the farm I used to work at, back in West Yorkshire," he boasted proudly. Nate agreed, and Pvt. Filmore Alexander was carried to the Englishman's cabin. As they left, Nate went over to the hapless mule. The poor beast was still kicking his hind legs as it gasped for breath. His stomach was ripped open and the entrails were slowly seeping out onto the frozen ground while dozens of deep bite marks covered the animal's legs, flanks, and neck.

"Po' bastard!" Nate aimed the Spencer at the mule's temple as the the beast's big eyes stared at him, and pulled the trigger.

The Englishman had stitched up Private Alexander's face and wrist and had made him as comfortable as possible. The West Yorkshire man also offered his bunk for as long as Private Alexander required rest. Nate was pleased that among the hundred or so white workers at the camp, at least one of them came forward and offered to help. To soothe his pain, the Englishman gave Alexander as much gin as he wanted, and his patient had grown quite fond of this drink. Filmore Alexander felt that the alcohol had a numbing affect on his stitched wounds, and helped him ward off the cold. More importantly, he found that gin made him gay in nature and less vulnerable to the boredom and monotony that plagued all military frontier posts, no matter how large the garrison. As a result of spending a week with the West Yorkshire man, Private Filmore Alexander, who had never consumed alcohol in his life, and who prided himself as a religious man, had slowly become subservient to gin to get him through the day and night.

Nate was writing in his journal while sitting in the corner of the railroad dugout where the squad had made the dark room into their living quarters. Nate thought that the interior resembled a sod house. The dugout had a potbellied stove in the middle of the room, a dirt floor, and one tiny window. With the exception of required daily duties such as taking care of the horses and guard duty, the men spent all of their time, day after day in the dark dugout if it was too cold or if there was too much snow for outside duties and patrols.

I am concerned about Private Filmore Alexander. He is a good man and fine soldier who is now facing a crisis. He had been with me when we rescued Jesse from the railroad cut hole, and had proved to be reliable in battle when we beat off the attacking Dog Soldiers. Now, the man has become dependent on drink to get him through the cold and long winter days at the railroad camp which was deeply affecting his performance to behave like a soldier. I am no stranger to the consequences of men falling prey to the bottle. During the war, I saw many men, enlisted and officers alike, black or white, who either got themselves killed while being drunk, or had destroyed their health and mental well being. The worst crime is an officer that gets drunk and leads his men into battle. The stupid fools get men killed.

After Filmore Alexander had left the West Yorkshire man's cabin, he started to frequent the ever-present smiling booze peddler, and spend his pay on gin, or whatever other forms of spirits was available, to get drunk. I found him last night passed out while he was on night guard duty, and although every punishment I have inflicted, such as making him stand from reveille to tattoo, on the edge on top of a barrel, blind-folded, with his hands tied behind his back and his feet bounded together, Filmore has failed to stop drinking. I have tried talking to him at first, then attempted to belittle him into shame. I have also unsuccessfully sought to locate Filmore's bottle stashes, and finally, I had to resort to more and more physical punishment to at least keep the trooper sober during the period of his castigation. All to no avail.

I have received complaints from some of the other troopers that certain articles are missing from their personal effects, and although I can not prove it, I know it was Filmore Alexander stealing to sustain his alcohol addiction. The last straw came however, when I found him wandering through the railroad camp without his great coat in the middle of the day. Private Alexander had sold his winter coat to the greedy whiskey peddler and had become completely inebriated. I had to buy back the great coat from the thieving liquor pimp at a profit, so Filmore Alexander wouldn't freeze to death. I ordered two troopers to drag him off to his bedroll and make him sleep it off. I have decided that the only way I can force Private Filmore Alexander to get off the booze is to send him away from the railroad camp. Clearly something has to be done in order to save this man from the ravages of drink. It pains me to see what has happened to a good soldier within a few months of living on the frontier during the winter.

"You drunk now, boy?" asked Nate as Private Alexander stood in front of him at attention outside the ravine dugout.

Although Filmore Alexander was hungover, he tried to hide the fact from the sergeant major. "No, Sarge, I ain't drunk."

"Maybe you feel like shit though, eh?" scoffed Nate, in Filmore's ear. "Well boy, I'm sendin' you on a mission," added Nate as he slowly circled Alexander as if he was sizing up a potential prey.

"What, what, kinda mission?" stuttered the trooper.

"The courier that came in from Wallace last night was supposed to push on this mornin' to Fort Gibson and deliver dispatches and the mail. But the boy came down with dysentery and can't go on." Nate paused for a moment and noticed that Filmore Alexander's face was showing signs of great concern. "So I made up my mind that I'm goin' send your sorry ass on military business."

Filmore Alexander's eyes popped wide open, and his heart started to beat more rapidly. For a moment, he no longer felt hungover. "Sarge, Fort Gibson is hun'reds of miles away! I, I, never been a courier 'fore," begged Private Alexander.

"This is your last chance to prove that you're a soldier and a man, boy! I'm sendin' fo' your own good. And I goin' be checkin' your saddlebags fo' any liquor 'fore you leave. Now get ready and report back to me in an hour."

Private Alexander grudgingly rolled up his bedroll and packed up all of his gear into his saddlebags and checked his Spencer repeater and army Colt revolver. Nate inspected his horse, making sure the animal's shoes were secure and then gave Alexander an extra bag of feed. He also handed the dispatches and mail pouch to Alexander and made him strap the bags to his back. As the trooper mounted, Nate opened up a map.

"Listen up, boy." Nate traced the route with his index finger on the map where Private Alexander would have to travel to reach Fort Gibson. "Yo'll ride southeast, toward de Arkansas River and ford de river, right about here. Now you watch it when you ford de river. Watch de currents, pick your spot on de bank and take your time, you hear!? You'll then follow de river till you reach de fort and report to de commandin' officer. Any questions, trooper?"

Filmore Alexander sat in his saddle silently. He felt sick and he looked at Nate with sad eyes, hoping to draw sympathy. He sighed and asked Nate how many miles it was to Fort Gibson, which was south of the Kansas border in Indian Country.

" 'Bout three hundred and fifty miles," replied Nate.

"Sweet Jesus! I'm never goin' make it," whined Alexander.

"Yes you are, boy," said Nate with assurance. "You're a cavalryman in de U-nited States Army! Now, go do your duty." Nate slapped the rump of Alexander's horse, the animal bolted, and cantered out of the railroad camp toward the southeast and the Arkansas River. Nate yelled to him as he departed, "And don't you be sellin' that army coat, yeah hear!?"

FEBRUARY 1868

Nate was lying in his bedroll thinking about Jesse. He missed his friend's conversation and regretted that he was unable to be with him to pass the time. Jesse however, had to spend the winter at Fort Riley and recover from his wounds. Winter was slowly coming to a close and Nate looked forward to March and his return to Fort Riley.

Although the days were becoming longer and there were times when the temperature rose above freezing, the loneliness of the winter still continued to weigh heavily on the troopers' and railroad civilians' minds. There were no signs of Indian activity for months, and the only two distractions that the camp had was the omnipresent whiskey peddler, and a bunch of whores that were lodged in a portable building that followed the railroad. They were very successful in milking the bored and horny workers for money in return for satisfying their carnal lust. Although the portable bordello was a crude, drafty wooden structure that leaked, the concept was ingenious. Like a circus, the building was disassembled and reassembled as needed, whenever the Union Pacific Railroad moved west. The structure had five bedrooms and a large central room that served as a parlor where customers and the "horizontal workers" met each other and discussed terms with the pimp, a fat Creole from Baton Rouge by the name of Antonio Vasco.

These "Nymphs du Prairie" were the same assemblage of harlots that Nate had encountered on the outskirts of Hays City. When they had first arrived at the railroad camp, Nate was unaware that they were the same group that he had seen at Hays because they would stay cooped up in their bordello. He had thought about the young half-breed on many occasions and wondered if he would ever see her again in much the same way as he thought about finding his long-lost half-sister. It was only when he recognized the gaudy pimp did he realize that this was the same bunch, but he had not seen the young half-breed woman. Nate had learned through one of the whores, that the pimp was of Portuguese descent, and his mother was an African who came from Angola. He was an uncouth man with olive skin and jet black hair that was greased back and Nate thought the top of his head resembled a helmet. Antonio Vasco had a huge girth and always wore silk embroidered vests. He carried a gold pocketwatch in his right slit pocket, its heavy chain festooned across his protruding paunch.

Antonio Vasco had eight whores and a young girl who was his half-breed housekeeper and harlot assistant, by the name of Cara de Cuervo Zarata. Her father was a leader of a Mexican scalp hunting band and her mother was a Commanche squaw who was captured by the scalp hunters and forced to be a servant and concubine for the leader of the band. As a consequence of their carnal union, a girl was born and her mother gave her daughter the Mexican father's last name and called her Cara de Cuervo, Spanish for Raven Face. The mother decided to call her that because her coal black hair and large, penetrating dark eyes shined as if she were a raven. When the girl was twelve years old, her father sold her to Antonio Vasco for a few pesos and she became his concubine and servant while traveling with the whores from the Rio Grande to the Upper Missouri.

Cara de Cuervo Zarata had toiled for Vasco for seven years while being abused as if she were a homeless mangy dog with fleas. Vasco not only forced her to clean and serve as a maid for his precious whores, but compelled her to be his sex slave whenever he became drunk and felt like abusing her. Cara de Cuervo often thought about fleeing, but backed down after contemplating that she had no idea where to go or how she would survive alone on the frontier. Her mother had disappeared with the scalp hunters, so she was completely isolated and had become dependent on the fat Creole pimp.

As Nate stared at the ceiling of the dugout, he thought about the young woman half-breed at the traveling bordello that he had finally seen again during one of his morning rides. She was emptying bedpans and had brought the laundry in a wicker basket to wash in a cast-iron cauldron in the cold. From that moment on, his mind became preoccupied with her. He wondered where she came from and why she would work for a man who abused her. Although Nate was a very handsome and strong man who made women's heads turn whether they were black, white, Mexican, or Indian, he was not interested in the affairs of the heart. He avoided women and preferred to put his energies into work and self-betterment rather than expending energy pursuing skirts. His detachment from women was partially due to the experience that his mother had undergone with Blood Hound Jack and his lost half-sister, but also largely due to a traumatic experience he had when he was thirteen years old.

Although Nate loathed thinking about it, he often found himself wondering in abhorrence at the time when Mas'a Hammond had forced him to copulate for the first time with one of his prize young slave girls that he had reserved for breeding. Mas'a Hammond was impressed with the woman's big hips and large physique and decided to reserve her as a slave baby maker in order to produce strong bucks to work on his fields in the future. Nate considered the episode as one of the more ghastly experiences he had to endure while he was a slave. The girl was a virgin and Nate was still tormented in the way he had treated her. It still made him wince in disgust whenever he relived the experience of behaving as if he were a young eager stallion mounting a frightened mare. The young slave girl screamed and fought when Nate mounted and penetrated her, and during the middle of the act, blood poured forth from her vaginal organs. This revolted Nate so much that it was years before he had a woman again, and that was during the war when he visited a contraband camp with a bunch of other black noncoms.

The half-breed girl who worked as a servant at the traveling bordello, however, appealed to Nate like no other had before. Several times when he rode past the mobile bordello in the mornings, he would catch her outside near the washboard doing laundry and other chores. She would stop what she was doing and give him a smile with her crooked mouth while her bright, dark eyes looked at him with great intensity. He would tip the visor of his kepi politely and move on, because he did not have the courage to accost her.

This changed one morning when Cara de Cuervo wished him good morning in Spanish, *"Buenos días, Señor Sargento Mayor."* The way she said it, in that raspy tone of voice with an air of provocative solicitation, seized Nate's attention. This morning ritual continued for several weeks until Nate decided that he would properly introduce himself the next time he saw her.

After the usual breakfast of fried beans, salt pork, and dry bread, followed by the morning presentation of the colors in front of the ravine dugout where the cavalrymen were quartered, and seeing that the horses were fed and groomed, Nate polished his hightop boots. This morning however, he polished his boots with an extra air of enthusiasm. He had never felt this way before. A combination of euphoria and inner dread affected him. When he had completed brushing his uniform and preparing to mount his horse, he spoke to himself softly as he held the reins with his left hand and placed his boot in the stirrup, "I ain't nervous. I ain't nervous."

Cara de Cuervo Zarata was scrubbing clothes against the washboard. It was late February and the sun was extremely bright. Its warm rays were slowly melting the layers of winter snow and drifts, while the sounds of trickling water could be heard everywhere. Cara was wearing a large sombrero to shield her round face from the strong early spring sun and to prevent the heat from escaping her body. Underneath her well-worn French trapper coat, she had on a plain buckskin dress that fell to her ankles and little deerskin booties covered her tiny feet.

As Nate approached on his horse, she was wringing out the last bit of linens from the wash. Ever since she had laid her eyes on the big, *Sargento Mayor Negro*, she felt her heart pound, and her eyes transfixed on the man. She looked forward every time that he would canter by with his squad or by himself in the morning. For Cara de Cuervo Zarata, this was her favorite time of the day and what kept her going during the winter months as she tended to every dirty whim from her Creole master. She remembered fondly the time when Nate had rushed to her assistance when she had fallen from the wagon and loved Nate's uniform and the big chevrons on his sleeves as he sat erect in the saddle. She was impressed by the way the *Sargento Mayor* moved with his mount, appearing as if he were one with the horse. This time however, he was headed straight for her rather than just cantering by. Her penetrating dark eyes stared at Nate while she loosened the chin straps on her sombrero. Cara de Cuervo could see the horse's nostrils twitching and the rear hooves kicking up a combination of melting snow and mud as the animal and rider approached her.

Nate halted his horse by simply pulling back his hands gently on the reins. He never believed abusing a horse's mouth if you could help it. He always figured that a horse would respect you more if you are easy on the animal's mouth, rather than pulling abruptly or jerking on the reins.

"Mawnin', ma'am," said Nate nervously as he tipped the visor on his kepi.

"*Buenos días, Sargento Mayor.*" Cara de Cuervo raised her head and Nate could see that her face was flushed. He was amazed how bright her eyes were.

"Finished with the wash are ya, ma'am?" Nate felt terribly clumsy, and was at a loss to find something to say. Sensing his awkwardness, Cara de Cuervo gently removed her sombrero and slid the hat down the back of her neck while adjusting the straps so the hat hung halfway down her shoulder blades.

"You go for ride, *El Gran Caballero?*" she said teasingly, her crooked smile showing her bleached white teeth.

"Eh, yes, ma'am. Eh, it's a nice mawnin' fo' that," replied Nate, as he stared off to the horizon while his horse started to chomp on its bit.

"*Sí.* I see you every morning," she added, in a raspy Spanish accent. She approached the horse and gave the animal a pat on its neck.

"Like horses?" Nate finally found a subject that he could discuss without feeling maladroit.

"Sí, very much!" she responded eagerly as her little head bobbed up and down.

"Maybe we can go and ride . . . together, sometime?" He could not believe that he asked that question. He felt like a wet-nosed kid asking for buttermilk from a stranger while his big toe drew circles in the dust. He decided to change the subject. "My name's Nate, Nate Gordon. What's yours, if I may inquire?"

Cara de Cuervo Zarata was stunned. She could ride of course, and would have liked nothing better than to go on a leisurely excursion on horseback with the *Sargento Mayor*. Her mother, a Commanche, and her father, a former Vaquero, taught her to ride like the wind considering that her family were scalp hunters and had to move expeditiously. The problem was that she could never leave the railroad camp, and Antonio Vasco would never give her permission, especially to spend time with another man!

"*Cara de Cuervo Zarata,*" she finally answered, preoccupied by the fact that she was trapped and could not break free from her tyrannical and abusive employer. Nate looked a little perplexed. He was not used to hearing Spanish names and although it sounded beautiful, she said it so quickly that he was not able to distinguish any of the words.

"It means, "Face of the Raven," she clarified, as she took her hand and moved it in front of her face in a quick circular movement.

Nate smiled and nodded in approval. After an awkward moment of silence he asked again if she could come riding.

"*El hombre . . . ,*" she responded, turning her eyes toward the building.

"I see. Vasco won't let you go," said Nate as he tilted his head in the direction of the bordello. She did not know what to say and a long silence overcame the two of them. Nate's horse was pawing the ground nervously and snorting.

Cara de Cuervo also nodded in the direction of the bordello and gave Nate a look that told him that she was a virtual prisoner to the fat Creole.

Nate dismounted from his horse and turned to the beautiful half-breed girl. He was only a few feet away and could smell Cara de Cuervo's body aroma. He felt the hairs on the back of his neck suddenly spring up, and a heightened sense of stimulation.

"I'll go an' talk to the man." He tipped his kepi and made for the front door of the bordello.

Antonio Vasco was pouring hair oil on his scalp and rubbing the liquid into his jet black hair as he gazed at himself lovingly in the mirror of his vanity table. He then took both of his palms and smoothed back the hair until it rested completely flat on his scalp. Satisfied that he looked the part, he adjusted his pink silk cravat.

The whores were still sleeping it off from a long night of satisfying customers and Vasco was wondering where Cara de Cuervo was. The Creole pimp looked at his heavy pocket watch, and became angry when he noticed that it was past nine-thirty and no sign of the half-breed girl with his habitual morning coffee. This irritated him greatly. "Where's di bitch?" he asked himself. "She should have finished di wash by now." He stared at himself in the mirror and then cracked, "Looks like I will have to smack dat Indian-Mex bitch some more." He threw down his towel in the washbowl and started to make for the door to see if she was outside. As he was about to reach for the doorknob, Nate pushed in the door from the outside, nearly knocking over the obese Creole.

Vasco stumbled backward, but managed to grab the end of a table and remained erect. He was blinded by the bright morning sunlight that poured through the opened doorway and had to cover his face with his hand in order to see the frame of the big man that had just entered the room. Nate shut the door behind him as if he were going to give some uppity trooper a richly deserved dressing-down.

"I know that you're de *man* here," said Nate contemptuously.

Nate towered over the Creole. The sight of this coal-black man dressed in a perfectly-fitting shell jacket, hightop cavalry boots polished to look like glass, and the butt of Nate's big Walker-Colt protruding from his left hip, was quite intimidating to the mulatto pimp from Baton Rouge.

"De girls are asleep, come back later . . ."

"I ain't here fo' no whores," interrupted Nate, offended that the fat Creole would assume that he was a whoring man. Nate stood at attention and removed his kepi, revealing his closely cropped hair.

"Oh? Then why are you here?" responded the Creole, irritated that Nate was taking up his time.

"I'm here to tell you that I'm goin' . . . court that Spanish gal . . ."

"*My half-breed Commanche bitch?*" exclaimed Vasco, bemused that this big nigger with sergeant stripes had the nerve to be so impertinent. Nate, on the other hand, was appalled that this fat pimp referred to the girl he was rapidly falling infatuated with, as a breed-bitch. It reminded him of slavery days when the whites and even many of the quadroons and octoroons treated blacks who were darker as if they were livestock, as beasts of burden or sex objects to be abused at will.

"*Your a Gawddamn breed yo'self, you cursed idiot.* Or maybe you was a house nigga toadyin' up behind some mistress's' skirttails, Now hear this! 'Cause I ain't goin' say it twice. If I catch you abusin' that gal, I'll come back with my squad and burn this cursed place down to the ground like I used to do durin' de war. And furder mo', I'm goin' court her, and you got nothin' to say 'bout that!" The artery on Nate's neck was bulging, and his eyes became wide with anger. It had been a very long time since he felt such rage. Not even during the war or during the recent fights with the Cheyennes did he feel such animosity. Nate had always remained composed in battle and not take the fight personally. This odious man, however, was so repulsive to him, that his usual self-controlled demeanor was being severely tested. He wanted to place his hands on the pimp's corpulent neck and raise the bastard off his feet and throw the swine outside where he could really give him a thrashing.

Antonio Vasco was shaken and taken aback with this vicious tongue lashing. Realizing that he faced the prospect of his establishment being burned to the ground was enough for him to relent. "*Halto! Halto!*" he responded, waving his hand as if he were chasing away some mad dog. He then added, as he cracked a sly smile. "You have my permission, *Sargento Mayor.*"

Pvt. Filmore Alexander was shivering in his saddle as he tried to warm his numb fingers by rubbing his hands together. He had traveled over two hundred and fifty miles in the middle of winter to bring dispatches and the mail to Fort Gibson. His horse, weakened by the long ride in the cold and wet weather, stumbled along with its weary rider cursing every step. Ever since he left the railroad camp his fingers and toes had been deadened by the intense cold. He would ride as long as possible during the day and endure the unwavering pain inflicted by the low temperature and high winds. When the agony would become too great to endure, his frozen hands would tug at the reins to command his horse to halt. He then would slowly lower himself down from the stiff McClellan saddle and dismount to stomp his feet which were encased in boots that were too tight for him, and rub his hands together to get the circulation going.

Private Alexander had managed to sneak a pint of 190 proof Kentucky corn liquor under his forage cap which was the only place Nate failed to search before he left that dreary railroad camp. Incredibly, he made the booze last for two days and finally dropped the empty bottle on the trail with much sorrow. He was now sober for the first time in weeks and he despised it. At least when he was drunk he felt warmer. He cursed Nate for ordering him to go on this God-forsaken courier trip in the first place, and damned the sergeant major even more for not letting him take at least a full bottle of liquor with him.

The Northwest winds would cut through his great coat, long johns, and wool uniform as if he were naked. He would keep his scarf close to the lower half of his face but by the end of the day, the rag had become encrusted with ice because his breath would slowly freeze on the wool thus making the garment very uncomfortable to wear next to his face. Every night he would find a tree, ravine, or gully, or anything else that might provide some shelter against the elements, and bivouac. He would make a fire from damp twigs and keep it going for as long as possible and try to dry out his wet clothes and feel the warmth of the tiny flickering flames on his face and hands. After he had fed his tired mount, he devoured a plate of beans and hardtack for supper, and spend most of the night in his bedroll shivering from the cold and staring at the sky counting stars, in an attempt to keep his mind preoccupied. He would stop counting, however, when he heard the prairie wolves howl in the distance. It brought back the dreadful memories of his recent encounter with the predators at the corral. Every time a wolf would cry out, Pvt. Filmore Alexander would murmur to himself, "Please don't come, please don't come."

He had made good time however, in spite of the wind, snow, and cold. His small bundle of the written word, strapped to his back, was a precious commodity for the soldiers that resided at Fort Gibson.

Newspapers from back East and letters from families and loved ones were greatly welcomed by the troopers.

Pvt. Filmore Alexander had followed the Arkansas River for most of the way south and Fort Gibson was about twenty miles away, located at the point where the Verdisgris and Grand Rivers join the Arkansas. Alexander veered eastward, leaving the Arkansas and proceeded toward the Verdisgris River which he would have to cross in order to reach the post. It was the beginning of March and most of the region's streams, rivers, and creeks were swollen from the melting snows and early spring rains.

As he approached the Verdisgris he could hear the sounds of rushing water. This alarmed him, because he did not like to cross streams in general, but now with every body of water swollen to capacity for hundreds of miles around, he really dreaded this last stage of his ride. He knew however, that he had no choice but to ford the river if he wished to reach the post. He had searched for about an hour for a place in which to cross but was unable to locate a spot. It was late afternoon and he wanted to spend the night at Gibson. "I'm not spendin' anoder Goddamn night outside," he said to himself as he spurred his reluctant mount toward the Verdisgris. He was looking forward to getting intoxicated and hoped that he would not have a problem locating a bottle. He had to admit though, that the ten days of forced sobriety had been good for him from a health and mental point of view. He enjoyed waking up without a splitting headache or stomach pains that resulted in diarrhea. Therefore, justifying this recent good behavior, he decided that after he had delivered the mail pouch, he was "gonna get stinkin' drunk," as a reward.

The currents of the Verdisgris were strong and unpredictable during most of the year, but with the additional spring rains and water from fast-melting snows, the river was much more treacherous than usual. Pvt. Filmore Alexander was tense but felt that if he kept his mount moving at a consistent speed through the river, he should be able to ford without too much difficulty. He halted his horse at the river's edge and gave the body of water a good looking-over. The sounds deriving from the millions of gallons of rushing white water reminded him of the noise made by a passing train. He checked upriver to make sure that there were no floating pieces of debris heading downstream that might knock his horse over. With the exception of some small branches that were floating by, the trooper was satisfied that the debris in the river would not affect his crossing. He urged his horse forward to where he thought the animal would have little trouble descending the bank. The black gelding shied abruptly, however, and started to retreat away from the river and Alexander had to vigorously spur the horse and curse the animal to regain control and proceed down the bank into the Verdisgris. Finally, the gelding relented and slowly descended the sandy bank, using his hindquarters for traction. The horse halted however, right at the waters' edge and lowered his head to sniff the river. Alexander allowed him to do this for a brief moment then started spurring the horse and ordering him to move into the water. The gelding again refused to move forward and Alexander had to use the barrel of his Spencer to beat the hapless beast on the rump. This did the trick. The black gelding hesitantly moved into the water and started to cross the river while Alexander kept spurring the horse, trying to ford as rapidly as possible. The trooper felt that his mount was becoming unsteady as the animal waded deeper and deeper into the Verdisgris and fought to keep the swift currents from pushing him over. The horse, already weak and exhausted from the long ride, found the crossing a struggling challenge. The white water was now up to the trooper's hips, and with the exception of the animal's tail, head and back, the body was completely submerged. Alexander was now becoming fearful and nervous that the water would continue to rise. His mind was racing, and he felt his heart pound against his chest. What would he do if the rushing water unhorsed him, or if his mount stumbled and disappeared under the water?

He was now past the halfway point and the water started to recede. He felt more confident and started to relax knowing that he was going to make it. For a while there, he really thought he would be swallowed up, and not being able to swim, it would have meant certain death. Alexander gave another glance upriver to see if any debris was coming his way, and he noticed to his horror, a very large tree stump, thick with branches, being torn from its mooring by the eroding river currents about thirty feet away on the opposite bank. "Jesus Christ," he shouted desperately. The cut-off trunk started to revolve violently in the water as if it were a large wheel turning with jagged protruding edges. The stump, propelled by the currents, was rapidly moving in the direction of Alexander and his tired mount.

Realizing that he had a real deadly problem at hand, he started to beat his horse's rump with the barrel of his Spencer. The black gelding tried to push on but began stumbling and lost more time attempting to get out of the water than if Alexander would have just let the animal advance at his own speed. The stump was approaching fast and the closer it got, the larger the object became.

"Come on, boy; come on!" shouted Alexander frantically, as he smacked the barrel of the Spencer on his struggling mount's rump. The trooper became more and more desperate. Every step that his horse took, the lethal spinning cut-off trunk advanced as if it were following him. He was only about fifteen feet from the other side of the Verdis- gris, but his horse had drifted so far from where he thought he could safely cross over to the eastern side, that he was now forced to search for another location. He decided to turn his mount downriver and locate a spot where his mount could climb over the sandy bank, when the free-wheeling trunk with protruding sharp branches slammed into his horse's rear flanks thus forcing the gelding underwater while dis- lodging its rider.

Both the horse and Pvt. Filmore Alexander were now caught in the currents. The trooper still held onto his mount's reins but it was to no avail for he was unable to remount or even get close enough to at least hold onto the horse for support. His training as a cavalryman taught him to never, ever, let go of the reins of his horse if there was not another trooper to watch his mount. His gelding however, was being dragged by the rapid currents and Alexander was having great trouble keeping his head from being dunked as he took several mouth- fuls of Verdisgris white water which started to choke him. In addition, the heavy mail pouch that was strapped to his back did not make matters any easier, as it became a burden and hindered his ability to remain afloat. He now tried to let go of the reins in an effort to try and paddle toward the eastern side of the river bank but found that his left hand had become entangled in the reins. Private Filmore jerked at the reins frantically while his mount struggled to keep his head above the water line as the currents of the river rushed around him and his horse and pulled them below the surface for longer and longer periods of time. Pvt. Filmore Alexander gasped hopelessly for breath, but his lungs had filled up with water instead, and within a few moments he was dead, his body being dragged downriver by the drowning black gelding.

Nate and Cara de Cuervo were out riding a few miles from the railroad camp. The day was warm enough for them to be free from layers of clothes and Nate just had on his wool shell jacket and Cara de Cuervo had slipped on a Commanche blanket that had an opening for her little head. Every day since Nate had brow-beaten the Creole pimp into relenting his hold on Cara de Cuervo, they had gone riding. Sometimes they would ride in the mornings after Nate had completed his morning duties, or in the early evenings, to watch the sunset. They were growing closer to each other with each passing day, and Nate was slowly falling in love with the half-breed. He loved to be with her and every time he smelled her body aroma he felt a tingling sensation in the back of his neck and lower skull. For Cara de Cuervo, Nate was a godsend. Although she continued to perform her duties as Vasco's servant, the beatings and his drunken sexual abuse of her had ceased ever since Nate threatened to set fire to his bordello. For the first time in her life, she felt protected and secure, and most importantly, she felt happy whenever she was with the "*Sargento Mayor.*"

Spring on the plains was a welcome event, and Nate thoroughly enjoyed riding among the new growth, and smelling the fresh spring air. He loved seeing the grasses sprouting back and listening to the sounds of new life. The squad, the railroad workers, and even the whores at Vasco's traveling whorehouse all relished the warm weather and smells of new grass. After a long, cold, dark winter with much snow and ice, the warmth of the sun and bright light lifted the spirits for all those who had spent the winter months in dark and lonely semi-hibernation.

Nate behaved like a perfect gentleman when he was with Cara de Cuervo. He had only touched her when he assisted her to mount the horse he had procured for her and always tipped his kepi whenever he greeted her or said good-bye. Cara de Quervo in turn became delighted with Nate's treatment of her. She had never been treated with so much kindness and consideration and dreaded returning to the bordello where she had to fight off dirty men who always grabbed, kicked, slapped, and even punched her whenever they became displeased with her service, or more frequently, when she rebuffed their sexual advances.

"Over there. . . ." pointed Nate at a small herd of mule deer that were grazing on young grass shoots. Nate enjoyed pointing to objects of interest on the prairie.

"*Sí los cuervos,*" confirmed Cara, as she pulled back a strand of hair that was dangling loosely against her right cheek and tucked the raven black hair back into her sombrero.

Nate smiled every time he heard her speak Spanish. He found her voice charming and soothing and the manner in which she pronounced words with that sharp Mexican accent always got his attention.

"Got my orders today," said Nate seriously as he bowed his head. The two of them were riding side by side, and the horses were walking at a fast pace while flicking their tales at a steady rhythm and relishing the spring air. "De squad has to report to Fort Riley in a week." There was a long silence as the horses plodded along, and Cara de Cuervo became melancholy. Nate felt that she had become sorrowful and decided that now was the time to reveal his little plan.

"I want you to come with me, Cara." Nate had started to call her Cara only a few days before, after she had given him permission to do so. "You can come with me when de squad moves out and go on to Riley where I'm sure I can find you a position as a laundress at the post. See, each comp'ny is allowed to have four laundresses who are enrolled on de comp'ny roster and there are authorized rations and quarters for them." Nate paused, and then added optimistically. "You can make a little money, 'cause you can make seventy cents per soldier and a dollar fo' de officers and their wives. I know it ain't much, but . . . you see, I want you to come with me. I wanna get you outta this bad place."

Cara de Quervo was both pleased and sad. She was happy that the *Sargento Mayor* wanted her to come and go with him, and the possibility of escaping her Creole tormentor was very appealing. But that was the problem. She knew that Vasco would not let her go freely. Maybe Nate could buy her from him, or now that Vasco was no longer sleeping with her, he might lose interest and release her from him.

"I would like to come with you. But Vasco, he will not let me go, I am afraid," she finally responded shaking her head. Cara had to strain to look up at Nate. Her horse was smaller, and her riding companion so tall, that Nate appeared to look like a giant in the saddle.

"I will take care of Vasco," said Nate grimly. "The question is though, will you come with me to Riley?"

Cara looked up at Nate again, her tiny face overwhelmed by the wide sombrero, and smiled. "*Sí! Absolutamente,*" she responded smiling, as her flashing ravenlike eyes stared at the man who she was falling in love with.

Antonio Vasco knew that he was going to lose his half-breed, but was determined that he was not going to let her go for free. After all, he was a businessman and had purchased the breed bitch, fair and square. He was going through his morning ritual of oiling his hair and perfuming himself in front of the mirror of his vanity. He was admiring himself as he buttoned his embroidered silk vest when he noticed that Cara de Cuervo was carrying a blanket that held her possessions folded to form a bundle.

"Yo no go nowhere!" ordered Vasco. Cara halted, she was clutching her bundle and could smell the cheap eau-de-cologne that permeated the room.

"I'm finished being your *puta* and *criado*!" she responded defiantly.

Vasco became immediately furious at this impertinent rebuttal. Never before had she been so insolent. He knew it was that interfering nigger sergeant that had instilled this newfound independence in her and he resented him for that. He raised his right arm with the palm of his fleshy hand wide open, and was getting ready to strike her when the front door creaked open.

Nate was standing in the doorway leering at Vasco. He had left the squad outside mounted and ready to depart for the return trip to Riley. He had halted his troopers in front of the bordello, and ordered them to remain at ease while he went to go and fetch Cara. He knew that Antonio Vasco was about to slap Cara when he saw the Creole's raised arm. "I told you, I'll not tolerate you touchin' that woman!" he warned Vasco sternly in a low tone of voice. Seeing a man strike a woman always made Nate's blood run hot and his normal patient demeanor disappeared. He was always reminded about the time when he was very young and witnessed the mistress of the plantation strike his mother because she had slightly overcooked some biscuits.

"You can't take her!" scoffed Vasco defensively, as he placed his arms by his side and tried to change the topic. "I paid good cash money fo' her and she's mine!"

"I'll buy her freedom from you. How much?" demanded Nate, trying to control his temper.

"One hundred dollars," responded Antonio Vasco without blinking an eye.

"One hundred ...!? *You thievin' bastard.* I'll give yo' half-black ass, thirty dollars. Dats all I got, an' dats dat." Nate was outraged that he even had to pay money to free Cara. She was not a slave, and the fact that Antonio Vasco was half-black and demanded money for her release really angered him. "Thirty dollars. Take it or I'll take her right now and leave you greedy ass with nothin'!"

"One hundred dollars, not a penny less. I gots to make a profit, I'm a businessman." Vasco remained stubbornly adamant.

Nate moved to where the Creole pimp was standing and placed his face squarely in front of Vasco's as if he were some insolent green trooper. "You are a flesh peddler!" growled Nate—his eyes became huge and Vasco could smell his breath. He then added daringly, "I'm takin' de woman with me, and if you show your sorry face out de door, my boys outside have orders to blow it off!"

This unnerved Vasco for a moment. He had not been prepared for that. As he stood there stunned, Cara made a move to be next to Nate, but Vasco blocked her attempt to cross the floor and grabbed her arm, squeezing the limb which made her cry out.

"*Eres un cerdo!*" she screamed, cursing him. Nate unbuttoned the holster flap of his Walker-Colt so swiftly that the Creole did not see him make the movie, and the next thing he was conscious of was when he felt the blow at the back of his skull being whacked by the big pistol barrel of Nate's Walker-Colt. He staggered, blinded and disoriented from the blow, and fell forward on the bordello floor, as if he were a felled tree cut down by an ax.

Cara ran to Nate and wrapped her arms around his waist as if she were a child that needed to be comforted. She was free at last from the yoke of servitude and from the abuses of Antonio Vasco. Nate reholstered his pistol and buttoned the holster flap. He calmly gazed at Vasco's pudgy body that resembled a dead sow, and commented as if he were reminding some wet-nosed kid that I told you so, "I warned you that I wouldn't tolerate bad behavior."

Twelve

The year of 1867 is proving to be an atrocious period for folks living on the Kansas frontier. Wells Fargo stage stations, sod hut homesteaders, ranchers, railroad laborers, wood and hay cutters, travelers, surveyors, prospectors, military patrols, and army posts are all vulnerable to vicious and sudden attack on the Kansas prairie. Hundreds of folks have suffered greatly at the hands of the Cheyennes as the Dog Soldiers commit such acts as burning, looting, torture, mutilation, and the indiscriminate murder of women and children. Dozens have been made captive and have experienced a separate horror that usually led to a violent death after much anguish.

The Hancock War of 1867, named for its commanding officer, Major General Winfield Scott Hancock, was a complete failure in putting a stop to these depredations, and in fact, made the situation worse by the general's conflicting speeches between war and peace, and by his threatening military maneuvers that made the Indians greatly suspicious. Considered as one of the finest tactical masters of the Civil War, and beloved by millions of Yankees as the man responsible for stunting George Pickett's frontal assault against the federal center on that third and final day at the Battle of Gettysburg, Hancock was the epitome of the American warrior.

Known as "Hancock the Superb," this demigod-General carried the responsibility for convincing the Dog Soldiers to cease their attacks against the settlers and sign peace treaties, or failing that, force the Indians to abide by the laws and customs of the United States by utilizing threats, and an overt willingness to use brute military force to intimidate the tribes of the plains into submission. I have read in the newspapers that this botched military expedition had cost the United States Treasury about one hundred million dollars, and not only failed to convince the Arapahoes, Commanches, Lakotas, and Cheyennes to cease their ravages against the settlers, but had actually provoked greater reprisals on the part of these tribes, and the Cheyennes in particular, were in the vanguard in expressing their outrage at the arrogance of white incursions on their traditional homelands.

As a result, I predict that 1868 will prove to be worse than the year before regarding continued Indian ravages against folks along the Saline, Solomon, and Republican River valleys. The promised government annuities were very late in coming because the congress, rather than promptly ratifying the Medicine Lodge Treaties promptly, as the tribes of the plains had done in October of last year, decided to amend and debate the treaties! The fools! They have no idea what is going on here beyond the newspapers and the cities. This delay, as I had predicted, has enraged the tribes, who had gathered at the vicinity of Fort Larned and had fully expected to receive the agreed-upon supplies. Indian agents were unable to quiet the disgruntled, hungry braves, and the eagerness of greedy bootleggers to supply whiskey, only furthered aggravated the explosive situation.

The United States Cavalry and the Kansas militia, underequipped and poorly supplied due to a weary populace that just went through four years of war, were given the task of "disciplining" the hostiles. But both the army and state militias have been constantly out-maneuvered and out-numbered by the Dog Soldiers on the field of battle and we are unable to take the Cheyennes by surprise.

General William Tecumseh Sherman, commander of the Division of the Missouri, has replaced Major General Winfield Scott Hancock with General Phil Sheridan. "Little Phil" has his own concept of how to wage war on the hostiles. According to what I have heard from Colonel Armes, he has decided to mobilize small, heavily armed ranger units to seek and destroy Dog Soldier war parties and follow the pattern that had worked so well in bringing about the collapse of the Confederacy: Engaging in a scorched earth policy against the tribes of the central and southern plains by directly attacking and annihilating their villages, wiping out their stores, and killing all of their ponies, preferably during the winter months.

I am concerned about Private Filmore Alexander. I have been informed that he never reported to Fort Gibson with the mail. He has been declared a deserter. This pains me. I did not think that the boy would do that. But with his boozing problem and the harshness of the winter and all, maybe he did have his fill and deserted. Or maybe, I hope, he died as a soldier. Maybe the Indians got him, or he froze to death on the trail.

Nate, the squad, and Cara de Cuervo had arrived at Fort Riley in the last week of April. The grass was lush so the horses were putting on weight and the weather was clear and cool. The group had made good progress along the trail as they smelled the blooming aroma of millions of wildflowers that carpeted the prairie. General Sheridan had ordered the regiment to assemble at Fort Riley and await further orders for deployment on the frontier.

Nate found lodgings for Cara with the negro laundresses who worked at suds row some distance from the fort. As they walked together on rickety planks that served as a crude walkway for the shanty town, they felt they were more among friends than at the fort where the wives of the officers paint their faces and wear fine clothes. The laundresses came from many different backgrounds. Mexican, black, low-class whites, and half-breeds. Cara felt secure among these physically tough, independent women who had a seasoned appearance.

"Dese *mujers?* Dey hav' *hombres?*" inquired Cara as she watched barefoot children run around the huge cast-iron kettles that were kept in backyards with boiling water fueled by wood fires.

"Oh, most of them are de wives or girlfriends of noncommissioned officers," replied Nate matter-of-factly.

"Non . . . com . . . miss . . . ?" responded Cara perplexed.

"Noncommission . . . means like me," smiled Nate, as he slowly said the word while pointing to his chevron stripes.

Cara smiled and understood. She also felt something inside of her that made her think . . . who knows?

Suds row's chief laundress was a large, black as coal matron and former slave. "Mah name is Matilda Pugh Daniel, an' ah comes from Eufaula, Barbour County, Alabama," she exclaimed, eye-balling Nate. Then adding as if she wanted to make the point, "Ma mistress wa'nt goin' to let nobody wash dem julep glasses but me, soz iz de bestest wash woman white or black, on dis side of de Mis'ip'i, an' ah ain't scared of nothin'!" Matilda agreed that she could use the additional help and reassured Nate that she would watch out for Cara. "Ain't nobody goin' touch dis child. Now yo' git your impo'tant black ass ov'r to da fort where yo' belong," she ordered, as she used her huge body to maneuver Nate out the door.

As Nate was walking his horse toward the stables he heard a man yelling at some trooper inside the stables for not properly grooming and hoof-picking his mount. He recognized the voice immediately. He released the reins of his mount and tiptoed into the stables and sneaked up to the yelling man from behind. He managed to sneak up to him and was only a foot away. The soldier was a noncommissioned officer and was still dressing-down the trooper, so Nate decided to observe him for a moment.

"What the hell do you think goin' happen to your sorry ass if this animal throws a shoe out there on the plains when a hundred Dawg Men are comin' at you with pointed lances?"

"I say it sounds like a *dead man* to me," mocked Nate loudly, startling the noncom.

"What the *hell*?" The sergeant jumped, and turned to face Nate.

"Jesus Christ! How are you, *boy*?" exclaimed Jesse, as he embraced his comrade whom he had not seen since last fall. Nate also wrapped his arms around his friend and the two big sergeants resembled two embracing grizzlies. They laughed and back-slapped each other vigorously.

"When you git in?" inquired Jesse.

"Jest now," responded Nate, smiling. He paused for a moment and gave Jesse a good look. He had put on weight and looked healthy. Nate, on the other hand, had lost weight and felt tired. "It was a hell of a winter, Jess! A hell of a winter."

"Well, Iz sure yo' woul'nt have traded places wid me!" teased Jesse. He started laugh. "Hell, m'ah winter was so borin'. While yo' was freezen in some gawd-forsaken railroad, end-of-the-line camp, eatin' vittles dat ain't fit fo' a dawg, an' puttin-up wid wild Indians an' white shit, whil' I'z forced to stay close to a nice warm stove wid de other noncoms an' eat as much as I liked while waitin' fo' de weather to warm up."

"Yeah *damn right* I wouldn't have traded asses with ya," retorted Nate with a big smile. "You're almost as fat as a hog," said Nate as he pointed mockingly at Jesse's belly with a disapproving look. So what if his friend passed a relatively comfortable winter at Fort Riley becoming overweight by sitting near a potbellied stove while shooting the breeze with the other black noncoms? After all, he was in love with Cara, and would not have met her if he had spent the winter at Riley.

Col. Benjamin Grierson was expecting Sgt. Maj. Nate Gordon to arrive at his regimental headquarters office at any moment. He was standing by the window looking out and watched the signs of spring that were coming to the plains. He looked forward to seeing his preferred noncom and expected to be relying on him for the special assignment he had in mind. Grierson had received orders from General Sheridan to see if he could locate and negotiate the release of six white captive women from the Northern Cheyennes. The captives were believed to be held on the upper Smoky Hill River about eighty miles from Fort Wallace.

The white women and young girls had been taken last fall after a

Dog Soldier raiding party attacked an immigrant train, killing four men, stealing most of the stock, and abducting the women and girls. Appeals were made from the surviving members of the families for the army to do something in order to secure the release of their loved ones, and a pathetic letter written by one of the older captured girls that had been recently smuggled out of camp by a half-breed, begged the authorities to rescue them. In response, Sheridan pledged to act in the spring, and selected Colonel Grierson for the task.

"Enter," responded the commander of the Tenth Cavalry, crisply. He knew who it was.

After Grierson and Nate dispensed with the usual military formalities, the colonel got down to business.

"Six white captives . . . all women, three under nine years of age and their sisters . . ." Grierson paused for a moment. He knew that those young white women were probably forced to be sex and labor slaves to service the base needs of the warriors in a Cheyenne village, and the thought made him uncomfortable. Grierson seemed lost in deep thought, and Nate felt as if he had to say something.

"Sir, you were sayin'?"

"Eh . . . yes, Sergeant . . . ," responded Grierson, as if he had just been awoken from a dream. He shook his head slightly as if to chase away some cobwebs that were in his mind, and continued. "The other three women are young ladies from back East. All six of them were captured when their wagon train was attacked by the Dog Soldiers last September. They were last reported to be held in a Northern Cheyenne village on the upper Smoky Hill River, and I have been given orders to attempt to rescue them through negotiation."

"Does the colonel believe that they might have made it through de winter?"

"One of the scouts, a half-breed, delivered a note to the post that was written by one of the captives. That is how we know that at least a few of them survived the snows and cold . . . and brutality. We also know, more or less, the general location of the Cheyenne camp where the captive women are located."

"Do we know if it is Roman Nose and his Dog Soldiers, Colonel?" Nate was thinking about that Dog Man that had tried to run him over with his painted war pony in the fight near the banks of the Saline. He still had a vivid picture in his mind of how he almost dispatched the Dog Man with his bowie knife when he was stopped by another brave riding a fast pony. Nate was impressed with Cougar Eyes' agility and the way he leaped on that galloping pony. He recalled how he saw him again at the fight in the Valley of the Beaver. There, Cougar Eyes boldly charged the top of the ravine and fired into the skirmish line. Nate wondered if he would encounter that warrior again in battle. And if so, he would try and kill him.

"We are not certain who the leaders are, but we suspect they are part of Bull Bear's band." Grierson scratched his beard near where his scar was located on his cheek and added, "but as you probably know, Sergeant Major, it is very difficult to know who leads these bands of hostiles. In any case, you are to accompany me with Sergeant Randolph and a squad from H troop. We will depart in two days for Fort Wallace and from there, pick up the scout, William Comstock, and proceed toward the upper Smoky Hill River, and attempt to locate the captives."

"Beggin' de colonel's pardon, would that be Medicine Bill from Custer's Seventh, sir?" asked Nate anxiously.

"I believe that the man goes by that name, yes, that is correct, Sergeant Major," responded Grierson, a little surprised. "You know this scout?"

"Yes, sir, I knows Mister Comstock."

"Any thoughts on his capabilities?" inquired Grierson in his professorial manner.

"Yes, sir, he's a fine man and from what I knows, a good tracker and interpreter."

"We will need him." Grierson sat back down on his desk chair and ran his fingers through his thick hair as he gazed at the mounds of paperwork. With the exception of Nate and a few other noncoms, most of his men were illiterate and the regiment was still short of officers available to assist him. "That is all for now, Sergeant Major, you are dismissed."

"Aye, aye, sir." Nate saluted and was in the process of turning on his heels and leave the room when Grierson stopped him.

"One moment, Sergeant Major." Nate noticed that Grierson's face became melancholy. His eyes seemed sad and his mouth tightened. "I have bad news. It is about Private Filmore Alexander. Two weeks ago, a patrol from Fort Gibson found his body along the banks of the Verdisgris."

"Indians, sir?" interrupted Nate, who was sure of his assessment.

"No, Sergeant Major," replied Grierson as he gently moved his head from side to side.

"Then . . . how, sir?" pleaded Nate, his face exhibiting surprise.

"Private Filmore Alexander drowned in the river. There was not much left of him, you know. But if it is any consolation, the mailbag was still strapped to his back and might have been the reason why he failed to negotiate the currents. He died doing his duty."

"Yes, sir. I guess he died a soldier's death after all, sir."

"Yes, Sergeant Major. That is all," confirmed Grierson, eager to end the conversation.

Nate saluted and left the room thinking about Filmore Alexander. "Well, drunk or no drunk . . . de boy died like a man."

Cara de Cuevro was firmly gripping a very large smooth wooden paddle with both her hands while she stirred the heavy laundry that was soaking in a cast-iron cauldron. The steam from the boiling water made her perspire and even though she had covered the top of her head with a bandanna, she still had to wipe her face periodically with her sleeve to keep the dripping sweat on her face from running down her nose. The big Negress, Matilda Pugh Daniels, had kept her very busy doing laundry, but Cara did not mind the work. She was free from Antonio Vasco, and most importantly, Nate promised to see her every evening. It was past eight o'clock and she was expecting *el gran Sargento Mayor* to come by after his duties were completed at the post. The trumpeter had just sounded tattoo and the loud, gruff voices of the first sergeants, calling troopers' names from their rosters, could be heard from Fort Riley's parade ground.

"Chil', yo' go an' gits yo'sef cleaned-up af'er yo' finished scrubbin' dem linens. I knows dat yo' wants to look nice fo' dat sergeant a yours when he come a callin'," bellowed Matilda Pugh Daniels from the back door entrance of the cabin.

"*Sí, Señora Daniels,*" replied Cara, relieved that she was through for the day. She finished hanging the load of wet linens on the long laundry line and hurriedly placed the clothespins on the various articles so they would not blow away in the strong prairie winds. Completing this last task, she went inside the cabin and started to prepare herself for *el gran Sargento Mayor.*

The usual custom for officers, enlisted men, and noncoms after the evening Dress Parade and when Retreat was sounded by the trumpeters, was to quickly return to their quarters and remove their confining and stuffy dress uniforms. Nate, however, preferred to keep his on for the visit with Cara. He fully realized that he had to tell her that he must depart for Fort Wallace in two days and then penetrate the country on the upper Smoky Hill River to search for the white captives. As he made his way toward suds row, Nate pondered the possibility of having Cara come to Fort Wallace and serve as one of the laundresses for the company that he would eventually be assigned to once he returned from his sortie with Grierson and Comstock.

As he walked along the path leading toward suds row, he noticed that there were hundreds of colorful wild flowers blowing in the breeze. The moon was out, lighting up the prairie as if a giant lantern was held over the landscape. He decided to stop and pick a few. He felt very self-conscious and awkward, for he had never picked any flowers before, and he looked around to make sure that no one was close enough to see him stoop like a child and gather them into his bearlike hands. The moment reminded Nate of his mother, who at times, when she was not too tired or occupied, would gather a few wild flowers that grew along the banks of streams and near the rice fields at the plantation.

Cara was outside the shack waiting for Nate. She was combing her hair with the bone comb that her mother had given her. As Nate approached the shack of Matilda Pugh Daniels, he was astonished how beautiful Cara looked in the moonlight. As he approached her, he noticed that her olive face gleamed from the light of the lantern that hung near the doorway and when the breeze slightly lifted her raven-colored hair, he felt that peculiar sensation in the back of his neck.

"*Hola, Sargento Mayor!*" She greeted him with a provocative smile that made her face even more striking.

Captivated by her beauty, Nate had forgotten that he was holding the bouquet of wild flowers in his hands. He stared at Cara in clumsy silence until she asked, "*para mi?*" and pointed at the flowers.

"Oh yes, ma'am!" Nate quickly removed his kepi and held out the bouquet of prairie wild flowers as if he were a shy little boy, and was not sure what to say next, or how Cara would react.

"*Gracias, Sargento Mayor,*" responded Cara, delighted that the flowers were for her. She felt like a little girl receiving a gift from a conquering war hero. She raised the bouquet to her nose and smelled it. The aroma was so sweet that her dark eyes widened.

"Will you walk with me a ways?" asked Nate, still holding his kepi.

"*Seguro,*" responded Cara as she clutched her tiny bouquet of wild flowers between her breasts. Her long, thick black hair kept lifting in the prairie breeze and Nate could not help noticing how beautiful she seemed to him, and how fortunate he was to be in her company. As they walked along side by side, Nate kept smelling her strong body aroma and it aroused his senses. They chatted about mundane things such as what had happened to them during the day, and both agreed that the beautiful, clear, star-filled sky was stunning in its expanse. Cara pointed out several stars that she knew, and Nate enjoyed explaining how during the war, he had to rely on the stars to maneuver at night while seeking out rebs.

"I gots to leave again," said Nate finally, after much contemplation on how he should phrase his thoughts and convey them to Cara. He found it interesting how he never had any problems expressing himself to white officers or conveying orders to enlisted men. Even with most women, whom he avoided if at all possible, for he thought they were the source of more problems than they were worth, communication with the opposite sex was always brief and noncommittal. When he was with this particular woman, however, he felt very self-conscious and concerned that every statement he uttered be carefully constructed so he would not seem awkward or boorish.

"When you leave?" The smile on Cara's face vanished and she felt her heart sink.

"In two days." Nate bowed his head, and for the first time since he had met Cara, dared to gently seize her arm affectionately. He delicately clenched her firm left arm with his right hand in an attempt to express his tender feelings for her. His hand on Cara's arm felt reassuring, and she stepped closer to the *Sargento Mayor*. Following her lead, Nate also moved closer, and within an instant, both of them found themselves locked in a tight embrace. Cara's head only reached up to Nate's stomach so she pressed her left cheek firmly against his heaving chest. She could smell the wool of Nate's shell jacket and hear the rapid beat of his heart. They embraced for a long time. Nate was content just to hold her, while Cara felt secure and protected in the huge and strong arms of her *Sargento Mayor*.

"Soon as I'm situated at Fort Wallace, I'll send fo' ya." Nate paused, he felt a little hesitant, but then added, "Would you like that?"

"*Seguro!*" Cara de Cuevro felt reassured, and although she would miss Nate while he was away, they would soon be reunited.

Cougar Eyes, Roman Nose, and Bull Bear, along with some of the medicine men of the tribe, were deliberating around a roaring fire that the *berdaches* had prepared in the Council Lodge. The tribe's four sacred arrows were fastened to the central lodge pole and one of the ceremonial pipes was being passed around, its bowl refilled by the designated pipe handler whenever the tobacco burned out.

"We have received word that the chief of the *Mo' ohtae-Ve' ho' e* pony soldiers with the aid of the scout, Comstock, are on their way to talk with us about the white captives," said Bull Bear in a grave and pensive tone of voice. Although he was the chief of the Dog Soldiers, he had always tried to restrain the more militant Roman Nose who had vowed to kill General Winfield Hancock in front of all his blue coats.

"I will kill them as soon as they come near our lodges," scoffed

Voo' xenehe, as he dipped his horn spoon into his meat soup and brought the implement to his mouth with great eagerness. The tall warrior was ravenous after a day of hunting and was devouring the contents of his bowl which consisted of dried prickly-pear cactus, red turnip, and buffalo meat,

"Will you kill the scout, Comstock, as well?" retorted Bull Bear, cynically.

"No! He understands our ways and speaks the language of the people. He can go free and tell the other *Ve' ho' e* how they will die if they come close to our camp." Roman Nose slurped the last bit of his beef stew and placed the smooth wooden bowl in front of him.

"I feel my brother's anger and understand it. But you must not kill the soldiers that come to talk to us about the captives. They come in peace, they do not come to us to make war." Bull Bear was trying to convince Roman Nose that by killing the soldiers who came in peace would just make matters worse between the people and the Americans.

"Will they return the lands that they have stolen from us if we surrender the captives?" demanded Cougar Eyes angrily. The white women were his captives and he resented that Bull Bear and some of the other chiefs had talked to him about giving them up. Cougar Eyes had been the leader of the raid of revenge against the settler wagon train that was composed primarily of German immigrants. The Dog Soldiers had killed several of the immigrants and had successfully seized the hysterical women and rode off carrying them on their swift war ponies as if they were dead antelopes.

"It was the chiefs that gave our lands away to the whites without consulting the people," added Roman Nose, resentfully. He took a deep hit on the ceremonial pipe and passed it to his neighbor. The *berdaches* were elegantly placing additional logs on the "skunk" which was a very large fire in the middle of the Council Lodge.

The *berdaches*, who were called *hemaneh*, meaning Half-man–half-woman, were transvestites. These men were highly revered by the Cheyenne and had many roles. They served as masters of ceremonies, doctors, and intermediaries of love because they possessed the knowledge to make love potions and were trusted by the younger members of the tribe. They also practiced self-abstinence as a means of storing their virility. The Dog Soldiers would sometimes invite them to accompany them on their raids because the warriors believed that the *hemaneh* would be a psychological benefit due to their stored up semen that resulted in greater virility, thus giving the Dog Soldiers an edge in any fight.

"I trust the scout Comstock," stated Bull Bear. "Let us meet with these men and hear what they have to say."

"They will make threats and speak lies," derided Cougar Eyes as he too took a toke on the ceremonial pipe. The Council Lodge was becoming very warm due to the large fire, and Cougar Eyes was becoming tired of listening to Bull Bear's talk of caution. He decided to get some fresh air. He raised himself from his place in the circle and walked out of the Council Lodge.

"Cougar Eyes is right," added *Voo' xenehe*. "The whites steal our land, murder our people, and break all the treaties that the chiefs had signed." Roman Nose paused and took a deep breath in order to control his growing rage. He raised his head and looked into Bull Bear's eyes. "Out of respect for you, old friend . . . I will not kill the chief of the *Mo' ohtae-Ve' ho' e* pony soldiers. Let them come within our camp . . . if they can find it."

"They will find us. The scout, Comstock, will see to that," replied Bull Bear, as he gently grasped the ceremonial pipe that was passed to him by Roman Nose.

Col. Benjamin Grierson and Medicine Bill Comstock, along with 1st Sgt. Jesse Randolph and Sgt. Maj. Nate Gordon were standing around the dying bivouac fire devouring their dinner of salt pork and beans. They were accompanied by a squad of troopers bivouacked along the north bank of the Saline River, about twenty-five miles from Fort Wallace. They had left the post at first light and proceeded cautiously due north in the direction of South Fork Creek in the northwestern corner of the state.

Colonel Grierson was fully aware of the dangers involved regarding their task of locating and negotiating the release of the captives from the Dog Soldiers. Medicine Bill Comstock, nevertheless, had assured Grierson that they would not be attacked, and felt confident that he could find the Cheyenne camp. Comstock, drawing on his immense experience among the nomadic tribes of the plains, learned to be vigilant regarding the volatility of Indian behavior and remained alert to the possibility of attack. Grierson was impressed how the scout's keen eyes were constantly surveying the terrain, searching for any signs where a possible ambush might be launched against them. During the march, Comstock would point out to Grierson and Nate certain ravines and other topographical sites that were ideal for concealment and characteristic of the High Plains.

"Well, Comstock, do you think that we have any chance of locating Bull Bear's camp by tomorrow?" inquired Colonel Grierson as he wiped his mess-tin plate with a damp cloth.

"Well, Colonel, if I know an'thing, it's Injuns," responded Medicine Bill. He took a long sip from his canteen and gently pushed back the cork stopper into the spout. "I know that Bull Bear's camp is somewhere on the banks of South Fork Creek, and I have confidence dat we'll run into some of dem Dog Soldier scouts by noon at the latest."

Grierson and his squad had gotten an early start the next morning. The horses were feeling frisky and Nate and Comstock were out in front of Grierson and the squad scouting the terrain and searching for signs of Indian activity. It was a gorgeous spring morning, and there was not a cloud in the sky. The air was fresh and the men enjoyed feeling the sun's warmth on their faces. Grierson ordered the troopers to ride their animals at a walk so the squad appeared non-threatening in case they were detected by any Dog Soldiers or scouts that were patrolling the outer perimeter of their villages.

"So! Still like fightin' Injuns, Sergeant?" inquired Comstock, as he cracked a smile that twitched his thick and closely-cropped Mexican-style mustache. He was wearing buckskins and his head was crowned with a well-worn broad brimmed hat. His thick long black hair was combed behind the ears, and when the wind blew, several strands would lift up and wander about the side of his face. He was riding his favorite

mule, and Nate envied how well-behaved the scout's beast was in com-
parison to his own unruly mount. Comstock's thin and strong fingers
held his mount's reins as if he were holding a deck of cards. As Nate
watched Medicine Bill ride his mule as if he were on his way to a town
social, he was reminded of Mas'a Hammond's mules on the plantation,
and how they were the work-animal of the South and stood up to the
searing heat and humidity much better than horses. Nate often pondered how if it was not for black slave labor and the trusty, reliable
mule, the southern plantation owners would never have gotten so rich.
In a way, Nate felt a closer bond with the mule rather than the horse.
After all, the slave and the mule were used as beasts of burden and
both were considered stubborn and the butt of jokes and insults by the
white man.

"Sure different then fightin' Secesh," replied Nate, matter-of-factly.
He reflected for a moment as he bowed his head and thought out in
his mind what to say. As they rode side by side, Nate's gelding and
Comstock's big mule started to snort and sneeze as they negotiated the
buffalo grass and sandy ground beneath their hooves. "Durin' the war,"
Nate finally stated in his usual melancholy voice that he used whenever
he spoke aloud " 'bout the war," "I saw a lot a good men, black and
white do a lot fool things that you might say was brave." Nate then
shook his head as if he were recollecting some bad memory. "But the
Injuns," he added, "they . . . brave, and what spooks me, is that they do
it, like nothin' "

"Oh they brave, all right. But they treacherous too!" retorted Comstock, as he swatted a big fly that had landed on his face.

Nate thought for a moment then made his own retort. "Maybe the
Injuns are no mo' treacherous than white or black men."

Medicine Bill snickered for a moment and was about to respond
to Nate's comment by saying something along the lines of, "ain't that
the Gawddamn truth," when he noticed two mounted Indians moving
slowly on top of a ravine about three hundred yards away in the northwest. His eyes focused on them as if he were a bird of prey and Comstock struck out his hand to signal Nate to look in his direction. Nate
immediately saw the Indians and reined in his mount.

"Dawg Men!" stated Medicine Bill, as if he were waiting for signs of confirmation since the squad moved out from their bivouac area several hours ago.

"Scouts frum Bull Bear's village?" Nate pulled down the visor on his kepi to secure the hat on his head, and touched the pommel and hammer of his Walker-Colt with his right hand to make sure that the piece was ready for action.

Medicine Bill's eyes remained transfixed on the two Indians.

"Been expectin' dem bastards all mornin' long.... Yes, I believe dare hare to escort us."

"I gots to alert the colonel," said Nate as he firmly tugged at his left rein while he gently rubbed his right spur against his animal's flanks to turn the horse a hundred and eighty degrees. He cantered the animal toward Colonel Grierson who was riding next to Jesse and pulled along next to them.

"Beggin' to report, sir!"

"Yes, Sergeant Major?" inquired Grierson, as he pulled on his reins to signal the horse to slow down. He responded in that familiar schoolmaster tone of voice that Nate thought was so typical of his demeanor. Nate also realized by the tone of Grierson's voice that neither the commander of the Tenth Cavalry nor 1st Sgt. Jesse Randolph had seen the Dog Men scouts riding on top of the big ravine in the northwest.

"There, Colonel! In de distance!" Nate stood up in his stirrups and twisted his body. He then raised his right arm and pointed in the direction where the Indians were. His kepi was cocked over his right eye and he was wearing knee-high cavalry boots that were splattered with mud and caked with dust from the ride. "There, sir ... toward de northwest." He pointed to where he last saw the Cheyenne scouts, but by the time Grierson and Jesse had looked to where Nate had indicated, the Dog Men had disappeared behind one of the ravines.

"How many, Sergeant Major?" inquired Grierson calmly but with an air of concern.

"Two, sir. They be de scouts from the village."

"Have Comstock report to me," ordered Grierson as he threw his arm in the air to halt the squad.

"Sir!" Nate galloped his horse ahead of the squad and rejoined Medicine Bill. He told the scout that the colonel wanted to see him, and with a quick flick of his right wrist that slightly jerked the reins, the scout turned his mule a hundred and eighty degrees and cantered back to Grierson. Nate's horse, however, was being unruly and excitable since the animal had smelled the Indians' ponies, so Nate had to dig his spur into his mount's right flank and tug on the left rein to get his animal turned around again to catch up with Comstock's fast moving mule.

Colonel Grierson was conversing with Comstock when Nate reined in his horse to the left of his commanding officer. The eyes of Grierson, Comstock, Jesse, and the whole squad nervously searched the tops of the ravines and horizon for the Indian scouts.

"They know that we detected dem, Colonel," said Comstock after a few moments. The men were silent and remained motionless, and with the exception of the flicking of flies from the tails of the horses, the place was completely silent. "Best we keep a movin' Colonel, the Indian scouts will show themselves when they get good an' ready."

Grierson nodded and ordered Nate to quietly signal the squad to continue to advance. Comstock was now riding close to Grierson, and Nate and Jesse were riding behind them in front of the squad. After a few minutes, the Cheyenne scouts reappeared. The two warriors were sitting on their ponies on top of a large ravine in the southwest. Nate was a little dazzled by the fact that the last time they appeared, the scouts were ridding their ponies toward the northwest. That meant that they had ridden perpendicular to the squad without being discovered. This time Grierson noticed the Indians immediately and raised his arm to halt the squad.

Comstock turned to Grierson. "They don't seem hostile, Colonel. They are not carryin' war lances an' shields, an what's more, dem bucks ain't wearin' war paint. I thinks that fer sure, dey were told to lead us to de village. I think I should go an' parley wid dem."

"Go see," ordered Grierson. Medicine Bill nodded in approval and walked his mule toward the two braves who remained so still that they appeared as if they were statues. It was mid-afternoon and the day was very hot. The flies in particular were very bothersome to the horses and the men. This made it difficult for the troopers to remain motion-less as Grierson had instructed. With the exception of the colonel, all the men, in addition to Nate and Jesse, were sweating profusely in their wool shell jackets and all had been thirsty for most of the morning. One trooper made a movement to reach for his canteen when Nate calmly told him to refrain from touching it.

"But Sarge . . ." said the trooper in a whinny voice.

"Shut up boy and pay attention. Keep your hands on your reins and think 'bout your Spencer."

Grierson and the troopers watched as Comstock approached the two scouts. They saw Medicine Bill raise his hand as a sign of peace as he approached the braves. The Cheyennes responded in kind and although the troopers could not hear the conversation, they could tell by the way Comstock and the Indians waved their hands and arms that their scout and the warriors were engaged in some negotiations. Finally, after about a minute, Comstock turned his beast around and left the two braves who were still standing in a statuelike position on top of their ponies and walked the mule back to the squad as if he did not have a care in the world.

"Well, Comstock?" Although Grierson remained calm, he was clearly anxious, as were the rest of the men, about what Medicine Bill had to convey regarding his brief conversation with the two Cheyennes.

"We're to follow them two warriors, Colonel," said Comstock as he patted his mule's neck.

"Do you trust them?" responded Grierson skeptically as if he was questioning some student that had come up with a new approach to a long-established concept.

"Yes, sir! One of dem boys is Bull Bear's nephew. I knows him since he was a pup when I visited his uncle at his lodge years ago. We're not far from the village, Colonel." Comstock paused for a moment then added, "Colonel, dey hav' been expectin' us."

"Very well, we will follow them at a safe distance."

Comstock waved his arm in the air signaling to the two Cheyenne scouts to lead the way. The warriors simultaneously turned their ponies around and would have disappeared behind the ravine if Grierson had not ordered the squad to canter so they would not lose sight of the two

Cheyenne scouts. Medicine Bill's eyes remained transfixed on the two Indians, and urged his mule to follow them. He was way in front, while Grierson and the squad spurred their mounts toward the Cheyenne village.

Grierson and the squad were only a few miles south of the Cheyenne camp and Bull Bear, Roman Nose, and Cougar Eyes had already been informed by the village perimeter scouts that Comstock and the pony soldiers were on their way.

"Where are the captives being held?" inquired Bull Bear as he took the last chokecherry from his clay bowl. They were just completing a little midday meal that consisted of fruit from the prickly pear, thistle, and a tuber known by the French name, *pomme de terre* that was also called an Indian turnip.

"I gathered the *Ve' ho' e* in one of the smaller lodges," replied Cougar Eyes as he nibbled on some thistle.

"Have they been fed?" inquired Bull Bear. His tongue was wrestling with that last chokecherry that had managed to become lodged behind one of his back teeth.

Cougar Eyes shrugged his shoulders and scornfully quipped, "That is for the squaws to take care of."

Cougar Eyes was against the return of the captives. He considered them legitimate spoils of war and retaining the captives suited his unquenchable thirst for revenge against the whites. Roman Nose, on the other hand, wanted to return the six white captives because he feared that their presence in the camp would contaminate the pure traditional and ancestral Cheyenne medicine that he had sworn to uphold. Bull Bear, the oldest of the influential men of the tribe, wanted to use the captives as a negotiating chip. He had already decided that the captives should be released as a gesture of goodwill, while using the occasion to lecture one of the chiefs of the pony soldiers how it was that the whites were stealing their land, slaughtering the buffalo, breaking the treaties, and killing their women and children as they had done at Sand Creek.

The perimeter scouts had informed them that a small detachment of white and black men were escorting the chief of the pony soldiers.

Cougar Eyes was eager to meet these *Mo' ohtae-Ve' ho' e* blue coats who were led by the whites face to face. Perhaps that big black man with the wide yellow stripes on his blue coat would be among them. He wanted to talk to this man who he deemed as a worthy opponent and if the opportunity should arise again, he would kill the big *Mo' ohtae-Ve' ho' e* pony soldier and take that shell jacket with the wide chevron stripes.

As Grierson approached the Cheyenne lodges which were located along the sandy banks of Sappa Creek, the guard dogs of the camp started to bark. Within a minute several dozen warriors had leaped on their ponies and had completely surrounded the small detachment. Nate kept repeating to the troopers to remain steady and not show any signs of fear or concern. He admonished one trooper for letting his eyes wander about rather than looking straight ahead. Grierson was right behind Comstock who was conversing with another warrior who had rode up to him at a gallop and only halted his pony within a few feet of Comstock's mule. Grierson remained stoic, his closely-cropped beard gave him an appearance of wisdom and authority which impressed many of the older braves. Jesse, however, was becoming more and more nervous and was beginning to have flashbacks. His mind wandered back to the time when he was trapped in the railroad cutting hole. He kept thinking about how his body was repeatedly stabbed by those lance tips while the Dog Soldiers howled and shouted with glee outside of the hole. Warriors were now circling the squad but refrained from touching them as they pretended to count coup, while others shouted expletives and dared the troopers to make the first move.

The detachment was now almost in the center of the village and Nate noticed the plumes of blue smoke from dozens of little campfires that dotted the camp's landscape. There were countless buffalo hides being dried out and scraped by the squaws, and several suspended antelopes were in the process of being butchered. There were also numerous racks of beef jerky strips drying in the hot sun. Nate was a little stunned however, when he saw an average-size dog roasting over a slow fire. The animal's coat had been removed from the carcass and a little girl, dressed in an attractive beaded buckskin dress, was slowly turning the spit. The rod was rammed through the dog's mouth and emerged through the hapless animal's rectum. The girl, along with other young females of the camp, were preparing for the up-coming dog feast that was to occur this evening and was much anticipated by all the members of the tribe. The little Cheyenne girl, who was quite pretty and in a way, reminded Nate of Cara because she had raven-colored hair, smiled at him. Nate however, had to look away in disgust. "Jesus Crist!" he whispered to himself, "Mas'a would never had tolerated a dawg bein' roasted like a hog!" Nate did not really know why he thought about Mas'a Hammond and the plantation, but somehow in his mind, this Indian village scene reminded him of the days of slavery.

In many ways, with the exception of the roasting dog, the Cheyenne camp reminded Nate of the Nigga Qua'ters on the plantations, as they were referred to by the whites back in Louisiana. The open cook fires, barking dogs, modest lodgings, women working at domestic tasks, and bands of wandering "young-ins" or "pickinninies" were all familiar to him.

Bull Bear, Roman Nose, and Cougar Eyes emerged from Bull Bear's lodge just as Comstock was dismounting from his mule. *Voo' xenehe* was dressed in a breechclout, leggings, and in an elaborate hair-fringed war-shirt that had tassels of scalp hair attached to the chest. It was his favorite ceremonial piece of garb because the scalp tassels represented the souls he had captured in battle. Cougar Eyes was dressed in a simple fringed buckskin shirt, breechclout, and rawhide leggings with black fringe. Both Roman Nose and Cougar Eyes carried heavy-bladed knives in superbly decorated sheaths dyed in bird quills. Bull Bear's manner of dress however, was more sophisticated. He wore an elegantly painted deerskin shirt that fell past his waist. The front of the garment was decorated in groups of painted stripes crossed with symbols such as arrows, hoof marks, and tobacco pipes that represented his past war record.

While Grierson and the squad remained in their saddles, Nate gently turned his head and gazed at the swallowtail regimental guidon. The banner flapped smartly in the wind and seeing the stars and stripes blowing whenever there was a strong breeze always gave Nate confidence. As he stood erect in the saddle, his right gauntleted hand rested on his hip just above the pommel of his Walker-Colt. Sergeant Major Nate Gordon looked every inch the soldier. He was not only the tallest man in the squad, but with the exception of Roman Nose, the biggest man in the Cheyenne village. Even some of the braves and gawking children were in awe of seeing a huge black man in hightop boots, mounted on a big black gelding. Several of the warriors noticed the immense Walker-Colt holstered on Nate's right hip, and itched for the weapon. Their eyes and facial expression reminded Nate of the faces in the saloons at Hays when men lusted after the prostitutes.

Bull Bear stepped forward, separating himself from Roman Nose and Cougar Eyes. All three warriors had their long hair sharply parted in the middle of their scalps and divided the hair into two thick braided strands that hung down their chests. All three men also had eagle feathers tucked into the back of their hair. Bull Bear had just one huge eagle feather that protruded from the right side of his head in a horizontal manner, while Roman Nose and Cougar Eyes had several, smaller eagle feathers that stood up vertically at the back of their heads.

"If Comstock and the pony soldiers come in peace, you are welcome." Although he was smaller and older than Cougar Eyes, and Roman Nose towered over him, Bull Bear, *Hotoanahkohoe*, was still physically strong, and enjoyed the respect of the tribe.

"We come in peace, *Hotoanahkohoe*," proclaimed Comstock, as he raised his hand to greet his old friend. Bull Bear also raised his hand and Comstock then added, "We are here to convince you to release the *Ve' ho' e* captives."

"We will talk. Come, invite the beard face and we will talk in my lodge."

"Wait!" yelled Cougar Eyes. "I want the big *Mo' ohtae-Ve' ho' e* blue coat to come as well." He pointed to Sgt. Maj. Nate Gordon.

Nate was stunned. He had not recognized Cougar Eyes when he had come out of the tipi, but now as the Dog Soldier aimed his arm and index finger at him, it became clear that this was the same warrior that he had fought along the banks of the Saline last year and at Beaver Creek.

Comstock motioned Nate to dismount and join them in Bull Bear's lodge while Jesse was given the unenviable task of remaining with the squad. Bull Bear entered the lodge first and was followed by Grierson and Comstock. Roman Nose, who so far seemed indifferent to this meeting with the hated white enemies, entered the lodge after Comstock. Only Cougar Eyes and Nate remained at the entranceway. Both men glared and sized up the other. Nate towered over Cougar Eyes but that did not impress the Dog Soldier. He had killed many men who were taller and larger than he was. Nate thought about how he had almost dispatched this savage son of a bitch with his bowie knife only to be saved by a fellow brave that whisked him away on his fast pony.

The two enemies stared at each other intensely. They were so close to each other that they smelled the other's body aroma. Finally, Bull Bear shouted something from inside the tipi and Cougar Eyes responded by slipping through the lodge entrance. His gaze, however, never left Nate's face. Nate reflected on Cougar Eyes' hostility and silent bravado for a moment and shook his head. He then whispered to himself, and cracked a little smile, "de boy sure seems to think he's som'tin'."

Bull Bear's tipi was one of the largest in the camp and Nate was surprised to find the air inside the lodge was much cooler than outside. Made from twenty-five buffalo hides, *Hotoanahkohoe*'s tipi, as was the case with all tipi's that are properly equipped and pitched, was cool during the hot summers and warm during the harsh winters. The conical shaped structure was far superior to the wretched log cabins and "soddies" that dotted the frontier, and certainly superior to drafty army tents. In addition, the tipi was relatively free of insects, vermin, and small animals which was a far cry from crude sodhuts that usually became infested with bugs during the summer months. Well ventilated, highly mobile, roomy, and comfortable, the tipi was designed to withstand gale force winds, snow drifts, and searing heat. The Cheyenne tipi, like their brother tribe the Lakotas, was based on a tripod pole foundation. The poles, ideally, would be yellow pine and were found in the Black Hills. Like most well-pitched lodge's, Bull Bear's home possessed an interior lining that insulated the interior from cold and heat. If the weather would be especially cold, dried prairie grass would be stuffed in between the outer skin and the interior lining. The space between the two walls also had the advantage of providing extra food storage space. *Hotoanahkohoe*'s lining, however, was beautifully painted with stripe designs at each pole which reminded Nate of the wallpaper at Mas'a Hammond's big house.

Lighting was provided by maneuvering the size of the space at the smoke hole which was controlled by flaps, or ears, and additional lighting and ventilation was provided by raising the cover on the windward side during sultry days, as Bull Bear's squaws had done in anticipation of the additional body heat that the tipi would have to accommodate because of the meeting. Nate thought that the tipi looked very cozy. Certainly more comfortable than most places he had lived in all his life, whether that was on the plantation, or in army tents during the war, or more recently, spending most of last winter in that dank railroad cut-out.

Hotoanahkohoe's lodge had not only numerous buffalo skins that served as blankets, floor coverings, and robes, but Nate noticed a whole collection of furs that would make his friend Jean le Fou, green with Cajun envy. Scattered about were hides from a wild cat, red and gray fox, coyote, dog, black and brown buffalo calves, wolverine, bear, fawn, possum, horse, elk, moose, and Bull Bear's favorite fur, a splendid mountain-lion skin. Other items such as beautifully adorned war shields and eagle-feather bonnets, lances, and quivers filled with arrows, were neatly stashed at various stations around the tipi. Additional accoutrements such as straw baskets, clay bowls, and rawhide-making tools and implements made from buffalo bones, could be seen neatly arranged at various places about the lodge. Bull Bear was a rich man. Not only did he possess many horses, but owned such exquisite items as colorful embroidered beaded bags and boxes. His willow-rod backrests however, were his favorite pieces of furniture and were just as comfortable as a rocking chair.

The interior of the tipi, as is the custom for the Indians of the plains, is systematically arranged. All sleeping, conversing, eating and other activities takes place in the rear of the lodge, as far away from the door flap entrance as possible. The fireplace area is located a little off-center from the smoke hole, while the altar occupies central position in the lodge. Bull Bear had three beds that were slightly raised by pallets of buffalo hides and as was consistent with tipi etiquette, sat and leaned back on his willow-rod backrest at the far left of the half-circle, while Roman Nose and Cougar Eyes were to his immediate left.

What really captured Nate's eye, however, was not the beautiful furs and splendid beaded accoutrements, but something far more foreboding. As he took his place on the far left end at the half-circle, he noticed something glistening right behind where Cougar Eyes was sitting. The light that poured down from the smoke hole vent shined on a brass box-like object. Nate squinted his eyes to identify the article for a moment and when he finally realized that the object was the brass magazine of a relatively new lever action Henry .44-caliber repeater, he became astonished. He refrained from manifesting any signs of surprise on his face, but Cougar Eyes however, had noticed that Nate had seen the Henry. The Dog Man smiled slightly as if he were a little boy that just showed up one of his peers. The rapid action rifle was leaning on its stock, while its octagon barrel rested against one of the lining poles behind Cougar Eyes. The Henry repeater carried fifteen rounds, more than twice the number of a Spencer, thus Nate was taken aback when he saw a weapon that not even the U.S. army had enough of, but somehow this deadly weapon found its way into the hands of a hostile. He thought to himself while trying not to shake his head, "Gawd help us if we have a scrape against that kinda fire power." Then he remembered how he had heard that during the Fetterman fight with the Sioux, two civilian employees from the fort had requested permission to join the command to try out their new Henry's. The weapons were definitely put to the test on that bloody afternoon. Rumor had it that when they found the bodies of Captain Fetterman and his eighty men, over sixty-five pools of blood were observed around where the two civilians had made their last stand but no bodies were found because the Sioux had removed them. While he sat in a lotus position to the right of Grierson, who in turn, was sitting next to Comstock, Nate wondered if it was possible that Cougar Eyes was present at the Fetterman fight. Or did he trade for the weapon?

There was a moment of awkward silence. Roman Nose was sizing up Colonel Grierson as if he was preparing to kill him. Nate ignored

Cougar Eyes' intense gaze and made an effort to be completely relaxed while thinking about his Walker-Colt in case the party might have to blast their way out of the camp if the Cheyennes decided to be treacherous. Sensing the intensity in the lodge, Bull Bear reached over and gently grasped the ceremonial pipe that was resting on the altar. The pipe had a deep and narrow bowl made of polished stone and an eagle feather hung a quarter of the way down the long stem. *Hotoanahkohoe* filled the bowl with tobacco from a pouch made from the scrotum of a buffalo. As he stuffed the stone bowl, Grierson started to speak. He was uncertain about how to proceed, but felt that something had to be said in order to establish a dialogue. He turned to Comstock and asked him to translate the following.

"As you were informed . . ." Grierson was all business, but with a touch of civility, knowing that he was in the heart of the enemy's camp. He also wanted to remain conscious about the gulf of cultural differences that separated the two races. "We have come to you in peace and seek the release of the six female white captives. . . ."

"First, we smoke the pipe so the spirits will bless this meeting between us," interrupted Bull Bear in English. His voice was reassuring and sounded slightly lyrical. "There is much tension here, much hatred and hostility. We will smoke the pipe and then we will talk."

Bull Bear placed the pipe tip to his lips and lit the bowl with a piece of straw and started to vigorously puff on the pipe. Within a few moments, the lodge was permeated with the smoke of burning tobacco. As the ceremonial pipe was passed to the left, each member of the meeting took a toke from the pipe. The tobacco seemed to have a calming influence over Cougar Eyes and Roman Nose, who now softened their gaze at Grierson and Nate.

After all the members of the group had held and smoked the ceremonial pipe, Bull Bear turned to Medicine Bill Comstock and inquired in his native tongue, "Ask the bearded face if he is the chief of the *Mo' ohtae-Ve' ho' e* pony soldiers?"

Comstock nodded, and turned to Grierson and posed the question. Grierson turned to Bull Bear and spoke very slowly while Comstock interpreted.

"My name is Grierson. And yes, I am the chief of the men who you call the black and white soldiers." Grierson paused and with that schoolmaster reflection added, "although these men are black, they are men like we are all men, whatever the color of our skin."

Hotoanahkohoe nodded and voiced his approval at Grierson's words. This *Ve' ho' e* chief was unlike the others who he had met. Men like *Tsehe esta ehe*, (Custer), and that fat chief Hancock, who *Voo' xenehe* wanted to kill in front of all of the blue coats last year, were arrogant, demanding, and greedy.

"Tell the bearded one if he truly believes his own words then why do the whites make war and break all of the treaties?" asked Bull Bear in a stern tone of voice as he eyed both Grierson and Comstock.

Grierson dreaded this question. He knew that the history of his government's treatment toward the Indians was less than equitable, and the Indian agents and traders were corrupt. As a soldier however, he was charged with implementing government policy toward the Indians whether he approved of their actions or not. Like many officers who served on the frontier, they were responsible for implementing treaties that were broken even before the congress would amend the documents to death. Frontier officers detested that it was the Indian Peace Commissions and the politicians who were responsible for managing the "Indian problem," and not the military. Every time difficulties developed between the tribes and whites, it was the army who was called upon to clean up the mess.

"The whites and the tribes have experienced many problems in the past. We have much to resolve if we are to live in peace." Grierson looked straight into his hosts' eyes and tried to be as sincere as possible. He wanted to treat Bull Bear as an equal and not behave as if he were a patronizing ignoramus, as so many of the younger members of the officer corps in the West were. Grierson remembered Captain Fetterman's boast two years ago when the young upstart graduate from West Point declared that he could "ride through the whole Sioux Nation with eighty men." Well, the braggart got his opportunity against the Sioux and was promptly baited, ambushed, and massacred by Crazy Horse and hundreds of warriors within an hour just beyond the hills of Fort Phil Kearny. Grierson did not want to be associated with such officers. He believed in being firm and accomplishing his tasks with peaceful negotiations rather than engaging in bloody conflict. He had seen enough death during the war, and much preferred to talk rather than reach for the sword. He hoped, however, that it would not be a long before he could get on to the subject of the six white female prisoners. He disliked defending his government's Indian policy, but realized he might have to parlay with the Cheyennes for quite some time before bringing up the captive question.

After the pipe had been passed to everyone, the last person who smoked it (who was on the far left) had to return it to the head man. Nate was the last one to take a toke, which he thoroughly enjoyed. He found the flavor of the tobacco to be excellent, and was gratified that he was able to take a deep hit of it into his lungs.

"You gotta return the pipe to Bull Bear," instructed Comstock. "It's proper tipi politeness," he added. Nate was holding the pipe, the stem pointing to the left. After he had taken his toke, he was unsure whether he should pass the pipe back to Grierson or hold it until someone removed the item. To return the pipe back to Bull Bear, Nate would have to raise himself from his lotus position and walk over to Bull Bear while passing Cougar Eyes and Roman Nose. He slowly raised his huge body and stood up. His erect frame became momentarily silhouetted by the light that poured through the smoke hole of the tipi and he looked like a giant. As he moved catlike toward Bull Bear, he stared at Cougar Eyes, who in turn, stared back at Nate. Both men eyed each other, waiting for the other to make the first move. Nate approached Bull Bear with reverence, however, and stooped to hand the pipe to the head man. Bull Bear nodded and took back the ceremonial pipe. As he clasped the article, he gave Nate a good long look. He was intrigued by this man's black-as-coal skin color and huge muscular body, but impressed that this *Mo' ohtae-Ve' ho' e* walked as gracefully as a wild cat and showed respect in his demeanor. Bull Bear decided that Nate Gordon was different than the usual white pony soldier who he considered weak, stupid, and disrespectful.

As Nate slowly walked back to his spot, Cougar Eyes suddenly seized the front of Nate's left boot with the palm of his left hand and called out for him to halt. The warrior's hand moved as swiftly as if he was catching trout from a stream with his bare hands. Nate paused and Cougar Eyes sprung up from his sitting position. Both men now stood face to face with only a foot between them. Cougar Eyes then held out the palm of his right hand and moved it gently against Nate's chest where his heart was located. The tipi was completely silent. Bull Bear, and Roman Nose, and even Comstock knew what Cougar Eyes was doing and were not really concerned. Colonel Grierson and Nate, however, were completely perplexed. While Grierson nervously watched, Nate remained cool and continued to stare down at the Dog Soldier. Each man could smell the other, and see every detail in each others' faces. After a few moments had passed, but which seemed much, much longer to Nate and Grierson, Comstock decided to intervene.

"He's listenin' to the beat of your heart," said Medicine Bill smiling, trying to reassure Nate and Grierson that the sergeant major was not in danger.

"I know it!" responded Nate, still staring down at Cougar Eyes.

"The *Mo' ohtae-Ve' ho' e* heart shows no fear. His heart beats slowly," commented Cougar Eyes as he turned to Roman Nose and Bull Bear.

Roman Nose and Bull Bear simultaneously acknowledged this fact by nodding their heads and expressing agreement. They were impressed with the calm of the big white and black man.

"He heap big son-of-a-bitch!" cracked Cougar Eyes in broken English. It was a phrase that the Cheyennes had learned from the fat white traders who sold them guns and whiskey and was often repeated among themselves as a form of verbal amusement. The tipi roared with laughter, and even Grierson had to chuckle at Cougar Eyes' comment. Nate remained stone-faced, but after a moment, smiled. His brilliant white teeth flashed in the mellow light that softly poured through Bull Bear's lodge smoke hole.

Cougar Eyes sat back down and Nate walked to the far end of the semicircle and retook his place next to Grierson.

Bull Bear placed the ceremonial pipe back on the altar, and then turned to Colonel Grierson and Comstock.

"The people will return the captives to the bearded face because I feel he is a just man and I hope he will speak on our behalf to those who make the treaties." Bull Bear was solemn in his speech and was afraid for the future of his people. He was one of the first Cheyennes to encounter the white man when he was a boy. Every year that he could remember, he had seen more and more whites come and he knew change was coming. All he wanted now was to stop the killing between his people and the whites and live out the rest of his days in peace.

"Tell Bull Bear," commanded Grierson to Comstock, "that I appreciate his gesture, and that I will always favor talk over war."

"It is good that you believe that," responded Bull Bear after Medicine Bill had translated. "Our people have suffered much, and after Sand Creek, we do not trust you anymore." *Hotoanahkohoe*'s voice grew more sharply now, as he thought about the relatives and friends he had lost during the past few years after the whites made promises of peace.

"I pray for the day when there will be no more war between our peoples, but your young warriors raid farms, ranches, and steal property." Grierson paused for a moment and gently ran his fingers through his beard and lowered his eyes. "Your young warriors . . . they have killed many whites, and this must stop."

"It's the pony soldiers that have killed our relatives, and stolen our land!" clamored *Voo' xenehe*. His gaze, filled with hate and anger, became fierce. The tipi became tense again. Bull Bear wanted to avoid a screaming match between Grierson and Roman Nose, but before he could say anything, Cougar Eyes pointed to Nate and asked, "Why do you . . . *Mo' ohtae-Ve' ho' e*, fight with the blue coats and help them steal *our* land?"

Although Nate was taken completely by surprise by this abrupt question, he knew what to say. He centered his gaze on Cougar Eyes and with his right index finger and thumb, pinched a piece of wool from the sleeve of his shell jacket. "It is not in my heart to make another a slave and this is de *uniform* that fought for my freedom and my people's freedom! I honor this uniform with all my heart." Nate placed his right hand on his chest near his heart and paused. "Once, I was a captive. Like the white women you now hold as slaves." Nate stood up at attention and his huge erect frame almost dominated the entire interior of the tipi. "*No man* should own another human being." Nate's deep baritone voice filled the tipi as if he were a fire-and-brimstone black preacher. The Cheyennes became stunned by his statement and by his sudden move to stand up and look down at them and by the tumultuous, commanding sound of his voice. Even Comstock and Grierson became surprised and concerned that Nate's action might anger their hosts. But the Cheyennes became mesmerized by Nate's sudden movement and the tipi became silent. They were surprised to learn that this man, who was once a slave and now obviously a formidable warrior, might also possess great medicine. "When I was a slave," Nate continued in a controlled voice, "I had only one name. Like a dog, or any other animal, and I was expected to serve my mas'a like an ox or a dog." The Cheyennes listened to Nate with great interest, and as Comstock translated, they became more and more intrigued. Here was a man with a unique story to tell and they wanted to hear more. "After de war 'tween de white man . . . my people became free, and I took de name Gordon, so I can be called Sergeant Major *Nate Gordon* and be respected!" Bull Bear and Cougar Eyes nodded in approval at the *Mo' ohtae-ve' ho' e* speech while Roman Nose remained completely motionless and unimpressed. To him, Nate was an enemy who should be killed.

"Now . . . we . . . will give you another name!" interrupted Cougar Eyes in broken English. "We call you . . . *HOTOA'E GORDON!* You look, fight . . . like . . . angry, *Hoto a 'e* . . . buffalo!" Nate's eyes widened. He felt honored that his enemy considered him as fierce as a buffalo. The fact that Cougar Eyes also associated his blackness with the noble fighting beast, the bison, did not bother him.

"It sounds like a worthy name, Sergeant Major," stated Grierson, as he cracked an approving smile while stroking his beard.

"Aye, sir." Nate returned the smile and repeated the name, *HO-TOA'E* GORDON, BUFFALO GORDON, softly to himself. He liked the way it sounded and he couldn't wait to tell Cara about it.

The six young white female captives were German immigrants who spoke virtually no English. They had been snatched away after Cougar Eyes' Dog Men had killed their parents when their small wagon train was camped for the night along the banks of the Smoky Hill River. When the Dog Men attacked the immigrants in the early morning hours, the Germans were taken by surprise and slaughtered within a few minutes. Cougar Eyes spared the girls from the same fate as their parents because he preferred to enslave them, and now after months of living with the Cheyennes as captives, they showed all the signs of their harsh detention.

They were a pitiful sight. The German girls were filthy and emaciated. Their blond hair was caked with dirt and hopelessly entangled while their faces, necks, arms, and legs were severely sunburned and marked with many hideous gashes and bruises. Dark streaks of tears marked their faces from the incessant crying that they broke into whenever they were together at night, and their clothes were in tatters. Barefooted, their feet and ankles were covered with cuts, festering open wounds and insect bites which were aggravated by intense scratching. When Nate saw them he shook his head and couldn't help whispering to Jesse, "Them po' white girls is de sorriest sight I've seen in a *long* time."

When the German girls realized that they were going to be released from their horrendous state of captivity, the two eldest started to weep uncontrollably and kept repeating over and over again, "*Danke schön, danke schön.*" The youngest, who was only seven and still sucking on her thumb, slowly walked up to Nate and placed her arms around his knees and hugged the big black man for dear life. Nate felt awkward and was unsure how to behave under such emotional circumstances. Jesse noticed Nate's awkwardness and offered to take the girl, but Nate waved him away and Jesse then told him to, "Let's put the chil' in your arms." Nate glanced at his friend and wanted to say, "I've never done that before," but then decided that it was good advice. He lifted the child as if she were a porcelain doll and sat her on his left arm as he held the girl's tiny hands within his huge right palm. Nate forced a smile and repeated, "Is goin', be aw right, now. You're safe now. Ain't nothin' that's goin' harm you now!"

Thirteen

FORT WALLACE, SEPTEMBER 1868

Colonel Grierson and his tiny command had returned to Fort Wallace with the newly freed German captives. On the return ride to the fort, the girls had doubled up on the supply mules that had accompanied the squad. While they were on the trail returning to Wallace, Nate and Jesse did the best they could to clothe the young women, make them comfortable, and coddle them at night when they would sob uncontrollably or cry out because some of them were experiencing nightmares about their recent ordeal with the Cheyennes and the brutal death of their parents.

After a week of rest at Fort Wallace where the post's surgeons examined them, and where the hapless young immigrant women became the subjects of mass gawking, loose gossip, and much consternation among the men, officers, and family members of the post, the girls were told they were to be sent back to St. Louis where anxious relatives awaited their arrival.

Nate and Cara de Cuervo, who had just arrived from Riley along with some other laundresses escorted by a company of troopers, would visit the little girl every evening. The beautiful pig-tailed child had adopted Nate ever since she had wrapped her skinny white arms around his knees that day, when he appeared through the tipi door flap to rescue her and her sisters from the Cheyennes. Although she was only eight years old, Nate reminded her of a knight, saving her from the barbarians. Nate would read passages from the Bible, to her as his mother had done. The big burly sergeant major had grown genuinely fond of the little German girl, and had developed a paternal protective instinct toward her. Cara and Nate saw her off when the girls took the stage for Fort Hays that was escorted by a squad of hand-picked troopers that Nate had selected himself. He felt saddened by her departure. He turned to Cara after he saw the stage disappear over the horizon, and in a melancholy tone of voice expressed his sense of resignation.

"Don't think I'll ever see her 'gain."

Cara de Cuervo, with several other laundresses, had reached Fort Wallace several days before. She had managed to become attached as a laundress to Company H tenth Cavalry, which was Nate's company. The sergeant major was delightfully surprised to find her at Wallace when he had returned with the captives. When word was received at the post that Grierson and the German captives were approaching, Cara was in the middle of washing officers' blouses. She was in the process of wringing out the linens as beads of perspiration poured down from her forehead onto her cheeks and chin. Her tiny hands struggled to wring out the soap from the laundry as the water boiled in cast-iron cauldrons. When she was told by another laundress that the *Sargento Mayor* was approaching the fort, she ran to the main gate and waited for him, her eyes searching the ravines and horizon. When she spotted the guidon flapping in the wind, rising just above the crest of a ravine, she cried out, "*Dios mio! Mi Sargento Mayor ha llegado!*"

Cara had made up her mind several days earlier that she was going to lure Nate into having him inside of her. She desired *el Sargento Mayor* like a mare that ovulated when she smelled a stallion miles away. During the day, when she was washing dozens of shirts, linens, and socks for the officers of H Company in the bright Kansas sun, she would think about Nate. As her tiny but nimble hands reached into the hot cauldron and pulled laundry item after laundry item from the soapy creek water and beat and rubbed the heavy wet clothing, sheets, towels, and other items against an old washboard to squeeze the excess water, she longed for *el Sargento Mayor's* return.

While Nate, Colonel Grierson, and Medicine Bill Comstock were engaged in negotiating the restoration of the hostages, Cara waited, night after night, for Nate's return. She longed to hear his voice and feel his strong presence. She craved to breathe his strong body odor through her nostrils and pondered what her spine and "hot spots" would feel like when he caressed them. Although Nate had never touched her breasts or any other part of her body, her nipples nevertheless ached for his huge but gentle hands to squeeze them. When she pondered how it would feel when *el Sargento Mayor* would caress and softly pinch her nipples, and how it would feel to have him inside of her, thrusting against the walls of her womanhood as if he was a raving *"Toro"* mounting a *"Vaca,"* the juices from her body flowed.

She made arrangements with the two other laundresses who were sharing the small, windowless suds row shanty to be absent, thus giving her the privacy and opportunity to seduce Nate. She became determined to carry out her plan the very night that he should return to Fort Wallace. She decided to prepare a late night supper and procured some candles which she placed strategically around the room to provide a soft atmosphere, something that she had learned when she was with Vasco and his traveling whores.

Nate finally arrived a little past nine, after the bugler had sounded tattoo. The fall air was brisk and when Cara opened the door to let him in, a breeze made the candles flicker and she felt a chill. Nate's army greatcoat was draped over his shoulders and the kepi was in its usual cocked position over the right eye. The light of the full moon shined on Nate's back, silhouetting his huge frame within the wooden doorway. Cara paused for a moment as she contemplated the way her *Sargento Mayor* looked. She thought that he had a demigodlike appearance which heightened her senses and made her face slightly blush. Before Nate could remove his kepi, Cara had gently reached for his left hand and urged him to enter the shanty so she could close the door and check the draft. Nate had a slight smile on his face and as he entered the shack he could feel the warmth coming from the potbellied stove and noticed that the many burning candles gave the interior room a soft glimmering glow.

Nate threw his army greatcoat on a large construction nail that protruded from the wall near the right side of the door frame and surrendered his kepi to Cara. As she scurried to place the hat on a rickety night table that had a soiled white doily drooping over the top, the sergeant major now noticed how beautiful she looked this evening. Her long raven hair was combed down all the way to the small of her back and was very straight. She was wearing an ankle-length bright red wool dress that she had traded from a Blackfeet squaw. The dress was her favorite because it was decorated with hundreds of brass beads arranged in four separate rows across the yoke and the wide elbow-length sleeves of the dress. Under the last row of the tiny brass beads, a string of thimbles were tied to colorful light blue and white glass beads which dangled along the length of her tiny waist and across her sleeves, giving her the appearance of an iridescent exotic bird.

Cara had placed a clean white tablecloth that she had "borrowed" from one of the officers' wives' laundry and had set the small table that was in the center of the room with tin plates, knives and forks, and two whiskey shot glasses because she was unable to locate any thing more appropriate. She did however, have two Indian feast bowls made from maple in which she planned to serve the soup that she had concocted from thistle, pomme blanche, and fruit of the prickly pear cactus, which she had split, deseeded, and dried. This was used as a thickener for the soup, and gave it a hearty taste. For the main course she had prepared two bison steaks, reserving the very large piece for her *Sargento Mayor*.

They feasted on these delights and for dessert, Cara served some canned peaches that she had procured from the post's butler's store. Although Nate did not say very much, he was clearly very content to be with Cara. He felt both relaxed and rejuvenated by her presence, but remained naive in what Cara de Cuervo had in mind. When Nate was polishing off the last bite of his bison steak, he told Cara about the scene in the tipi with Roman Nose and Cougar Eyes, and how the Dog Soldier had named him Buffalo Gordon out of respect. In fact, Medicine Bill Comstock and Colonel Grierson started to call Nate Buffalo Gordon on the way back to Wallace and it did not take long before quite a few of the enlisted men started to refer to the sergeant major by that name. The black troopers of the Tenth Cavalry identified with this title that was bestowed upon one of their leaders out of reverence by the enemy. As a consequence, they were slowly earning a reputation as bona fide Indian fighters because of their stubbornness on the battlefield while confronting hostiles and the respect the Cheyennes had placed on their fighting prowess.

Cara listened very closely to Nate's recounting of the incident in the tipi with the Cheyennes, and she especially enjoyed the part when Cougar Eyes placed his hand against Nate's chest to feel the rhythm of his heartbeat to determine if his enemy was calm or nervous. She was not overly surprised by this act. Being a half-breed and growing up with her Commanche mother, she often heard and witnessed many things that were typical of Indian behavior. When searching for the truth, Indians were motivated to find what was inside of a man's heart by either looking deeply into the eyes, or by touching, listening, and by talking honestly about one's feelings.

As if she wanted to demonstrate how physical and personal an Indian can be, she quietly rose from her chair and approached Nate with her head slightly bowed, forcing her long hair to fall delicately against her cheeks. The strings of the colored glass beads in which the brass thimbles were attached on her dress gently jingled as her sensual body swayed and moved across the rickety floor boards of the shanty as she approached Nate who was still sitting on his chair. She looked into his eyes and with her left hand pushed the table backward so she could face him. She then lifted the hem of her Blackfeet red wool dress and climbed on top of him by placing her right arm on his shoulder and using her knees to mount his lap. Then by squeezing her thighs, maneuvered herself on top of his balls. She threw back her hair with a twist of her head and sensitively placed her tiny hands on Nate's face as she advanced her lips toward his. As Cara pressed her mouth against Nate's, she could feel his huge cock rise and press against his tight wool army britches. She worked her tongue into Nate's mouth so forcefully and seized his tongue with such vigor that his head became pressed against her face and he felt that his tongue would be sucked down Cara's throat. Nate was momentarily stunned by Cara's physical aggressiveness but events were happening so quickly and the feelings that he was experiencing so overpowering, that he simply surrendered to her will. As Cara started to dig her thighs and squeezed her buttocks against Nate's huge cock, he wrapped his arms around Cara's waist and pressed her toward his chest. He could feel her plump breasts rubbing against his chest, her nipples were hard and she began to pant and rub her hands all over Nate's closely cropped hair.

Both of them were becoming very excited and the air in the room became steamed with their perspiration. Cara was thrusting harder and harder as Nate started to respond with his pelvis by thrusting upward from his sitting position. The dowels of the chair started to squeak and become loose, and Nate, for a moment, became concerned that the chair might collapse from their combined weight and intense physical activity. He was feeling extremely warm, and wanted to rip off his wool shell jacket to partially get some air, and at the same time, get closer to Cara's breasts. He thought to himself, that not even during the war, when he had to fight zealot Confederates in a burning sun with thousands of screaming men and horses in a cloud of black powder and dust that burned eyes, throats, lips, and mouths, did his body feel so hot! Not even when he was engaged in battle against the Cheyennes did he feel so soaked with perspiration. His mind became confused and started to wander. He thought about Cara's bright red Blackfeet dress and the rows of brass and glass beads that rubbed against his chest while the miniature thimbles jingled against his jacket as the panting and breathing became louder and louder. He also experienced brief flashbacks into the past when he was a slave. His mind raced to the time when Mas'a Hammond instructed his overseer to force Nate to "breed him with that tall, plump wench with the wide thighs." He pondered to himself how different this experience was compared to that miserable slave cabin where he was commanded to behave as if he was a steer with a ring in its nose. Unlike that time however, Nate now really wanted a woman and he wanted this woman. He did not know if it was love but what he did know was that it was lust that was driving his desire. As his emotions became increasingly more intense, his cock felt as if it was on fire and as hard as a stallion's erection.

Nate had not taken off his brass army spurs. As he drove the spiked edges of the ball of the spurs into the floorboards in order to reach maximum elevation to pivot the rear chair legs and swing back and forth as Cara rubbed her spot against his organ, the sharp edges started to dig into the wood. While he was engaged in this activity, Cara, as if she were an expert pickpocket, maneuvered her fingers on her right hand to undo Nate's fly buttons one by one. *"Dios mio!"* she exclaimed, when his organ emerged from the opening of his trousers and underpants. Her juices were flowing so profusely that when she seized Nate's penis she had no trouble placing the huge, hot, pulsating black organ inside of her. With every thrust, Cara would moan and cry out with little noises that Nate thought sounded as if she was becoming some kind of small animal. At her urging, he placed his hands underneath her buttocks and started to lift her petite body gently up and down as the wooden chair squeaked and rocked back and forth while his spurs continued to dig into the wooden floorboards.

Nate was panting and his chest heaved with excitement. Cara's now nimble hands started to work on Nate's shell jacket but the garment was so tightly worn that the brass buttons stubbornly resisted her efforts. Nate tried to help and managed to unsnap his tall collar but this was not fast enough for Cara. Frustrated that this process was taking far too long, she clasped Nate's hands and softly said, *"Alto, mi amor!"* Then, instead of grappling with the brass buttons, she grabbed the tunic where the buttons were sewed and pulled it apart, popping three of them and exposing Nate's undershirt which also met the same fate as the jacket. The curly dark hair on his huge chest made Cara's eyes widen with delight. She plunged her hands onto Nate's chest and directed her fingers to claw at the hair and rub the skin and muscle with her palms.

The dowels of the rickety chair were now slowly becoming ominously loose. Nate was digging his spurs into the cottonwood floor planking with such vigorous rhythm that tiny pieces of wood splintered off and two grooves were slowly being chipped out where the balls of his spurs rested on the floor. Great pressure, therefore, was being placed on the hind legs of the chair, and with every squeak, the horizontal dowels that supported the four legs were become looser and looser. Cara was riding Nate now like a rider cantering a horse on the open prairie. As she moaned and made those sounds that Nate thought sounded as if she was a small animal, the tip of one of the horizontal dowels became free from its groove. Nate noticed that the chair was becoming increasingly unstable but he could not be concerned with that right now. Cara was screeching and moving her body in such a fashion that it reminded Nate of the women voodoo dancers he had seen back in Congo Square in New Orleans. As he thought about those octoroon and quadroon half-naked dancers, he felt his semen getting ready to erupt. Cara sensed this and reached with her left hand for Nate's balls and gently massaged them as if she was caressing a delicate fruit. Nate moaned as he ejaculated and felt his body stiffen, and just when he was about to recover from his orgasm, the rear lower dowel of the chair broke loose and within a split second, the two hind legs of the chair collapsed, sending both of them straight to the floor.

Nate was on his back but he held on to Cara as the chair fell backward. With the exception of heavy breathing resulting from intensive sexual exertion, there was a moment of stunned silence as they stared into each other's eyes. Then Nate smiled, and Cara started to giggle. Within a moment, they were both laughing.

Fourteen

Maj. George "Sandy" A. Forsyth and his fifty well-armed civilian ranger-scouts were under siege by seven hundred to a thousand Cheyenne Dog Soldiers and their Arapaho and Brulé Sioux allies. The scouts had been ordered by General Sheridan to seek out and engage marauding bands of Cheyenne Dog Soldiers along the upper Republican River.

They had left Fort Wallace a few days earlier and had struck a hot trail of hostiles who had murdered several Mexican teamsters and slaughtered their oxen. Instead of locating and surprising the Dog Soldiers however, it was the hostiles that found and surprised Forsyth and his scouts. The rangers had made camp the night before on the banks of the Arikaree River which was a fork on the upper Republican in the territory of Colorado.

In the very early morning hours of September 17, hundreds of hostiles charged out of the east, and stampeded many of the command's pack mules and horses, and the surprised scouts were fortunate to have escaped with their lives. If it was not for their expeditious thinking and reaction to quickly fall back to a sandbar in the middle of the Arikaree River, they would have been overwhelmed by the Dog Soldiers and their allies who were camped nearby and had plenty of reserve warriors.

The brainchild of Gen. Phil Sheridan, the hand-picked frontier scouts were to be experienced horsemen and form a fast-moving, hard-hitting assault force that was designed to operate independently from the army but assist in the government's efforts in subduing the Central Plains Indians.

457

"Sandy" Forsyth was technically a line officer in the Ninth Negro Cavalry since the summer of 1866, but General Sheridan, who had become close to him during the war, had chosen "Sandy" to become part of his staff. Major Forsyth however, longed to see action and have his own command. During the war, he had participated in many engagements and rose to become a brevet brigadier general of volunteers through his courage, competency, and leadership qualities. In addition, he was one of the two cavalry officers who had accompanied "Little Phil" on his famous twenty mile gallop from Winchester to Cedar Creek to rally retreating federal troops and turn the tide of battle against the attacking Confederates led by General Jubal Early. So when Forsyth approached Sheridan and asked for a field command, "Little Phil" rewarded his protégé by giving him command of the fifty scouts.

Major Forsyth and his fifty scouts went out looking for a fight and found much, much more than what they had prepared themselves for. It was evening now, and the snipping from the nearby hills had died down and the scouts were crouched in their shallow rifle pits as if they were cornered bobcats. They spent their time deepening their rifle pits, caring for the wounded, burying the dead where they had fallen by covering them with a little sand, and stripping sections of meat from their dead horses and mules and squirreling them in the dirt for future use. Although the scouts managed to repulse three heavy charges against them, thanks to their Spencer repeaters and Colt revolvers, the command however, suffered heavy casualties during that first day of heavy fighting with the Dog Soldiers led by Roman Nose and Cougar Eyes.

Three scouts were dead from gunshot wounds, and fourteen were severely wounded by bullets or arrows. Most tragically, the scouts' second in command, 1st Lt. Frederick H. Beecher, who was the nephew of abolitionist Henry Ward Beecher, died from a mortal gunshot wound to the side and died at the feet of his commander. Before he died, the youthful, slender man, who had a face that resembled a painter, rather than a warrior, had called out for his mother. Forsyth himself was seriously wounded and in horrible agony. In addition to receiving a scalp wound, the commander had taken a bullet in the right thigh that had ripped his flesh wide open, and when the surgeon, Dr. Mooers was attempting to attend to the major's wound, Forsyth was hit by another lead bullet in the left leg. Later that afternoon, while Dr. Mooers, the former surgeon at Fort Hays, and who had joined Forsyth's scouts because he wanted to see real live, wild Indians, received a mortal bullet to his forehead as he was shooting his Spencer in a rifle pit. All in all, the command suffered nearly fifty percent casualties during this first day of fighting.

Some of the wounds that were inflicted on the scouts were just as ghastly. One scout received an arrowhead in his head but continued to fight on with the shaft protruding from his face. Another scout had his left arm smashed by a rifle ball, while another was shot through the hip, and still another was shot through the eye, the bullet lodged in the back of his head.

There were other problems. In the rush for the sandbar, the scouts had abandoned all of their medical supplies and food packs in favor of the ammunition. What was more ominous, however, was that all of their horses and mules were either stolen by the warriors or had been shot or slowly killed by multiple arrows as they stood tethered on willow and plum tree branches on the northeast end of the island. Therefore, with no horses or mules alive, all possible means for quick escape were cut off, leaving the possibility that the men could be in for a prolonged state of siege with the prospect of starvation looming. In addition, because all of the medical supplies were left on the opposite bank, those men who suffered wounds such as Major Forsyth, were facing death by slow infection.

Although his scouts had successfully thrown back three mass attacks, Major Forsyth knew that without food and medical supplies, the men could only hold out for so long. No one knew where they were or for how long they were suppose to be out looking for hostiles, so the prospect of being rescued was not a possibility. His only chance was to risk sending out two men on foot, at night, through country crawling with Dog Soldiers to Fort Wallace and get help. The main problem though, was that Fort Wallace was about a hundred miles away!

He decided to send Pierre Trudeau, "French Pete," who was sixty years old, and Jack Stilwell, who was only eighteen but had already spent years on the frontier, was fluent in Spanish and could handle a gun with deadly accuracy, to Fort Wallace to seek succor for his imperiled command.

Cougar Eyes and Bull Bear were in the ceremonial tipi watching *Voo' xenehe* slowly die from a bullet wound that he had received in the small of his back. The great warrior had led the last and final charge against agains the *Ve' ho' e* invaders and had been shot after he had nearly trampled some of the scouts that were hiding in a rifle pit among the tall buffalo grass.

The mood inside the tipi was grim. Some of the squaws, bunched together in the southwest corner of the lodge as if they were geese, were weeping while the medicine men chanted near the fire and sought purification from the spirit world for their fallen hero. Present with Bull Bear and Cougar Eyes were other members of Roman Nose's Dog Soldier society. Their faces were still painted for war and they remained attired for battle.

Although the Cheyennes and their allies inflicted heavy casualties on the whites and were in complete control of the surrounding countryside for hundreds of miles around, the Indians had failed to take control of the sandbar in the middle of the Arikaree, and had failed to run down the whites in three massive charges. Most devastatingly though, was the loss of Roman Nose. The warrior had been visiting a nearby Brule Sioux camp when the whites were sighted. Eager for glory and prestige, several of the younger warriors had attacked the whites without waiting for instructions from the chiefs. Roman Nose had missed the two initial assaults when he was found by runners who were sent to find him and bring him to the battle site because many of the warriors needed his leadership and strong battle medicine. *Voo' xenehe* however, knew that his medicine had been broken. He did not want to engage the enemy because he had found out that a piece of bread that he had recently devoured was cooked in an iron frying pan. The fact that the cooking pan was made by the *Ve' ho' e*, and that *Voo' xenehe* consumed the food from the pan, destroyed his medicine and invincibility in battle. According to his spiritual mentor, Ice, he was told that if he should touch anything that is made by the white man, it would contaminate the pure Cheyenne medicine and render him no long impervious to bullets. Roman Nose knew that if he engaged the whites, he would be killed. Nevertheless, he mounted his white stallion and rode to the battle site.

When he arrived he dismounted behind the hill that overlooked the sandbar and pondered his fate. It was too late for any purification ceremony and he knew that he could not simply stay out of the fight when so many braves looked up to him and needed his courage. When it became clear to Cougar Eyes and some of the other *Hotame-Ho' nehe* that had rode up to meet Roman Nose, that *Voo' xenehe* was hesitant to lead the next charge which they hoped would overwhelm the whites, they started to ask him questions.

"*Voo' xenehe!* Why are you not leading the charge when so many of our brothers have fallen in expectation that you will lead us to victory?" demanded Cougar Eyes. He had killed two of the scouts that day and had ridden over a rifle pit unharmed and counted coup with his lance. He was excited from the heat of battle and could not comprehend why Roman Nose was reluctant to mount up and lead the next attack.

"My medicine has been broken," he finally responded solemnly. "In the Sioux camp...I ate some bread cooked in a *Ve' ho' e* pan," he further explained. He then turned his gaze away from Cougar Eyes and stared at the sky as if he was asking the spirits to forgive his transgression. "If I go into this fight, I will surely be killed," he said with resignation.

Cougar Eyes and the other braves understood what that meant. "Could you not engage in the purification ceremony?" Cougar Eyes knew that the process was a lengthy one but he could not think of anything else to say.

"Too late!" responded *Voo' xenehe*. Some of the other braves begged him to lead the charge anyway, knowing that it would place his life in jeopardy. They felt that they were close in breaking the stubborn defense that the whites had put up on the island, and they believed that with Roman Nose's participation in leading the next charge, they would kill all of the invaders.

Roman Nose walked over to his white stallion and removed his war bag. He untied the bundle and prepared to paint his face in red, black, and yellow which his mentor, Ice, had told him were the holy colors of the Cheyenne for battle. As he painted his face, he requested a scalp shirt which was promptly given to him while the other warriors offered him beautiful moccasins and leggings. After he had completed painting his face and stallion, he untied the knot on his fine parfleche to remove his famous war bonnet with the single buffalo horn protruding from the center of its crown. He placed the sacred bonnet on his head and made sure that the long twin feathered tails were free from entanglement so they would flow freely in the wind when he charged. The other Dog Soldiers were encouraged and some of them started to blow on their war whistles and shouted that they were going to ride down the whites and that their squaws were going to remove all of their enemy's privates.

Cougar Eyes moved his white-faced mustang behind Roman Nose's stallion and waited for the great warrior to give the command to proceed toward their objective. As *Voo' xenehe* prayed to the spirits for guidance and forgiveness for deviating from the path of living a pure Cheyenne way of life, the braves mounted their war ponies. Then in single file, the warriors moved out from behind the hill that overlooked the Arikaree and prepared to charge the scouts on the sandbar.

The final Indian assault came quickly. As Roman Nose, Cougar Eyes, Dog Soldiers, Sioux, and Arapaho braves urged their ponies toward the banks of the Arikaree, the scouts greeted them with enough gunfire that it resembled a horizontal rain of lead mixed with smoke, dust, and the deafening sound of Spencer repeaters and army Colt revolvers. Although the assault was impressive in terms of the number of charging Indians howling at the top of their lungs as their ponies dashed toward the scouts, this last determined mass attack was over very quickly. The concentrated fire from the well-disciplined scouts proved too much for the Indians. Several warriors were shot off their ponies and many of their mounts had been killed or wounded as they rode toward the sandbar. The fire power from the scouts broke the charge and the attackers were once again forced to ride around the island as if they were a great ocean wave broken by a huge rock. Roman Nose, however, still managed to gallop his enthusiastic stallion and ride over some of the scouts. When he rode past, some of the scouts rotated their bodies in their rifle pits and shot at him with their Spencers. One bullet hit *Voo' xenehe* in the lower back, but the great Cheyenne war leader barely flinched when he realized he was severely hit. He slowed down his mount and guided the stallion to the rear where the squaws helped him down from the back of his horse. They then gently transported him and moved the body to the tipi were he was now breathing his last gasps of air.

Capt. Louis H. Carpenter and seventy troopers of H Company were bivouacked for the noon rest at Goose Creek near the Smoky Hill Road close to the territorial border line of Colorado. They had departed Fort Wallace the day before and were tracking down marauding bands of Dog Soldiers. Carpenter's orderly, Private Reuben Waller had just completed watering and grazing his commander's horse and had spoken to Nate who instructed him to inform Carpenter that all of the horses had been watered and fed and that the men had finished their noon meal.

"Suh, Sergeant Major Gordon has tol' me to inform you that the horses and men have done all their noonin'."

"Have the sergeant major report to me immediately," instructed Carpenter as he sipped some steaming coffee from his tin cup.

"Yes suh," responded Waller in his usual crisp fashion.

Carpenter was with his chief of scouts, Jack Peate, who was a friend of William Comstock. Jack Peate was a very competent scout but lacked the finesse, sensitivity, and knightly quality that Medicine Bill possessed. As was the case with most frontier scouts that served as the eyes and ears of the cavalry, Peate was a greasy boor. Carpenter and his scout were discussing which direction the command should take in order to strike the trail of the marauding Dog Soldiers, when one of the pickets suddenly shouted, *"Riders comin' in."*

Immediately, the camp became alive with curiosity as two troopers galloped into the camp and rode up to Carpenter and Jack Peate. The black troopers had been sent by the commander of Fort Wallace to locate Carpenter and H Company to deliver dispatches. Their horses were thoroughly lathered up and they were exhausted from the long hard ride. After they had caught their breath somewhat, one of the troopers' blurted out, "Captain, dispatches from Wallace." The trooper handed over the envelope to Carpenter and dismounted his spent horse. He had a wild look about him and looked like a man eager to talk.

"Beggin' the captain's pardon, sir! As we left Wallace, was run into two of Major Forsyth's men not far from Wallace . . . Suh, they were on foot and half-starved . . . Forsyth and his scouts are in a real fix, suh. . . . Somewhere up on the Arikare . . .'bout fifty miles from here toward the northwest. French Pete and a young boy by the name of Jack Stillwell, were jest 'bout crawlin' on the Smoky Hill Road towards the fort yesterday seekin' help. They be in a mighty po' condition, them two . . . but they walked a hun'red miles all the while hidin' from the Indians. They told us that Forsyth is wounded real bad and that the second in command is dead, an' that they have lots of wounded. Suh, they done tol' us that the command is sur'ounded by t'ousands of Cheyennes, Sioux, and Arapaho and that the men could be *wiped out!*"

Carpenter anxiously turned to Jack Peate. "Do you think we can locate them in time?" By now Nate and Jesse had joined Carpenter and Jack Peate in the middle of the camp. Louis H. Carpenter thought about his friend of Maj. "Sandy" Forsyth. They had served together with General Sheridan in the Battle of the Wilderness and in other engagements. He felt a personal responsibility to rescue his companion.

"I reckon we ken," responded the greasy scout as he stroked his filthy beard. "But we gotta move, Captain!" added Peate as he spat out the tobacco wad from his mouth that he had been chewing for hours. His teeth were yellow and Nate was reminded of his old nemesis, Bloohhound Jack.

"Sergeant Major!" Carpenter turned to Nate.

"Sir?!" responded Nate, a little startled. He was thinking about Bloodhound Jack and the time when he had to kill him in the bayou.

"The troop will move out at once. Get the men ready," barked Carpenter.

"Aye, aye, sir."

"Oh, and Sergeant Major! I want scouts thrown out ahead of the column as far forward as possible," added Carpenter anxiously.

As the bugler sounded the call to mount up, the troopers from H Company rushed to their horses and formed two columns. It now became a race against time. The command had to move quickly in order to rescue the scouts on the Arikaree from being butchered by the Indians, but they were completely unfamiliar with the territory north of them, so the troop had to be careful not to be ambushed themselves.

Maj. "Sandy" Forsyth was facing death and his command was in wretched condition. The scouts had now been on the sandbar for almost a week and all of the food had been devoured days ago. They were, however, successful in digging a shallow well to gain access to water which was their only link to survival. After the death of Roman Nose on that first day of heavy fighting, and with the exception of one faint charge the following day, the Indians had pretty much called off their siege on the scouts.

Forsyth's men, however, were facing new horrors. Hunger pains plagued all of the men. After they had finished the meager food contents in their saddlebags, the scouts were reduced to eating putrid horse and mule meat spiced with gun powder in order to kill the stench and to disguise the rank taste of the rotted meat. The fifty dead horses and all of the mules slowly rotted away in the September sun. The animals had remained unburied, and after a few days, the grossly bloated carcasses started to reek from decomposition. The ghastly, disgusting odor became so offensive to the scouts that many of them threw up the remains of their stomach contents in the tall buffalo grass and gagged from the stink in their rifle pits until they became acclimated to this fragrance of decaying flesh that permeated the air.

Those scouts that had been killed were only superficially buried where they had died. Because the defenders were under siege and had no entrenchment implements, they used tin cups, plates, and their hands to cover the bodies with sand. Consequently, parts and limbs of the cadavers, such as a nose, a finger, or a knee would protrude from the sand and attract flies or even trip-up one of the men when moving about on the tiny island.

In addition, the elements were not kind to the injured. The

mortally and gravely wounded suffered severely as the days were hot and the cold September nights added to the general misery of those men who were suffering from gunshot and arrow punctures. Major Forsyth's gunshot injury to his leg was so rotten that maggots had taken up residence in the wound and he knew that if help did not arrive soon, he would certainly lose his leg and possibly his life within a very short period of time.

Not only did the wounded have to endure perpetual agony and delirium from their injuries, but millions of flies harassed them as the insects were drawn to the blood-soaked makeshift bandages. Hundreds of avaricious flies would congregate on a bleeding wound and feast on the red flesh and there was nothing that the scouts could do to drive them away.

Although the bulk of the Cheyennes and their allies had left the area, there were still roaming bands of Dog Soldiers and the scouts were not certain if the hostiles had left the vicinity or were possibly laying low and preparing for another attack. In any case, Forsyth's men were on foot and because of the injured, the scouts were not prepared to make the hundred mile trek to Fort Wallace while dragging mortally wounded comrades through Indian country. So when one of the scouts removed his tattered blue sailor's blouse and attached the garment to a cottonwood pole and implanted it into the soft ground as a sign of defiance, the scouts had made up their minds that they were either going to be rescued or bravely face a grisly death.

Capt. Louis Carpenter had advanced his column thirty-five miles within six hours and had now bivouacked the command for the night near the south fork of the Republican River. Company H had moved rapidly during the last half of the day alternating between trotting and walking while proceeding cautiously in hostile country. As Carpenter ordered, Nate and Jesse had placed additional pickets along the perimeter and Nate, along with Reuben Waller, had verified that the horses and pack mules were well-tethered for the night. The men were ordered to have no campfires to avoid being detected, so eating hardtack dipped in water to soften them or chewing on beef jerky if one was fortunate enough to have some, was their only option. The horses and pack mules were fed oats and watered in nearby Goose Creek that was almost dry but enough water remained at the bottom to allow the animals to have their fill.

The next morning, the command had moved out at first light and with flankers and scouts thrown far forward, the column searched for any signs of Indian activity or signs of Forsyth and his command. By mid-morning, Carpenter was becoming increasingly concerned and frustrated that the scouting parties that he had sent in various directions had only found a dry riverbed and no signs of hostiles or Forsyth.

Nate and the scout Jack Peate however, had found the trail. They were scouting about three miles northwest from the column when they came upon what Jack Peate described as a "hell of a fuckin' hot trail." Indeed, after Nate and Peate discerned the number of ponies and deep ruts made by hundreds of travois, they concluded that there must be at least two thousand warriors on the move within a short distance of the command.

"We best alert the captain!" observed Nate as he took out his bandanna to wipe the dust and perspiration from his face. He was staring at the wide and deep Indian trail and thought about Cougar Eyes and where he could be. After Nate and the chief of scouts had galloped back to the command and impressed upon Carpenter that the company could possibly face thousands of Cheyenne warriors, Carpenter decided to circle his supply and ambulance wagons as a precaution and ordered a squad to accompany him to where the trail had been located and reconnoiter the area.

Nate requested Jesse and his squad to accompany Carpenter, and the commander concurred. The captain, Reuben Waller, Jack Peate, Nate, Jesse, and the troopers dashed to a nearby hill where the fresh Indian trail was first sighted and gazed at the surrounding country, surveying the terrain. What they saw in the distance astonished them.

About a dozen Cheyenne burial scaffolds were erected to hold the dead warriors. They were all wrapped in buffalo robes and surrounded by their prized possessions and war accoutrements.

"Captain, I think it behooves us to investigate the bodies of dem dead Cheyennes an' see how dem braves died," suggested Peate, as he placed a wad of fresh chewing tobacco in between his lips and gums.

Carpenter at first was a little stunned by this un-Christian suggestion but after a moment of reflection, agreed. They approached the
burial ground with caution and Nate felt uncomfortable. He really did
not want to engage in what he viewed as grave robbing. Jack Peate
however, had no problem with grave robbing, and looked forward to
the many souvenirs he was going to acquire. He was the first to dismount his horse and commenced pushing on one of the vertical sup-
ports of the scaffolds. After a few violent pushes on one of the poles,
he looked up at the troopers and derided, "Well? Am I goin' do dis
'lone?" Nate looked at Carpenter and the commander nodded his head.
Nate dismounted and instructed two troopers to do the same. Together,
they managed to topple the scaffold, sending the body of the dead
warrior tumbling to the ground and scattering his personal possessions
in the buffalo grass.

After Jack Peate eagerly unfurled the tightly bound buffalo robe
skin from the carcass, revealing the dead warrior's fine leggings, moccasins, and war shirt, the scout searched for the cause of death.

"I knew it! Here it is . . . a bullet wound in the right side," barked
Peate triumphantly.

"How fresh is the wound?" inquired Carpenter.

"Well, Captain, I figure 'bout a couple of days at de most," responded the scout after he spat some of his tobacco wad near a prickly
pear bush.

"Examine the other bodies," ordered Carpenter, as he pulled out
his white handkerchief from the inside of his blouse and placed the
item against his nose to cover the stench of the dead Indian who was
in the beginning stages of decomposition.

Systematically, the men went over to every burial scaffold and
tipped the structures to the ground and unfurled the hides to get to
the bodies. In every case, the bodies revealed that the cause of death
was by gunshot. It was a grisly task. Each body that was unfurled was
soaked in blood, and in some cases, maggots had taken over the body.
Two troopers were so revolted by the stench and goulish task of un-
covering the dead, that they had to step back and throw up their breakfast.

"No doubt 'bout it, Captain. Dem bucks were kilt by our boys in de last few days," stated Peate as if he were some great physician commenting on a specific medical question.

Carpenter, however, was preoccupied. He was looking through his binoculars when he noticed a white tipi on the horizon. "Peate, take a look at that wigwam." Carpenter handed the binoculars to the scout and pointed in the direction where he saw the white tipi.

"Interestin', Captain! Very interestin'. A lodge dats made from white buffalo skins means *big medicine*. Prob'ly a burial tipi for a chief or a great warrior."

"Let's go see!" instructed Carpenter, as he gently spurred his mount toward the mysterious tipi that resembled a bleached tomb in the middle of the prairie.

The lodge was indeed white. Carpenter thought maybe the lighting had distorted the true colors of the skins, but that was not the case.

"Sergeant Major!" cried Carpenter as he waved his right arm in air to signal the squad to halt.

"Sir!?" replied Nate.

"Go see!" ordered the commander. Nate dismounted and handed the reins of his horse to Reuben Waller. He unflapped the cover of his holster and pulled out his Walker-Colt. As he approached the tipi flap door, he raised his weapon in the air and cocked back the hammer all the way. With his left hand, he pulled back the flap door of the lodge and cautiously stepped inside. Because the smoke flap was wide open, the interior of the lodge basked in the soft late-afternoon light. In the middle of the tipi was a burial scaffold that was about eight feet high and supported a dead warrior. Nate approached the body and noticed that the brave was wrapped in several beautiful buffalo robes. His war bonnet, with a polished buffalo horn in the middle of the crown, was on his head and a war shield and a large ceremonial drum was located near his feet. Other items that were placed on or near the scaffold were such articles as arrows, a lance, and an ornately painted parfleche.

Nate approached the corpse and looked into the face of the dead warrior. His eyebrows lifted slightly and he remained motionless for a brief moment as he stared into Roman Nose's face.

"Well, this big buck won't bother nobody no mo'," sighed Nate as he retired his Walker-Colt back into the holster. He then stepped back outside to report, "All clear, sir."

Carpenter and Jack Peate entered the tipi and examined the body. They unfurled *Voo' xenehe*'s buffalo robes and noticed that this man had also been shot. Carpenter was curious about the ceremonial drum above Roman Nose's head and decided to investigate. He lifted the instrument from the scaffold and turned the article around in his hands. The commander liked the painted detail that adorned the drum and ran his right hand against the tightly stretched buffalo hide that covered the top.

"Like de drum, Captain?" smirked Jack Peate, showing his yellow teeth. "Make a nice souv'nir fo' sure," he added.

"Yes, it would," responded Carpenter, a little embarrassed that his scout, Jack Peate had assumed that he was going to take it. He respected the gruff scout, but disliked his crude insolence. "I think we have seen enough. Sergeant Major, we will return to the column."

"Aye, sir." Nate saluted as he exited from the tipi.

Captain Louis H. Carpenter was the last to leave the lodge, and as he stepped out of the tipi, Nate noticed that his commanding officer was holding Roman Nose's ceremonial drum under his left arm.

SEPTEMBER 25, 1868

The troopers of H Company were in the process of saddling their horses and checking their weapons when one of the pickets shouted, "Riders comin' in!" The early morning fog was slowly burning off and the men had just completed a light breakfast of hardtack and beef jerky. The horses were feeling frisky, and snorted and pulled on their picket ropes in the cool September morning air. Nate had just hoof-picked his horse and Jesse was lecturing one trooper who was talking and laughing too loudly. Captain Carpenter's orderly, Reuben Waller, had finished packing his commanding officer's eating utensils into one of the pack mule's bags, and Jack Peate was chewing on a fresh wad of tobacco as if he were an old bull chewing cud.

The five riders that were fast approaching the bivouac area were first noticed by the pickets when they appeared on a nearby hill toward the south. Nate noticed that the lead rider was on top of a little mule and that his feet almost touched the ground because the beast was too small for the rider. The rider, who was now frantically waving his right arm in the air as if he were half-mad, was Jack Donovan. He had been sent, along with another scout, by Forsyth the day after "French Pete" Trudeau and Jack Stillwell left the besieged scouts on the Arikaree to seek help. After experiencing painful ordeals on foot, Donovan and the other scout finally reached Wallace but found the post virtually deserted because most of the soldiers had left with the fort's commander to find Forsyth after Trudeau and Stillwell had sounded the alert. Although Jack Donovan was exhausted and his feet severely swollen, he borrowed a mule, because all the horses had left with the relief force, and convinced four other civilians to accompany him to find either "Carpenter's Brunettes" or the large column that had departed with the post's commander in search of Forsyth.

"Praise God that I've found you!" shouted Donovan as he slipped off his small mule. Carpenter, Nate, and Jack Peate gathered around the bearded Coloradian as the frantic man explained his recent ordeal on the Arikaree and his long painful walk to Wallace and consequent ride on the mule in search of Carpenter or the Fort Wallace relief force. The exhausted scout had gotten lost but was extremely fortunate to have stumbled upon Carpenter's column. He informed the commander that he believed that Forsyth's scouts were located farther north from their current position and Carpenter immediately ordered the company to move out at once.

The troop alternated between a trot and a gallop for Carpenter felt that they were now close to reaching Forsyth, and the senior officer of H Company did not want to lose any more time in view of the desperate situation that his friend was facing. Morale among the men was high. They felt that they were close and that their efforts would pay off by rescuing Forsyth's embattled scouts. At around ten o'clock, the troop came to a high ridge that rose above the Arikaree River and Jack Peate suggested that they have a "looksee." Carpenter, Peate, Donovan, and Nate scaled the ridge that overlooked the river and Carpenter once again pulled out his binoculars. He focused his glasses down the river while Donovan stared toward the western part of the Arikaree.

"I'm not quite certain, Captain . . . but I think the island must be further up the river," said Donovan anxiously. He was concerned that they might be too late to rescue his comrades whom he had left nearly a week ago. More than any body else, the Coloradian knew how desperate the situation was. He had explained to Carpenter that his companions were not only surrounded by hordes of Cheyennes, but that the men were starving and the wounded were dying because there were no medical supplies.

"*Captain! Over there,*" exclaimed Jack Peate pointing his finger as if he saw a revelation. The scout was looking toward the northeast where some hills were located, and saw two men walking down the hill about a mile and a half away. Jack Donovan trained his gaze toward the northeast and stared, his eyes frantically surveying the terrain. He then jumped up as if he were a child that had just been told he was going to have a piece of cherry pie, and shouted enthusiastically, "*By Jesus, there's de camp.*"

Carpenter trained his binoculars on the sandbar and noticed a tattered banner attached to a crude pole that listed downward.

"Sergeant Major!"

"Yes, sir!" Nate knew exactly what Carpenter was going to tell him but awaited for the orders anyway.

"Have the company advance at a gallop and order the ambulance and supply wagons to come up as quickly as possible."

"Aye, aye, sir." Nate galloped down the ridge and instructed Jesse to order the wagons to "Hurry them up!" He then was joined by Jack Peate, Carpenter, and Reuben Waller. The four of them took the lead, racing toward Forsyth's scouts.

Maj. "Sandy" Forsyth had been alerted by some of his scouts that they had spotted an ambulance and what looked like cavalrymen in the northwest. The major was partially buried with sand in his rifle pit and was facing death. Nevertheless, when told that relief had finally arrived, he meekly seized his saddlebag and with his right hand reached inside one of the bags as if he were a sick and suffering old man searching for a bottle of pills. He finally located what he was looking for and pulled out a copy of *Oliver Twist* that one of the men had found in a saddlebag of a dead horse. He opened the book and placed the well-read novel near his chest, as if he was reading, and was just resting for a moment. "Must remain calm," he whispered to himself.

Jack Peate's horse was faster than Nate's or Carpenter's, so he was the first to arrive on the island. The scouts on the tiny sandbar erupted with such joy that the scene could have been mistaken for the second coming of Jesus Christ. When Nate, Carpenter, and Reuben Waller arrived, the scouts begged for food and frantically grabbed at saddlebags searching for jerky, hardtack, or anything that would fill their aching stomachs. No sooner had they wolfed down a piece of jerky, than they would demand more. Reuben Waller couldn't hand out his food fast enough. He felt great pity for these white men who, although looked like death, were heroes nevertheless. To the tired, starving, and wounded white men however, it was the troopers of Company H Tenth Negro Cavalry, who were the heroes of the moment.

When it finally became apparent that their deliverers where black, several of the scouts were taken aback.

"*By God! Niggers,*" remarked one scout as he eagerly chewed on some jerky that Nate had given him. "We been saved by the darkies," yelled another scout as he ran up to one of the troopers and begged for food.

Capt. Louis Carpenter had found his friend in his rifle pit. He was shocked at his condition, but found it interesting that a copy of *Oliver Twist* lay open on his chest. Carpenter removed his gauntlet and offered his hand to Forsyth as if he was greeting an old friend at a tea party.

"Sandy, I moved as quickly as possible . . . I, I hope you are all right! All of my supplies are at your disposition . . . I will do every thing in my power to assist your men." Carpenter was visibly shaken by the sight of his companion's deteriorating condition, and by now, the stench from the rotting dead horses and mules started to affect the troopers.

"Thank you, Louis," responded Forsyth meekly. It took every ounce of restraint for the major not to break down and weep like a child. He was so tired and weak from the loss of blood and his leg was on the verge of gangrene, but at the same time he was so overwhelmed by joy to see that help had finally arrived that he choked back tears in his attempt to remain calm as if he were at a picnic.

By now all of the troopers of Company H had arrived on the scene and urged on by Jesse, the supply wagons and ambulance were not far behind. The black troopers kept feeding the demanding avaricious scouts and as the white men devoured the food, they danced, shouted, cried, and gave thanks to the lord and to the cavalrymen who have come to save them. Nate was not offended that quite a few of the scouts were calling the men of the Tenth, niggers, darkies, and brunettes. As far as he was concerned, his boys proved that they were up to the task, and he was proud of the fact that they had ridden their horses for over fifty miles within two days in unknown and hostile country and had rescued these white men, who had gotten themselves into a fight that nearly cost them all of their lives.

First Sergeant Jesse Randolph however, became offended. One of the scouts, a Jew from New York City by the name of Sigmund Shlesinger, and the youngest man in Forsyth's command, had offered Jesse a piece of putrid mule meat as a joke and to call attention to the fact that this was the kind of food that the scouts had been eating for nearly a week. Jesse was so offended by the sight and smell of the putrescent piece of mule flesh that he nearly drew his Colt revolver and told him, "You gets that goddamn piece of rot outta my face 'fore there be one less Heb in the world!"

The next day the main relief force from Fort Wallace arrived and additional succor was available to the survivors of the island fight. After Forsyth's scouts had been properly fed and attended, Carpenter's H Company, the relief force from Wallace, and the scouts left the area for the return trip to Wallace. Jack Peate, Jack Donovan, and Pierre "French Pete" Trudeau, who had returned with the relief force, were riding well in advance of the column while Nate and Reuben Waller were following close behind with a squad of flankers ahead of the main column. The men had just passed the remains of a Cheyenne corpse that had been partially devoured by wolves during the night. Jack Peate, Jack Donovan, and "French Pete" had come across four warriors the day before. One of the braves, who was on foot, failed to escape the wrath of the white men. The warrior moved very quickly and dropped all of his accoutrements on the prairie in order to gain speed while running in an irregular zigzag pattern. The scouts gave chase as if they were hunting down a prairie jackrabbit. They shot at him with their Colts and Spencers, the bullets kicking up sand and dirt as the brave ran for his life. While Donovan and Peate fired their Colts wildly at the hapless Cheyenne and yelled and hollered with glee, "French Pete" took careful aim with his Spencer and fired. The .52-caliber bullet hit the Indian above the right knee. He hobbled for a few feet and sat down. He then revealed a .36-caliber Navy Colt revolver and raised the weapon at the on-coming scouts. He pulled on the trigger but the cylinder failed to revolve and the weapon would not fire. Perplexed but remaining calm, he looked at the Navy Colt as if he were a child who had just broken a toy. He decided to discard the weapon by throwing it away in the buffalo grass, and began to chant his death song. The scouts of course, showed no mercy. They executed him as if he was a rabid dog and Jack Peate promptly scalped him.

The advanced parties were returning to the area where the large white tipi and burial scaffolds were located. Jack Peate and some of the other scouts, including Sigmund Shlesinger, the little Jew who almost got his head blown off by Jesse after he offended him with his putrid piece of meat, dismounted and commenced a systematic pattern of plundering the scaffolds and removing items. Buckskins, bonnets, parfleches, bowlances, and other personal articles from the decomposing bodies of the warriors were eagerly pilfered by the surviving scouts.

Nate and Reuben Waller were sickened by the sight of these men feasting in an orgy of grave robbing. When two of Nate's men dismounted without permission and joined in the looting and pilfering of the bodies for trophies, he lost it.

"You two sons of bitches get back on your horses now, 'fore I whip your asses and put you all in the guard house."

"Sarge we wants to get some souvenirs," retorted one trooper, defiantly.

"Yeah thats right! Them scouts are a helpin' themselves and we gots de same rights as they..." added his companion who was holding an engraved clay bowl.

"*They be not army, you stupid fools.* Killin' the enemy is one thing, robbin' the dead is another! Suppose somebody did that to you?! Now mount up, or do I have to pull my horse pistol?"

The two troopers grudgingly remounted their horses, but they did manage to sneak away with some items such as a war charm made from a piece of buffalo intestine, some raven feathers, and the engraved clay bowl.

Nate however, could not stop the looting and desecration of Roman Nose's burial tipi. Jack Peate and some of the scouts looted and ransacked the white lodge with no regard that its dead occupant was a great warrior and that the body should be respected rather than defiled. The person who really surprised Nate however, was little Sigmund Shlesinger. Nate was told by one of the scouts that the frail Jew from New York who wore spectacles, had expressed horror only a few days before when he saw some of the scouts tearing off Indian scalps with their hunting knives. Now to see him degenerate into a state of barbarism in partaking in the looting and grave robbing, confirmed for Nate that the Indian was not alone in committing acts of outrage. As Nate watched Shlesinger seize Roman Nose's war bonnet and remove the swallowtail article, he noticed that the little Jew became stunned when he saw that maggots covered the crown of the war bonnet and Roman Nose's forehead. That did not stop him though. He removed the warrior's earrings and tin finger rings and grabbed Roman Nose's beaded knife scabbard and other items that he could snag in the rush by the scouts to steal everything in sight.

"Gawd almighty! Life's cheap and dirty, here on the frontier," exclaimed Nate to Reuben Waller, as he watched the scouts loot the dead bodies while the stench from the rotting corpses permeated the air.

"Not even durin' the war have I seen such," responded Reuben Waller who had seen the slaughter of black federal troops at Fort Pillow at the hands of Nathan Bedford Forrest's ruthless cavalrymen.

"Let's keep movin'," responded Nate as his mount became increasingly nervous from the foul smell coming from the dead Cheyennes and the hundreds of flies that swarmed about. "My horse, nor I fo' that matter, can stand much mo' of this stench of death, an' dese fuckin' *flies*!"

Cougar Eyes and two other Dog Soldiers were out scouting toward the northeast, a short distance from the main army relief column. They were part of the rear guard that volunteered to protect their people's departure from the lands that boarded the Arikaree River. Cougar Eyes was sad at the death of his friend and mentor, *Voo' xenehe*. He felt that he had died in vain because they had failed to overwhelm the whites on the island. Although he kept pondering why the spirits had not been with the people, he strongly felt that with one more determined charge, the warriors would have stormed the island and slaughtered all the remaining defenders. He was skeptical regarding Roman Nose's assertion that their medicine became useless because he had devoured some food from a cast-iron frying pan.

Nate was the rear flanker for the column. Carpenter had ordered that flankers be sent out to watch for any signs of hostiles. He still feared that the relief column might be suddenly attacked by hordes of Cheyennes. At the very least, Carpenter was concerned that snipers might harass the column by hiding among the ravines and grass while taking shots at stragglers and at the mules and horses.

As Nate's horse plodded along, he kept a clear eye on the horizon and watched the ground for tracks. Although alert, his mind was preoccupied with thoughts about Cara. Especially that night when they made love in the chair. Nate kept grinning and even chuckled when he thought about how their lovemaking became so intense that the leg of the chair snapped off, causing the couple to fall suddenly to the floor laughing. He still remained amazed at what they had done and how Cara expertly orchestrated the whole event. "She sure is a take-charge woman!" Nate whispered to himself. He had never had such a pleasant sexual experience before. The time that Mas'a Hammond forced him to have intercourse for breeding purposes and the feeling of disgust regarding his mother's rape by Bloodhound Jack, had made Nate's sensuous desires anemic. Nate realized that Cara had changed him. Now he wanted to be in bed with her all the time and worshipped the moments he was with her. The notion of marriage came to mind and he thought how proud his mother would be if he did marry and started to raise a family in freedom. Here, in the West, where opportunity abounded and a man's color seemed to face less discrimination. He longed to return to Fort Wallace and feel her tiny but strong arms squeeze him while he breathed her intoxicating body aroma and felt her thick raven-colored hair in between his fingers. Nate felt fortunate that he had such a woman. He considered her strong, dependable, self-reliant and strong willed, like his mother. Yes, she is the perfect mate, he acknowledged to himself, and whispered to himself, "and when I return, I'm going to do something about it."

A contorted skeleton of a large mule deer came into view as Nate descended a ravine. He gazed at the bleached bones that lay partially disassembled in the buffalo grass and his mind turned to remembering those killed over the past twelve months. Nate thought it was important to remember the dead. He particularly thought about Sgt. William Christy and Pvt. Filmore Alexander and how they were good men with dreams and that they paid the ultimate price. He thought about how it was a shame that they were not present to participate in the rescue, and how the event made all the suffering of the past winter and the forced marches in the stifling heat, fighting thirst, flies and Dog Men, all worthwhile.

Nate decided to gently spur his mount toward another tall ravine. This particular ravine had a sharp incline and Nate had to shift his weight forward in the saddle and encourage his horse up the steep slope. He wanted to get a good look at the surrounding countryside and see if he could spot any signs of the hostiles or maybe locate the main retreating body of Cheyennes. When his mount crested the top of the ravine, Nate halted and surveyed the terrain. He shielded his eyes with his right hand and gazed toward the west as his horse shook his head to chase away flies. He slowly rotated in the saddle and searched the ground all around him. Satisfied that the land was void of any signs of life, Nate was about turn his reins and descend back down the ravine when he spotted what appeared to be long slender poles protruding from behind a ravine toward the northeast. He quickly estimated the distance between himself and the moving poles at three hundred feet away while his horse suddenly started to act up. He rubbed his eyes and attempted to focus on the objects that were moving at a good clip along the uppermost part of the opposing ravine when he noticed that the poles had bright colored feathers attached to them and that the tips were sharply pointed. "Lances! Dawg Men!" he whispered to himself as he steadied his increasingly nervous horse. Nate's first instinct was to leave the area and report back to the column, but he decided to see if he could determine their exact number and if worse came to worse, he knew he could out run them.

Cougar Eyes and his companions also wanted to take a look at the surrounding terrain. So he led the band quietly up to the crest of the ravine where they had been walking their war ponies close to the edge and emerged at the top.

When Cougar Eyes saw a big *Mo' ohtae-ve' ho' e* sitting quietly on his horse staring at him on top of the opposing ravine, he became dumbfounded. He stared back and immediately saw the big chevrons on Nate's sleeves and realized that it was *Hotoa' e Gordon*. Nate remained calm as he watched the Dog Soldier's face him on the opposing ravine but tightened his hold on the reins in case he had to order the horse to bolt if the warriors decided to give chase.

"*Haaate! Hotoa' e Gordon,*" cried Cougar Eyes, raising his bowlance into the air as his painted war pony pranced around nervously. His companions wanted to chase Nate and slay him but Cougar Eyes told them that he alone reserved the honor to kill this *Mo' ohtae-ve' ho' e* himself. *Taenanotse*! demanded Cougar Eyes, instructing one of his braves to remove the arrow that he had started to fasten to his bowlance.

Nate had not initially recognized Cougar Eyes when he appeared over the ravine because all of the warriors had their faces painted and were dressed in war regalia with turbans and headgear decorated with large feathers. The greeting and the way the warrior said his name in Cheyenne, made him realize that it was his old nemesis.

"*Hotoa' e Gordon!*" yelled Cougar Eyes again, raising his bowlance to get Nate's attention.

Nate remained composed. He was bemused by this spectacle and uncertain what to do next. He decided that the Dog Men would have already started to pursue him if that was their intention, so he made up his mind to stay put for the moment and watch Cougar Eyes and see what would happen next.

Cougar Eyes was in awe with Nate's *sang froid*. The normal reaction of the blue coats when discovering a superior number of mounted Dog Soldiers was to run.

"*Hotoa' e Gordon novana' xaetano,*" remarked Cougar Eyes to a companion.

"It is true," responded the companion. "The *Mo' otoa'e-ve' ho' e* seems calm and serene. His medicine is strong."

"I think I will not kill *Hotoa' e Gordon* today," replied Cougar Eyes as if he had absolute power to determine life or death.

Nate noticed that the Dog Men were conversing among themselves and he wondered if they were trying to make up their minds what to do. After watching them stare at him for a minute, he decided to raise himself in his McClellan and lifted his right arm and hand and say one of the few words of Cheyenne that he had learned during the past year, which was, "until the next time."

"*Nestaevahose voomatse.*"

Cougar Eyes and his companions were taken aback. Cougar Eyes especially, was pleased that *Hotoa' e Gordon* had responded in Cheyenne. He smiled and waved his bowlance. "*Nestaevahose voomatse.*"

"*Noheto!*" commanded Cougar Eyes, ordering the party to move on.

Nate watched Cougar Eyes and the other Dog Soldiers disappear down the opposing ravine. "*Nestaevahose voomatse,*" whispered Nate to himself. "That's right, my man. We'll see each other again, real soon."